ROUGH contact

BETH BOLDEN

Publisher's Note: This is a work of fiction. Names, characters, places, and incidents are a product of the author's imagination. Locales and public names are sometimes used for atmospheric purposes. Any resemblance to actual people, living or dead, or to businesses, companies, events, institutions, or locales is completely coincidental.

Book Layout © 2021 Beth Bolden

Book Cover © 2021 Cate Ashwood Designs

The people in the images are models and should not be connected to the characters in the book. Any resemblance is incidental.

Ordering Information:

Quantity sales. Special discounts are available on quantity purchases by corporations, associations, and others. For details, contact Beth Bolden at the address above.

Rough Contact/ Beth Bolden. -- 2nd ed.

PROLOGUE

FEBRUARY 2021

It was the shortest field goal of Neal Fisher's life, and also the longest.

His breath came in choppy, uneven pants as he jogged onto the field with the rest of the kicking unit. He couldn't calm himself, no matter how much he tried to slow both his breath and the uncooperative heart thundering away in his chest.

He'd kicked this distance a thousand times, probably more, but he'd never done it under these circumstances—even though the Los Angeles Riptide had won plenty of games on his leg alone before. But they'd never won a Super Bowl when he was the one responsible for the three extra points that would put them on top.

Last year when they'd won, it had been all Sam Crawford and Chase Riley. They'd done their best this time around, too, hoping they might do what very few teams in the modern era of professional football had done—repeat Super Bowl wins—but it hadn't been quite enough, and Sam and Chase had come up short. "It's okay, it's good," Sam had chanted when he'd returned to the sideline, "Fisher's gonna get it done for us."

Almost always when Neal kicked, the world retreated into a fuzzy approximation of reality, but maybe there was just way too much fucking reality happening today, because right now, he couldn't get back into his own head again. The noise of the crowd was deafening, a loud cacophony ringing in his ears, reminding him of every single person who was watching here, at the stadium, and also of all those millions watching on their televisions.

The hardest people to forget were his team, all braced on the sideline, relegated and resigned to the act of observation. All of them, counting on him to do the job for which he was paid very well—to kick a ball dead straight for forty-four yards. That was all. *Piece of fucking cake.*

He could make this kick a hundred times in a row in practice. A thousand. But in front of millions, with the whole game riding on him? *That* was why he was one of the highest-paid kickers in football. Still, it was hard not to sweat, not to feel the pressure begin to press in on him.

Neal thought he caught a flash of blond hair out of the corner of his eye. Sam must have taken his helmet off, and kneeled, as he often did, when their games came down to one of Neal's kicks.

Right now the announcers would be analyzing the distance of the kick—forty-four yards—the angle—pretty much dead center—and the wind—a slight breeze but nothing Neal was particularly worried about—and they'd be putting up stats on the bottom of the screen, talking about how he'd never missed a kick in a big-time situation. Of course, he'd never kicked to win a Super Bowl, but he'd kicked and won them a playoff game, once, three years ago. In their Super Bowl run last year, he'd been merely incidental, only being called on to kick the extra points as Sam threw the touchdowns that had led to their victory.

"You good?" Jon, the long snapper, nudged him with an elbow. Aware, as they always had to be, that not only were their actions observed by everyone, but there were some crazed weirdos out there that tried to read their lips, too. Nothing was secret on a football field. Especially not *this* football field.

"I'm good," Neal said, and meant it. Maybe he hadn't been in this exact situation before, but he wasn't going to let the pressure get to him. He was going to make the kick. He could already feel his foot hit the ball just right, could already see it soaring through the uprights. Could feel the way Sam would smack right into him, in some approximation of a bear hug.

It was already all there. It existed somewhere, in some version of some reality. Neal just had to make it happen in this one.

The referee indicated it was time, and since the Miami Piranhas, the opposing team, didn't even have a timeout left, there was nothing to do but to watch—they couldn't even "ice" him, or force him to make the kick a second time by calling a timeout at the last second.

Jon got set, and Neal nodded down at the holder—who was also their punter, Ian. He was set too. Everyone was set. Neal tamped down the sudden nerves that swamped him. It was just another day, just another kick.

Kicks always went so fast. Jon snapped the ball flawlessly, Ian caught it and then suddenly he was kicking it, right where he needed to, right as he'd intended. The moment it left his foot, it felt perfect, just like he'd wanted it to, just like it had felt a hundred times before, a *thousand*.

Except, then, suddenly the ball veered off to the right, then hit the crossbar, and Neal stared disbelievingly as it fell forward.

His first thought was, *that's a mistake.* Then he realized, a half second later, as the Miami Piranhas poured joyously on the field, *that was* my *mistake. I missed it. The single biggest kick of my entire career, and I just fucking blew it.*

Somehow, Neal got pushed to the sideline, though he wasn't even sure how he'd made it from the center of the field to the Riptide's side. He couldn't force his head up because he might be forced to see the wrenching disappointment in everyone's faces. He thought Sam came up, the flash of blond hair too distinctive, and felt, for a brief second, the press of a hand on his shoulder pad. "It's alright, dude," Sam might have said. Or it might have been a, "Fuck you." Neal wasn't sure he could distinguish, not right now, not when suddenly, inexplicably, he'd gone from the most important person on the team to the least.

He'd known then that things were going to change. But he'd never guess that a single missed kick would alter his whole life.

• • • ● • ● ● • •

"I'm glad you could come by today." Michael Turner, the assistant director of player personnel for the Los Angeles Riptide, propped a hip on the corner of his desk.

Every single time Neal faced his boyfriend across the expanse of office carpeting, done in gaudy shades of teal and aqua, he found it awkward. He'd known it would be when they'd started to date, but even though he'd learned to tamp most of his reaction down, he still felt the echoes of it.

But today? The awkwardness was back in spades, and it had been from the moment Neal had missed that stupid fucking kick less than a week earlier.

Everything had changed in a second, and in the five days since. It hung there, unspoken, when Neal had gone to clean out his locker. When he'd done a few workouts in the player facilities. When he'd been in the steam room after a particularly brutal set of reps, and a few of the defensive players had come in and taken one look at him and hadn't said a goddamn word. It had been there, ugly and pervasive, between him and Michael. Like Michael couldn't quite look at him, not in the eye. Neal couldn't even blame him, because he couldn't look at his own self in the mirror. Not anymore.

There was a rumor that one of the Piranhas had tipped the kick, but Neal hadn't been able to bring himself to watch the footage to see for himself. He'd rather walk barefoot over hot lava.

"Yeah," Neal said shortly. What was he supposed to say? *No, I'm not coming? I know what you're going to do and I can avoid it forever if I avoid coming here?*

"You're a valuable member of this organization," Michael said kindly. *Lied* kindly.

Neal *had* been a valuable member of his organization, signed right out of college when the Riptide had been an expansion team. He'd played for Los Angeles for his entire career. He'd been rock solid, never missing when he needed to make it. He might not be able to routinely kick the sixty-yard field goals that were the new norm, but he could reliably kick in the high fifties, and there weren't a lot of kickers out there who could say that.

But all it took was one miss. And a miss in front of millions? It erased every good thing he'd ever done. Neal felt empty inside, as Michael smiled, full of cold sympathy. "I told them I wanted to do it, because it'd be easier coming from me."

Neal hadn't ever come out officially, but he and Michael, who *was* out, who'd been one of the first gay executives in professional football, were an open secret. When they'd started to date, Michael had made lots of promises, both to his boss, and to Neal. *We'll never let our personal and professional relationship intersect,* he'd vowed, and Neal had agreed because that was something he'd wanted, too.

Except now, they weren't separate at all. They were intertwined, staring at him in the corner, the ugly elephant in the room.

"Is that really what you think?" Neal asked. He'd told himself when he'd dressed this morning for this meeting that he'd take the punishment. But that was when he thought he'd be meeting with Michael's boss.

"That it doesn't have to be hard? Of course it doesn't. You can just turn around and walk away, and things will go back to the way they were before."

Except Neal already knew that couldn't happen. He could see it in Michael's eyes, which had gone inexplicably cold.

It was salt in the wound that it was going to be the man he loved, who he'd *thought* loved him, who was going to be the one to tell him that his services were no longer required by the Riptide. The only team he'd ever known. Before this moment, he'd even stupidly believed they were like a family.

But family didn't come and go. Family didn't judge. Family accepted you, even when you fucked up. Even when you fucked up at the worst time imaginable.

It was his own goddamn mistake, Neal realized, he'd forgotten what it was that ran this league. Money. And he'd just lost the Riptide a whole fuckton of money.

"Well, not *exactly* how it was before," Michael added, still painfully sympathetic, but at least he was being more honest now.

In the two years since they'd begun dating, his blond hair had started to gray at the temples, and trying to marshal his temper, Neal focused on those silvering strands. Because he knew what Michael meant. Knew that it wasn't just his job he was losing.

He'd known because Michael couldn't even look at him anymore. How could you have a relationship with someone who blamed you every single moment of every single day?

"I didn't think so," Neal growled.

"At the time, it was a good fit," Michael said. "But now . . ."

Neal stood abruptly. He was a grown man, but he felt like a goddamn child, anger flaring through him, burning through all his self-control, unleashing things that he'd only thought about in the dark of night, when he couldn't sleep. "Is that what I was to you? An *accurate*, reliable convenience?"

"You were a valuable member of the Riptide organization . . ." Michael said smoothly, then stopped abruptly, in the middle of his fucking platitude, no doubt realizing what he'd just said.

Were.

"Yeah, I thought so." Neal shoved his hands into the pockets of his khakis. "I fucking thought so."

Michael's handsome face didn't flinch. "Now, there's no need to get angry. You know . . . you *know* we can't keep you on this team. Not after . . ." He couldn't even say it out loud. *After you lost us our place in history, the only modern team to repeat Super Bowl wins.* "After what happened," Michael finished awkwardly.

"After I missed the kick?" Neal ground out. "You can *say it*, it's not going to kill you."

Just me. It's only gonna end up killing me. Everyone else will go on, move on, focus on next year, but I'll be stuck there forever, in that moment.

"There's plenty of teams that are going to want you, Neal," Michael said.

Neal wondered if he'd written down a whole list of painful platitudes to recite ahead of time. Wondered if he'd made Gavin, his assistant, put them on notecards, and he'd memorized them that way.

That seemed like exactly the kind of shitty, heartless thing that Michael would do. At some point, Neal had found it amusing, the bloodless way he went about his job, how he was all cool, clear-cut logic. But that was before Michael had turned all that logic onto him, and Neal discovered that he didn't give a shit if it cut him and left him a bloody fucking mess.

It was like seeing him for the first time; and realizing that maybe he'd loved something that had never really existed at all.

"But not you," Neal countered.

"The Riptide are going in a different direction next season," he said. His face softened, just a little, but it felt so calculating, and the veil had been lifted from Neal's eyes—he'd never be able to see Michael again, with those gorgeous blue eyes, and be able to see them as anything other than painfully cold.

"And you?"

"Me?" Michael had the nerve to sound surprised, like he couldn't believe that Neal was dragging their relationship into this. Like he hadn't just fucked Neal into the mattress and dried his tears only a few days ago. Like he hadn't seen how destroyed Neal was after the game. Like he didn't know just how much Neal wanted to forget and had done his best to help him.

"You," Neal retorted. "That's what we're talking about, right? Because every single fucking sports reporter, when they're not covering Colin O'Connor's victorious retirement, is predicting how fast the Riptide is going to release me."

"We talked about this," his boyfriend said carefully, "that we wouldn't let our relationship intrude into Riptide business."

He had. He'd promised. And then when the time came to let Neal go, to put the final nail in his coffin, he'd volunteered to hold the hammer.

It was impossible not to take that personally. Michael could say all he wanted to that he thought it'd be easier if he delivered the blow himself, but he wasn't stupid. He knew Neal. Almost better than anybody else, which was particularly galling in this horrible moment.

"Yeah," Neal said shortly. "Exactly."

"What are you trying to say?"

"I'm trying to say, you sure didn't waste any time twisting the knife you just shoved in my back," Neal sneered.

"That's not . . ." Michael stopped abruptly. "Maybe it's better this way, anyway. I was going to give you some time to adjust, but yes, maybe you're right. Maybe it's better to just kill two birds with one stone."

The sudden shift in his tone—resolute and resigned, like he'd always planned it would happen this way—was like an ugly kaleidoscope, further revealing what he was really capable of. How had Neal never seen it before? He didn't know, but he was furious now. Furious that he'd opened himself up to someone who had turned out not to give a single shit.

Someone who could sit there while he cried and plan how to further ruin his life.

"It sure fucking is better this way," Neal spat out. "I can't fucking believe that I ever thought you cared about me. Not when . . . not when . . ." He found he couldn't finish the thought, that voicing how much he'd *thought* Michael cared about him but never had, hurt like fucking hell.

He'd thought missing that forty-four-yard field goal in the Super Bowl was the most humiliating experience of his entire life, but no, it was this.

Realizing that the man he'd thought he loved was a dead-eyed stranger, who couldn't wait to briskly dismiss him, like he'd meant nothing to him or to the team he'd loved.

"It's over," Michael said, and Neal knew he meant *everything*.

Neal's gaze fell on the framed photo on his desk. The one he'd given him for his last birthday, or was it their anniversary? He couldn't remember, and suddenly, even seeing it, their arms wrapped around each other, celebrating the first LA Riptide Super Bowl win, rings flashing on their fingers, was too much. He grabbed it, the wooden edges digging into his palm.

"What are you doing?" Michael asked, voice guarded. And *yeah*, Neal thought with vicious victory, he actually sounded worried now. "Do I need to call security?"

Neal stared at him. "You gonna kick me out?"

"If you're going to make a scene, yes." Michael's hand strayed towards the phone on his desk, and Neal knew he'd do it no matter what, because not only was their relationship an open secret, he wouldn't be surprised if every single person in this whole facility thought he should be punished for his crime.

What could be more of a punishment than dragging him, disgraced and alone, out of his ex-boyfriend's office?

"I'm taking this," Neal said.

"You can't, because that's mine," Michael said, extending his hand.

He didn't know how they'd ended up here, fighting over a picture in a ten-dollar frame. Just a week ago, before the game that had changed everything, they'd exchanged "I love yous," like they had hundreds of times before. Michael had told him that he believed in him. But had he really? Neal thought of his older sister, Ella, and how she'd never really warmed to Michael. How he'd never really understood her lack of acceptance and her reticence. And now, it all made sense. She'd seen it, long before he ever did.

"Actually, it's *mine*," Neal said. "It was mine before, and it's still mine." It was so stupid to fight over this stupid goddamned picture, but there wasn't much left of his shredded, tattered pride and he was going to *own* whatever still existed.

"Neal." Michael uttered it warningly, and suddenly there was a discreet knock on the door and then it opened and Terry, the head of security for the Riptide, walked in.

"Everything alright?" he asked, glancing from Neal to Michael.

"Neal was just leaving," Michael said smoothly, like he fired his boyfriends all the time. "And he's leaving that behind." He pointed, indicating the picture in his hands.

Neal's grip on the frame tightened. Was he really going to make a point of this? After everything?

Terry reached out and, with an apologetic look, tried to pluck it from his fingers. Neal didn't really blame him; after all, Michael was kind of *his* boss, too.

"Come on, Neal, don't be childish," Michael said patronizing-ly.

"*Childish*?" Neal spit out. "Oh, for fuck's sake. Take the fucking picture." He was a kicker for a living—not a pitcher—but he prided himself on being in excellent shape. He flung the picture, just to the left of Michael's stupidly handsome face, and fucking *finally*, felt something that wasn't resignation or anger or disappointment. A savage sense of satisfaction swept through him as his ex flinched, and the picture crashed into the wall in a shower of wood and glass splinters.

Michael gaped first at him, and then at the shattered remnants of the frame. His expression hardened and then he pointed to Terry. "Get him out of here," he said, and that was how Neal Fisher ended up not only being let go from the Los Angeles Riptide, but escorted off the property.

CHAPTER ONE

It was hard for Jamie Wright to believe this was where he was supposed to be.

He'd been so fucking thrilled to get the phone call after the draft—asking him to come to LA and tryout for the open spot on the Riptide roster. He, like everyone else in the entire universe, had watched as Neal Fisher, the Riptide's longtime kicker, had missed the potentially game-winning field goal in the Super Bowl.

Seeing his often-forgotten-about position become the talk of sports media for the next month? It was an unpleasant reminder that everyone forgot about kickers until they fucked up. His dad had pointed out how his business degree from Stanford was good, and he could get a job anywhere. He didn't *have* to go into the NFL. He didn't have to potentially be bounced around from team to team, trying to find a permanent spot. He was good at lots of things; not *just* kicking.

But even though he'd gone practical for his degree, and had promised his dad that he would look for a job if the tryout didn't work out, he *wanted* to be a kicker. He loved the smell of the freshly cut grass. He could even get into the new artificial turf they were putting in all the stadiums now. He loved standing on the sideline. Watching as his team made a particularly sweet offensive play, or made a drop-dead stop on defense was incredible. Even jogging out, with all the pressure riding on him to do his own job was a high that he couldn't seem to replicate anywhere else.

Ironically, he'd looked up to Neal Fisher forever, because he was so beautifully consistent. He always kept his head down until right when he was needed to make a kick, and then he never missed it. That consistency had kept him on the Riptide roster for thirteen years, which was an eternity for a kicker, and would probably earn him a spot in the Hall of Fame—or at least it *would* have, until he'd missed the most important kick of his entire career.

Maybe he would still end up in the Hall of Fame. Jamie hadn't been surprised at all that the Riptide had released him, but he had been surprised that he'd headed into July and veteran camps without being on *any* team.

Jamie shook his head, trying to clear Neal Fisher from it. But that was tough for two reasons: *one,* the guy had been his idol ever since he'd traded soccer for football at the beginning of high school, and *two,* because nobody at the Riptide facility seemed particularly interested in letting go of the past and moving on.

It was weird; he'd come to LA expecting to compete against a handful of other guys, likely a mix of rookies and veterans. But when he'd reported to the facility this morning, and walked into the equipment room, he'd seen *seven* other kickers, all of whom he'd recognized from various camps and also their YouTube highlight videos.

"Yeah," Dylan, a kicker from Michigan State that he'd texted on and off with over the summer, said when Jamie's jaw dropped, "and this isn't even all of us."

"What?" Jamie couldn't believe it. Eight kickers competing for a single spot was unheard of—and Dylan said there were *more*?

"Yeah, there's two veterans, they're already in the cafeteria." Dylan dropped his voice, leaning closer to Jamie. "I think this is all because Fisher fucked them up."

If the Riptide had brought in *ten* kickers to compete for a single spot, it was hard to deny: Fisher's missed kick *had* fucked them up.

"Wouldn't it fuck up anybody?" Another kicker that Jamie barely recognized, leaned in, joining their hushed conversation. "They lost a fucking Super Bowl because of that egotistical prick."

Jamie had never been lucky enough to meet Neal Fisher in the flesh—he'd fantasized about it plenty though, because god damn, that man was hot as hell, even though he had to be almost forty—but he'd never gotten an egotistical prick vibe from him.

"Is he really that bad?" Jamie wondered.

Dylan grinned at him. "Got the hots for Fisher, J?"

"I mean, all you gotta do is *look* at him," Jamie pointed out. "And it kinda sucks that he misses *one* kick, and that's all anybody gives a shit about. He made hundreds over his career."

The other guy shrugged. "It's the way it is, no point in fucking bitching about it."

Jamie liked Dylan a lot, but this other guy—he didn't recognize him—gave him a weird vibe. "Yeah, I know, but it still sucks. Nobody drops a quarterback for missing a throw or tossing an interception."

"Yeah, if that was the case, Crawford wouldn't still be on this team," the other guy said with a bitter edge to his voice.

And yeah, Sam Crawford, the Riptide's quarterback, had experienced his share of growing pains, but Jamie could tell he would eventually be a great player. "He won a Super Bowl and he almost won another one," Jamie said. "When you pull that kind of stunt off, you can bitch about him."

The guy looked surprised, and not only because Jamie had basically told him to shut the fuck up. The real reason why became very clear a second later.

"Hey, that's nice," a voice said behind them and Jamie glanced up to see Sam Crawford, blond hair falling to his shoulders, blue eyes bright and amused, in the flesh, standing in the doorway to the equipment room.

The guy Jamie didn't know paled. "Oh shit, man, it's good to see you. I'm Shane," he said, extending a hand, clearly trying to suck up to the de facto leader of the Riptide. Crawford might not have any real say about who the new kicker might be, but it wasn't ever a bad thing to get on the starting quarterback's good side.

But Sam just looked at him, eyes still amused, and skirted around Shane, to come to a stop right in front of Jamie. "Hey," he said, pointedly extending a hand towards Jamie and Jamie alone, "I'm Sam."

"Hey, Sam, I'm Jamie Wright. Hoping to make it on the team as your new kicker," he said, and then knowing that Sam went to USC, added, "Went to Stanford, hope there's no hard feelings."

Sam's smile was quicksilver as they shook hands briefly. He had a good, firm handshake, and even though Jamie would've been predisposed to liking the guy—after all, he'd literally *come out* in the middle of the Super Bowl celebrations, by kissing his boyfriend on the trophy presentation stage—Jamie found himself admiring him even more. And not just because he'd said a pointed *fuck you* to all the homophobic assholes who thought Colin O'Connor had been a fluke in the league.

And then the next year? There'd been *two* out and proud queer quarterbacks in the Super Bowl, and that had been even more fucking awesome. Sam and Colin had led the way to Jamie coming out himself, before his senior year at Stanford.

"Nope, not at all. You're here now," Sam said. "Always good to have a fellow PAC-12 guy here. Heath will eventually have to eat his words." Heath Harris, Sam's boyfriend, had been the Riptide's quarterback before Sam, and he'd famously gone to Auburn, and then proceeded to tear up the league with his fierce intensity, before injuries had finally led him to retire after the Riptide had won their Super Bowl.

"Fuck the SEC," Jamie said jokingly.

"Amen, brother," Sam agreed. "Hey, we're having a get-together later, a big veteran-rookie pool party at our house. Find me after practice, and I'll give you our address."

Jamie could feel Dylan's jaw dropping next to him, shocked that Jamie had managed to befriend Sam Crawford before he'd even set foot on the practice field. But Jamie's dad had always taught him that loyalty paid you back in spades, and it had here. He'd defended Sam from Shane's shitty gossip, and that had obviously meant something to the guy.

"Sure, that'd be great," Jamie said. Like he was going to pass up an opportunity to visit Sam Crawford and Heath Harris' house and actually *meet* them.

"Awesome," Sam said. "I'll let you guys get to it."

"Holy shit," Dylan said when Sam ended up at the front of the line, almost definitely because he was the Riptide's quarterback.

"Suck-up," Shane grumbled, but Jamie knew he was just jealous and the words didn't bother him.

"Seriously though," Jamie said, deciding to change the subject back to the one that really interested him, "I can't believe they brought in *ten* kickers."

"It's gonna be weird," Dylan said. And that was a painfully prophetic statement, because everything got weirder when they finally finished up getting their equipment and headed to the team-wide meeting held in the big amphitheater at the center of the practice facility.

Coach Rodriguez was standing at the front, in front of a gigantic television screen, accompanied by several polo shirt-wearing men, who were likely the other assistant coaches, as Dylan and Jamie took a pair of seats towards the back.

As the crowd of players quieted, Coach Rodriguez raised an arm. "Welcome back, everyone," he said. "I know last season didn't end like we wanted it to, but I don't want to hide from our problem. I want to face it head-on. I want to embrace it and then fight it." Then suddenly, the screen came to life, but rather than the traditional welcome video that Jamie had expected, having sat through five seasons of this in college, instead it was footage from last year's Super Bowl loss.

Specifically, a room of a hundred Riptide players watched in silence as Neal Fisher lined up to kick a forty-four-yard field goal and missed.

"I told you so," Dylan hissed at Jamie. *"Fucked up."*

It was hard to argue with Dylan's analysis of the situation. When Jamie had initially gotten the call from the Riptide, he'd fielded other calls, from other teams, but this was where he'd wanted to come. When his dad had questioned whether that was the smartest choice, Jamie had convinced him by reminding him that the Riptide would *definitely* be in the market for a new kicker. This wouldn't just be a way to put an existing kicker through their paces and make sure they had the best available choice. There was a real opportunity for a job here.

Jamie just didn't know if he wanted it anymore.

"Fuck," Dylan repeated as Coach R segued into talking about the upcoming season. "This is going to be fucking wild. Ten kickers. This obsession with a missed kick."

When the welcome meeting finally ended, instead of heading over to their own field to do their thing, Coach Toby, the special teams coordinator, led them to the main field.

"Warm up," Coach Toby said gruffly. "We're gonna start out with some drills."

"In front of the entire team?" one guy asked tentatively.

Jamie had never been to an NFL tryout before, but even he thought this was strange. In college, he and the other special teams guys had always practiced at a separate field from the rest of the team. They'd often do some kicks at the end of practice, to push their distance capabilities. But right now? At the beginning of practice?

Everything here felt weird and was getting weirder.

Jamie did his standard set of stretches, loosening his knees and his hips, getting set to make whatever kick they decided.

In the end, he should've guessed. Coach Rodriguez's speech had made it way too obvious.

"We're going to kick from here," Coach Toby said, indicating a certain spot on the field. "One at a time, down the line."

Jamie did a quick mental calculation.

Yep, it wasn't forty or forty-five yards. It was forty-four right on the nose.

"Fuck," Dylan said again. Jamie was beginning to wonder if he had any other words in his vocabulary, but truthfully his brain was pretty full of four-letter words, too. This was insane. So much of kicking was mental, and to put this kind of pressure on every single guy here? Was Coach Rodriguez intending for them *all* to snap?

The first guy went, one of the veterans, and his kick went way wide, which was unsurprising, because Jamie had seen his face before the kick, and he hadn't seemed confident at all. But then, how could he be when the coaching staff wasn't setting him up to feel that way?

Bad energy crackled on the field after that first miss, and it didn't get any easier as the guys went down the line and most of the kicks weren't even remotely good.

Dylan went second-to-last and managed to *just* squeak the ball past the left upright, which was surprising—or maybe not at all—because he was a distance specialist, and Jamie had watched him nail field goals from sixty yards plus on a regular basis, even during games. Forty-four wasn't really that far, but it was also really fucking long because of the emphasis the coaching staff had placed on that particular distance.

If Jamie thought they were interested in actually setting themselves up for success, he'd have said something to Coach Toby, but it was clear, this was a designed response to what had happened in the Super Bowl, and there was nothing to be gained by trying to tell the coaching staff that they were all fucking idiots.

It definitely wouldn't get Jamie this job.

He went last.

His palms were sweating, and he rubbed them against the slick fabric of his athletic shorts, emblazoned with the Riptide logo. How long would he be wearing them? Not very long, not if he couldn't make this kick. Not when there were nine others who were all capable if the mental pressure didn't defeat them first.

Jamie lined up, watching for the signal from the holder, because *of course* they were being asked to do this with both a holder and a long snapper who were brand new to them, and there was no established rhythm. When it came, it all happened in a blur, and to his own surprise—and that really said it all, didn't it, that he was *surprised*—the ball hit his foot exactly right, and sailed right between the uprights, almost dead center.

If that was a test—and it almost certainly had been—Jamie knew he'd passed. But how long could he keep this up, and block out all the negative energy that was threatening to overwhelm him and all the rest of the kickers trying out? He didn't know, but he knew if he wanted to become the Riptide's kicker, he was going to have to figure it out *fast*.

• • • • • • • • • •

"That was a good kick."

Jamie was pushing his damp hair back from his forehead, when unexpectedly Sam Crawford stopped in front of his locker.

Well, maybe not *unexpectedly*. Sam had told him he would, to give him the address of the house he shared with Heath, so Jamie could come to their pool party tonight. But Jamie had mostly believed that he'd forget about it—and about him—because who was he? One kicker out of *ten*, and a rookie who, despite having a good leg and a decent head on his shoulders, would probably start the regular season sitting on his parents' couch. That was exactly why his dad had tried to convince him it was a mistake to come down to LA, because no team carried more than a single kicker into the regular season. He'd have a lot better luck coming in a few games in, if one of the thirty-two kickers faltered and a team thought it was worth making a switch.

Jamie was realistic about his chances, and also realistic about Sam Crawford.

But here Sam was, anyway.

"It was decent," Jamie agreed. It had gone through the uprights, which was all he could fucking ask for, after being forced to kick on command like that. He was one of only four kickers who'd made it.

Of course, then the group had retreated to their own field, where Jamie had watched all of them nail kicks from fifty yards plus.

It was the pressure; a coach as experienced as Rodriguez *should* know that piling more onto kickers was a recipe for disaster.

"It went in, didn't it?" Sam said, leaning against the empty locker next to Jamie.

For a split second, Jamie considered defending Neal Fisher, who wasn't even here to defend himself—not anymore, anyway—but if he wanted this job, the last thing he should bring up was the man who'd failed them.

"It did," Jamie agreed instead.

"I meant it, about coming to the party," Sam said, and pulled out his phone, asking for Jamie's number. "I'll text you the address," he said. "It starts about six and goes til whenever, though since we have practice tomorrow, probably not *that* late."

"Makes sense," Jamie said. If his dad was here, he'd tell him it was a mistake to go to a party at all, when he had practice to prep for the next day, but Sam had made a point of inviting him *twice*.

It would be stupid to turn him down.

"Well, I hope to see you tonight," Sam said, shooting him another dopey grin. "I really want you to meet Heath."

It was a little overwhelming to realize Sam's boyfriend was *Heath Harris.* He'd known that, of course, because he and the rest of the universe had seen them kiss at the Super Bowl a year and a half ago. But meeting him? Seeing them together, in their own house? Jamie felt a little starstruck, but he knew the moment he *seemed* it, it would make everything weird.

"I'll be there," Jamie said.

After Sam walked away, Dylan pounced almost immediately. "Fuck," he said, "that was Sam Crawford *again*. Do you think he likes you or something?"

Dylan was supposedly straight, but he'd always been accepting of Jamie's sexuality. Better even than some of the players on his own team. "Don't be ridiculous," Jamie said. "He's got a boyfriend. You know, *Heath Harris*? You might've heard of him."

"Oh, that's right," Dylan said. "Now I remember." Like anyone was ever going to forget that moment with Sam holding the Vince Lombardi Trophy and casually, utterly destroying a century of homophobia in sports by leaning over and kissing his boyfriend right there on the stage, surrounded by a metric ton of confetti.

"You're an idiot," Jamie said, but smiled anyway. He *liked* Dylan and it sort of pissed him off they were competing for the same job.

"Well yeah," Dylan agreed. "So are you gonna go?"

It would be smarter to go back to his soulless hotel room, watch some film, get prepped for what would undoubtedly be a mentally grueling practice day. He'd gotten the impression that Coach Toby and Coach Rodriguez were just getting started.

"I don't know," Jamie confessed. "I *want* to."

"Then you should. And you should anyway," Dylan said. "It'd be good for your chances."

Jamie rolled his eyes, shoving his shower sandals into a side pocket of his duffel bag. "I don't think Sam Crawford gets to pick who wins the kicker spot."

"No, but some goodwill in that corner can't hurt," Dylan said.

He had a point. "Why are you even giving me this advice? Aren't we supposed to be competing against each other?" Jamie teased him as he picked up his bag and they made their way out of the locker room.

"Is it really a competition?" Dylan wondered under his breath. "*Ten* kickers. That's not even fucking legit. That's like . . ."

"It's a farce," Jamie agreed. "It's not about us at all."

Jamie knew exactly what it was about. Rather *who* it was about.

He and Dylan parted ways at the parking lot, each headed to their rental cars. "Go to this party," Dylan told him. "If only because I wanna know how Sam Crawford and Heath Harris live."

"I think I will," Jamie said, and knew, deep down, that his curiosity wouldn't have ever kept him away.

•　•　●　•　●　•　●　•　●　•　•

"Dude, you're pathetic."

Neal lifted his head at the accusatory voice. The room was gloomy and dark; the shades drawn against the bright California sun outside.

"I don't want to hear it," he said dryly, except that Olive wasn't going to stop, because this was *Olive,* and she'd come out of his sister's womb unstoppable.

"No," Olive said, striding into the room, and before Neal could stop her, she'd yanked up the shades, sending way too much unrelenting sunshine spilling into the room. Neal rolled over in bed and groaned aloud. "No, you don't get to do this anymore," she said, reaching for his covers, but before she could whip them back, he gripped them tightly. He used to sleep in the nude for a reason—*Michael*, that name still hurt, still stung every time he thought it—but now he just did it because he was too lazy to put clothes on.

Olive moving in last week because school was about to start should have motivated him to try to . . . *do* something, but it turned out when you'd spent six months doing fuck all, it was hard to break that particular habit.

"Mom was worried you'd turned into this lonely, sad hermit man, and she was right," Olive said. "I know you don't want to hear this, but you *are* totally, absolutely pathetic."

"Thanks," Neal retorted. He didn't need Olive to tell him; he already knew.

"It wasn't a compliment," Olive said.

"I wondered why your mother let you come to LA a few weeks early; now we know. She was hoping you could badger me to death," Neal said, pulling a pillow over his head, but also not letting his grip on the sheets go. God knew what Olive would do; he should've predicted all of this, but he'd gotten fuzzy and soft, hiding in his house for the last six months.

At first it had just been easier; he didn't have to face anyone who knew what he'd done—and the whole fucking world knew what he'd done. Or what he *hadn't* done. Then it had just gotten to be a habit. He'd always known that money could buy everything, and it could definitely buy a lonely, sad hermit existence. He'd had anything he needed delivered and had stopped leaving the house completely. Some days he found it difficult to even get out of bed. When he showered, he'd stopped turning the lights on, because then he didn't have to look at his pale, gaunt, *guilty* face in the mirror.

Olive whipped the pillow off, exposing him again to all that brutal light. "Do you want me to call her?"

If Olive was unstoppable, then her mother, Ella, was a force to be reckoned with.

"No," Neal said.

"Then I want you to get up, and take a shower, and then take me to Heath and Sam's house."

Neal groaned again. "I'll do the first two, but hell is freezing over before I go over there. There's gonna be a ton of Riptide players. And none of them want to see me."

"That's not true," Olive argued. "Nobody blames you."

"If they don't, they *should*," Neal muttered.

"Don't be ridiculous. Heath texted me *specifically;* they both want to see you—well, you *and* me."

Neal didn't know how his college-age niece and a thirty-year-old retired quarterback had become such good friends, but he kind of regretted introducing them in the first place.

"Then *you* go," Neal said. "I don't feel like going."

Olive perched on the edge of the bed, her long dark hair pulled over one shoulder. "You haven't felt like doing anything for six months. It's time to cut it out. You missed one field goal. You didn't murder anybody. You didn't cause a global catastrophe."

"That depends on your perspective," Neal retorted.

"Seriously?" Olive said incredulously.

"Okay, fine, I'm wallowing, but I'm allowed. I got dumped."

"Did you dump Michael or did he dump you?" Olive wondered. "Because I'm not sure you throwing a picture of the two of you at his head really counts as getting dumped."

That was Olive: always interminably *unstoppable.*

"Fine, fine, fine," Neal said. "Get out of here so I can haul my naked ass to the shower."

Olive sprung off the bed, her pretty features twisting into a grimace. "Gross. You are so gross, Uncle Neal."

"Believe me, I know," he said.

Chapter Two

Jamie felt confident—at least *a little* confident—until the moment his Uber pulled up to the address he'd copied from Sam's text message.

He was from Palo Alto, which was full of tech geniuses who liked to outdo each other, but there was something about this house, and how it took up nearly an entire block, and how the street was full of everything from Mercedes to Range Rovers to even a few Maseratis, that made Jamie nearly turn around and climb back into his Uber.

He wasn't even a player in the NFL—not yet, anyway—what was he even doing here?

Hesitating at the foot of the enormous driveway, full of cars that all cost more than what the Riptide were paying him for this chance, Jamie wondered if he even belonged here.

Sam wanted you to come, his brain reminded his heart. *Are you really gonna argue with Sam Crawford about whether you belong?*

He started to walk up the driveway. Sam had said it was a pool party, and so Jamie had worn his swim trunks, throwing on an old Stanford t-shirt. He was glad he had, because he could hear the sounds of water splashing, even though the entire backyard was surrounded by a tall stucco wall, keeping any curious eyes out.

The front door was gigantic, two huge slabs of wood, hand-carved with intricate designs, the wrought iron handles the size of his whole arm. "Geez," Jamie muttered under his breath, wondering if he should knock or ring, or maybe just . . . maybe just go in?

"I'm sure more intimidating doors exist, but I've personally never seen any." The unknown voice was dry, so dry a single flame would start a fire in it, and rough, like it wasn't used to speaking, and *deep*, so deep that Jamie felt the sound way down in his gut. At the base of his stomach, where arousal flickered to life. He'd always had a thing for voices, and this one wasn't changing his mind.

Jamie turned, sure that he'd be disappointed when he saw the man with that unbelievably sexy growl. But he couldn't see anyone, not through the lush gardens that surrounded the house in the front. He craned his neck, and finally could make the figure of a man, who looked to be sitting on a bench tucked in between several large bougainvillea bushes, ripe with bright fuchsia blossoms.

"It makes me wonder if I should knock or lay siege," Jamie said.

The man laughed, low and dark, and heat bloomed inside Jamie.

"I've wondered that too," he said.

Jamie walked over to where the man was shielded by the blooms. Maybe it wasn't right, and he would almost certainly be disappointed, but he wanted to see who was talking. Maybe it was even a guy from the team that he'd met today—but at the same time, Jamie knew that if he'd ever heard this voice before, he'd have remembered it, a visceral sense memory.

"Are you hiding out? Or maybe you're allergic to water?" Jamie wondered.

The man chuckled, and Jamie's stomach clenched. "No. If anything, I'm probably allergic to people."

"That'd be too bad," Jamie said regretfully, because goddamn it, he wanted to meet this guy. Even if he was ugly. Even if he was straight. That didn't matter. He just needed him to keep talking.

He considered trying to skirt around the bougainvillea, but it was clear that there was another *actual* entrance to the tiny private garden where the man was sitting. He had a feeling that Sam wouldn't be very happy if he trampled through their landscaping, just because he wanted to know the man who had the sexy-as-fuck voice.

"But is it?" the man wondered, the question clearly rhetorical.

"I think it would be," Jamie said firmly.

"My niece told me I should come—she practically dragged me here—but going inside? That's a whole other problem."

Jamie wanted to ask him why he didn't want to, but he had a feeling if he pushed, the man would never reveal himself. He'd evaporate into thin air, leaving Jamie aching and curious.

"Sam invited me," Jamie confessed, "but I think it had to be a mistake because I'm nobody."

"Ah, but Sam doesn't think that way," the man said. "He's way too egalitarian for that. Must be because he started as the backup."

He was desperate to ask how he knew Sam, and *how well* he knew Sam. Maybe this was Heath? But no, Jamie had heard Heath speak plenty of times, in interviews and in press conferences, and his voice had never done anything to him, not the way this man's was.

"Well, I'm not even the backup," Jamie said wryly.

"Still trying to make the team, huh?" he asked. "A rookie?"

"Yeah," Jamie admitted.

"Well, good luck," the man said, and Jamie had a feeling that was the end of it. He could either figure out a way to breach the garden, even though the man had said fairly bluntly he wasn't interested in interacting with anyone, or he could walk into the house and join the party.

But, that voice in Jamie's head said, *he* did *interact with you. Even though he said he was probably allergic to people.*

"You sure you don't want to come in? The water's fine."

The man laughed, and goose bumps ran up Jamie's arms. "You haven't been in the water yet."

"Okay, it's *probably* fine," Jamie said. "At least if it's anything like the rest of the house."

"I might," he said. "If I can decide I can stomach it."

"Come find me if you do," Jamie said and knocked on the door, hoping for a quick exit after he'd made his interest so obvious that even a straight guy couldn't miss it.

The door opened almost immediately, and it wasn't Sam or Heath. It was a girl with curly blond hair, and a wide smile on her face. She was carrying a pink plastic cup with glittery writing that read, "Sip Happens."

"Hey," she said.

"I'm Jamie, Sam invited me?" he said hesitantly. With the man grown silent behind him, Jamie had suddenly rediscovered his nerves. *What was he doing here?* Suddenly, he didn't have a single fucking clue.

"Ah, yeah, he mentioned that one of the new guys would be coming," she said, and she waved him inside, the door shutting solidly behind him. "I'm Felicity, Sam's sister."

They shook hands briefly. "It's nice to meet you," Jamie said.

She glanced down at his emerald green swim trunks. "Good," she said with an approving nod, "you brought your swimsuit."

"Sam said it was a pool party?" Jamie said.

She laughed, tossing her wild hair down her back. Her swimsuit was bright cherry red, the straps crossing across her tanned back. Jamie hardly knew Sam very well, but he could still see the strong family resemblance. "You'd be surprised at how many of Sam's teammates show up without one. Heath started buying them in bulk, because he hates not being prepared."

She'd led him through the gigantic foyer, with its soaring vaulted ceilings, and into a large kitchen. Beyond the eating nook, a whole wall of glass opened up onto a stamped concrete patio. The pool was a few steps down into the garden and it was full of people. Screams of kids and adults echoed through the kitchen. The matte gray concrete kitchen counters were full of food, some of it half-eaten, some of it barely touched.

"I can see that," Jamie said. "Is it always like this?"

Felicity waved to a chain of coolers sitting out on the patio. "Drinks are out there, and they're *labeled*. Yes, it's always like this because *he's* always like this. Though, he certainly used to be worse."

"When he was still playing," Jamie guessed, figuring out they were talking about Heath, who was notorious for his lengthy game preparation—that he'd apparently now transferred to party prep.

She turned to him, gaze suddenly hot and fierce. "Yes," was all she said, but Jamie thought there was a multitude contained in that one word.

Sam and Heath had not done much press since the Super Bowl kiss that had shocked the world. They kept their relationship private, even though they'd come out in the most public way possible. Since that day, Sam gave a few interviews, usually about football, but Heath didn't. He'd retired, and now he gave no interviews at all.

"He's happier this way," Jamie guessed.

"He wasn't happy at all before, and now he is," Felicity said simply. "That's all that matters to me."

It occurred to Jamie then, that while Sam might have invited him to his house, Felicity was the real test. She wasn't just the person who'd been closest to the door, the younger sister who liked pink glittery wineglasses, but the protector, and if Jamie's guess was right, she'd appointed herself.

"Me too," Jamie admitted. "I wasn't sure I could come out, even after O'Connor did, but that kiss at the Super Bowl? It changed the world. It changed *my* world."

Her smile warmed. "You make sure to tell him that," she said.

He'd intended to; it was one of the reasons he hadn't chickened out, in the end, and he'd actually walked up to that fucking gigantic set of double doors. He owed Heath and Sam something. How much and what kind of currency? He wasn't sure yet.

"I will," Jamie promised.

"Good," she said and like she'd just decided, wrapped an arm around his shoulders, surprising him. "Come on, I'll introduce you."

Heath Harris, his imposing frame still as impressive as when he'd thrown so many precise touchdowns, threading the ball between defenders, was sitting on the edge of the pool, a wild grin on his face, hair slicked back.

Sam was in the pool leading what seemed like an entire football team of kids in a rousing game of Marco Polo.

"Heath," Felicity said, "I've got someone you should meet."

Heath glanced up, and Jamie saw he still had a little of that old intensity about him, the intensity that Jamie remembered from a hundred post-game press conferences and pre-game interviews, but it had softened. Felicity's words resounded through him; he hadn't been happy, and now he was. The evidence made the truth of that difficult to deny.

"Hey," Heath said, extending a hand but not moving. His hand was big and his grip was firm, if a little damp. "I'm Heath."

"Jamie Wright," he responded. "I'm one of the new kickers they brought in."

"Oh yeah," Heath said, his faint Texas drawl still evident in the corners of his words, "Sam mentioned you."

"No idea if I'll still be on the team after the next few days," Jamie admitted wryly. "Lots of us here for camp."

Heath rolled his eyes. "Coach is smart, but sometimes too smart, if you get my drift."

Jamie did. "It's a hard thing, to lose like that." He personally didn't know how that felt yet, to have everything ripped away in a single heart-wrenching moment, but he wanted to believe that if he did, he wouldn't let it get into his head like that. But it was impossible to predict; that was one of the reasons why football was so popular.

Heath shrugged. "Yeah," he agreed, "but it doesn't excuse acting like a fucking maniac about it."

That was sort of what Jamie thought too, but he hadn't wanted to say it so bluntly, considering that Heath was now on the coaching staff of the Riptide, and it was hard to say which side he'd come down on. Jamie should've guessed he'd be a hell of a lot more reasonable than any of the other coaches.

"Hey, Heath, have you seen my uncle?"

They both glanced up at a young woman with long, dark hair pulled back into a ponytail, forehead creased with concern.

"I don't think so," Heath drawled. "I hadn't realized he'd come with you."

She sighed, clearly more annoyed than worried. "He's probably hiding somewhere."

"I hope he knows he doesn't have to," Heath said, getting to his feet. "We don't judge here."

Throwing up her hands, she grimaced. "Oh, he knows. Other people's judgment isn't nearly as painful as his own, apparently."

There was something familiar about her face, about the shape of her hazel green eyes. Jamie couldn't quite place it, but obviously her uncle was a football player.

"If I see Neal, I'll let you know," Heath said.

It hit Jamie like a lightning bolt to the chest. *Neal. She has to be talking about Neal Fisher.* That's why the girl had looked so familiar, and those eyes? Jamie was kicking himself for not recognizing them immediately.

"Neal Fisher is here?" Jamie stammered. His first thought was *awkward*, and his second and overriding thought was, *oh god, I might actually get to* meet *him.*

Heath's gaze turned on him instantly. "Is that a problem?" he asked. He still sounded calm, but everything about him had suddenly sharpened, and Jamie was reminded of the Heath Harris he'd seen so many times, right before he'd thrown a touchdown pass.

"No, no, of course not," Jamie said. "I'm . . . honestly, I'd love to meet the guy."

Heath's expression relaxed into a smile. He clapped a damp hand on Jamie's shoulder. "Then I'll make sure you do. But first, let's get you some grub."

As they walked towards the house, Heath glanced over at him. "Don't see many kickers who look like you," he observed quietly. It was not the first or the last time that Jamie would probably hear about this, but he had to give Heath credit for not just demanding to know what a guy who looked like he did was doing playing football.

"Nope," Jamie said. "But that just makes me memorable."

Heath grinned. "That it does."

"My parents adopted me from India when I was a baby," Jamie said. "And before you ask, because almost everyone does, *yes*, I see them as my parents."

"People actually ask you that?" Heath sounded annoyed, which was yet another point in his favor.

"You'd be shocked at what people think they can ask me."

Heath sighed. "Just when I think we've made some good strides in the right direction, I'm reminded that there's a long way to go." He clasped hands with Jamie. "Well, know you're always welcome here. Always."

At the grill, he met Felicity and Sam's father, who apparently owned a whole chain of Los Angeles restaurants but on the weekends liked to man Heath and Sam's backyard grill.

It felt surreal to be surrounded by so many people he'd only watched on TV. There was Bran Phillips, the famous center for the Riptide, just over there, a small girl balanced on his shoulders, and they were both laughing. Rashad Green, the best running back in the league, was sitting on a chaise lounge, sipping something fruity and frozen from a plastic margarita glass. And then there was Heath, making sure he got something to eat, and introducing him to everyone who they met. "The new kicker," Heath said several times, even though it was hardly like he'd won the job. But then Heath would know that better than anyone, because he was on the coaching staff and he knew how many kickers they'd brought in to try out. But every single time he said it, Jamie felt like giving an addendum of *not quite yet, but maybe, hopefully? If everything works out.*

But he didn't, because even though Heath was more relaxed than Jamie had ever seen him, he was still Heath Harris, and he contained so much goddamn confident certainty that after meeting most of the people at the party, it was *hard* not to think of himself as the Riptide's new kicker.

You're getting ahead of yourself; you still gotta make it happen, he reminded himself. *Tomorrow is the day you're gonna have to prove yourself, again. And then you're gonna have to do it over and over again, and then probably a couple hundred more times, for good measure.*

Maybe then Coach R and Coach Toby might be satisfied.

He was sitting on the edge of the pool when suddenly he felt a body drop down next to him. He was half-expecting it to be Heath or maybe even Sam—which was surreal because he'd never imagined he'd be in the kind of position to be sought out by either of those guys—but then when he glanced over, he nearly fell into the pool.

It was Neal Fisher, and he was just in a pair of navy blue trunks, with little green palm trees scattered across the fabric. He was pale, like he'd spent too long inside this summer, but he was still undeniably handsome, his green eyes glowing in his gorgeous face, offset by his dark hair. It fell into his eyes a bit, probably because it needed a trim.

Jamie's hands tightened on the edge of the pool and he prayed he didn't make a fucking fool out of himself. He was just meeting his idol, that was all, and a guy he'd probably spent way too much time fantasizing about over the years.

Do not tell him you've jerked off to him about a thousand times. Do not even think about it.

"Hey," Neal said casually. So casually that Jamie had a feeling that he didn't know who Jamie really was. "You told me to come find you." He smiled then, and though it was only a shadow of his former smile, which Jamie was embarrassed to admit he was intimately familiar enough with to tell the difference, it was still a smile. He poked Jamie in the shoulder. "Found you."

"You did," Jamie said. He grinned back, because he could not fucking help it. God, *Neal Fisher,* he was the one with the insanely sexy voice. Why hadn't he noticed in all those interviews he'd watched that Neal's voice was literal fire? Why was he even surprised anymore? Fate seemed to have it in for him. "I'm Jamie." He extended a hand towards the man, feeling a bit like he was walking on eggshells.

Should he tell him the truth, that he was only in town because he was trying to win his old job? Should he tell him he'd worshipped and admired and adored him from afar? That when Neal had missed the kick in the Super Bowl, it had felt like he'd been kneed in the solar plexus, that he'd felt sick for days as it became increasingly clear that Neal didn't care if the ball had been tipped, he intended to take every ounce of blame?

He should definitely not say *any* of that.

"Neal," he said shortly, not bothering to take his hand. "But then," he added wryly an awkward moment later, "you probably already know that. Not the greatest thing to be known for."

"For being a fucking amazing kicker with an enviable career, all with a single team?" Jamie wondered. "I'd think so."

Neal rolled his eyes, but didn't leave like Jamie was worried he would. "Don't even start."

But Jamie was just getting going, even though he still hadn't figured out when would be the best moment to tell the truth. *I'm a kicker, too, and I'm here for your old job.*

It should have been easy to say the words, but they stuck in his throat.

"I mean it," Jamie said.

Neal glanced over at him, and his expression had warmed slightly. "I think you might, actually."

"Have . . ." Jamie hesitated. "Have people been shitty to you?"

Duh, of course they have, you idiot.

Leaning back, Neal glanced up at the sky. It gave Jamie an uninterrupted view of Neal's torso and all the muscular ridges and nooks and crannies that Jamie knew a kicker didn't really *need*, but that Neal had anyway. Why? Probably because he'd been put on this earth to drive Jamie insane.

"Can they be if you don't give them a chance?" Neal wondered. "I've kinda been hiding."

"You came here," Jamie said, even though technically, he *had* been hiding, in the front yard, behind the bougainvillea. But he wasn't anymore, and in a fantasy he'd probably indulge in tonight, Jamie believed that he'd come out just for him.

"My niece, she made me come," he said. "I haven't been . . . getting out much."

"I think I met her, briefly," Jamie admitted. "She seems nice and uh . . . determined?"

Neal laughed dryly. "You are not wrong." His gaze swung back to Jamie, and suddenly he was sweating, despite that the sun had almost completely set in the last hour. "I probably would have stayed there, if you hadn't shown up at the front door."

Jamie's heartbeat accelerated, and he couldn't tear his eyes away from the guy next to him. *God, you need to tell him,* that annoying voice in the back of his head insisted. It sounded like a weird meld between Dylan and his dad. *He's gonna be pissed that you kept it from him.*

"And look," Jamie said, waving around. "You're fine. No judgment, no nasty comments, nobody died."

Neal's chuckle was humorless. "Not yet, anyway."

"Sam and Heath don't blame you," Jamie argued. He couldn't say the coaching staff didn't care, because the fact that he was *here*, in Los Angeles, proved they did. But he didn't want Neal to think he wasn't surrounded by friends, because from the hour or two he'd spent chatting with some of the other Riptide players and their families, he knew this was a good group of people.

"No." Neal let out a sigh. "You know how it is. The toughest critic is always yourself."

Jamie knew. Same way he knew that if he didn't make the team after this camp was over, he'd never really forgive himself. Same way that every single missed kick he'd had playing for Stanford had haunted him for too many late nights.

And none of them had been even remotely as momentous as Neal's miss had been.

Jamie didn't like to think how Neal slept, or if he even slept at all.

Maybe he sleeps naked.

"Why did I make you want to come in?" Jamie asked, because the last thing Neal needed was to keep dwelling on negativity. And if the solution to that was to flirt with him, Jamie was hardly going to complain.

"You just reminded me of . . . I guess *me*, a long time ago," Neal said contemplatively, stretching his legs out into the water, the tan of them barely visible through the rippling water.

Even though Jamie knew exactly how old Neal was—and he thought his age and wisdom only made him way hotter—he nudged him in the side. "You're not that old," he teased.

"Then why do I feel so fucking ancient?" Neal wondered. "Maybe because I'm looking at some very young hotshot, someone who shouldn't be wasting his time with an old man."

If Neal was *old*, then Jamie was a goddamn monk.

"Seriously?" Jamie said incredulously.

"What?" Neal's voice was self-conscious. "Any moment now, Heath is gonna come arrest me for flirting with a minor."

"I'm twenty-three," Jamie informed him. "Totally legal."

"Twenty-three," Neal muttered under his breath. "Goddamn."

"Besides, I think Heath is gonna be happy you're out here, and you're actually talking to someone."

Neal smiled, an unexpectedly wild grin, with a feral edge that had Jamie's pulse thrumming just beneath his skin. God, he'd never in a million fucking years imagined that he'd meet Neal Fisher and Neal Fisher would *flirt* with him. And he would flirt *back*.

"Heath and Olive, both," Neal admitted. "And me too, if I could get my head out of my ass long enough to admit it." He hesitated. "So, I bet you were happy to be drafted to LA," he said.

Jamie was a smart guy; he knew exactly why Neal thought that might be, and what he was digging for.

Was this the moment he admitted he hadn't been drafted at all, because teams only rarely drafted kickers?

It was a no-brainer to ignore the voice in his head telling him he was being stupid by continuing to lie by omission. Neal Fisher was *flirting with him.* Neal Fisher wanted to know if he was interested in guys. And the moment he discovered that Jamie was a kicker, and Jamie was in LA to try out for his old job, Jamie was fairly sure that their conversation—and any possibility of more—would end.

"Yeah, actually," Jamie admitted. "It was Heath and Sam who gave me the courage to come out in college."

Neal nodded absently. Jamie knew he'd never officially come out, but then, he also played the kind of position that everyone forgot about until the game was on the line. But Jamie had heard lots of times that while Neal had never officially made any statements, he'd been living fairly openly as gay.

He'd even heard a rumor that Neal had dated a guy in the Riptide organization. Jamie didn't know if that particular rumor was true, but if it still was, he had a feeling Neal wouldn't be sitting next to him in Heath and Sam's pool.

"Sometimes I wonder whether I made a mistake not making more of a point of it," Neal said. "But then, nobody ever gave a shit about me. Not like Sam or Heath."

Jamie laughed. "Maybe if you'd planted one on the holder on the fifty-yard line."

"Have you seen that guy?" Neal said, his voice conspiratorial. "He was *not* cute."

Jamie actually had. He'd seen him today. He'd held the ball for a bunch of kicks Jamie had made.

This is the moment. You have to fucking tell him, now.

But he didn't get a chance. "Hey, Jamie. Neal. I wondered when you two guys would migrate together." It was Sam, and he was holding a bottle of Corona in one hand. His swim trunks were bright pink.

Neal glanced over at Jamie, confusion clear in his expression. "Why?"

Jamie opened his mouth. It was better to be honest *now* before Sam exposed him, but Sam just laughed. "You're both kickers."

Neal looked like he'd just been shot. "What?" he exclaimed. A second later he was standing up, water running in rivulets down his muscular legs. "What? You're a kicker? You're here . . ."

"There's a tryout," Jamie said grimly.

He couldn't even be angry at Sam for revealing the truth, when he knew that he should've told Neal the whole story—even *part* of the story—when he'd first sat down.

"Shit," Neal said, and turned away. Jamie scrambled upright and grabbed at his arm.

"Listen," Jamie managed to get out before Neal shed his grip surprisingly—and embarrassingly—easily.

"This was a mistake," Neal said, reaching down and grabbing a pair of flip-flops. "I'm getting out of here."

"Will you just wait a minute?" Jamie didn't know where his stuff was, but he wasn't willing to let Neal out of his sight to go look for it. Instead, he trailed Neal through the house, and towards the front door.

"We don't have anything to say to each other," Neal said firmly. "I'm . . . I'm like fucking kryptonite."

"What? And I'm Superman?" Jamie retorted. "An Indian-American Superman who kicks balls for a living? That'd be a unique twist."

Right when he got to the door, Neal turned, faced him. "You knew and you still came up and talked to me."

"Not before, not at the beginning," Jamie said, "and then it didn't matter."

Neal looked exasperated. "How can you say that?"

"I've only been a fan of yours forever. When you missed . . . it killed me, too. I . . . just want to talk to you. Pick your brain a little.

I'm way out of my league here, I think, and I want this job. Don't you want someone to take it who deserves it?"

Neal laughed bitterly. "You really think I give a fuck who gets it?"

"Yeah, yeah I do." Jamie looked at him steadily. Neal was handsome even when he was angry. He'd been handsome when he'd chucked his helmet on the sideline after missing the Super Bowl kick. He'd even looked handsome in the photos someone had taken of him being escorted out of the Riptide facilities after being released.

"You've got more issues than I can help you with, then," Neal said. "Why the fuck would you want *my* advice, anyway? You've got coaches coming out your ass and I'm sure some consultant, who is gonna tell you how you should do everything."

"Yeah, but they didn't do this for thirteen years," Jamie said. "I paid attention. I always paid attention to you."

"God." Neal sounded wretched. "You really *are* a fan."

"You were my idol. You're *still* my idol," Jamie said bluntly. "The only one who thinks you're not worth anything is you."

"You'd be surprised about that, kid," Neal said, and wrenched the door open. It creaked on its humongous hinges. "Good luck, 'cause you're definitely gonna need it."

Chapter Three

THIS WAS A HUGE mistake; I never should've gone.

Except that as Neal stomped to his car, anger and hurt and disbelief surging through him, he already knew that wasn't true. He'd regretted it at first—the moment he and Olive had driven up to the house, he'd known he wasn't going to go inside. So he'd lingered at the car, and watched as Olive had gone inside, excited and distracted that she was going to see her friends again. Instead of following her, he'd skirted around the side yard, because he knew there was a nice hidden bench where he could observe who came and went, but not be forced to interact with anyone.

And if Olive bitched that he'd come to the party, but not actually *come* to the party, he could argue that he'd literally been on Heath and Sam's property, and that was all she'd technically required.

Of course, she'd probably still argue that he hadn't really *gone* to the party. He'd hidden out, not talking to anyone.

Was that why he'd seen the kid walking up to Heath and Sam's door, expression awed and nervous and unsure, like he couldn't quite believe he could belong here, and he'd spoken to him? Was it because he'd seen himself, so many years earlier, not at Heath's door but at so many others?

Through the bushes, he'd seen the kid, all long lean muscle, mussed dark curly hair, just a touch too long. He'd wanted to see his face, and Neal hadn't been sure if that was because this was the first guy he'd really seen besides the one who delivered his groceries, or if it was the first guy he'd seen since Michael that made him want to *look*. Or maybe it was because he couldn't be more different than Michael was. Even the thought of hooking up with another blond guy made him want to vomit in his mouth a little.

But this one? He was dark-haired and had a gorgeous olive cast to his skin.

So he'd talked to him, telling himself the entire time, even as their conversation turned more flirtatious, that it didn't mean anything. He was still allowed to just *talk* to a cute guy. Even if he had no idea if the cute guy was straight or not. While both Heath and Sam were gay, plenty of straight football players came to their parties. But as they bantered back and forth, it had become more obvious that this guy was either oblivious or queer.

It was not his proudest moment, but that was the realization that made Neal cut the conversation off. He wasn't ready. He was a fucking wreck, even as he tried not to ever think about *why* that was. If it hadn't happened to him, he'd never have believed that five seconds could destroy a life, but five seconds had destroyed his.

Then the kid had disappeared into the house, and Neal had been left alone again.

He'd gotten used to being alone; had even regretted it when Olive had moved in early for school. But suddenly, the concept was less appealing. *Come find me,* the guy had said. An invitation so blatant that even Neal couldn't miss it, despite his admittedly pathetic state.

He had, and now he was regretting doing even that.

"Goddamn it," Neal muttered to himself when he reached his Tesla. "A *kicker.*" God or Fate or whatever the hell was up there calling the shots must be having a real laugh at his expense. "Was it not enough to ruin my life?" he wondered out loud, even though he knew nobody was going to answer him.

Neal groaned and leaned against the door, not even bothering to open it. If Jamie hadn't been a kicker, if he hadn't been here in LA for *his* old job, maybe he'd have suggested they find a quiet room somewhere, and he could've let the cute kid with the expressive eyes and the bright smile burn away some of his sadness for a while.

Would he have let that happen, though? Neal wasn't sure. Wasn't sure he deserved to feel anything besides the unrelenting guilt.

And then the kid's request! Neal groaned again. Why would anyone want him to help them? He was worst choice in the world right now to help anyone, but something Jamie had said came back to him. *The only one who thinks you're not worth anything is you.*

Maybe that was true. Maybe he was wallowing. Olive certainly seemed to think so. His sister would too, if he got up the courage to call her—and there was a reason he hadn't. Maybe because it was easier to sit in his house and feel sorry for himself than it was to figure out what it was he was going to do with the rest of his life.

Because as much as he wanted to believe it was over, deep down, he knew that wasn't true. Jamie had proved that it wasn't true.

"Fuck me," Neal muttered. Of course the guy who made him want to *live* again was a reminder of everything he'd lost. Someone, somewhere, definitely had an ironic sense of humor.

Before he could even finish his debate with himself, he discovered his legs were moving, and he was walking back to the house, skirting around the back again, through a side door that he knew would be unlocked during one of these parties. He'd spent a lot of time here in the last two years, and he used that knowledge to get back into the house without drawing any attention to himself.

His exit had been too obvious; Jamie chasing after him way too blatant. But Jamie had gone back inside, he hadn't left yet. He was still hanging out with Heath and Sam and whoever else at the pool.

I just want another look at him, Neal told himself, even as he knew it was a lie. He wanted way more than a look. He wanted

Jamie to touch him, and he wanted to touch him back. And he wanted Jamie's fierce belief in him to begin to melt away all the insecurities that had developed in the last six months.

I'm still worth something. I'll prove it.

The kitchen had been abandoned entirely in favor of the patio and the pool. A lot of the players with kids had left, leaving Heath, Sam, Rashad, Felicity, Olive, and a few others like Chase Riley, lingering in the shallow end, their laughter echoing through the backyard, lit with at least a dozen strands of twinkly lights, lanterns set every few feet around the edge.

He'd spent too many evenings here to count. He'd have even called Heath Harris a good friend, and he and Olive had grown close too, over the past year. But now? Neal knew Heath and Sam and most of the team didn't blame him—shit *happened*—but how did he stop blaming himself? Shouldering the guilt they'd refused to pick up?

Neal didn't know. Maybe that was why he was here, because once he'd started, he didn't know how to stop. Maybe there weren't any answers in Heath and Sam's backyard, but Neal didn't know where else to look.

Jamie was sitting next to Olive, chuckling at something she'd said. He wanted to know what it was, and even though he knew he'd probably burn in a new and different hell for eavesdropping, he skirted closer to the shadows, being careful to avoid the lights.

"I wish I could tell you what they've got planned for you," Heath said to Jamie then, the edge of his tone ripe with disgust.

What plan? What was happening with the tryout? Neal had been deliberately sticking his head in the sand about the empty kicker spot he'd left behind, but it sounded like it wasn't just the regular kind of tryout he'd expected the Riptide would hold. "But I've got no fucking clue."

"It was nuts today," Sam added. He was cradled against Heath's chest, periodically kicking a foot out to splash his sister. "I can't believe what they made them do."

Oh god, what did they make them do? Neal took a few steps closer. He both was desperate to know, and dreading the moment he found out. He didn't want to feel any worse about what had happened.

"The forty-four-yard kick down the line . . ." Sam continued, shaking his head. "Fucking brutal, man. But yours was the best, absolutely dead center."

"I saw it," Heath said, and Neal watched as Chase and Rashad nodded along. All players who had some vague idea of the kind of pressure that would've put on the kickers they'd brought in.

Neal believed that Coach R would be insane enough to make all his potential kickers try from forty-four yards. The man was a fucking perfectionist. Of everyone, the person in the organization who had taken the Super Bowl loss just as acutely as Neal was probably him.

"Still bullshit," Rashad muttered. "Putting you on fucking display like that. Did they *want* you to miss?"

It was a good question.

Jamie just shook his head. "I think . . . I think they're just messed up about it. Kickers aren't important, until they are, and that's all anyone's thinking about now."

"They never should've let Neal go," Heath cut in with a fierce defense that Neal hadn't expected at all. He'd cost the man Heath loved a chance at immortality, preserved in the record books. Heath was the kind of guy who didn't just *let that go*. Even the new version of Heath wasn't that forgiving. But he had, anyway. Neal bowed his head, gritting his teeth against the sudden onslaught of emotion rushing through him. Yeah, he and Heath were friends, but he'd never expected . . . *this*.

"I fought for him," Sam said, his voice was raw. "Nobody listened to me."

"They should've," Heath said, because naturally, Heath was on his boyfriend's side. "But they wouldn't listen to me either."

"God, people suck," Jamie said, sounding genuinely regretful.

"I've tried to get him to see that you guys don't blame him," Olive said. "But you know how he is."

The chorus of agreement made it clear that *yes*, they all knew how Neal was.

"He wants to take the burden of everyone's suffering," Heath said softly. "I know how it feels to be obligated to do that."

Neal watched as Sam pressed a kiss to his lover's arm. "I wish there was something we could do."

They didn't know it, but they were already doing it. It wasn't like they hadn't said all these things to him already. They'd flooded his inboxes—email and text and voicemail—after the Super Bowl, every single message one of unconditional support, but Neal hadn't been ready to hear any of it. He'd been too busy doing exactly what Heath said: trying to shoulder all the blame and all the responsibility for the loss.

But maybe that wasn't what he should be doing. Maybe he cared what happened to his job. Maybe he really fucking cared, and also, maybe he *could* help.

"I like you," Heath said to Jamie grimly. "I just hope you can outlast the onslaught Coach R and Coach Toby are about to bring."

It wasn't a decision so much as an inevitability.

"I think I could help with that," Neal said, strolling out into the light, casually, like he hadn't just been listening to a group of his friends talk about him.

Sam smiled. "I thought you might." He didn't look surprised at all.

"You are not nearly as sly as you think you are," Heath added with a chuckle.

Neal shrugged and dropped down onto the pool deck, right next to Jamie, their thighs touching just enough to make his nerves skitter with awareness. Jamie glanced over at him, eyes warm and dark, the lights reflecting gold in their depths. "I'm glad you came back," he said softly, "and not just because I want you to help me."

"I'll see what I can do," Neal said. "But if they're deciding to make this insane, there's not much I can do to change that."

"I can make the kicks," Jamie said, and Neal's heart clenched—god, he had been just like this thirteen seasons ago. "But I'm gonna need to keep steady."

"Without the pressure, you're just kicking a ball," Neal said.

Rashad stood, stretching his arms behind his head. "Come on," he said, gesturing to Riley, and to the few other players remaining. "We've got practice in the morning. We gotta be fresh."

The party thinned out after that. Olive and Felicity disappeared into the house, chattering about something, and even Heath and Sam got up, starting to clean up.

It left Neal and Jamie, not really *alone*, but alone enough.

Neal felt his heart rate accelerate in his chest. It would be a mistake to start something with this young kid—*I'm twenty-three*, he'd said, *totally legal*—but he *could* help him. He'd done this for thirteen years. He'd never imagined coaching before, and he didn't think he wanted to go into it, not like Heath had done, becoming Sam's mentor and his coach and his lover. But could he impart some wisdom to get Jamie through the next few days? Absolutely.

"Tell me about the tryout," Neal said. "Everything that's happened so far."

"Well, there's ten of us," Jamie said wryly, and Neal gaped at him.

"*Ten kickers?*"

Jamie nodded, and Neal swore under his breath. "What the fuck are they thinking?"

"Uh, I don't think there's much *thinking* happening," Jamie said. "And then, you heard about this a little, but before the warm-up or any practice, they lined us up in front of the rest of the team, and had us all kick."

"Forty-four yards," Neal said grimly. *"Jesus fuck.* They're trying to weed out anyone who might vaguely fold under pressure."

"That kind of pressure?" Jamie said. "Anyone would. There's not going to be any kind of consistency, not if they keep wrenching it tighter, and since that was just the first day, I expect it'll get worse."

"You sure you want this job?" Neal asked, laughing humorlessly.

Jamie braced his hands on his knees. "I . . . I think so. It's crazy, maybe. But someone has to take it. And I want it to be me."

"Why?" Neal wondered. Why would you want to take a job with basically the *most* scrutiny of any kicker in the league? Why this one when you already *knew* the coaching staff was fucked up over something that had happened last season?

Jamie shrugged. "It's close to my parents. They live up in Palo Alto. And I want to kick in this league."

"So? There's lots of spots."

"Yeah," Jamie said, flashing him a sudden grin. "But there's only one Los Angeles Riptide."

Neal rolled his eyes. "Might've meant a little more if we'd repeated."

"It was still an incredible accomplishment, to even make it that far," Jamie said, voice hushed. Supportive. Neal believed he meant every word he was saying. Was it a little naïve? Oh, definitely. He didn't know yet that this league would chew you up and spit you out. He'd seen it happen with way too many players, kickers and other positions alike. It took guts, and it took grit to stick.

Did Jamie have what it took? Neal supposed the next few days would prove that one way or the other.

"Don't let them make it into some kind of boogey monster, that forty-four yards," Neal advised. "It's just another kick."

"Just another kick," Jamie repeated slowly.

"Here," Neal said, pulling his phone out of his pocket. Just an hour earlier, he'd been hoping to exchange numbers for another reason, but he told himself, *this is good, too. Just . . . not as fun.* "Give me your number, and I'll text you."

Jamie's gaze was something near worshipful. Awed. Neal wanted to tell him there was nothing particularly special about him, but the hero worship felt like a balm to his soul after so many months of being convinced he was worthless. Would it fix everything that had gone wrong in his life? Would it fix all his wallowing? No, but it was a good reminder that everything wasn't only pain and guilt.

Jamie repeated his number, stumbling over the digits twice. He gave Neal a sheepish smile. "I can't believe I met you," he said, and he reached over and hesitating a little, brought his hand down on

Neal's leg, resting it on his knee, just below where his swim trunks ended, so he was touching bare skin.

Neal sucked in air, surprised and floored by the single touch. Clearly it had been way too long since he'd even *thought* about sex, if this kid was affecting him this strongly. Already his cock was stirring in his shorts, and they were a thin material, and wouldn't hide a thing if Jamie kept pressing his fingers into his skin that way.

Who knew the knee was such a fucking incredible erogenous zone?

"I think you really mean that," Neal said.

Jamie's grin was sunshine-bright, white teeth flashing against his tanned skin. "Oh, I do."

"We should . . ." Neal was trying to formulate exactly what they *should* do, but the words weren't really coming. Instead, they felt jumbled in his head, the sudden sexual tension between them making everything fuzzy.

"We should . . .?" Jamie wondered.

"*You* should focus," Neal said, finally, firmly.

"Ah," Jamie said, but didn't move his hand. Instead, it felt like his grip tightened. "Okay."

"You're . . . uh . . ." Neal *wanted* to say: *you're making me think about your hand sliding higher, just high enough that you could feel what you're doing to me. To my cock.*

"I'm what?" Jamie asked. Amusement seemed to have joined the awe. He knew what he was doing to him, and he didn't seem particularly inclined to stop.

With the sun setting, the air had grown much cooler, but Neal began to sweat anyway.

"You're . . . maybe *I'm* the distraction," Neal finally admitted, embarrassed at how totally pathetic he sounded. He was a grown man, but he apparently couldn't handle a little bit of flirting. Before this, and before Michael, he'd have made sure Jamie was legal and then had all kinds of fun with him.

But something about this night, and this guy, made him feel like an unsure teenager again.

"You definitely are," Jamie teased lightly, "but at least you're a *fun* distraction." He swallowed hard, his Adam's apple bobbing in the dim light of the pool. His hand squeezed Neal's knee again, and he leaned another inch closer.

Nobody would care if Neal leaned over and kissed him. After the Super Bowl that had changed the world, many NFL teams had finally joined the twenty-first century and had written explicit instructions into their code of conduct that two players were not allowed to be "physically" or "emotionally" involved. When they'd dated, Neal and Michael had received special dispensation from the Riptide coaching staff and the executive board—but it had been less of an issue because Michael technically wasn't a player, he was an employee.

But Neal, he wasn't a player either. Not anymore. He could be, he supposed, if he ever called his agent back about all those outstanding offers sitting on the table to try out for other teams. Besides, it wasn't like Sam or Heath, who'd carried on their own torrid affair under everyone's noses, gave two shits what happened in their backyard.

Neal could do anything. Well, not *anything*. But he could definitely lean in the rest of the way and nibble on Jamie's full lower lip. Run his hands through Jamie's unruly curls. Nobody would care, and it would feel so good. The best thing he'd felt in forever.

"Uncle Neal?"

Fuck, Neal had forgotten about Olive.

That was unusual and a testament to how unbelievably attractive Jamie was—and how unbelievably attracted Neal was to him. "I'm here," he said, and as the moment was already broken, he pushed himself upright, Jamie's hand falling from his knee. It wasn't pressing into his skin anymore, but he could still feel it, like a brand, permanently etched there. Olive's presence had at least reminded his cock it was not playtime, and it deflated—though Neal already knew what he'd be doing when he got home.

"Sorry," she said, apologetically, standing out on the stamped concrete patio, just outside the kitchen. "I wasn't sure where you were."

"Right here," Neal said, trying not to sound frustrated, but it was hard, because frustration was cascading through him. God, he wanted more than anything to lean down and press his mouth to Jamie's. But that wasn't why Jamie had tried to stop him from leaving earlier. He'd wanted his advice and his support—and yes, Neal couldn't deny it; from the last five minutes, it was obvious

Jamie wanted something else, too. But that wasn't happening tonight, and it maybe wasn't happening ever.

"Hey," Neal said, leaning down, and *not* giving in to temptation by kissing Jamie, like he'd been dreaming about. "Hey, I gotta take Olive home, but . . . text me okay? I'm here for you."

Jamie smiled, his eyes crinkling at the edges. "Okay. I will. Thanks."

Neal walked around the pool to where Olive was standing. "We didn't have to leave right now," she said. "I just wasn't sure where you'd gone."

"I hadn't moved," Neal pointed out wryly. "But it's okay. It's late. And I know these guys have practice tomorrow morning."

"I'm just glad you came, and you actually *came*," Olive said, surprisingly throwing her arms around him, hugging him tightly. "I was . . . I was worried about you."

"I'll get over it," Neal said, even though before this evening he'd have argued fiercely with that theory, but as much as he hated to admit it, Olive had been right about getting out. He felt marginally less pathetic than he had this morning.

"I know you will, you're so strong," Olive murmured into his shoulder. "And you should call your agent."

He knew he should. It did not surprise him she'd added that, because he wouldn't be surprised if Alec had contacted his sister Ella, and then Ella had recruited Olive.

He couldn't even leave the house; how was he supposed to go to a different city and a different team and try to pick up the tattered remnants of a career again?

"We should go say goodbye to Heath and Sam," Neal said firmly. He wasn't going to talk about his agent or all those offers with Olive, because if he was stupid enough to do that, he'd probably end up making *her* his agent, in the end. And he loved his niece dearly, but the last thing he needed was her deciding she was not only in charge of his life, she was in charge of his career, too.

"Sure," Olive said. He wasn't naïve enough to think she'd dropped it, but at least she'd let it go for now.

Heath was packing up the food, putting it away in neatly labeled containers. Sam was lounging against the counter, reading something on his phone.

"Hey, we're about to take off," Neal said.

Heath glanced up. "Oh, already?"

"Yeah," Sam added, "you are absolutely free to stay in our backyard for as long as you like, as long as you keep flirting with the new kicker."

"He's not the new kicker yet," Neal argued. Because he wasn't going to touch Sam's flirting accusation with a ten-foot pole. Mostly because he was *right*.

"If you help him, he *could* be," Sam said slyly.

"I'm going to," Neal said. "I told him I would."

"Good," Heath said, sounding pleased by this turn of events. "I was hoping you'd see sense."

"Don't get any other ideas," Neal warned.

"What other ideas?" Sam asked innocently, when he wasn't innocent at all. Not even close. Neal knew how he worked.

"Like, *matchmaking* ideas," Neal said firmly.

"We'd never do that," Heath said steadily. And maybe the old Heath wouldn't have—wouldn't have even *dreamed* of it—but this new Heath? The happier, lighter version? The one who was head over heels in love with his boyfriend? Neal wasn't sure he'd be able to resist.

"Of course not," Olive chirped.

Neal knew they were all full of bullshit.

"Well, I guess I'll see you guys around," Neal said, suddenly awkward because he wouldn't be going to practice tomorrow—not like everyone else was. It reminded him for the millionth time that everything had changed in the last six months.

"Yeah, you will," Heath said very firmly, coming around the counter, pulling him into a brief, tight hug. "Don't be a stranger."

"Don't worry," Olive promised, as Heath hugged her next. "I won't let him."

Neal was afraid she was definitely telling the truth.

· · · ● · ● · · ·

When they got home, Olive retreated to her suite above the garage—she'd appropriated the guest suite when she'd moved in last year for college, and Neal liked that it gave both of them some privacy.

He hadn't really gotten into the pool, but he drifted towards the bathroom and the shower anyway, his blood already heating at the thought of putting his hands on himself. How long had it been since he jerked off? He couldn't even remember the last time. The urge had faded over the last few months, but now it was back, and he already knew who he was going to think about.

Flipping the water on hot, he watched as the steam began to fill the space. He imagined if Jamie had come back to the house with him, and they'd ended up here, eyes glued to each other as they stripped their clothes off.

Jamie was slender, but strong, and as Neal pulled off his t-shirt and pushed down his swim trunks, he let himself remember the way his biceps had bunched when he'd pushed himself up from the edge of the pool. The way his strong thighs had tensed when Neal had sat down next to him.

He groaned when he stepped into the hot shower, fisting his already hardening cock in one hand, bracing the other against the tiled wall. Jamie's body had been undeniably attractive, and Neal didn't even want to pretend he didn't want him. But the trusting, awed glow in his dark eyes? The way he'd bitten that full bottom lip between his even, white teeth as Neal had flirted with him? That had him moaning as he stroked himself faster, pleasure spiking through his system. He hadn't done this in so long because he hadn't wanted to, but also because he'd been afraid that Michael would intrude. But right now? Michael was the furthest thing from his mind. The only person he was focused on, dark curls falling over his forehead, a bashful yet determined smile on his face, was Jamie.

Maybe it wasn't right to be using his memory—and his fantasies—like this, but it felt too good to stop. Neal imagined Jamie going to his knees, eyes begging for it, his hot mouth wrapping around Neal's cock, and sucking him deep. It would be so good. So good it might even burn away so much of the wretchedness that had dogged him these last few months.

Jamie and his fantastic mouth, even in Neal's imagination, couldn't fix everything, but as his orgasm crested through him in a dizzying rush, he knew it didn't matter. He'd made him feel *good*, instead of bad, and Neal was going to take that, at least for tonight.

He finished washing his body and hair quickly, toweling off after stepping out of the glassed-in shower. For the first time in a very long time, he stared at his reflection in the mirror. He looked pale and gaunt, the sadness evident in the depths of his eyes, in the purple bruises underneath them. He wondered what Jamie had thought when he'd looked at him. He mustn't have thought Neal was pathetic; if he had, why had he flirted with him? Why had he wanted to kiss him?

Walking back into the bedroom, Neal retrieved his phone from the bedside table. When he unlocked it, he saw that Jamie had texted him back.

With trembling fingers, Neal opened the conversation and stared at the screen. His text to Jamie had been simple and straightforward. He'd said, **Hey, it's Neal.** But underneath Jamie had written practically a novel.

Stumbling to the bed, Neal couldn't tear his eyes from the screen.

When you talked to me at the front door, I thought I could listen to your voice for the next hundred years. In bed, and out of it. And when you came and found me, I thought you were even handsomer than you were that day six months ago. When you agreed to help me, I knew you were someone special. I meant what I said. You're not worthless. You're not washed up. You're bright as a star in the sky, your brilliance is just a little faded right now.

And under that romance novel of a text, was another one. **Sorry if that was too much . . . if I hadn't been a kicker, I think I'd have been a writer. Unusual choice of profession, yeah? Anyway, thanks for agreeing to help me.**

Neal didn't know what to say to either message. He didn't know how Jamie could have watched that kick six months ago and still believe everything he said. But he did, that much was crystal clear.

He stared at his phone's screen for long enough that his towel eventually fell away, and his hair dried in a bird's nest on his head. But somehow it seemed wrong to not acknowledge all the things that Jamie believed that Neal wasn't sure he could, yet—but how to do it? Neal didn't know, and he sat there for a long time, trying to figure out how he felt, and then how to put those feelings into words.

I think you see a different version of me than anyone else, he finally typed out. **Thank you for looking deeper. And you were right, I DO care who takes my spot. It should be you.**

It didn't matter that he'd never seen Jamie kick—though he quickly remedied that problem, because after sending the text, he pulled YouTube up on his phone, and binged about a season's worth of Jamie's field goals—he knew he was going to help him succeed. Not just because he deserved it but because for the first time in way too long, Neal felt like he was something other than a ghost, just waiting to fade away.

He lay back in his bed and watched another handful of Jamie's videos. He could see why the Riptide had called him to try out. He was consistent, with excellent textbook form. He'd made some tough kicks—up in Oregon, at Autzen Stadium, with the rain pouring down like a whole litter of cats and dogs; in USC's Coliseum, to win a particularly contested game—and he was a smart kid.

Too smart, probably, to get into kicking. Maybe Neal should encourage him to give writing a try, though it was hardly like that was a professional path more guaranteed to find success.

Still, Jamie had a way with words. A way that had captured Neal's attention as nothing else had for months. And when he fell asleep a little while later, he did it with a smile on his face.

Chapter Four

"So, how was the party?" Dylan asked as they went through a series of stretches, first thing the next morning.

"It was fun," Jamie said. He already knew he couldn't tell Dylan—or anyone—about meeting Neal. Except he was dying to; dying to scream it from the rooftops. *I met Neal Fisher, and he's hot and sexy and kind of sad, and there's nothing I want more than to make him smile.*

He'd known that text he'd sent was *way* too much, but then what was the point of meeting the guy you'd fantasized about forever, in the flesh, and experiencing that kind of electric sexual attraction, and *not* doing anything about it? If it backfired, and Neal thought he was a weirdo, then what was the worst that would happen? He wouldn't help him through camp? The chances of them ever running into each other again by accident were slim, if practically nonexistent, especially if Jamie didn't make the Riptide.

It had made sense to take the chance last night, but this morning, when he'd read Neal's response, his stomach had fluttered with a thousand butterfly wings. He hadn't hated Jamie's words; he'd even *appreciated* what Jamie had said, and how he'd felt. Maybe he'd even felt some of the same thing. After all, he'd sought Jamie out *twice*, when he'd not even wanted to go to the party in the first place.

"That was it? It was fun?" Dylan wondered. "I'm disappointed, man."

Jamie shrugged. "I got to meet some of the guys on the team. Rashad Green was there, and Chase Riley, and Heath and Sam, of course. And Bran, and a few others. It was great. The food was good. The pool was gorgeous. You wouldn't believe Heath and Sam's house, it's fucking incredible."

"I'm so jealous," Dylan said with a reluctant sigh. "You gotta get me some of the dirt, though. I'm dying for it."

Neal Fisher was there, and he's gonna help me make the team. He also nearly kissed me, and even though it didn't happen, it still made my entire life.

"It was just a fun time," Jamie said. All true. He wasn't lying to Dylan. It *had* been fun.

"Boo, you suck," Dylan said.

"Probably not as much as today will," Jamie said, changing the subject on purpose. He didn't trust himself, because the confession that he'd met Neal was right there, on the tip of his tongue.

"Oh god, you're not wrong," Dylan agreed. "Fuck, I sat in my crap hotel room last night and thought, *what are you doing here? You could've been in Green Bay, trying to best Mason Crosby.*"

Jamie didn't bother to hold back his eye roll. "Yeah, you could've gone to Green Bay, but that wasn't gonna happen. No offense, dude."

"It wasn't, which is why I came to LA instead." Dylan paused. "Still, if I'd known what this camp was gonna be like, maybe I wouldn't have."

"I think . . ." Jamie looked out over the field where the rest of the kickers were gathered. "I think we might have already lost a few?"

"You think so?" Dylan went through the motions of counting off the guys who'd joined them the day before. "Damn, yeah, we've lost two. Unless they left because this is so fucked up."

"They both missed that kick yesterday," Jamie said thoughtfully.

"But so did I, and a couple of others did too," Dylan said, his voice taking on a frustrated edge. "Fuck, I could make that kick in my sleep, but with all that pressure . . ."

"They're not setting us up to succeed. You can't blame yourself," Jamie said, his own voice getting hard. It was one of the reasons he'd tossed and turned last night, sleep coming in fits and starts when he finally managed to fall asleep. Did he really want to join a team that didn't really trust him? Who was just sitting back, watching and waiting for him to fail? He wasn't sure. But it hadn't only been his indecision on what the right path was, it was Neal, smiling at him, eyes sad and thoughtful and glowing, when Jamie had reached out, putting a hand on his knee. When Jamie had flirted with him, and he'd flirted back.

Coach Toby coming over, clapping his hands to gather everyone's attention, interrupted their conversation and yanked Jamie's focus back to what mattered—doing the best he could today. Even if he didn't make the Riptide, other teams might be interested in him if he was a finalist for the spot.

"We're trying something new today," he said, a guy that Jamie didn't recognize walking over to stand next to the special teams coordinator. "This is Ned Palmer from TrackBuddy. He normally works with golfers, to improve the angle and velocity of their swing. But we're going to use his setup to test your kicks."

Dylan made a scoffing noise under his breath, just low enough that Jamie, standing next to him, could hear.

"There's all kinds of data we can get from the sensors we put on the ball," Ned said, nodding at Coach Toby. "Data that should help you make smarter, better kicks."

"Smarter kicks?" Dylan muttered.

As Jamie glanced around at the rest of the assembled kickers, he saw a lot of the same disbelief he was feeling. He'd never heard of this before, not in all his years kicking, both in high school, and then in college, at Stanford.

"In case you hadn't noticed," Coach Toby said, the amusement in his voice falling flat, "we're serious about finding a new kicker."

We noticed, Jamie wanted to say, but he had a feeling that anything and everything was going to be used to make the final determination. How else would you pick from such a huge field of candidates?

Still, he couldn't wait for their lunch break, when he could grab his phone from his locker and text Neal about this latest insanity.

"This is *nuts*," Dylan said when they broke apart to get ready to work on extra-point kicks. "What the fuck are they thinking? Who cares about how fast the ball is going when it comes off my foot? If it's gonna go in, it's *gonna go in*."

"I don't know," Jamie said, but couldn't help the frisson of panic he felt when faced with the ball covered in all its electronic sensors. He knew he wasn't perfect; if he'd been better, more visible, he'd have had a chance to actually get *drafted*, which sometimes happened to the most promising kickers in a class. Hell, the Patriots had even drafted a punter two years ago. It *could* happen. But while he always wanted to improve, and make himself better and more consistent, the last thing he wanted was to be confronted by a set of data—"data never lies" his father always liked to say—that informed him (and the Riptide) that he was an impostor, and actually not a very good kicker after all.

He could do extra points in his sleep, but he was so keyed up, extra sensitive to every part of his process, that he nearly shanked the hell out of his first one.

"Shit," Jamie muttered as he returned to the group standing around. "Shit, shit, shit." He needed to get himself together, find his focus, and not let this increasingly weird crap throw him.

What would Neal say?

You can make these—you've never missed one in a game, he'd say. And he'd be right.

He took one deep breath, and then another, trying to find his calm and his normal zen state.

"You got this," Dylan said, after he'd made the next two. "You can't let that data shit fuck you up."

He couldn't. But it was hard not to think about it; even tougher not to *overthink* it. Because that was what the Riptide were doing, wasn't it? Massively overthinking.

By the time they got to their lunch break, Jamie *thought* he'd done alright, but without the data, how could he really know? And that was massively fucked up, because he hadn't actually missed a kick yet—and he could tell from the way Coach Toby kept eying him that he was one of the front-runners. Normally that would be a little pressure added to the general pressure of a tryout, but there was so much additional pressure being heaped on, that the additional weight barely made Jamie blink.

He grabbed his phone from the locker room and quickly typed out a message to Neal. **Going good this morning. Worked on extra points. They brought in some golfing system called TrackBuddy, and they're getting some kind of data from the ball.**

Neal's answer came back almost immediately, his phone buzzing in his pocket as he hurried towards the cafeteria to join the other kickers. He glanced at it when he was waiting in the buffet line. **Have you missed yet? Looking up that bullshit now. God damn these idiots.**

It was impossible not to smile at the text; Jamie could practically *hear* Neal's exasperation.

"You're looking perky, considering how we spent our morning," Dylan said when Jamie sat down with his tray of food. He'd missed once, and then Jamie could tell he'd thought about that miss every single kick afterwards. That was the danger in missing—sometimes you couldn't quite shake off that bad energy and move on.

It was the theory behind why teams let go normally consistent kickers when they missed once. They were always afraid the kicker would get too much into his head and wouldn't be able to get out again.

It was definitely why the Riptide had felt obligated to let Neal go—and add to that the fact he'd missed on the biggest stage imaginable and his release had been painfully inevitable.

"You need to get over that you missed," Jamie said. "Seriously."

"I don't know why you're giving me advice," Dylan said, frowning. "Though maybe I should be listening to you, 'cause you're clearly winning so far."

"I've had a few close calls," Jamie said. He had. But he'd shaken them off, Neal's voice in his ear the whole time, reassuring him that he could do this. Maybe it wouldn't have been so easy to listen, except that deep down, he *knew* he could.

"I'm dreading seeing those reports," Dylan groused.

That was something Jamie couldn't argue with. He'd made all his kicks, but had he made them with the right data backing him up? He had no fucking clue.

His phone buzzed again, and he glanced at it, unable to help his grin when he read the message. Actually, there were *two*. One, right after the other, in rapid fire.

I'm reading about TrackBuddy now.

Then, **WHAT THE FUCK ARE THEY DOING WITH THIS GARBAGE????**

"Who's that?" Dylan asked casually. "You're smiling so hard I think your face is gonna break in half. We're in the middle of hell, you shouldn't be so goddamned happy, even if you're the front-runner."

"Am I, though?" Jamie wondered. "I'm not the only guy who hasn't missed."

"No," Dylan admitted. "Shane, that guy who was a dick yesterday, he hasn't missed either."

"And that veteran, Kieran," Jamie said. But he already knew Kieran tapped out his max distance at about fifty yards, and Jamie could kick farther than that, because he'd grown up in an age when kickers were constantly pushing themselves to kick longer and longer field goals. Kieran was a few years older, and hadn't had that pressure, and as a result, hadn't put in the practice and work to push himself to the next level. Now, he would probably pay for it by losing this job.

If it came down to it, Jamie knew he could beat Kieran. Shane, too.

"Seriously though," Dylan pressed, "who are you texting with?"

"It's nobody," Jamie said. "Nobody important."

"Sure seems important. Important enough to go grab your phone from the locker room," Dylan said slyly. "Did you meet someone at the party? Seriously, you're glowing like that time in New Orleans at the Senior Bowl, when you met that one kid."

That one kid was Adam, a punter who he'd spent a few memorable nights with, and then they'd gone their separate ways. They still occasionally texted, but Adam hadn't left nearly the impression on him that Neal Fisher had—and they hadn't even kissed. *Yet.*

Yeah, Neal had tried to claim he couldn't get distracted, but what he didn't seem to understand was that he was *already* distracted. Avoiding the inevitable would probably only make that distraction worse. At least that was what Jamie told himself, and what he had every intention of telling Neal when he finally got him alone again.

"If I met someone, it's not like it's gonna last, not in this business," Jamie admitted.

Dylan's grin was sincere. "Then you gotta make the team, don't you?"

Dylan was right; if he made the team, he wouldn't leave southern California. He wouldn't leave Neal. At least not before Jamie figured out if this was all just remnants of hero worship or if it was something else entirely. All he knew now was that he wanted Neal to smile again—*really* smile—the dark shadows in his eyes and under them finally vanishing for good. Whether it was Jamie who made that happen or not, it didn't matter.

Jamie typed out a text back. **I don't know. I wish I knew. They're saying something about results at the end of the day.**

He'd felt the tremor that had washed over the group of assembled kickers. *Results?* Obviously this was all a test, which would be hard to miss, but specific results? Usually the only time you got results was when you were the last one standing.

"Seriously, though," Dylan continued, "if I were you, I wouldn't be sure this is even what I want."

I don't know if it is.

"You're not wrong," Jamie said slowly. "What do you think of this whole TrackBuddy thing?"

"Ugh, it's a fucking joke," Dylan said. "What does velocity off the foot matter? What does miles per hour matter? And this results thing? *Total fucking bullshit.*"

"It's a bad idea," Jamie agreed. "Let's heap some more pressure onto an already stressful situation."

"No fucking joke," Dylan muttered.

Jamie's phone buzzed again. **RESULTS? WHAT THE FUCK**, was what Neal had sent this time. Then another text right after it. **See if you can get a copy.**

God, that would *definitely* put the Riptide off—sharing the results of their super secret kicking tryout with the kicker they'd released after he'd missed the biggest kick of his career. But, Jamie decided, what the Riptide didn't know wouldn't hurt them, and he had no intention of the team finding out that he'd managed to both meet and befriend Neal Fisher.

· · · ● · ● ● · · ·

The afternoon brought a new set of horrors.

After lunch, Coach Toby brought them back to the main practice field, and Jamie mentally prepared himself for the same exercise they'd done the first day—lining up and kicking a forty-four-yard field goal, one at a time.

But this time when they lined up, Coach R stepped up and stopped the process before it could begin. It was foolish to hope that they might get a reprieve—and so Jamie didn't even consider it.

Instead, Coach R motioned above his head, and suddenly the music playing over the practice field's sound system cut out. "There's something they do at the Masters," Coach R said, "when a major putt is going to happen. They call it the Augusta silence, and I want to try it today. So everyone needs to be totally silent, and let these guys focus on doing their job."

But Jamie already wasn't sure he trusted the Riptide coaching staff, not after the last two days of bullshit, and he didn't really trust what Coach Rodriguez was saying. Was this "Augusta silence" a way of helping them focus on the task at hand? Or just another way to ratchet the pressure just a little tighter, to see who would persevere under it and who would break? Jamie had a feeling it was definitely the latter.

This time he ended up third in line. *Way less pressure*, Jamie told himself, trying to be optimistic. It was definitely harder to go further down the line. But then, a slight lessening of the already-intense level of stress wasn't really much in the scheme of things.

This time he also had more familiarity with the holder and the long snapper, which definitely helped. He knew their rhythm and how they did their jobs, so he could do *his* job better.

But this time, there was a third factor at play. There was a different but still compelling reason for him to want to make this kick. If he made it, he could keep seeing Neal. If he missed it, he might be packing his bags and heading back to Palo Alto tonight.

Maybe he'd never get that kiss after all. Maybe he'd never know how Neal's eyes lit when he was smiling and *happy*.

It was silly, and he shouldn't have even been thinking it, but he was, and before he realized he needed to stop, and *focus*, his timing was a little sluggish, and he barely got the ball off the right way, and he'd overcompensated, the ball veering to the right, and just barely squeaking in, nearly grazing the right upright.

"Shit," Jamie muttered. He'd almost fucked up. He'd let himself get carried away with thoughts he had no business thinking right now. So what if he stayed in LA? Neal might never want to see him again. He was here, at this camp, not for Neal, but for *himself*. He'd wanted to make this team—any team, really—but he'd determined that he'd have one of the best chances of winning a spot here. Maybe Neal was right after all—he shouldn't let his dick distract him. Not when there was something this big on the line.

More kickers made the field goal this time around, so maybe the Augusta silence wasn't quite the insanity that Jamie had assumed. Or maybe they were just more used to all the bullshit by now. The only miss was one of the guys who already seemed to not be able to handle the pressure. Dylan made it, Kieran made it, and Shane definitely made it. And even worse, his kick was the best of the bunch, straight and confident, with plenty of leg on it. Coach Toby clapped appreciatively.

Dylan shot Jamie an apprehensive look. Yeah, his front-runner status had just been supplanted.

They went down the line two more times, and Jamie was proud that each of his kicks was better than the last, but Shane seemed to have taken the pressure and somehow used it, because every single one of his kicks was textbook perfect. Jamie's weren't terrible, but they weren't as good as Shane's, and he knew it.

At the end of practice, they filed into the locker room, and Coach Toby pulled them aside, letting them know that the results would be posted in a few. "Results of what?" he heard Kieran say, mystified, after Coach Toby left the locker room. "They're gonna take one of us and leave the rest. That's how it works."

It was weird enough to be a rookie and experience this, but Jamie didn't know how a veteran who'd been to multiple of these tryouts, but likely never one like this, would handle it. *Not well*, was clearly the answer. Because Kieran had been distracted and losing ground all day.

"Fuck if I know," Dylan muttered back to Kieran. "Fuck if I know what any of this has been about."

And it did seem unnaturally hard to possibly pick the best kicker when there were too many to look at. Maybe that was what the "results" were for.

After showering, Jamie grabbed his phone, hoping to be able to take a picture of the results that he could send Neal.

He found Dylan and the other guys gathered around a set of printouts taped to the hallway wall outside the locker room.

Moving closer, Jamie noticed that basically every guy had his phone out, snapping photos, so Jamie followed suit. He glanced at the printouts. He was in second place, behind Shane, but the points they'd used to come up with the totals seemed . . . off. Were they taking off points for almost-misses? Because he'd had two today. But then Shane had had one yesterday, so how was he three points ahead? Were they getting points for the Track-Buddy data? None of that data was actually posted, but there were comments next to each name. Next to Dylan's: "Improve MPH off the foot." Kieran had "distance concerns." Jamie's said, "Ball trajectory a possible concern."

He could tell from Dylan's expression that he was unhappy with his comment. "Fuck, how does miles per hour even matter?" he said, as he and Jamie walked to their cars a few minutes later. "If it's going in, it's fucking going in. They're overanalyzing this so hard they're going to end up with some shit kicker like Shane, who's great at jumping through all these weird-ass hoops and not someone who can get the job done."

"You think he can't?" Jamie asked, though secretly, he'd wondered the same thing. While the Riptide were trying so furiously to recreate the pressures of a game situation, all they were doing was tying these kickers up in knots until cracking was inevitable.

"Who the fuck knows what he's capable of? I don't even fucking know what *I'm* capable of anymore," Dylan said, sounding angry, and Jamie couldn't blame him for his frustration. Dylan had been one of a class of about five kickers coming out this year that were actually really pretty good. Jamie had been another one. Shane had not even been *on* any major rookie kicker lists this year. And yet here he was, possibly going to win the starting Riptide job.

"Guess Green Bay and besting Mason Crosby is looking better and better," Jamie said.

"Actually," Dylan said, and then hesitated. "Actually, my agent called. He wants me to fly to Green Bay tonight. He thinks there's a solid chance I could end up on the practice squad. Crosby's not as young as he once was, and I guess the coaching staff wasn't particularly impressed with anyone they brought in."

"You should do it," Jamie said. "You should go. This is a clusterfuck, and not worth your time."

"Yeah, that's what my agent said, and you know what?" Dylan shrugged. "He's probably right."

"Seriously, you should go," Jamie encouraged. It was too much to imagine Dylan wasting a potentially promising NFL career by letting the Riptide sink it before it had even begun.

"I think I will," Dylan said. "But you're staying." His words were more a statement, less a question.

"Someone's got to keep Shane honest," Jamie joked.

"I'm serious," Dylan said. "You're better than he is, even on your worst day. You know that. The only ones who don't know it are the fucktards running this tryout."

"Maybe," Jamie said. If Dylan was really leaving, then maybe he could . . . *No,* that voice in the back of his head said firmly, irrevocably. *You can't tell him about Neal. He's a friend, but you can't trust anyone with this.*

"Go meet up with your new 'friend' you can't stop texting with," Dylan said, smacking him on the shoulder blade. "At least one of us should have some fun."

"Enjoy Green Bay and say hi to Rodgers for me," Jamie said with a grin, and laughed as Dylan rolled his eyes.

"Not all of us can be buddy-buddy with the quarterback," Dylan said, but he was smiling.

"I'm not buddy-buddy with Sam Crawford," Jamie protested.

"Yeah, you just keep tellin' yourself that," Dylan insisted. "But seriously, *take advantage* of that. Even though I hear Sam likes just about anyone."

Sam does, Jamie wanted to say, *but not Heath. Heath's cautious, and he was just as welcoming as Sam was, maybe more. He saw you and he knew you'd be a good fit for this team. That's why he kept telling everyone you were the new kicker. You gonna let him be a liar?*

The voice had morphed from his dad's distinctive baritone, to Neal's gravelly deep tone, and after Jamie slid into his rental, he remembered to text Neal the pictures of the results.

There was a minute or so delay and then before Jamie could even start the car to go back to his hotel, his phone rang.

"What the ever-living fuck are these?" Neal's voice came across the speakerphone, without a second of preamble.

"The results?" Jamie said.

"I've never even heard of this Shane Ferguson kid," Neal said. "And . . . *ball trajectory?* What the fuck are they thinking? Your ball trajectory is glorious."

Butterflies bubbled in Jamie's stomach. "You watched some of my kicks."

"Well, *yeah*," Neal said. "You think I'm gonna offer to help some rookie who I've never seen kick before? You've got real potential."

"Thanks," Jamie said, his face heating up. Thank god they were just on the phone and Neal couldn't see him flush.

"But honest to god, what does all this garbage *mean*?" Neal wondered.

"I don't know . . . I kinda hoped you might," Jamie admitted.

"I don't have a fucking clue, except that they have seriously jumped the shark here," Neal said. "It's a little reassuring that as fucked up as I am about that goddamned missed kick, at least they're right there with me."

"I think so," Jamie agreed.

"So you meant it," Neal said, changing the subject whiplash-quick. "You want me to help you win the spot."

"Yes." Easiest answer that Jamie had given all day. Probably all week.

Neal sighed. "I still think it's a risky idea, but I just looked up that Shane guy before I called, and he is *not* the guy to take my spot, that's for goddamn sure."

Jamie had the fleeting thought that Neal and Dylan would get along like a house on fire.

"And I am?" Jamie wondered.

"Jury's still out, kid," Neal said, "but like I said, you've got potential."

"Thanks," Jamie said, and meant it. He still couldn't quite believe that Neal had looked him up, but then it made sense. Why would you agree to help someone if you didn't know what you were working with?

"Come over tonight, and we're gonna do some strategizing," Neal said. Hesitated. *"Just* strategizing, okay?"

"Okay," Jamie said. His cheeks still felt hot. How had he managed to be so aggressive the other night when even the thought of going to Neal's house tonight for "strategizing" made his knees feel weak?

"I mean it," Neal said firmly. And that was all kinds of fantasies that Jamie didn't need. Neal telling him in *that* voice to get on the bed. To get on his knees. To make him feel good. To make him forget.

Fuck.

Jamie cleared his throat. "Alright. Text me your address."

"And come hungry," Neal added right before he hung up. "Olive's cooking."

Chapter Five

Jamie knew he should feel relieved that Neal had followed through on his promise to help him, but instead, the whole drive back to his hotel, Jamie was nervous and sweating. He felt the vibration of his phone in his pocket, and assumed that must be Neal, texting him his address. His palms, damp with sweat, slipped slightly on the faux leather of the steering wheel, as he finally pulled into a space in the hotel parking lot.

"You're fine," he told himself. "It's just . . . it's just Neal Fisher. No big deal. You flirted with him yesterday, didn't you?" But he'd flirted with him yesterday because he'd been hoping he could convince Neal to help him, and because he'd been hoping, more than a little bit, that Neal would ignore his better judgment and come back with him to his hotel room.

The problem was he'd never expected it would work, and the idea of going to Neal's house, where they'd probably be all alone, both thrilled and terrified him. What was he doing? He was just

Jamie Wright, who'd been a kicker for Stanford, and wasn't even guaranteed an NFL job. By this time next year, it would be a miracle if he wasn't out of football completely. Instead, he was hoping to . . . *what?* Seduce Neal Fisher? Let Neal Fisher seduce him?

No, he told himself firmly as he wiped his damp palms onto his shorts, *you're going there and he's going to help you figure out how to beat Shane. That's it. There's nothing to be nervous about.*

Still, he went up to his hotel room, dumped his bag off, and actually considered taking another shower because he felt like a sweaty wreck.

Neal's text read: **Here's my address, come whenever.** He'd written the address below, and Jamie wasted no time in mapping it. It wasn't near Heath and Sam's enormous house, so that made him feel a *little* better. For a split second, he almost considered googling the address, just so he'd know what to expect when he got there, but he didn't, telling himself that it didn't matter if Neal's house was twice the size of Heath and Sam's. He was still the guy with the too-sad eyes who looked like he didn't get out of bed and also hadn't slept well in six months.

He ran a hand through his still-drying curls, threw on a different t-shirt, this one from his Stanford days, and resolutely walked out, refusing to look at the mirror again. After all, Neal had thought he was cute yesterday, hadn't he? And he'd made zero effort then. This wasn't a *date*; this was for work.

• • • ● ● • ● • • •

When he pulled up to the house, Jamie was pleasantly surprised.

It *wasn't* enormous, like Heath and Sam's. Instead it was further out of town than Jamie had expected, and had more land around it than most houses in LA did. It was an extended remodeled bungalow, just one story but sprawling, painted a cool ocean blue with dark navy shutters and crisp white trim.

The landscaping was pristine, not a blade of grass too tall, not a stone out of place. At least this front door, Jamie thought as he approached, was not intimidatingly gargantuan. It was polished hardwood, the grain beautifully rich, with a string of small cutout windows, all trimmed in dark blue, running down one side.

Maybe it wasn't the kind of door you'd put on a castle, but Jamie had a feeling it was custom and it hadn't been cheap.

He rang the discreet doorbell on the side, and waited only a second for Neal to pull the door open.

Had he been waiting? Jamie had texted him in response to the address and had told him he was on his way. Still, had he been hanging out by the door, just waiting for him to show?

"Hey," Neal said. He was wearing a pair of khaki shorts and a green t-shirt, tightly fitted to his muscular torso. He'd done something different to his hair, pushed it back maybe, making his eyes stand out and nearly *glow*. Jamie thought maybe they looked a little less sad, a little more rested than they had the day before.

God, he is so gorgeous.

"Hey," Jamie said uncertainly. He still wasn't sure what he was really doing here. He knew what he wanted—*everything*, his mind whispered unhelpfully, *you want everything*—but it was difficult to imagine Neal wanting even a fraction of what Jamie did.

"I see you found it okay," Neal said, pulling the door open wider so Jamie could step inside. He was immediately struck by two things: the faintly citrus-y scent of Neal's cologne, and the fact that he hadn't worn any yesterday, but he was now, and the huge expanse of polished hardwood floors that stretched out as far as he could see.

Everything was wide open, like they'd torn out every single wall, turning what was once probably a fairly cramped-seeming ranch into an expanse, one room melting into another. The start of the kitchen was in the back, the rest around a corner, next to a casual-looking dining room. The foyer segued seamlessly into a living room, with a TV that took up an entire wall. And everything was painted in faintly muted cool tones, blues and turquoises and greens.

Jamie turned to him. "I love your house," he said.

Neal smiled, his pleased expression warming his face, and even reaching those stunning eyes. "Yeah, me too."

But still, as Jamie took in the living spaces, not a pillow out of place, not a speck of dust to be seen, he thought it was designed to be lived in but it *wasn't*.

"Here," Neal said, suddenly stiff, "we should find Olive."

"Olive?" Jamie said, hating how stupid he sounded. Why had he sent that text message last night? He'd known then that Neal was going to help him win the starting job, and he'd sent it anyway, even though he'd realized he'd have to face the man again. But imagining it in his hotel room was so much different than experiencing the bloom of awkwardness in person.

"My niece, she's living with me while she goes to school," Neal said, leading him through the living room towards the kitchen. "I think you might have met her yesterday."

Jamie remembered a young woman with long dark hair, who'd been worried about her uncle. And he couldn't exactly fault her for that, because he barely knew the man and he was worried about him, too. "Yeah," he said.

"She lives in a little apartment, over the garage," Neal said. "We both get a little privacy."

Jamie wasn't entirely sure if Neal was telling him so he'd know they'd have as much solitude as they wanted, or if he was using her as a buffer.

It occurred to him as they walked around the corner into a big, open kitchen, that maybe Neal didn't know either.

It made Jamie feel a little better that it seemed that Neal didn't quite know what to do with him, either.

"Olive," Neal said, and the girl turned, a white and yellow striped apron covering her tank top and cutoff shorts, her dark hair pulled back into a ponytail.

"Oh, hey," she said, smiling hugely, clearly pleased to see him again. "I was so happy when Neal said he was inviting you over."

"He needs help," Neal said, his stiffness returning. "The Riptide have gone off the fucking deep end."

Her green eyes—nearly a match for Neal's—narrowed. "Yeah," she said, "you wouldn't know anything about that, would you?"

He flushed, rubbing a hand on the back of his neck, right above the collar of his t-shirt. "Of course not," he said. "Come on, Olly."

Her ponytail whipped around her as she turned back to the stove. "You know I hate that nickname," she said.

Neal chuckled dryly. "Yeah, I'm aware."

"Do you like tacos, Jamie?" Olive asked, changing the subject.

"Doesn't everyone?" he asked.

"Oh good," she said. "Chicken tacos, they're my specialty."

"Or the only thing you know how to cook," Neal said, amused, as he slid onto one of the barstools. There was a bunch of papers, scribbled with notes, and a large tablet, and as Jamie joined him, he realized with a jolt that the picture he'd snapped of the results was on the tablet.

"Hey, Olive, get us something to drink, why don't you?" Neal asked.

She didn't answer, and Neal sighed. "She's a good girl," he said, grinning, "but a little stubborn."

"A *lot* stubborn," Olive said, still not turning around. "You've got legs. The fridge is right there."

"Fine," Neal said, glancing over at Jamie. "What's your poison?"

"Anything is fine," Jamie said, feeling more than a little out of his depth. Both in this gorgeous house, and with such a gorgeous man, and also with the painfully clear affection that uncle and niece shared with each other.

"Beer? Pop? Lemonade? Water?"

"Uh," Jamie said, uncertain and not expecting to be faced with so many choices. "A lemonade would be good, actually."

"Yeah, I think so, too," Neal agreed, and reached into a cupboard for glasses. "It's hot today."

No, that's just you.

"Yeah," Jamie agreed.

"Though not why you were probably sweating it out at practice," Neal said, setting a glass of lemonade in front of Jamie. "This results thing is complete fucking madness."

"Language," Olive said, her back to them still as she sauteed something in a huge skillet.

Neal rolled his eyes. "*Okay*, this results thing is complete *freaking* madness." He hesitated, and then sorted through some of the scribbled papers, finally unearthing one and sliding it toward Jamie. "I think most of the notes they came up with are from the TrackBuddy thing, though, I can't figure out this point system," he said. "You said you didn't miss any kicks today, and neither did Shane, so why does he have more points than you?"

"I don't know," Jamie said, frustration leaking into his voice. "But I feel like he's not really suited to game-time kicks, just this weird-ass competition they've constructed."

"I'm sure they *think* they're trying to approximate the pressure of a game kick," Neal said wryly, sitting down next to Jamie. "But they're fucking *failing*." He paused. "Don't even say it, Olly."

"Fine," she grumbled.

"I think . . ." Neal said, staring at the tablet with the results on it, "I think you just need to pretend none of this is happening."

"Kind of hard to do that," Jamie said. "It feels like every time we turn around, they're throwing a new obstacle in front of us, trying to get us to mess up."

"But you can deal with this, you can *deal* with all of those things, but you can only do that if you don't focus on them," Neal said.

"That sounds easier than it actually is," Jamie said.

"There's a lot of things I can suggest to help make that possible," Neal said, and motioned to a stack of books sitting on the far side of the counter. "I got some books for you I think might help you out."

Jamie raised an eyebrow. "I thought we'd go kick, and you'd tell me what I'm doing wrong."

"Yeah, maybe, but your mechanics are good. Solid. Probably why the Riptide wanted you to come try out for the team. But most sports? Football? Kicking specifically? It's all mental. You've got to learn to focus on the positives and let the negatives go."

"Yeah," Olive said, gesturing to the set table in the nook, "I can't imagine how that might help *you*."

She wasn't wrong; it was hard to take Neal's advice, because he hadn't really taken it himself. At least not in the last six months.

"You want to know how I did this job for thirteen years?" Neal asked, and Jamie nodded. "I focused on the positives and let the negatives fall away. And a bunch of other stuff, but that was most of it."

"Let's eat," Olive said, setting a foil packet of tortillas on the table with the rest of the taco fixings. "You can go all mindfulness guru on him after."

Neal hadn't been wrong; Olive could make a good chicken taco. Of course, like he'd said—tacos were like pizza and blowjobs, it was hard to get a bad one.

"What did they teach you at Stanford?" Neal asked when they were almost done eating.

"They spent a lot of time fixing my mechanics," Jamie said. "And strength and balance training. That was huge."

"That's good. You've got a solid foundation. Like I said earlier, that's why you're here at all. But there's so much more," Neal said, leaning forward, his eyes gleaming like precious stones. "And I can teach you."

"But only if you open your mind," Olive interrupted with an eye roll. "Seriously, I love you, but you're a broken record."

"Hey," Jamie said, even though he could tell that Olive's teasing was loving, "this guy is a *legend*, anything he wants to tell me, I'm down to hear."

"Yeah, I bet," Olive said, smiling so wide her dimples were showing. "Okay, you two can get all cozy and talk about meditation and positive zones and all that, but I'm off to the beach."

"Beach?" Neal asked, raising his head, his expression suddenly alert, those incredible eyes narrowing on his niece's seemingly innocent face. "I thought you were sticking around here tonight."

He's totally using her as a buffer, Jamie thought. He didn't know whether to be relieved at this realization or disappointed.

Disappointed, his mind supplied before he could stop it. *You're totally, epically, disappointed.*

The one silver lining was that she was leaving anyway, and it didn't seem, from the way Olive was eyeing him forcefully, that Neal really *could* stop her.

"I think you'll have plenty to keep you occupied," she said pointedly, and Jamie couldn't help it, he flushed bright red.

Neal, finishing up his lemonade, choked a bit. "Well," he finally said, clearing his throat, "be safe, okay?"

"Remember, just put the dishes in the sink," she said, pulling her ponytail holder out, her long hair spreading across her shoulders, "and Maria will take care of them in the morning." She grinned at Jamie. "It was so great you came for dinner," she said, resting her hand on his shoulder, briefly. "You should do it again sometime, okay?"

"Okay," Jamie said. "I appreciate the home-cooked meal."

She smiled. "Of course, anytime."

She flounced off in a cloud of dark hair, whipping her apron off as she went out the back door.

"Well," Neal said awkwardly. "I guess we're on our own, then."

"I guess we are." Jamie stood, wondering if he should go. Wondering if maybe Neal didn't want to be alone with him, while at the same time he wanted it way too much.

Neal didn't say anything else, and gathered together the dishes to take them into the kitchen. Jamie decided he might as well help him, and when he reached the sink, he flipped the faucet on and began to rinse them.

"You don't have to do that," Neal said, setting another set of dishes next to the sink. "Maria will take care of it."

"Yeah, but Olive said she wouldn't be here until tomorrow morning." Jamie turned the faucet from cool to hot, beginning to wash the plates off. "You should at least give everything a rinse."

Neal leaned against the counter next to the sink. He wasn't quite hip to hip with Jamie, but he was close. "Yeah, we probably should, shouldn't we?" He sighed. "I'm not usually . . . well, honestly, before Olive showed up, I hadn't really been cooking for myself."

"Didn't really feel like it?" Jamie asked even though he already knew the answer. The sadness still lurking in Neal's eyes told the whole ugly story.

"I was *never* a big cook," Neal admitted with a wry chuckle, "but yeah, not really in the last six months. It was just . . . easier not to try."

Jamie thought that if somehow he got an invitation to Neal's bedroom, he'd discover that while the rest of the house looked barely touched, it would be obvious that was where Neal was spending all his time. His mother, Lila, was a professor of psychology at Stanford, and he knew the signs of depression in his sleep. Depression was an insidious thing; right now, looking at Neal, and spending time with him, he wouldn't have guessed immediately that he was depressed, but when faced with some of the symptoms, it was undeniable.

But even then, there were signs that he might be pulling out of the worst of it. Him responding to Jamie reaching out, agreeing to help him, spending all this time trying to decode the results the Riptide had posted. Though, Jamie could imagine his mother pointing out that getting involved in the very thing that had pulled him into his current state was probably not the best idea, but even though Neal wasn't playing, he was *still* a football player. That wasn't going to change, no matter how many field goals he missed.

"You were pissed off and frustrated and guilty and sad," Jamie said steadily, continuing to wash the dishes. "I don't think anyone would blame you for not wanting to try."

"Here," Neal said, shifting to the side, and opening the dishwasher. "We might as well load it."

Jamie smiled at him. It wasn't anything big—just taking care of his own dishes, but he was glad to see Neal care about something. Something other than football.

"Sure," he said, easily, and watched as Neal began to grab the rinsed plates and put them into the dishwasher himself. It felt good to be doing something together—and it was hard not to wonder if this was only the first time, and there might be more opportunities in the future. *Chances to get close, chances to . . .* But Jamie cut the thought off.

"You're a good kid," Neal said quietly as they finished up, Jamie grabbing a sponge and cleaning the cutting board and the area around the big commercial range, where Olive had cooked the chicken and it had splattered a little.

"Just trying to do my part," Jamie said. He didn't know how he felt about the nickname that Neal had seemingly adopted. Was it to remind himself that he thought Jamie was too young for him? Did he really see him like a kid? Because he *wasn't* a kid, and he would be one hundred percent ready to show Neal just how wrong he was.

"So, what else happened today?" Neal asked, and it seemed he wanted to keep the subject firmly on football. That was why Jamie was here, after all, even if he wished there were additional reasons.

"Dylan is going to Green Bay," he said. "I have a feeling they might pare more down than just him."

Neal looked thoughtful. "I wouldn't be surprised if it happened without them even trying to do it. Who wants to stay and continue to endure the torture if they know they aren't getting the job? Especially if they have another opportunity someplace else? I'd guess you'll show up tomorrow and half the guys are already gone."

"That makes sense," Jamie said.

"And, I wouldn't be surprised that if they have two good candidates—which is obviously you and Shane, your scores are way higher than anyone else's—they carry them into the preseason."

"Really?" It wasn't unheard of to do that—to try to get the kickers some real game experience so they could judge the final competition better. But Jamie hated the idea that another couple weeks could go by and he wouldn't be any closer to knowing where he'd be spending the year. He could even make it to the preseason and then be let go, in favor of Shane, or whoever else made it that far.

"It's going to be you. Don't worry," Neal said, leaning back against the counter and crossing his arms over his chest. It was tough not to be distracted by the way his biceps flexed; Jamie couldn't quite manage it.

"I'm not . . . I'm not *worried*," Jamie argued, as he followed Neal into the living room. "I knew it was an outside chance that I'd end up on an NFL team. But I . . . I had to try anyway."

Neal sat down on one of the gray couches, and patted the cushion next to him, like he wasn't sure if Jamie would've sat so close. And Jamie *wasn't* sure he would have. Not with the hot and cold signals that Neal had been giving.

"You had to try. You're good," Neal said. "Giving up would've been a waste of your skills." He paused. "But I think you've got a lot to learn."

"That's what I want," Jamie said, leaning forward, scrubbing his damp palms on his thighs. "I want to get better. Teach me."

Neal smiled. "Why don't we start here?" he said, and he reached for the remote, flipping on the enormous TV. When he navigated to YouTube, Jamie wasn't surprised to see that the most recently watched playlist was full of kicker videos—most of them featured kickers who were currently at the Riptide camp—but Jamie's highlight video was at the top of the list.

"Really?" Jamie wasn't sure how watching his highlights—these were all his best, greatest successes—was going to teach him anything. They should be watching his misses instead. Of course, those existed, in some corner of the internet. Jamie knew, because on bad days, he had to force himself not to watch himself miss over and over and over again.

Not that there were *that* many misses. Whoever had put the video together had had to dig deep into Jamie's history, even pulling out practice misses and misses from high school, when he hadn't really known what the fuck he was doing.

"Trust me, we're not going to talk about your mechanics. That can wait til another day, because yours are actually not bad, not bad at all, but there's something else you need to see."

Jamie glanced over at him in confusion as he clicked on Jamie's highlight video and it started playing. His dad had hired a professional videographer to put this together, as a calling card for NFL teams, and Jamie had helped to pick the kicks that should go in, but he'd never seen the finished product.

Jamie watched himself line up in Autzen Stadium, the home of the Oregon Ducks, rain pouring down, and it was impossible not to remember that moment—he'd barely been able to see the uprights through the sheets of rain, the lights reflecting weirdly on all the water. But he'd nailed it anyway, winning Stanford the game. A game that nobody had expected that they might win.

Neal had been silent all the way up to the kick, and then right after the ball sailed through the uprights, barely visible in all that rain, he paused the video.

"See?" he said, pointing to the screen, where Jamie was celebrating with his teammates.

"What?" Jamie wondered.

"There's thirty-five seconds left on the clock," Neal said. "You have to kick off, and you *know* you have to kick off, you knew it before you lined up to kick the field goal. And thirty-five seconds? Maybe not a lot of time, but for a team like Oregon? Even in a rainstorm? There's a chance they could've scored. But instead of focusing on the next task, you're hugging and high-fiving every-one."

"Well," Jamie said, fighting the urge to defend himself, "they thought I'd just won the game."

"You hadn't," Neal said. He tossed the remote onto the couch. "It was a fucking amazing kick, and it's exactly what you should've led with in this video. It was clutch, you were in a notoriously hostile stadium, the conditions were *terrible*, and you made it, right down the center. A textbook kick. But instead of turning your mind to the next task, you were . . ."

"Celebrating prematurely," Jamie finished for him. He looked at the screen. He didn't even remember the kickoff. Maybe it had gone out of the end zone, resulting in an automatic touchback, but maybe it hadn't. He honestly didn't remember.

"I looked it up," Neal said, like he knew that Jamie couldn't remember. "It wasn't a touchback. The clock ran out while Oregon was trying to drive."

At the time he'd probably been sitting on the sidelines, helmet clutched in his hand, rain pouring down as he waited to see if Oregon could pull out a better miracle than the one he just had.

But now? He didn't remember those thirty-five seconds at all. Back then, they'd probably felt like an eternity.

"Huh," Jamie said and flopped back against the couch. "Fuck, I didn't . . . *fuck*."

"You didn't know any better, because I'd guess that the special teams coordinator at Stanford didn't really care to teach you. He's all about returns, isn't he?"

"Yeah," Jamie admitted. "He taught me some basic fundamentals that I was lacking from high school, and we focused on accuracy, but . . . that's about it."

"That's about what I figured," Neal said. "I don't want you to beat yourself up about this."

Jamie shot him a frank stare, and Neal went pink. "Okay, that's fair," Neal conceded. "We all have stuff we can work on. Before, I might've been good at mindfulness, at not internalizing mistakes, but it turns out that the Super Bowl blows everything to hell." He hesitated. "At least it did for me."

"That's why you're not out there, trying out too?" Jamie wondered.

He'd wanted to ask, but it hadn't felt right until now.

Neal stared at the paused screen in front of them. "I'm not good for any team right now."

"You really believe that?" Jamie said incredulously. "You missed *one* field goal. For the thirteen years before that you were rock fucking solid."

"Yeah, for *thirteen years*," Neal said. "Maybe it's time to figure out what else I'm good at."

"Might be. You know, we haven't done much yet, but so far, I think you'd be a brilliant coach."

Neal grinned. "You do, do you? Why? Because we can't stay away from each other?"

Jamie flushed, because it was one thing to have that be unspoken between them, and it was another entirely to say it out loud. At least when he'd done it, he'd done it via text.

"Um, that might be *part* of the reason why," Jamie admitted.

"I thought so," Neal said, amused. "But even if I want to help you, I don't think I want to go into coaching. I don't have the patience."

"Heath did," Jamie pointed out.

"Yeah, Heath and Sam are their own little weird world." Neal shook his head. "Besides, I burned my bridges with the Riptide, so I'd have to start out someplace else, and honestly, I'm not interested in moving. I've been here thirteen years now. I like LA, I like this house, I like that Olive can live with me and commute to USC easily. So yeah, coaching is out. I'm not sure . . . I'm not sure what else I'm good at, honestly."

"Looking hot." Jamie spoke before he could retract the statement—a statement that was bound to make things even more awkward than they already were.

But Neal didn't say anything immediately, just leaned back on the couch, and regarded Jamie thoughtfully. "I think you mean that."

"Uh, *definitely*," Jamie said, and it was like his brain-to-mouth filter was just gone, because instead of shutting up, he kept going. "Cutest kicker in the league, that was for sure."

"Did you have a poster of me above your bed?" Neal teased.

"If they'd made one of you, I sure would have," Jamie said. "But you *were* my computer background, forever. Even before I came out. I always said you were the kicker I admired the most, and that wasn't a lie, but it was . . . it was also more."

"This is going to be a problem, isn't it?" Neal said, his voice dropping low, rumbling deep in Jamie's stomach. He reached out, and Jamie sucked in his breath as his fingertips traced the edges of the curls falling over his forehead. "A real problem," he mused.

"Yeah," Jamie said breathlessly. "Yeah, if you think it's a problem."

"It's complicated," Neal said finally, his hand returning to the couch between them. Jamie was so tempted to reach over and cover it with his own. "You're trying to make the team that couldn't hate my guts more if they tried."

"It's . . ." Jamie wanted desperately to say it wasn't like that, but it was, wasn't it? Every single coach, and maybe even a lot of the players, were still painfully hung up on Neal's missed kick. Otherwise, this tryout would've been a lot different than it actually was.

"Yeah, I thought so," Neal said morosely, turning his head away. And Jamie *hated* hearing him sound like that, like he'd internalized all that hatred, like he *believed* it. He reached out and took Neal's hand, and before he could turn away, tangled their fingers together and squeezed.

"Hey," he said firmly, "let's talk about this." With his free hand he pointed to the paused TV screen. "What should I have done instead? Tell me what you would've done."

"When I was in college?" Neal said wryly, but he didn't pull away, which Jamie took as a win. "I probably would've celebrated just like you did."

"Then let's say when you were in the NFL. What would you have done?" Jamie asked insistently.

"I'd have pulled away from everyone, almost immediately, and gone over to the sideline," Neal said, his voice unsure at first, but growing in confidence. Like he *knew* what the right path was, he'd just momentarily forgotten it. "I'd have sat by myself, helmet on, and done my kickoff visualizations. Probably consulted with the kickoff team, the special teams coach. Confirmed they were looking for a touchback. Thought about my execution and went through my progressions, to make sure I knew the optimal situation and visualized it. Done a few warm-up kicks into the net."

"And you'd stay away from everyone," Jamie confirmed. "Okay, that is definitely different than what I used to do."

"This game is physical, but it's mental too," Neal said. "And for us? It's almost entirely mental. Get any semi-athletic person off the street and with a few minutes of instruction, they could probably kick an extra point. But doing it when it matters? That's both physical *and* mental prep. And if you're doing the first, but not the second, you need to start."

"Is that what the books are about?" Jamie asked.

"Yeah, I mean, I watched this three times," Neal said, gesturing to the screen. "And you do it with a few of your kicks, there's footage of you hanging out on the bench, talking to teammates, and that's not *bad*, but you need to stay focused. More than anyone else on the team."

"Alright." Jamie nodded. "I can work on that."

"That'll help with this process, too," Neal added. "It's good that Dylan's going to Green Bay."

"Why?" Jamie wondered, though he had a feeling he already knew the answer.

"Because you don't need to be getting friendly with the competition, and I know you're friends with him," Neal said firmly. "You're not there to socialize. You're there to win the spot."

"I can do that," Jamie said. It *would* be easier with Dylan gone. He wasn't particularly friendly with any of the remaining guys—definitely not Shane, who was likely to be the last obstacle to winning the job.

"Here's the thing," Neal said, turning close to Jamie, pulling their joined hands onto his knee, and this time it was him, squeezing reassuringly. "You've got this. You've got the physical skills, and I'm not sure what else they can mentally throw at you. Technically, there's only one more day of camp. And this Shane kid? I watched some of his kicks, and he's not a game-time player, not like you. He's doing well, because this is a weird set of circumstances, and he happens to excel at them. If you make it to the preseason, you're gonna blow him out of the water."

Jamie would be lying if he said Neal's belief—and he *did* believe, the look in his green eyes was dead serious—didn't feel particularly sweet. He'd believed enough in himself before, but hearing Neal say it? That *meant* something. Because Neal was not only one of the hottest guys he'd ever seen, and he wasn't just dying to lean over and kiss him—he was also dying to learn from him. To keep having Neal teach him everything he knew.

"Thanks," Jamie said. "It . . . well, obviously it means something that you think so. And not just because I think you're cute."

"Cute?" Neal demanded, all faux affront. "I thought I was *hot*?"

"Can't you be both?"

Neal gazed at him, and it felt like he was staring right down into Jamie's goddamn soul. Maybe Neal was right after all, and this *was* going to be a problem. Because he didn't want just a night or two, he already wanted more, and this was the kind of relationship that wouldn't ever be easy. "Yeah," Neal said, squeezing his hand again, "yeah, you definitely can be."

"Good," Jamie said, grinning, "now that we've established that . . . you wanna give me any more pointers?"

"Oh yeah," Neal said, reaching for the remote. "I've got pointers. You might regret asking, though."

"Yeah, no. I really don't think so."

"Okay then," Neal said, and clicked play.

• • • ● • ● • ● • • •

They stayed on the couch for another hour, dissecting Jamie's kicking video and figuring out what he should be doing to better prepare mentally. And then, just as Jamie began to really, desperately, achingly hope that something might happen besides them only holding hands on this couch, Neal released his fingers and stood up, stretching.

"You've got an early day tomorrow," Neal said awkwardly, and Jamie knew then that he wasn't the only one who was afraid. "I'll grab you those books."

"Thanks again for dinner," Jamie said, when Neal returned, carrying the handful of paperbacks. "Make sure to tell Olive again that I really appreciated the invite."

"Alright," Neal said, and he stayed far enough back, just out of reach, that Jamie realized he was trying to keep this G-rated. Well, *PG-rated,* if any of the hot glances Neal had been shooting him between suggestions counted. And Jamie definitely thought they counted. "Well, good luck tomorrow."

"I won't need the luck now," Jamie said. "I've got this nailed down."

Neal smiled, slow and steady. "Yeah, you really do."

Jamie hated to leave, but there was nothing to do but go, and hope that this wasn't the last time they did this.

But Neal's words as he was walking out the door made his heart leap in his chest. "Next time," he said, "we'll go to a field I know, and work on your fundamentals."

Jamie wanted to ask if "working on his fundamentals" was a euphemism, and that maybe it really meant "mutual blowjobs" or "being fucked within an inch of his life" or even "making out until they couldn't stand up anymore"—but this was enough. It would have to be enough, at least for right now.

"Sure thing," he said. "See you around."

CHAPTER SIX

"YOU REALLY DON'T WANT to go to any of these tryouts?" Alec, Neal's agent, sat across from him at their favorite breakfast place. It was the first time they'd met in person since the Super Bowl—not because Alec hadn't made any effort, but because Neal had refused to return any of his calls or his texts or his emails.

Last night, after Jamie had left, Neal had leaned against the front door, fighting the urge to open it back up and pull him back in, pull him into his arms. He barely knew the kid, but he *longed* for him, and not just because for the first time in six months, he felt like he could face someone without feeling an ounce of judgment, but because Jamie reminded him he was *alive*. He wasn't just a mass of bone and muscle and skin and failure.

Even though he'd told Jamie it was a mistake for them to get involved, there was an inevitability to it. If they kept spending time together, eventually the feelings swirling through him would override his good sense. At some point, the risk would feel worth it.

When that moment came, Neal wanted to be less of a disaster zone. He knew he'd been hiding. He knew he'd been avoiding the world, because that had been so much easier than facing it. But even he knew it was time for him to stop. Olive's arrival had been the beginning of that realization. When she'd come for school, he'd begun to pull out of his funk, by the force of her personality and also the fear that she might tell her mother how bad off he was. But the pool party and meeting Jamie had been the line crossing the "t" and the dot over the "i."

When Jamie had left last night, Neal had known in his bones he needed to finish dragging himself out of this and one of the first steps of that had been a text to Alec.

He'd been inundating Neal with phone calls—all going to voicemail; texts—mostly unanswered; and emails—sent to the trash bin without a reply. Once he'd even stopped by, pounding on the front door for ten minutes before finally retreating to his car and sending Neal a text: **I know you're feeling pretty sorry for yourself right now, and that's okay, but when you're ready to stick your head up out of the sand, just let me know.**

Alec wasn't Neal's first agent, but the agent he'd researched and then sought out after he'd been in the NFL a few years. There'd been nothing technically *wrong* with Eric, his first agent, except a complete lack of morality and a grating laugh that made Neal contemplate justifiable homicide. Still, Eric had negotiated Neal's first two contracts with the Riptide, and then Alec had come on board, and had promised him as one of the foremost kickers in the league, he'd never have to worry about money again. And he'd delivered on that promise, without any of the nasty underhanded tactics that Eric liked to employ.

Most of all, Neal liked Alec because he left him alone. Or he had, before Neal had retreated into his house and decided that he didn't want to leave it ever again.

After the visit and the last text, Alec had continued to forward offers—and it had surprised Neal how many there were, considering how his last season had ended—but he'd stopped pushing for Neal to talk to him. He'd been willing to wait Neal out, and now Neal was ready to actually talk about it.

Well, *mostly*.

The waitress had said something offhandedly when she'd shown him to the table where Alec was waiting, and since Neal had kept the world at an arm's length during the last six months, he hadn't known how to deal with it. What did you say to, "I was watching the game, and god, it sucks to be you?"

Yes, it does suck to be me? Or, *it sucks less than you think. The Riptide still have to pay me four million dollars this year, for sitting on my ass and watching stupid YouTube videos?*

"I don't want to kick again, I don't think," Neal said, answering Alec's question as he sipped his coffee. He'd thought admitting this would be harder, but he knew it was the right thing, because he totally lacked the eager hunger that guys like Jamie had, fresh in the league and wild-eyed at the thought of proving themselves.

He wasn't sure he was done trying to prove himself, but the idea of joining another team and jogging out onto the field made him feel vaguely sick, so at least, for now, he was finished playing football.

"So, that's a no to all these great offers, then," Alec said, and this time it was more of a sentence than a question. "I'm assuming you read them; some of them really aren't terrible."

"I am not willing to be someone's PR grab," Neal said slowly. "And I don't need to use any of them to find my redemption or whatever."

"Good, because in my experience, that isn't a thing that usually works."

"PR grabs or redemption stories?" Neal asked wryly, setting his coffee down.

"Yes," Alec said. Neal had always liked the guy, but he'd especially liked his sparseness.

"Yeah, I don't know what the future holds," Neal admitted. That was much tougher to admit to than saying he didn't want to keep playing football.

"You've got lots of options," Alec said reassuringly. Deep down Neal knew that, but it helped to have a guy he respected say so. "You could coach, I'm getting some feelers out there for that. You could become a consultant. Lots of teams would jump at that chance. College and NFL both. Also, there's a somewhat unusual offer that you should consider."

"I'm not sure coaching is for me," Neal admitted, "though I guess I would be willing to consider some of the consultant gigs." Consulting would mean that he wouldn't be away from LA long, and the life he'd built here.

"The good news for you is that the Riptide is still paying you for the next two years," Alec said. "So you don't even *have* to do anything, not yet anyway. Probably not ever actually, with the way I know you manage your money."

Kickers didn't exactly pull in big contracts—even well-established kickers with a solid history of consistent results—so Neal had known early on that he was going to have to be careful about his money if he was going to retire before forty and be comfortable not only for the rest of his life, but to potentially help his family, *and* pay for his niece's education.

"Yeah," Neal agreed. "Probably not, but I'd go insane pretty damn quick if I didn't do anything." Now that he was on the tail end of his meltdown, he could see that he didn't want to repeat it again. Six months with doing nothing? That wasn't going to be something he could live with regularly.

"If you're not into coaching, then maybe this unique offer might be something you could consider," Alec said thoughtfully. "When it first came in, I wasn't sure it was serious, but after talking to the producers, I think they might be, and it might be a good fit for you."

The waitress appeared then, and they ordered, Neal telling himself repeatedly that she wasn't going to bring the Super Bowl up, because the last time she had, he'd clammed up completely.

Besides, this was good practice for going out in the real world more. Because by now, he knew he needed to. The hiding part of his recovery needed to be over.

Still, he was *not* expecting what Alec said next. "The offer is from ESPN, to join their Sunday analyst panel for the upcoming season."

Now, Neal understood that he *needed* to rejoin the world, but he wasn't thinking he wanted to expose himself to the world, either.

"Seriously? *The* panel. Sunday Morning Football. That panel?"

Alec's eyes gleamed as he nodded, which told Neal that this was exactly the opportunity that he was afraid it was.

"You mean, the panel where I'd be sitting between Jimmy Johnson and Terry Bradshaw?" Neal demanded. So much for trying to fly under the radar. Suddenly, the coaching thing didn't look so bad.

"They're looking for new blood. Some young blood."

"I'm almost forty," Neal said, and Alec rolled his eyes.

"You're thirty-seven, and yes, that is *young* compared to everyone else sitting at that desk."

Neal could concede that, at least. He wasn't sure what the average age of the panelists was, but it was definitely not young.

"They'd be looking for you to do some practice segments, some guest spots, to kinda get a feel for your style—though you've done plenty of interviews over the years, so they already know you're great on-camera."

"They're serious about this, aren't they?" Neal couldn't quite believe it. "They're going to put a special teams guy on the Sunday Morning Football panel?"

"You're not just a special teams guy," Alec reminded him. "You're Neal Fisher. You're going to end up in the Hall of Fame. You played for the same team for thirteen years, you won a Super Bowl with them and almost won a second one. You're handsome and charismatic and funny. You're a perfect fit."

"I think you're exaggerating more than a little," Neal said dryly. "The Hall of Fame thing isn't for sure, not now, anyway, and frankly the thing I'm most famous for right now is the worst miss in NFL history."

"Then lay that to rest. You haven't given an interview since the Super Bowl. Maybe it's time."

"It's not time," Neal said flatly. "It's never going to be time for that. I'll consider the panel idea, because even I realize that's a crazy, once-in-a-lifetime opportunity, but I'm not giving interviews. Not about the Super Bowl. Not now, not ever."

"I think it would help, but if you're not willing to consider it, I'll pass that along," Alec said. "But if you won't do that, think about adding a PR consultant to the team, especially if you're going to seriously consider this new job with ESPN."

"Ugh, really?" Neal liked his team small; it was mainly just Alec, who took care of a lot of stuff—or Alec's people did. But he liked just having to deal with Alec.

The waitress appeared with their food, and after refilling their coffee, left them alone again, and Neal, who had been dreading her reappearance and any other comments she might make, wished she wouldn't have done her job so efficiently. Probably because he didn't want to listen to Alec or acknowledge how right he was. Did he want someone to manage his public image? Not really. But he knew he might need it.

"I know, but you're going to need the social media help, old man," Alec teased. "I know you hate using it."

Neal hadn't liked social media before the last Super Bowl; now he made sure he never, ever went on it. He could only imagine the things people might feel emboldened to say to him. It was like they thought because they weren't face-to-face with Neal, and they couldn't see his reaction to their ugly words, that they weren't responsible for them. But Neal knew he'd feel every single nasty comment. It was hard to push all that garbage away and pretend that he wasn't tempted to believe it was true.

"If you hire someone," Alec continued, because he'd heard this particular opinion of Neal's more times than he could probably count, "then they could monitor it for you. Delete anything that got out of line. Block any trolls. You wouldn't have to deal with it, then, and it would be a good way for you to sort of 'reemerge' into the world without having to do it yourself."

"Except I need to," Neal said with a sigh. He pushed his eggs around his plate. He was hungry, but *not* hungry at the same time. He knew what he should do, but the idea of *doing* it still made him a little nauseous. "No interview. Not yet. I might . . . need some more time." *You need to feel less like what everyone's saying is true,* he thought. *Maybe if I spend more time with Jamie . . .* but Neal knew Jamie wasn't a magical solution. He believed in him, but deep down, the remnants of Neal's belief in himself still existed. He just had to find them again and dust them off. Resurrect them.

"You take all the time you need. But this panel thing . . . it's a bit more pressing. They want some kind of answer on your interest level."

Neal leaned back in his chair. "The difficulty is I want to say no *now* but I know in three months? I'll probably feel differently."

"Think of how many times you've bitched about how special teams isn't represented on ESPN or any of the other sports media networks," Alec pointed out. "This is your chance to *personally* remedy that."

"It's not a fix, but it's a start." Neal had to concede that point.

"The salary they're throwing out looks good too, so at the very least, you'll like the bottom line. *And* I know this is important to you: they're filming the show in LA going forward."

"Going forward?"

"Yeah, they were filming it in New York, but this year it's moving to LA. Part of their plan to bring in a younger, more involved audience."

"And I'm part of that," Neal said, contemplatively.

"That's the idea," Alec said. "It's a good idea, too. It's probably a gamble that's going to pay off big-time. And you could be part of it. Front and center. This could be the next big step that you've been looking for."

Neal honestly hadn't been sure *what* he was looking for, but he was afraid that Alec might be right—*and* that Jamie might also be another piece of that puzzle.

"Okay . . . tell them I'm interested. I'm considering it," Neal said. "I guess open negotiations. See how flexible they can be on the salary."

"And the PR component?"

Neal sighed. "Let's look for someone. You know the kind of people I like."

"Discreet," Alec said with a grin. "Loyal and discreet and hard-working. Yeah, I know."

And suddenly, as they were finishing up breakfast, Alec pulling out his wallet to pay, he realized something that might make him want to turn down the job completely.

"Hey," he said, "they know I'm gay, right?"

Alec glanced up at him, surprised. "Does who know you're gay?"

"ESPN, the producers of Sunday Morning Football, etcetera. You know, *that* whole group."

"You mean, if you ever want to come out, is it going to be a problem?"

Neal couldn't help but think of Jamie then; that he was already out. That he might not want to date someone who wasn't either. Neal didn't really want to make a big deal out of it, but also didn't want to push himself further back into the closet either. "Yeah, that's exactly what I'm saying."

Alec shrugged. "It's not exactly a state secret that you're not straight. I can't imagine they wouldn't know, and in today's sports climate, that it would matter enough to be a deal breaker. They might even like it better, if you did come out. More attention for their show."

"Ugh," Neal said, but understood that this was sometimes how the media worked. "Just . . . make sure, okay?"

"Why?" Alec said. "Are you thinking of coming out?"

"I'm thinking about of a lot of things," Neal said, and that, at least, was the truth.

• • • ● ● ● • ● ● • • •

The day before, Neal had spent a lot of time doing research for Jamie—watching his kicking package on YouTube a half-dozen times, making notes, digging out some of the books that had helped him when he'd first gotten started in the NFL, and finally, trying to make some logical fucking sense out of the stupid-ass "results" that Jamie had sent him.

Today, after he got home from his breakfast with Alec, Neal did two things: first, he stripped his sheets, and not even bothering to ask Maria to do them, stuck them in the washer himself.

"Oh, Neal, I could've done those," she said, when she came into the laundry room, and saw him trying to figure out the washing machine controls.

It had taken three months of constant reminding for Maria to call him "Neal" instead of "Mr. Neal," and now, after working for him for five years, he considered her a friend more than an employee.

"I know," Neal admitted, but after not letting her deal with his bedroom for six months now, he kinda felt like it was his responsibility to clean it up. "But I wanted to."

Maria came over, resting a reassuring hand on Neal's shoulder, squeezing it lightly. "You don't need to," she said pointedly, "and don't you dare apologize."

"I wasn't going to apologize," Neal said, futilely pushing more buttons. The washing machine still didn't come on. Except he *had* been just about to apologize. For the sheets. For being a recluse the last six months. For being a fuckup.

Neal figured a blanket apology covering all of that was probably the best choice.

"Of course not," Maria said dryly. "Here, why don't you let me start that?" she asked, and before he could move, she'd neatly hip checked him out of the way. "And," she added, "you should probably bring the comforter cover too."

"The comforter cover?"

Maria rolled her eyes. "That can be washed too, and probably *needs* to be washed."

Neal could definitely concede that. "Yeah," he agreed.

"I'm sure you have something you can do in the living room today," she said pointedly. "Because it's high time you let me into your room so I can shovel out all the grime."

"Really? I was . . ."

Maria shot him a look. "Just let me do it," she said. "Zero judgment, okay?"

Neal was still trying to figure out how to look in the mirror and hold back on his own particularly virulent form of judgment. But last night, he'd told himself he couldn't keep wallowing, and this morning, when he'd woken up, Jamie on his mind, wondering what it would be like to wake up next to him, he'd *known. You can't keep going like this*, he'd realized. *You don't even want to.*

That thought had gotten him out of bed and into the shower earlier than it had for months. It had gotten him to the meeting with Alec, and had forced him to consider what his agent had said. And now, it pushed him to nod, and agree to what Maria was suggesting.

Imagine if he got lucky enough to share his bed with Jamie and it was musty and gross?

Also, why did *he* want to stay in that musty and gross bed? He had standards too, and he'd been ignoring them because it was too hard to face any of them.

But it was impossible *not* to face them now.

"Zero judgment," Neal told her. "I'll be in the living room, if you need anything."

"Sure thing," Maria said, and swatted at him. "Now get out of here. Maybe call that sweet boy that Olive tells me came over for dinner last night."

Neal blushed. "He's . . . I'm just giving him some advice."

Maria's look was frank. "Maybe he could give *you* some advice," she suggested.

"Hey, I've still got it," Neal claimed. "I could go out there tomorrow and kick if I wanted to."

"Of course you could," she said, her expression softening. And maybe he could; but the problem was he really didn't want to.

It was definitely time to figure out what he wanted to do with the rest of his life.

This time when he settled onto the living room couch, he didn't pull up any of the kicking videos on his recently played list. Instead, he typed in "Sunday Morning Football" and was faced with a huge number of results. Blindly, he clicked on the first one, and watched as Terry Bradshaw and Jerry Rice broke down a particularly sweet Riptide play from last year. He'd thought it would hurt more, watching this—watching the game he'd loved, that he was pretty sure he *still* loved. But it didn't hurt at all. Instead, he felt exhilarated. He'd been on the field for that play. He'd watched it unfold in real time. Could still remember Sam's triumphant expression as he'd returned to the sideline. The pride in Heath's eyes.

Neal had never had much opportunity to watch the pregame shows because he'd always been on the field or in the locker room, prepping for the game. Occasionally, when the Riptide were on a bye week, he'd watch, but usually on those weekends, he liked to visit Ella and her husband, Mateo—and Olive, of course—and they'd do something that was decidedly not football related. So it turned out that he hadn't really watched these shows. He'd only heard about them.

He made some notes on his phone, questions he wanted to ask Alec about the proposal that he'd given the green light for them to hammer out. Over the years, he'd done a few guest appearances on different talk shows, with different kinds of formats, but he liked the panel aspect here. He didn't want to argue with someone every day, not like Shannon Sharpe and Skip Bayliss. He didn't want to be a sports evangelist like Stephen A. Smith. He had no interest in being a game commentator, even a really good one like Tony Romo had become. Neal thought, *I'd be really happy, just sitting there, next to Terry and Jerry and Jimmy.*

He wasn't dumb enough to believe that he'd be good right away, or that he really belonged on a stage with all those greats, but he *wanted* the opportunity.

First Jamie and now this; wanting things had never been a problem before, but post Super Bowl, he hadn't been sure he deserved to want them.

But now? He could feel himself waking up, coming back alive, and it was easier to push down and push away that insidious voice that kept telling him he deserved nothing.

By the time he looked down at his phone again, it was lunchtime, and not only was his stomach growling, he had a handful of texts from Jamie.

You were right, the first one said. **Only five of us here today.**

And, **You were right, AGAIN, it's a lot easier to focus if I'm keeping to myself.**

One last one: **Haven't missed today. But neither has Shane. We seem to be the front-runners heading into the preseason. They also did that bullshit silence again, and we had to kick 44 over and over again. The coaches here are WACK.**

Neal thought they'd honestly be a lot better off moving on, not focusing on this insane obsession with Neal's missed kick. *I'm moving on, why can't they?*

He went into the kitchen and pulled out the chicken taco leftovers from the fridge. He couldn't help but remember how sweet Jamie had been, insisting on doing the dishes and packing up all the leftovers. Neal didn't think he'd ever found responsibility sexy, but on Jamie? It was a good fucking look, and it made Neal want him to be back here tonight, hip to hip as they did the dishes together.

As he heated up the leftovers, he replied to Jamie's texts. **You knew they were wack already,** he said, **so that isn't really a surprise? But good job. I knew you could do it.** He hesitated, desperate already to see the guy again. Butterflies swirled in his stomach, making him feel like a teenager again. He couldn't remember the last time he'd felt like this, wanting to do so much more than hold hands and watch as Jamie's dark eyes glowed, his curls falling over his forehead. He wanted to pull him close, to feel that electric draw between them flare to life. He might barely know him, but he knew it would be so good. The best thing he'd felt in six long months.

It was that thought that pushed him to add the next few words, hitting send before he could change his mind. **Are you free tomorrow?** He already knew, because the Riptide were predictable, that Jamie would have two days off—and then the practices for the first preseason game would begin in earnest. But selfishly, even though Jamie probably wanted to not even *think* about kicking for those two days, Neal wanted to find a way for them to spend time together.

You could just ask him out to dinner. You could invite him here. You don't have to make it about football, a voice that sounded suspiciously like Olive's pointed out. *You're making this harder than it already is.*

But Neal wanted to be cautious. Take it slow. If things worked out, Jamie wouldn't be going anywhere, but he'd also be playing for a team that hated Neal's guts. Dating him would mean Jamie taking a chance that nobody would find out, and if they did, they wouldn't care anymore. But that was going to take time. More time than they probably had.

That was why it was important that Jamie went into this with his eyes wide open; that he knew the risks and knew the benefits. That he knew this was what he really wanted.

And Neal needed to know it too. Michael's callousness had cut deep, making him wonder if he could ever really trust a partner ever again, the way he'd trusted him. He still wanted that partner to be Jamie, but taking it slow meant he might learn to trust again. That Jamie could earn it, just by being himself.

He was just sitting down to eat when Olive waltzed in, hair piled on top of her head, still wearing her pajamas.

"Late night?" Neal questioned as she pulled open the fridge, grabbing a bottle of water and chugging half its contents. One of the things they'd discussed about Olive living with him while going to school was that he wouldn't be keeping tabs on her all the time. That's why he'd put in the separate suite over the garage and why she had her own entrance, so she could come and go as she pleased.

"Yeah," she admitted, sitting down at the table across from him. She grinned at him, dimples emerging. "How about you?"

"Jamie left about nine," Neal said. Which was the truth. He just left out the semi-pertinent fact that he'd almost asked him to stay about a hundred times. Maybe even a thousand.

Basically—a number that he was *not* proud of.

"Sure he did." Olive leaned back in her chair, still grinning at him. "He really is cute, you know. And he likes you a lot."

Neal *knew* it, but hearing her say it, out loud and blunt like that, still made the realization shiver down low, deep in his stomach, where he had no right to feel something for someone he barely knew.

You didn't even feel this way about Michael. There was a part of you that was always waiting to feel it, and you didn't.

"I like him too," Neal said, because he was sure that was going to be Olive's next pronouncement, and he might as well admit it before she forced him to. "But . . . you know it's complicated, right?"

Olive rolled her eyes. "Yeah, it is. But you shouldn't give him up, just because of that. You won't, right?"

"I don't think you were *ever* this enthusiastic about Michael," Neal muttered. Which made sense, because even though his ex had been perfect on paper, that perfection had never really materialized in real life. They'd been *fine*, he realized, but in the end, nothing particularly special.

"I wasn't," Olive said. "He was cold. Kind of . . . I don't know . . . way too logical for you. You deserve a little romance, you know?"

Neal thought of a text message sent before Jamie ever really knew him, a sweet and flattering and kind message. A *romantic* message.

You're as bright as a star in the sky . . .

"Maybe," Neal said, hedging because he already knew confessing everything to Olive would be a mistake. She'd probably be planning their wedding in a few days.

"You're tough, you know," Olive said, reaching out and snagging his half-finished taco from his plate. "But you're sensitive too. You need someone like Jamie."

"I'm glad you've already decided we're meant for each other," Neal said dryly. Except that he couldn't quite pull off the disinterest very well, because he kinda thought they *might* be. *You barely know him*, Neal reminded himself, but then he remembered how safe and peaceful yet galvanized Jamie made him feel. Like he could do nothing and that would be okay, and like he could do everything, and that would be just as fine.

"We'll see," Olive said slyly. "But I bet that you can't stay away from each other."

Right then, Neal's phone, sitting on the table, buzzed with an incoming text. His face must have lit up when he read it because Olive was standing up and nudging him. "Yeah," she said, as she headed into the kitchen, probably in search of more leftovers since she'd eaten most of them off Neal's plate, "yeah, you're definitely meant for each other. You should see the way your eyes glow. It's kinda gross."

But Neal was too busy replying to Jamie's text. It had simply said, **No plans, unless you have some.**

He typed out an answer, then deleted it, and then typed it out again, finally settling on: **You wanna check out the best practice facility in the country with me?**

Chapter Seven

"This can't be right," Jamie muttered as he turned his rental car into a weed-choked lane, a sign crawling with vines proclaiming he'd discovered some kind of sports park. According to the address that Neal had texted him, this was right. But it was totally nothing like what Jamie had been expecting. Neal had promised one of the best practice facilities in the country.

But if this had been a sports park at some point, it was totally abandoned now. Clearly nobody was maintaining this place, as each field Jamie drove by looked worse—tall, waving grasses, interspersed with some real monster weeds. There were some outbuildings, in the same disrepair, and some signage that Jamie could barely make out through the overgrown foliage.

Neal had told him to turn in and keep driving until he got to the field at the back. "You'll see what you're looking for," he'd texted cryptically, and now, thinking about that comment, Jamie couldn't help but roll his eyes. *The best practice facility in the country?* Jamie couldn't help but wonder as he drove through the increasingly bumpy, gravel-infested lots that maybe Neal's sarcasm was even drier than he'd imagined it was, because *nobody* would ever imagine that this place would win any awards, except maybe for least-maintained property in all of southern California.

Finally, Jamie pulled into what seemed to be the last lot, a sharp right-hand turn, and his jaw dropped. After passing field after field that was going to absolute shit, this last field looked as pristine as the day they'd probably built this place. The grass was a perfect, uniform green, and it even looked neatly cut, not a single weed in sight. These outbuildings had been repaired and then maintained, covered in a fresh coat of bright white paint, trimmed in navy blue. Even the field goal posts were painted, with what looked to be regulation NFL ribbons attached to the ends, so whoever was kicking could better judge the velocity and direction of the wind.

The rest of the parking lot was still empty, because Jamie, embarrassingly eager and also sure he was going to get lost, was early. His jaw was still dropped as he got out of the car, because the last thing he'd expected was this perfect jewel of a field. Especially after passing so many fields that were an utter disaster.

He was still staring at the perfect, uniform green grass when Neal pulled up in his Tesla.

"Damn," Neal said, his smile brighter than Jamie could remember it being, "I kinda wished I'd gotten here first, just so I could see your face. But then . . . I think I'm still kinda seeing it."

"Hey," Jamie said, a little sheepishly, because *yes*, he probably still looked shocked. "What *is* this place?"

"It's mine," Neal said, still grinning as he opened the back door of the car and pulled out an athletic bag. "God, it's fucking *hot* today. I always hate it when it's humid."

Now that Neal mentioned it, it was humid outside, the hot air damp and sticky. Jamie hadn't noticed because when he'd climbed out of his car and its air-conditioning, he'd been focused entirely on the field in front of him.

"Might get a big thunderstorm because of it," Neal added, glancing over at Jamie.

"It's yours?" Jamie said, still stuck on the fact that Neal *owned* this place.

"Yeah, it's kind of a long story, but this athletic park complex was built and developed by a group that went bankrupt. I bought it for pennies, because by then, I'd been in LA for a few years, and it was nice to get away from the Riptide facilities, you know? There's a lot of pressure practicing there, with everyone watching. Sometimes I'd just want to get away. So I bought this and fixed up the back field. Nobody would ever imagine it's here," Neal said. "Keeps the onlookers away, and anyone else who might want to use it."

"With the way it's buried back here, nobody would," Jamie retorted. "You could at least . . . I don't know . . . make the rest of it look less like an eyesore."

That would take money but then maybe Neal was right; why would you waste it on fields you weren't using?

"Someday," Neal said. "I always thought when I retired, I'd redo all of this and fix it up, turn it into a sports center for kids again."

And just like that, all of Jamie's righteous indignation faded away. Of course that was what Neal was going to do.

"At the time, I kinda thought it'd be a joint project between me and the Riptide," Neal added, "but I don't think that's gonna happen anytime soon."

"They treated you like garbage," Jamie said and meant it. Neal just shrugged, leaning against his car. Like he wanted to make sure there was a decent distance between them. Like they hadn't already held hands and practically snuggled on the couch. Like Jamie wasn't *dying* to kiss him already.

"From your perspective, maybe," Neal said thoughtfully. "Maybe from their perspective, I treated *them* like garbage."

It was hard to disagree with him when the entire Riptide special teams program seemed designed to not repeat Neal's mistake.

"Doesn't make it fair—or right," Jamie said staunchly.

"The sooner you get rid of the idea that any of this NFL business is going to be fair, you'll be better off," Neal said, pushing away from the car. He approached where Jamie was standing and tapped him on the shoulder casually—except that every touch between them was the opposite of casual and they both knew it—and said, "Come on, let's grab some balls and see what you can do."

Jamie followed him across the field, towards the pristine shed, where Neal typed in a code, and the door opened. The inside was lined with shelves, with various equipment neatly stacked on them, most of which he recognized from his time at Stanford. Neal unearthed a few kicking holders, and a big bag of footballs, which looked practically unused.

"Do you ever really use this place?" Jamie said, looking around. Even the shed was free of dust, like it was cleaned regularly. "It looks like nobody ever does."

"I do. Well, I *used* to," Neal said. "I think I . . . I guess I haven't been here in six months. At least. But I have someone who maintains it for me. Cleans it up, makes sure the grass is cut, that everything looks good."

"Well, it looks great," Jamie said. "I'm impressed."

"Impressed that I've been slacking for six months?" Neal asked dryly, juggling the bag of balls in one hand as he pulled the door shut behind him. "I wouldn't be."

"I'm impressed that it looks this good," Jamie countered. "I don't think even the Riptide fields are this well-maintained."

"They're used a bit more," Neal pointed out. "You wanna do a warm-up?"

Jamie glanced over at the guy next to him. "You gonna warm up with me?"

He wouldn't be surprised if Neal hadn't even been on a football field since the Super Bowl six months earlier, and he definitely hadn't kicked since then. Was he going to kick now? Or had he just brought Jamie here so *he* could kick without being in the pressure cooker of the Riptide practice field?

"Yeah, sure." Neal looked surprised—maybe that Jamie had asked, maybe that he'd agreed.

It turned out it was one thing to watch Neal stretch on TV, and it was another to have a front row seat to how he carefully and gradually stretched himself out, his long, lean muscles bunching and flexing as he went through his regular progressions.

Jamie tried to stay focused on his normal warm-up routine, but it was hard when Neal was *right there,* and also looked like that, his slightly too long hair growing damp at the temples.

He'd been sure that his glances had been subtle enough, but about halfway through his own set of stretches, Neal stopped abruptly and looked over at him, catching him right in the act. "See something you like? A lunge you're into? Or something else, maybe?" Neal teased.

"I . . ." Jamie had no good excuse. None whatsoever.

"I hope you don't usually get this distracted," Neal continued, smiling. "Otherwise I might be worried."

The thing was—Jamie *wasn't.* The thing that professional athletes always worried about when they had a gay player in their midst was that all the muscular prowess on display might destroy their focus and they'd spend practices and games ogling all the hot guys, instead of focusing on their job.

But Jamie had never had a problem with that—and he knew so many other queer athletes didn't either.

But then, he'd never practiced with Neal Fisher before, either.

"Trust me, it's not . . ." Jamie took a deep breath, embarrassed even though he shouldn't be, at admitting that he had a real weakness and it was just for the man in front of him. "It's not normally a problem. You're just . . . and I'm just . . ."

Neal grinned widely, his eyes crinkling at the edges. "Oh, it's just me, huh?"

"Yeah," Jamie admitted.

Neal didn't look perturbed, just really, really pleased. "I'm flattered," he said. "Just don't pull a muscle because you can't stop staring at my ass."

Jamie flushed, and it wasn't just because it was still way too fucking hot outside. He ran a hand through his hair and decided this was as good a time as any to grab his sweat band from his car. "I'll be right back," he said, jogging off towards where he was parked. When he returned, a minute later, after pushing his curls back with his favorite bright red sweat band, Neal had opened the bag and had pulled a ball out and was tossing it around, doing hand drills the way Jamie had seen some of the wide receivers and running backs do.

"Are you gonna throw it between the uprights?" he asked with a quick smile. Neal was surprisingly good at what he was doing; maybe he actually *could*.

"I started doing these," Neal said, after the ball finally fell to the ground, "because someone once threw me a ball at practice, and I literally dropped it. So fucking embarrassing, and now I do this, so that *never* happens again, but also because it feels good to get my mind used to focusing on the ball, on putting it exactly where I want it to be, not just with my foot but with my hands too." He tossed the ball in Jamie's direction—actually a fairly decent throw, which didn't surprise Jamie at all—and he caught it. "You wanna give it a go?"

Jamie chuckled. "Sure, but I'm gonna be terrible at it."

"It's okay. I was too, at first. But I learned it helps. Helps to focus my mind. Might help you too." Neal picked up another ball from the bag and balanced it on the edge of his hand, his grin daring him to try.

Before, whenever Jamie had thought of Neal Fisher, he'd seemed to be this super hot, larger-than-life guy, who always did everything right. Even when he did everything wrong—like missed a field goal in the Super Bowl—Jamie still thought he handled even the most difficult situations easily.

He'd seen him as a figure to look up to, practically perfect up there on his pedestal. But now? Watching Neal bumble the ball again, only a few seconds into his next exercise, it hit Jamie then that he was a real flesh and blood man. He wasn't always perfect, and didn't always do the right thing. He hadn't handled everything that had happened after the Super Bowl. Instead of facing what had happened straight on, he'd hidden from it. Couldn't face it.

Jamie had always thought if he made it to the NFL, he'd have the grace under pressure that Neal Fisher possessed in spades. But

Jamie was beginning to realize that life was way more complicated than that. Sometimes you hit things you couldn't handle, and it wasn't because you weren't strong or tough or smart. Because Neal *was;* he was all of those things. But he was also human.

"I think I believe you," Jamie said, tossing the football in the air and beginning to imitate Neal's movements. He'd been right about being awful at it, as he lost it on the third toss, and laughed as it fell to the ground.

"That it'd help you?" Neal wondered, keeping his own ball in the air with that precise sort of concentration that Jamie recognized all too well from all those years watching it on TV.

"That you suck at this," Jamie said with a laugh, as Neal glanced over at him in surprise, his ball falling to the grass.

"Thanks," Neal said wryly, "I think I actually had a good run going there, and you distracted me."

Jamie shrugged, feeling unrepentant. "I thought we were supposed to be able to block the world out," he teased.

Neal stared at him, somehow the air between them growing hotter and tighter with the tension that seemed to bloom between them. "You're . . . well, you're a little distracting," Neal finally admitted softly.

Jamie grinned widely, feeling joy spread through him. He'd known it wasn't just him; but it was so sweet to *hear* it. "Oh, so if I did this . . ." He reached up and tugged his t-shirt off. He was hardly an Instagram model or anything, but he'd worked hard for the beginnings of a decent six-pack. Neal's eyes, all those shades of green, pinned him in place.

Yeah, they'd met at a pool party and maybe neither of them had been totally clothed, but Jamie could feel the weight of Neal's gaze on him now.

"Don't like to play fair, huh?" Neal wondered. His voice soft and hushed. Secret. Like nobody would ever know what they did here, and Jamie thought he was right; nobody ever would. They were in this bubble, isolated from the world.

"Nope," Jamie teased. "Not when it comes to you, anyway. Besides, if I pull a hamstring checking out your ass, turnabout's fair play, right?"

Neal's smile was slow and wide, and it lit up his entire face. Even his eyes, banishing that last bit of sadness from them. Though Jamie could attest that sadness had been slowly fading away, anyway. But it felt good to be the one responsible for putting that kind of smile on Neal's face. For making him *happy*.

"Absolutely," Neal said. "Now, I wanna see some kicks. Show me what you got, big boy."

"Oh, I was a kid, and now I'm a big boy, huh?" Jamie laughed.

Neal nudged him with his hip, and a flash of heat rushed through Jamie. He craved him, *badly*, and the longer this painfully delicious tension dragged out, the deeper the craving dug its nails in. For a second he nearly reached out and dragged Neal against him, finally and irrevocably fitting their mouths together. But . . . he was waiting. Until he was ready? Jamie knew *he* was ready.

Until Neal was ready, he realized. He was waiting until Neal was ready. Neal had started out by setting the pace, and he'd let him, Jamie realized. He'd let Neal do just about any goddamn thing he wanted.

Even wait.

"You wanna play with the big boys, then, *yeah*, you are," Neal said.

"Alright then," Jamie said, and he picked up a football holder, positioning it, not on the forty-four-yard line—God knew he'd made enough kicks from that distance recently—but at the fifty-five.

"Ambitious," Neal pointed out, and Jamie glanced back, watching as he lifted his own shirt, wiping the sweat from his brow, giving him a split-second view of his own ripped abs. It was playing unfair, but then, Jamie knew he was also testing him. Could he focus? Could he be mindful? If he couldn't do either of those things right now, with just a tantalizing glimpse of Neal's stomach to distract him, then how could he do it in a stadium? To win a game? With a million fans watching?

Jamie turned back to where he'd set the ball on the holder. He did his visualization—he'd expanded it with the recent reading that Neal had given him; usually he just imagined the ball coming off his foot perfectly, and sailing right between the uprights, but now he went through an entire process—and then got ready to kick.

The world faded away, even Neal, standing behind him, and making sure his footwork was perfect, kicked the ball and sent it sailing through the uprights on the other side of the field.

Only when he saw it go through did everything slide back into focus, including Neal, giving him a low whistle of approval. "You've got a leg," he said, coming up to stand next to Jamie. "That could've gone another twenty yards."

The further a kick was, the tougher it was to be accurate. But in practice? It was easy to be accurate, because it was hard to simulate the stresses of a game kick during practice; there was usually no inclement weather, very little pressure, and the complete lack of an opposing team trying to tackle, distract or destroy.

But during practice? Jamie was proud he could sometimes kick a seventy-yard field goal.

"Yeah, that's not a problem," Jamie admitted shyly. "I could've gone seventy, easy." Maybe *easy* wasn't entirely accurate, but he was allowed to brag a little, right? Especially in front of the boy—*man*, he corrected, *Neal Fisher's a grown-up, hot-blooded, way-too-desirable man*—he liked.

"You can kick seventy? Really?" Neal looked like he wanted to see it and Jamie thought, *why not?* He leaned down and was about to grab the holder to move it back another fifteen or so yards, but then Neal reached out a hand and closed it around his forearm. "Not today," he said. "I want you to practice on something else."

Jamie looked at him questioningly.

"I've watched more of your video," Neal admitted. "I . . . I couldn't sleep, and it was something to do."

Jamie thought there might be more to the story than Neal was telling him, but he could be patient. He wanted Neal to tell him everything—but he was willing to wait until the time was right. *But it's never gonna be right, not if you don't win this job,* that pushy voice inside reminded him. *You gotta become the next Riptide kicker.*

That voice wasn't necessarily wrong, but he pushed the pressure aside, listening to what Neal was telling him about his mechanics.

"They're good," Neal said, "you've got a good pre-kick process, but I'd like you to focus more on making every single movement the exact same. If the Riptide job doesn't work out, that's something that teams will want to see—a consistency correlating to success."

"Am I not doing that?" It was hard to push the wave of embarrassment aside. He'd focused on doing exactly what Neal was describing when he'd been at Stanford, and he thought he'd done it, improving his completion percentage as he solidified his set of movements during the kick.

Neal shrugged. "You could be better. We could *all* be better."

"Okay," Jamie said, shaking off the remaining feelings of inadequacy. He'd asked Neal for his help. If he was already perfect—which he definitely wasn't—then he wouldn't need it, and he *knew* he did.

"Let's try a shorter kick, like an extra point," Neal suggested. "I want you to do it ten times. Think about your feet, your center, your hands, the angle of your shoulders, *everything*, during every single kick."

"Alright," Jamie said, and he glanced down at the bag of footballs at his feet. There were only seven left, after he'd already kicked that long field goal.

"I'll play ball boy," Neal said. He patted his flat stomach. "I could use the exercise."

Jamie considered telling Neal that if he got any fitter, he wasn't going to be able to handle it—but considering how many times he'd gotten caught checking him out today, he thought that probably wasn't much of a secret.

"Okay." Jamie reached down and snagged the football holder, and picked up a ball, giving it a few tosses in the air, refocusing himself on the task at hand as he walked towards the right yard line for an extra-point kick.

Neal jogged past him, body moving gracefully, and Jamie had to glance away. He was *so* distracting. Somehow Neal flustered and centered him, all at the same time.

He kicked ten extra points, catching each ball as Neal tossed it back to him, focusing this time not on just *making* it but on the exact set and placement of his body as he did it. At first, it was foreign to worry about where his arms were or which way his hands were facing, or the set of his shoulders, but by the end of the ten kicks, Jamie thought he'd gotten a lot better at it.

Neal jogged back to where Jamie was set up after the tenth kick sailed through the uprights.

"You're getting better," Neal said, stopping next to him, his breath coming in short pants. He reached up and stripped off his t-shirt. "Goddamn, it's hot. It's never this humid in LA."

Hot, Jamie's sluggish brain thought as he gazed at the sweaty streaks on Neal's skin. Paler than his own, but no less appealing. He wanted to lick all those damp, rippling muscles. *Down, boy,* he told himself firmly. It wasn't the time to get excited, it was the time to focus on the practice he needed to best Shane and get to keep the job. Maybe even earn the Riptide's trust, the way that Neal had.

Neal craned his head back, watching the rippling gray clouds that were congregating overhead. "I think we might even get a heat storm."

"Heat storm?" Jamie was still not following. Not staring and imagining putting his hands all over Neal's body was proving to be a trickier task than he'd imagined.

"They have them on the East Coast all the time, and in the South," Neal explained. "Usually when it gets super humid. My sister and her husband live in NYC, and I used to spend part of the year with them, before I went to college."

"Wisconsin," Jamie supplied, still painfully distracted. "You went to school at Wisconsin."

"Go Badgers," Neal said with a sly grin. "What'd you guys have? Oh, that weird tree thing."

"Hey, don't knock the Stanford Tree," Jamie retorted.

Suddenly a darker cloud passed over Neal's face and then a moment later, a water droplet hit Jamie square on the nose. "Well, shit," Jamie said.

"Yeah," Neal sighed. "It'll feel better after. Maybe if it doesn't rain too hard . . ." But just as he'd said that, the heavens opened up, sending a fierce deluge down to earth. Jamie was soaked within seconds, and he laughed, the rain unexpectedly cooling him off, and then he looked over at Neal and nearly swallowed his tongue.

The rain had drenched Neal too, and he shoved his dripping wet dark hair back, exposing his exquisitely handsome face, his eyes cool and green against his pale skin. And he was *laughing*.

"Fuck," he said, leaning over, his soaked athletic shorts conforming to his muscular thighs. Jamie swallowed hard. He'd never felt drawn to another man the way he felt drawn to this one.

"Heat storm?" Jamie finally answered.

Neal nodded. "I guess we'd better get everything cleaned up."

It didn't take long to get the footballs back into the bag and to gather up the rest of the equipment, carting it back to the shed.

"I'll text you the code," Neal said, as they put everything away, leaving wet, squishy footprints on the concrete floor. "So you can come whenever you like."

"Without you?" Jamie asked, without thinking that through.

Neal glanced up and the silence pulled taut between them, snapping into place. His green eyes wide and disbelieving, then settling into something hot and possessive.

"You don't want to come without me?" Neal asked carefully.

You don't have to push him, but you don't have to hold your feelings back, either. "No," he said. "No, I don't. I don't want . . ." He cleared his throat. *Be fucking honest.* "I don't want to do much without you, honestly."

Those gorgeous eyes widened and then softened. "God, you gotta stop saying shit like that," Neal said, pushing his dripping hair back again.

"Why?" Jamie wondered. Suddenly afraid that Neal would tell him he needed to stop. Because he didn't *want* to stop.

"Because I'm gonna . . ." Neal muttered and then dropped the balls in place, and suddenly his arm was hot and wet around Jamie's bare middle, and he could pick out every single shade of green in Neal's eyes as he stopped only a breath away from kissing him.

Jamie licked his lips nervously as Neal's fingers dug into his side. Not hurting him necessarily, but *there,* like he wanted to make sure Jamie knew it was him holding him so tightly. "You're gonna?" he questioned.

Maybe he'd say that this was a mistake again; maybe he'd warn them it was messy, and it was bound to blow up in their faces.

"Because I'm gonna do this," Neal said quietly, and leaned in, brushing his mouth gently across Jamie's. "Probably a whole lot."

"Okay, good," Jamie said in a breathless rush. "I won't argue with that." He slid his hands up to Neal's shoulders, gripping the firm muscles there, and tilted his head, slanting his mouth more forcefully against Neal's, and the kiss went from sweet to incandescently hot in a split second, before Jamie could even realign his world with the fact that Neal Fisher had kissed him.

That Neal Fisher *wanted* him.

Chapter Eight

Kissing. They were *kissing*. Neal felt a wave of panic-tinged euphoria crest through him. He'd known this would happen—it had felt inevitable that it would, when they both wanted it so much—but he hadn't imagined that it would happen *today*. But then, the rain had come, unexpectedly soaking them both to the skin, plastering Jamie's shorts to his legs and his hair to his forehead, his dark eyes shining in his wet face.

It was hard enough to resist the guy when he was *dry*. Wet? Neal felt all his good intentions to take it slow, to ease into this for both of their sakes, burn up completely.

He was a few inches taller than Jamie, and maybe not necessarily younger or stronger, but Jamie went boneless when he kissed him like this. Neal tilted his head, their mouths fitting together like they'd been made to kiss each other, and Jamie's back hit the door. He wondered, in some distant, disconnected part of his mind, that if his arms hadn't been holding on to Jamie's waist, whether he'd have slid weak-kneed to the floor.

It was a heady feeling, knowing that he'd done this, that just kissing was enough to unwind this confident, collected man, until he was putty in Neal's hands. His cock throbbed at the thought of taking Jamie to bed, of exploring all the tantalizing possibilities that existed. Neal didn't have many hang-ups when it came to sex—if he liked it, and it felt good, he did it—but the idea of making Jamie feel so good, to overwhelm him with pleasure, was enough to nearly make him fall to his knees *now*.

Jamie moaned into his mouth, his fingers digging into Neal's neck. He could probably feel his hard cock through the clinging wet shorts he was wearing, because he knew he could feel Jamie's. It was a hard, hot line against his hip, and the thought of it made him want to throw everything out the window. All his hesitation, all his concerns, *everything*, until it was just the two of them caught up in each other, existing in a bubble where nobody could touch them.

Except that wasn't true, was it?

Jamie was living in the opposite of a bubble. Every single thing he did would be scrutinized, in the next few days, as Jamie tried to make the team. Until they made that decision . . . even *after* they made that decision . . . he still had to win the kicking competition in the preseason games, if he wanted to be the guy they signed.

Neal pulled away, his breath sounding harsh and heavy in the small space. Jamie's chest was rising and falling, and he stared at

Neal, tongue flicking out of his mouth to lick his bottom lip. His full, red, *swollen* bottom lip. *You did that*, Neal's uncooperative brain announced, *and you could do it again.*

But he couldn't, he *shouldn't*.

"We shouldn't do this . . . *here*," Neal said, amending the sentence when he saw the disappointment bloom in Jamie's eyes.

"You could come back to my hotel with me . . ." Jamie offered, his voice trailing off. "Nobody would know."

"Except I'd know, and you'd know and well," Neal admitted, "once we start this, I'm not sure I'm gonna want to stop."

"But you already started it," Jamie said. And *yeah*, Neal deserved that. He *had* started it. He'd been way too confident in his own self-control, but after so long not feeling anything at all, feeling *good* had been too enticing of an attraction. He hadn't been able to resist, not when Jamie was staring at him like that, when he was looking at him like he was a mix of man and god, and he wanted to seduce the former and worship the latter.

"I know," Neal said. He swallowed back the apology, because Jamie deserved better than that, and also he wasn't really that sorry at all. "I just think . . . this is a critical juncture for you, that's all. Decisions are happening that could affect the rest of your career—the rest of your *life*. I can't be the person who fucks that up for you."

"So, you think you'd distract me," Jamie said slowly.

"If we had sex, I know I'd be pretty damn distracted," Neal admitted, the admission raw. Even saying the word *sex* in this charged air between them felt like a step too far. A step too close to letting it actually happen.

Jamie's gaze was fierce and knowing, and for a split second, Neal wanted to drop to his knees—either to beg forgiveness or to reach for the shorts currently plastered to Jamie's hard cock, he wasn't sure. Both seemed like the best idea that he'd had in forever.

Definitely better than six months of self-flagellation and the never-ending cycle of anger and guilt.

"You're . . . you're not wrong," Jamie said, finally glancing away, relieving some of the pressure, and most—but not all—of the temptation. "We'd end up in bed and not want to leave."

Exactly what Neal was both hoping and dreading, all in the same moment.

"Listen, this isn't . . ." Neal took a deep breath. Jamie was still too close, and far too tempting. "This isn't *no*, which you know, because you know I want you." He reached out and took Jamie's hand, and telling himself that this wasn't a monumental mistake pressed it to the front of his still-damp shorts, against his rock-hard dick, which strained at the idea of being touched. Of *Jamie* being the one doing the touching.

Jamie hissed—or maybe that was Neal. Either way, their gazes locked, and yeah, maybe it was a risk, but it was a calculated one. "I want you," Neal repeated. "Desperately. Which . . . you know, because you can feel it. All from one kiss."

"I'd give you more than one," Jamie said, and dropped his hand, which was probably for the best, because Neal felt like he'd dealt with all the temptation he was capable of handling. "I'd give you as many as you wanted."

God, he knew it. He knew it already. But hearing it? Way too sweet for Neal's current state of mind.

"Fuck, I would too," Neal ground out, and before he could stop himself, he was pulling Jamie back into his arms. This time though, Jamie's head came to rest on his shoulder, and they stood there for a long moment like that, listening to the rain hitting the metal roof, and held each other.

"Not right now," Jamie repeated softly, his words muffled by Neal's bare shoulder.

"I don't know when the right time is . . ." *Probably never, but I can't promise that, not when it comes to him.* "But we'll figure it out."

"Okay," Jamie said, taking a step back. It stung a little to lose the feeling of Jamie's bare chest pressed to his, and it stung even more to see that Jamie wasn't sure he trusted him that he was telling the truth.

Why did trying to do the right thing always suck so bad?

"Did they say when they were making decisions?" Neal wondered. He knew it'd be in the next day or two, because there was only a week and a half before the first preseason game, and they'd want to have the maximum amount of preparation time for their new kicker—or kickers, if Neal was right, and they ended up carrying two into the preseason.

But he already knew he was going to be right, because he knew Toby and he knew Coach R, and he knew what kind of twisted mindset they'd fallen into. Just any old kind of competition hadn't been good enough in camp; and it wouldn't be good enough going forward, either. No, they were sure to add a few extra additional wrinkles. To reassure themselves? To prove to the media they were doing their due diligence? To promise their fanbase that the Super Bowl kick would never happen again?

The problem was that there were no guarantees, not in football.

"I'm going in tomorrow morning and meeting with Coach Toby," Jamie said, leaning against one of the shelving units. "My agent is sure they're going to offer me at least a contract through the preseason."

"I think so too. And honestly, out of everyone they had at camp, you're the best choice. They'd be insane to sign Shane too, and keep you on edge for another four games, instead of letting you settle in and grow your confidence, but we know they're being stupid right now, so I think you're gonna be stuck with him. At least for a while."

"Probably," Jamie said with a reluctant sigh. "I don't mind him . . . I can block out the bullshit, *mostly* anyway, but I just want to know. Am I staying here? Am I leaving? Am I gonna be back on my dad's couch by the time the opening kickoff happens?"

"Nope, that's definitely not happening," Neal said. "Not if I have anything to say about it. You're good. And you're getting even better. You've got room to grow; Shane's already at his max."

Jamie didn't look convinced. And yeah, it hurt to no longer be that god, the one that he looked up to, the one whose word he hung on. Doing the right thing absolutely sucked. "I guess we'll see." He sighed again. "It's not that I don't think you're right; I'm just not sure anyone in that office is thinking clearly right now."

"They aren't." Neal could see that. He understood it, even, because he hadn't been, either. "But I still have to believe they're gonna make the right call."

"I guess I'll see tomorrow."

The rain was finally coming to a close; Neal could barely hear it now. "You'll call me when you find out, yeah?"

This time, Jamie's smile was wide and bright. "Of course. I can't say you'll be my *first* call, but you'll be on the list."

"That's all I want to be." *Lie*, that traitorous voice yelled, *you want to be way more than just some place on the list.*

"You got it," Jamie said, pushing off from where he'd been resting against the shelving unit. Giving them space, Neal realized. He'd been giving them space to cool down; to go along with what Neal had suggested. He felt a pang in his chest, and for a split second, he almost told Jamie, *never mind.*

"Hey," Neal said, "the rain's stopping now, I think. We'd probably be able to make it to our cars without getting drenched, *again.*" Jamie nodded, looking unsure. But Neal wasn't unsure—he knew what he wanted, and maybe if he couldn't have all of it, he could at least have *something.* So, as Jamie approached, assuming that Neal would open the door, he leaned down and kissed him again.

Jamie looked shocked, and Neal paused for a second. "We can have this," he reassured, "because if we can't, I'm gonna go insane." Jamie nodded once, and then again, like he couldn't help but agree.

This time when Neal kissed him, he wasn't so caught up in *oh god, this is finally happening*, that he could pay attention to every single little detail. Each and every detail that made kissing Jamie so different than kissing any other man. The way he sighed into Neal's mouth when he threaded his fingers through his hair and tugged, positioning him just right. The hint of citrus-y cologne under the smell of rain and the unique scent of Jamie himself. The shy dart of Jamie's tongue into his mouth, and then when he relaxed into it, the pliable way he could be coaxed back into confidence.

He ended the kiss before he could get too carried away, but arousal was already flaring in his veins again, lighting him up from the inside out, and when his fingers moved to rest on Jamie's bare chest, they were trembling.

"We can have that?" Jamie said, opening his eyes. They were filled with wonder. Like he'd experienced the same kind of unique beauty that Neal had. Like Neal was the first man he'd ever kissed. And Neal knew that couldn't be true. But it *felt* like that; like he was experiencing everything all over again. He'd thought it was just him, because he'd been so solitary during the last six months, that he was just remembering how to experience something other than pain for the first time in so long, it was like a long unused muscle stretching out again. But it was more than that. And Jamie was more than just the first guy he'd been interested in since Michael.

He could be everything, that voice told Neal, and *yeah*, that kinda scared the shit out of him.

•••••••••••

When he showed up at the Riptide facility, Jamie was led into one of the small conference rooms. Coach Toby was there and so was Coach Rodriguez, typing something distractedly on his phone.

"Glad you could stop by today," Coach Toby said, which was ridiculous, because what was Jamie going to do? Say, *oh yeah, I've got a full and busy schedule, not sure I could fit you in*? Not when this conversation was going to change his whole life—or at least *start* to change his whole life.

Truthfully, that kiss with Neal yesterday had *felt* more life-altering. Like every kiss he'd experienced before that one had been child's play and ultimately irrelevant. It wasn't like Jamie disagreed with Neal's assessment that he needed to focus on the job and the task at hand, but... truthfully holding back was *just* as distracting.

Wondering what Neal would feel like, sound like, *taste* like . . . it was killing him.

It wasn't that he wanted Neal *more* than he wanted to be the Riptide's new kicker. It was that he wanted *both*.

"No problem," Jamie said. "I was happy to."

"We've decided to carry two kickers into the preseason," Coach Toby said. Which was exactly as Neal had predicted. Jamie had assumed he'd be right, but it was still a jolt. He'd been *right*. "And we'd like you to be one of them."

"Thanks," Jamie said. It was a hard line to walk, because he was definitely appreciative that he'd won one of the two spots, but at the same time, he couldn't help but be offended that *Shane* was the guy occupying the other one.

He was way better than Shane.

Except, now it's time to prove it, he thought, *there's no excuses left.*

"I don't want you to think this competition is over," Coach Toby said. It took all of Jamie's self-control not to roll his eyes and return with *no shit, Sherlock.* "I want you to put all your effort and your work in during the next few weeks. Our intention is to come out of the preseason with a kicker for this season and hopefully for several seasons to come."

Seasons to come. Jamie perked up, immediately. That could mean a long-term contract, and even if Coach Toby had only dangled that possibility as a motivational tactic, it was still going to work. Because that was what all kickers wanted, right? To stop being so goddamned transient? To not be shuttled from team to team, never unpacking their stuff? To finally get some stability? That was what the Riptide was theoretically offering.

It was what Neal had had, when he'd been their kicker, and until the Super Bowl, that had paid off for both of them. It made logical sense for the team to want that again.

"I'm going to be your guy. I promise."

He couldn't really *promise.* But he was going to deliver on it anyway.

Because this was the job he wanted. It would mean so many things—the stability, but also the chance to stick around LA. To keep seeing Neal.

"Good," Coach Toby said with an approving nod. "That's what we like to hear, right, Coach R?"

Coach Rodriguez looked up for the first time during the meeting. Other than a brief introduction and a quick handshake at the beginning of camp, the only time Jamie had spent with the head coach was that first meeting when the Coach had proven that he was still painfully hung up on the way the last season had ended. But to Jamie's surprise, his gaze was warm and supportive.

Everything that Jamie had wanted these last few days of camp, that he'd had to seek from the very last person he probably should have.

"I have great confidence in your abilities," Coach R said. "You've kicked great this week. Really consistent. You've got all the things we're looking for in a great special teams player."

"Thank you, sir," Jamie said. Suddenly he didn't want to let this guy down; suddenly, he realized that Neal *had*. And Neal was still dealing with that, just like Coach R was still dealing with the aftermath that he had.

There were still a few things the Riptide were doing that he couldn't agree with, but he wanted this job now. Seeing Coach become human made him want it even more.

Maybe he should be taking this competition with Shane more seriously—but then it was hard to take *Shane* seriously. Shane hadn't been a high-end recruit, though Jamie knew that scouts could always be wrong. Look at Tom Brady, they'd definitely been wrong about him. But even so, Jamie hadn't seen Shane do anything that proved the scouts wrong yet. All he'd done was manage to ace the bizarre, non-game tests that the Riptide had thrown at them.

Would that translate to game time? Could Jamie beat him when it really counted?

Shane might be mediocre, but he was also the kind of mediocre that kept making kicks, too, so really how mediocre could he be? Jamie thought about this as he shook hands with both coaches.

"Make sure you head down to the equipment manager and finalize your number," Coach Toby said. "I know you've been wearing a temp one, since we've had so many guys in for camp. And we'll see you in a few days. Have a good rest, because we're going to work hard when we get back. First game's coming up soon."

He'd had to pick a number different from the one he'd worn at Stanford—there'd been that many extra players at the Riptide training camp. When he headed down to the lower level, to the equipment manager's office, he thought he would keep the same one he'd worn at Stanford. But then, when faced with Dan, the equipment manager, he found himself saying an entirely different number. Not his old one at all. But someone else's old number.

"Five," Jamie said to Dan. "Please change my number to five."

Dan eyed him dubiously. "You know . . ."

"Yeah," Jamie said. "I know."

· · · ● · ● · · ·

"Hey, Dad," Jamie said, leaning against his rental car, shading his eyes from the sun as he took in the bright afternoon. "I was hoping I'd catch you out of a meeting."

"When I know how big today was? I'm waiting," Dave Wright said, fairly impatiently. "Your mother is probably dying too, to find out how it went."

"I made the team, at least for the preseason," Jamie said.

"That's fantastic news," his dad said, and he sounded thrilled. Jamie was lucky in that his parents, while worried about what kind of lifestyle an NFL kicker might enjoy, were always unflinchingly supportive. He'd wanted to go to this tryout, even though he'd been unsure if he'd make the team, and though his dad had expressed some reservations, he'd also told him he knew Jamie could do it.

"You're tough, and you're smart," he'd said, right before Jamie left for LA. "If anyone can navigate the minefield that's probably the Riptide, you can."

His dad's statement had been surprisingly predictive. The Riptide *had* been a minefield, and he'd navigated it. At least so far.

"Your mom is going to be so proud," his dad said. "I can't wait to tell her."

"Oh, is she in class?" Jamie asked.

"Yeah, all afternoon, and then office hours, but I'll tell her when she gets home. You don't want to have to text her or leave a voicemail."

"Right," Jamie agreed. "Just be sure to tell her that for now, it's *just* for the preseason, but they're talking about a long-term deal, which could be great, if I could win it."

"You can," Dave said confidently. "I know you can."

"Thanks, Dad," Jamie said wryly. He'd been adopted when he was just a baby, but his parents had never made him feel any less special even though he wasn't their natural child. In fact, it felt sometimes to Jamie like they cherished him even more because he'd gotten lucky enough to be the kid they'd both dreamt of for ages.

"How is LA, then? Good so far?"

Jamie hesitated. There was a part of him that wanted to tell his dad about Neal, but while his dad *was* supportive, he was also notoriously risk-averse. He'd hate the idea of Jamie hanging out with the old Riptide kicker. "It'll make a problem for you," he could imagine his dad saying. "What if the team found out?"

His dad would also hate the fact that instead of choosing to wear his old Stanford number, he'd purposefully selected Neal Fisher's old number.

But what he didn't know couldn't hurt him either.

"It's fine," Jamie said. "Kinda boring, actually, when I'm not at practice."

"Well, that's a *good* thing, Jamie. Keeps you focused on what's important."

Jamie rolled his eyes. It was *not good* that his dad and Neal sounded so much alike.

He didn't need any lectures about distractions, thank you very much.

"I will," Jamie promised.

"Good," Dave said. "Maybe we could come down for one of the preseason games."

"I'd love that," Jamie said. He couldn't introduce them to Neal but maybe he could float the idea that he was seeing someone down here . . . someone he couldn't quite introduce them to yet . . . at least get them used to the idea there was more than one reason he wanted to stay in Los Angeles.

"Well, let me know the details," his dad said, sounding like he was in one of his many meetings.

"Sure thing," Jamie said.

"And don't be a stranger. It makes your mother sad," Dave added sternly, even though Jamie already knew that it bothered *both* of his parents if they didn't talk often.

"Right," Jamie chuckled. "I won't." His phone vibrated in his hands with another incoming call. "Hey, I've got to run, I think this is Grady calling." Grady was his agent—not a major, important one, like he knew Neal had, but he was perfectly good enough for Jamie.

"Alright, I know you've got lots to talk to him about," Dave said. "Love you, son."

"Love you too, Dad," Jamie said, clicking to switch the call.

"What the *fuck* were you thinking?"

Jamie nearly dropped the phone in surprise.

It was Neal; of course it was Neal.

"Huh?" Jamie was still reeling from the fact that it wasn't Grady on the phone. "I don't . . ."

"The number," Neal said. It was the first time Neal had ever seemed annoyed with him—and he was clearly more than annoyed, he was *angry*. "You fucking requested *my* old number. So I'll ask you again: what were you thinking?"

What had Jamie been thinking? He'd been thinking the way the Riptide had treated Neal was egregiously unfair. That not only had the way they conducted their camp and their kicker tryout made it more difficult for everyone involved, but that it was a giant *fuck you* to the guy who had been nothing short of consistently spectacular for thirteen long years. He'd been thinking *someone* should remember Neal. And that maybe he wasn't there to replace him, to erase Neal and his history, but instead to continue on Neal's tradition of excellence.

Maybe he'd gone a little far. The way the equipment manager had gone white and then red in the face at his request had made that pretty clear. Neal yelling at him? Left him feeling uneasy. Was it really such a mistake? *Probably,* but it also felt right, too. In the end, though, none of that mattered, because Jamie wasn't changing it.

"I'm guessing you don't like it, then," Jamie said flatly.

For a long moment, all Jamie could hear was Neal's breathing on the other end of the phone. It was frenzied, like he'd been running full speed. "I don't *hate it,* but what I do hate is the problems it's gonna cause you," Neal finally said.

"How did you even find out about it?" Jamie wondered. He knew gossip in the NFL traveled fast; still, it had been less than fifteen minutes since Jamie had even requested the number. Could it really travel *that* fast?

"Do you really think I don't have friends in this organization anymore? That everyone hates me?" Neal asked bitterly. "Dan is an old friend. I got him that job. He called me because he wasn't sure why you wanted it, or if I should even let you have it."

"That number isn't retired," Jamie pointed out. "I can have any number I want that isn't currently claimed."

"Yeah, but there's a reason why nobody else has it," Neal said ominously.

"Please don't say because it's cursed."

"I wasn't going to," Neal retorted, but Jamie had a feeling that was *exactly* what he'd been about to say, and if anything, that stupidity only made him want to wear the number *more.* To prove Neal's—and the rest of the Riptide's—silly superstitions wrong.

"Then what's the problem?" Jamie asked, because even though he had a pretty good idea, he wanted Neal *to say it.*

Neal made a frustrated noise. "You're thinking about *me*, not about what you should be thinking about."

He *wasn't* wrong. "What I should be thinking about—the job I've almost won, or the contract that I'm going to sign in a few weeks, or the preseason games that I'm going to kick great in?"

"None of that is guaranteed," Neal said with a resigned sigh.

"I know that, but that doesn't change anything. Doesn't mean that I'm not going to make all of it happen. And if I want to do it wearing your number, all that's going to do is prove to people that they were wrong about you."

"I don't give a fuck what people think of me," Neal said. Impatiently. "I . . . I care about you throwing this chance away."

Jamie couldn't help but wonder if Neal had wanted to say he cared about *him*, but he'd held back at the last minute. It *was* fast—probably anyone out there would tell him it was way too fast to already care about someone he barely knew, someone he'd only known for a week—but that didn't change how Jamie felt.

"I'm not throwing it away," Jamie argued.

"Toby isn't going to be happy," Neal warned. "And all they need is a stupid reason to sign Shane to that contract, instead of you. This would be a stupid reason, but it'd be a reason. Don't give them one. Not for me."

It was hard to deny the truth of Neal's words and Jamie *did* desperately want the job—for so many different reasons, but whether he liked it or not, Neal was tangled up in them, too. He'd been part of this since they'd met at Heath and Sam's house a week ago. But really, he'd been part of this so much longer. Jamie remembered the way his stomach had sunk, the vaguely sick feeling he'd felt when Neal had missed that kick six months ago. How conflicted he'd felt when Grady had included the Riptide on a list of possible teams that could host him for a tryout.

Neal Fisher had been a part of his life before they'd ever met.

"What if I explain my reasons for taking your old number?"

Neal laughed bitterly. "Because you like kissing me isn't a reason that's gonna change their mind."

"That's not why," Jamie said—though it was, a little. But it was so much more than that, too. "I've looked up to you, forever. I . . . I nearly took your number when I was at Stanford, but I couldn't, because Eli, our long snapper, already had it. And then I got used to being number eleven, but this afternoon, I realized I could change it now."

Neal sighed. "It's not going to matter *why*. But I guess I can't change your mind."

"It's bullshit the way they treated you," Jamie said stubbornly. "I just want to show them you're worth so much more than one kick in one game."

"Thanks, kid," Neal said dryly. "It's a sweet, but stupid, gesture."

"I think there's a compliment in there somewhere," Jamie teased.

"There is," Neal said. Sighed again. "It means something, it really does. I just don't want you to fuck this up."

"Trust me. I'm not going to."

"I . . . I guess I'll have to?" Neal said, his voice brightening. "But you made the team, so that's great. Congrats."

"Just me and Shane left," Jamie confirmed. "I was gonna call you right after I talked to my dad."

"Is he very proud?"

"Yes, though I think a part of him isn't sure why I'm doing this," Jamie confessed. "In his mind, I've got a great education, and that's way more of a sure thing than the NFL."

"You don't do this because it's a sure thing," Neal said quietly. "You do it because you love the game, and I know you love it, I can tell."

"I do," Jamie said.

"My sister didn't understand it either. I think over the years she began to 'get it' and then . . ." Neal trailed off.

"The Super Bowl happened," Jamie finished for him.

"Yeah," Neal said shortly. "Yeah, and now she just mostly worries, I think."

About me went unsaid.

"But I called for another reason, too," Neal continued, "because it turns out I've got to go out of town for a few days. And I didn't want to just . . . disappear on you."

Jamie was disappointed, even though he knew Neal didn't owe him a thing. Were they dating? They hadn't *been* on a date, yet. He'd kind of been hoping he could convince Neal they could do something in the next few days, but it looked like that wasn't going to happen. "Oh," he said. "Well, you could've texted."

"Not my speed," Neal said wryly. "I'm old-fashioned like that."

"Alright. Will you be back for the first preseason game?" Jamie wondered. Not that Neal could *go* to the game. But it'd be nice to see him before, if he could. Neal might not believe it, but he calmed and centered and relaxed him—almost as much as the books he'd lent him. Was he also a distraction? Okay, *yes*, a little.

"Yeah, I think so. A day or two before. At least if my meetings go well," Neal said. "I'm . . . I want to tell you what I'm doing, but if it doesn't work out, then I'd feel dumb, so I'm not going to."

"Okay," Jamie said hesitatingly. "Are you excited about it?"

"Actually," Neal said, pausing. "Actually, yeah. A lot."

"Then good luck," Jamie said. "I'll be here when you get back."

CHAPTER NINE

NEAL HAD MET A lot of famous football players over the years. He'd even played with some of them—Heath Harris, Sam Crawford, Bran Phillips, he'd even shaken Colin O'Connor's hand multiple times—but it was another thing entirely to walk into a conference room, and see Jerry Rice, Terry Bradshaw, and Jimmy Johnson, sitting around the end of the long table, shooting the shit.

He hesitated at the entrance to the room, Alec standing next to him, and took a deep breath. "Is this a mistake?" he muttered to Alec under his breath. "I'm not . . ."

And that was the moment Terry Bradshaw glanced up, a wide smile on his face. "Hey, look who it is! Our new special teams guy!"

Jimmie stood and walked over to where Neal was hesitating. He extended his hand and Neal took it. He'd met Jimmy Johnson a handful of times before, and had always been impressed with the guy. This was no exception. His handshake was brisk and no-nonsense. "We're glad you're here," he drawled, the South evident in the edges of his voice. "It's about time we got some young blood in here."

"Who you callin' old?" Jerry Rice retorted from the other side of the room.

"It ain't me," Terry crowed.

Neal had to smile; he couldn't help it.

"You willing to let this guy sit down with you?" Neal said, as he walked over. He shook both Terry's hand and Jerry's, thinking the whole time, *I don't belong here, I don't deserve it, I'm just a kicker who got lucky a few times.*

A lot of times, Jamie's voice echoed in his head. *A whole lot of fucking times, and yes you do, so stop bitching about it, and enjoy it.*

Terry waved a hand at an empty chair, and Neal sat, rubbing his damp palms on his khakis. Maybe he *was* young. He felt it compared to the giants surrounding him.

"How you been hangin' in there, buddy?" Terry asked, and Neal tried very hard not to flinch, but it was impossible. Maybe hiding himself away for the last six months instead of getting used to people's direct—and even their indirect—references to what had happened in the Super Bowl hadn't been the best choice. Because he still reacted. He didn't know how to brush it off kindly and casually, like it didn't matter to him. Maybe because it still did.

How did you learn to deal with failure? Neal had learned to live with success, but he'd never had to learn to live with complete and total failure. Until now.

"I . . ." Neal stuttered. Took a deep breath. "I guess I've been better."

Terry thumped a hand on his back. "You know you're not alone. We all done screwed up, right, guys? Way worse than you, and for the record, the way they tossed you out . . ."

"You way more than me," Jerry drawled, and Terry shoved an elbow into his middle.

"What we're trying to say . . . is we've been there, and also . . ." Jimmy grinned. "We could've made that kick in our sleep."

If anyone else had made that comment, Neal thought he might've punched them in the face. But this was *Jimmy Johnson,* and he was grinning wildly, and how could he punch someone who so obviously meant well? Who just wanted . . . *to tease him?*

Yeah, that was what he was doing. Diffusing the tension. Letting him know it was okay.

"Hey, me too," Neal said and found himself *smiling back.*

"Could've fooled me," Terry said, cackling, and slapped him on the back again. Neal relaxed. These guys might play around, but they were smart as whips, and knew exactly how to put someone at ease. He'd come in, semi-terrified, and not only sure he didn't belong, but dreading *talking* about the missed kick. And now he was *joking* about it.

Neal could barely believe it himself.

"You really want to join this circus?" Jerry asked, leaning forward, his eyes gleaming even as his expression remained serious.

"I . . ." Neal hesitated. He hadn't really been all that sure, before this moment, but now that he was in it, the answer was surprisingly simple. "I would be honored to," he said simply.

"If you're sure you're ready to hang up those cleats," Jimmy said.

"I'm done playing," Neal said firmly, and discovered again, he really meant it.

Terry nodded. "Not into revenge kicking. I like it."

"What has that ever got anyone?" Neal wondered. "And I don't want to be a PR stunt."

Jerry laughed. "You think you're not a PR stunt?"

"Those fuckers would turn anything into an event," Terry muttered. *"Anything."*

"Maybe at first, I might be," Neal said, and discovered he'd switched, almost naturally, into the argument he'd considered and prepared ahead of time. Because—and he'd thought about this—they were definitely interviewing him for the job, not the other way around. Neal wasn't stupid enough to think he was the only "young blood" they were considering for this job. If the producers were serious about changing up the panel, which had been fairly stagnant for several years now, they'd have covered their bases, and made sure there were several different options, if the chemistry between Neal and the other panelists wasn't just right.

"Maybe I might be," he repeated, continuing. "But I'm in this for the long haul, and it's time for special teams to get covered here.

It decided the last Super Bowl, didn't it? And no offense, but none of you guys know a fucking thing about special teams."

Terry nodded thoughtfully. "We don't. But then you don't know much about offense or defense, either."

"I've been sitting on the sideline, watching, for the last twenty years, haven't I?" Neal pointed out archly. "And I'm a quick study."

"He doesn't take your shit," Jimmy said with a chuckle. "I like him already."

"Let's get this meeting going," one of the producers announced, but Neal had a feeling that the important part of the meeting had just happened, and if he decided this was his future, he would get a chance to try it on for size.

• • • ● • ● • • •

"They loved you," Alec said, sounding excited as they headed down the hallway towards their hotel rooms for the night. "They fucking *loved* you."

Neal had had a few glasses of wine at dinner and was feeling relaxed. *Successful,* even. "I think they kind of did," he said, still a bit mystified that out of every ex-football player and coach out there, the guys on the panel had picked *him.*

"Not *kind of*, they were joking with you, and laughing, and oh my god, *teasing you*," Alec said. He sounded just about as mystified as Neal felt. "And you *smiled*, and did it right back," he continued. They'd shared the wine at dinner, and so Neal definitely wasn't alone. They'd dissected the conversation three or four times now, and they were no closer to understanding what had happened, but every single time, it took on more of an unbelievable sheen.

Or maybe that was just the alcohol they'd drunk.

"I did," Neal confirmed. He could barely believe it himself. There was a part of him that wanted to continue drunkenly dissecting the successful afternoon with Alec, and then there was a part of him that was desperate to call Jamie and tell him he'd *done* it. He'd faced down the demon of his missed kick and maybe not entirely vanquished it, but he'd laid it to rest, at least for a little while. Would it be easier to talk about it now? Neal wasn't stupid enough to believe everything was fixed. But did he feel better? Undeniably.

He wanted to share that with Jamie, and he wanted to find out how Jamie was managing at practice, and what other stupid bullshit Coach Toby and the other guys had discovered to throw at him.

Neal hesitated at his door, his key card in his hand. Alec was leaning against the wall, still grinning loopily. It had been a good day, and a good night. And what was wrong with keeping it going? *Nothing.*

"Hey, just so you know," Neal said, tapping the card against the door. "I might start dating someone."

Alec, who was still grinning like he'd had a bottle of red wine—and he *had*—tilted his head. "Is it going to be a thing?" he asked.

"Uh," Neal hesitated. A thing? It did seem possible that him dating Jamie—eventually publicly, because he knew that was what they both wanted, someday—would undeniably be a thing. Everyone would remember, because their memories were not *that* short, that Neal had been the Riptide's kicker. And Jamie would hopefully still *be* the Riptide's kicker.

"Your hesitation does not fill me with confidence," Alec said. "Maybe you should think about it more, before deciding if I should know about it."

"It's . . . it's not going to change the fact that I *am* going to date him," Neal said. Laying it out, verbally and bluntly, for the very first time.

"I'm not saying it has to," Alec said kindly, "but this would be a big step for you. Right when you're taking a lot of other big steps."

"It's the new Riptide kicker," Neal said in a rush, before he could change his mind.

Alec's shocked face was everything he needed to convince him, once and for all, that it was almost definitely a mistake of gargantuan proportions, and also that he was going to do it anyway, damn the consequences.

"Wow, okay, well, you are not fucking around," Alec said, and squeezed his eyes shut. "Oh, yep, I'm still here."

"Not a dream after all?" Neal was amused, despite the sudden panic streaking through him. Alec's reaction had been understandable, perhaps, and definitely not unexpected, but it still didn't feel very great.

"You mean a nightmare?" Alec rolled his eyes. "Well, at least give it some time, before you decide to go balls to the wall and tell the world, alright?"

"Alright," Neal said, clapping Alec on the shoulder. "And thanks for not letting me bury myself any longer."

"I didn't do anything. You had that shovel clenched tightly all by yourself. Something just . . . made you want to wake up and rejoin the living one day. I can't take responsibility for that." Alec paused and then grimaced. "It's him, isn't it?"

Neal had a pretty good idea who Alec was referring to, but he asked anyway. "Who?"

Alec sighed. "The guy. The kicker. He's the one who made you wake up one day and decide to drop the shovel."

"It was a lot of things, but is he the thing that made me want to remember what being alive felt like? Yeah. I won't deny that." Neal frowned. "Why? Is it that big of a problem?"

"No," Alec said mournfully, "not exactly. Just that I know that this won't be some minor crush that's gonna pass. You're serious about him."

"I . . ." *Was* he? Neal thought he might be. "We're just getting to know each other. It isn't *anything* yet."

"Yeah, you're totally serious," Alec said, despite what Neal had just said. "When you catch up to that realization, let me know. Now I'm going to alternatively celebrate and drown my sorrows in another bottle of wine."

"Drown your sorrows?" Neal wondered. "I thought we were celebrating?"

"We were," Alec confirmed. "And then you decided to fall in love with the worst possible person on the planet."

• • • • • • • • • •

It had only been a week, Neal told himself as he let himself into the hotel room and flopped down on the bed. A week and a half. He and Jamie barely knew each other. They weren't in love. *He* wasn't in love. Alec was just drunk and talking out his ass. That was all.

Still, he found himself reaching for his phone anyway, and dialing Jamie's number, because he couldn't stop himself.

"Hey," Jamie answered on the second ring. "I wondered if I'd hear from you tonight."

Maybe he's not that full of shit, Neal told himself as his heart sped up at just the sound of Jamie's voice.

"I wanted to hear how it went today," Neal said. He was trying to sound casual and not desperately eager, but the truth was, he was far closer to the latter than the former.

"Actually, just fine," Jamie admitted. "They mostly left us special teams guys alone. We were on the second, smaller field. Toby had us working on extra points today, and I think I did better than Shane, but it's hard to say. Neither of us missed."

Neal let out the breath he didn't know he was holding. "That's good, that's really good. You've just got to stay even with him until he gets into a game and freezes." He didn't *know* Shane was going to freeze, but based on his past, rather spotty record, Neal could still *hope*.

And that was absolutely what he was doing. He wanted Jamie to win this spot, and not just because it felt only fair that someone Neal cared about, someone Neal respected, take his spot on the Riptide, but because he wanted Jamie to stick around in southern California.

You want him close. Right there, pressed up next to you, leaning in . . .

Neal cleared his throat, trying not to think about the last time they'd seen each other, when they were soaking wet and had kissed.

"Yeah, we'll see if he does. I'll admit it," Jamie said with a reluctant sigh, "I was really hoping that one of the guys I could tolerate would be left, but on his best day, Shane is still an ass."

"Ugh," Neal said. He'd dealt with his share of nasty jerks that he'd been forced to work with.

"Yeah, that just about sums it up," Jamie said wryly.

"And nobody said anything to you about the number?" Neal was surprised that hadn't happened. But then, maybe they were both obsessed with him *and* also as eager as he was to leave last season behind.

"Not a word," Jamie said. "But I was wearing this neon yellow vest over my jersey, so maybe Coach Toby didn't get a good look at it."

"He's going to notice, someday," Neal said grimly. "And I meant it before, and I mean it now. Don't let your nobility interfere with your ability to get this job, okay? The moment this becomes an issue, I want you to promise me you'll drop it."

"I . . . yeah, I'll drop it," Jamie said. "I'm . . ." He cleared his throat. "I just . . . I miss you, okay? And it makes me feel closer to you. As silly as that sounds. I know I usually keep my sappy confessions to text, but I wanted you to know."

Neal breathed in and then breathed out, trying to control the sudden racing of his heart. Jamie's voice had sounded hushed and private, like he didn't want to speak his confessions too loudly. Afraid someone might hear. Afraid *Neal* might hear, maybe.

For a second he considered repeating his earlier warning. Considered telling Jamie that he just wasn't worth the price he might have to pay. But then he realized—despite the nickname he liked to call the guy, Jamie *wasn't* a kid, and he knew exactly what he was risking. Was he slightly naïve about the way the Riptide could be your friend one moment and your enemy the next? Of course, but then so was every single rookie.

The NFL's ruthlessness always took every rookie by surprise.

But by this point, Jamie *knew* what he was doing, and knew the risks he was taking. That he was still taking them *meant* something. And how was it any different from the risk that Neal had taken just a few minutes earlier, confessing who he was dating to his agent?

"Are you . . . was that okay?" Jamie asked, snapping Neal out of his reverie.

"It was more than okay," Neal said simply. "I loved it."

"Oh, okay," Jamie said, and he could *hear* him smiling over the phone.

"Two days here, and I'm already ready to come home," Neal admitted. *I'm ready to come home to you.* Maybe that was too much to say just yet, but he had a feeling Jamie heard the unsaid words, anyway.

"Did it at least go well?" Jamie asked.

"It was fucking extraordinary," Neal confessed. "It's hard to believe I deserve the chance, but I'm getting better at accepting that it's gonna happen. I think it will anyway. Alec—he's my agent—is over the moon."

"You going to tell me what it is yet?" Jamie wondered.

"I . . ." Neal hesitated. He wanted to see Jamie's face when he told him. Wanted to kiss him afterwards. It didn't feel right to do it now.

"I'll be home in a few days," Neal continued, "and I'll take you out to dinner and tell you."

"Dinner?" Jamie said skeptically.

"I know lots of places we can go where we'll fly under the radar." It was amazing how much money could smooth the way. But Neal discovered that it was important that he do this right. Maybe they couldn't really date in the traditional sense, but he could still treat him the way he deserved to be treated.

And that meant taking Jamie out to dinner, not just taking him to bed.

"Alright," Jamie said. Hesitated. "Would this be like a date, then?"

Neal's smile was so bright and wide, it felt like his facial muscles were stretching and straining in a way that they hadn't in a very long time. Six months, to be exact. "It would be exactly like a date."

"I'd like that a lot," Jamie said, voice still hushed. Reverent. "I can't believe it sometimes."

"That I'm Neal Fisher?" he asked wryly.

"No," Jamie said. "No, that you're *you*."

•・•・●・•・●・•・●・•・•・•

Jamie felt like he floated into practice the next day. Felt like everything that he'd wanted and dreamed about for so long was about to come true. He was going to win his dream job, as a kicker for the Los Angeles Riptide, and he was going to go on a date with *Neal Fisher*, who it turned out wasn't a jerk at all, but a genuinely kind-hearted, dryly funny, incredibly sweet guy who also looked like he belonged on the cover of *GQ*. How had he gotten so lucky? Jamie wasn't entirely sure, and as he jogged out onto the practice field, he had no comprehension that his luck was about to turn.

"Hey, you! Hey there!" Jamie heard the shouts from behind him, but kept jogging over to the other practice field, the one he and the rest of the special teams guys had spent so much time at the last few days.

He figured there was almost no chance anyone was talking to him—he barely knew anyone, because he hadn't even technically won the job yet and so while he might be on the team for *now*, there was no telling if he'd *stay* on the team. And so as a result, most of the regular team guys had kept their distance. Jamie even understood it. He'd kept his own distance from some of the walk-ons at Stanford, before he'd known if they'd make the team. There was little point in trying to bond with people you didn't know would stick around.

"Hey, number *five*."

For a split second, Jamie considered turning around to see what the commotion was, and then suddenly, it hit him—*he* was number five. He'd taken that as his number, even though Neal was furious that he'd done it.

He turned.

Coach Toby was standing there, a perturbed look on his face, and the expression Coach Rodriguez was wearing? Thunderclouds might have been an apt description.

"Goddamnit, freaking *listen* once in a while," Coach Toby scolded him, coming over and poking a finger right into Jamie's chest—right where his number was emblazoned on his practice jersey. "What is this bullshit?"

"What bullshit?" Jamie asked slowly, even though he was afraid he already knew.

Coach R walked over, the pissed-off look on his face deepening. "What are you doing?" he demanded to know.

Jamie shrugged. "Jogging to the practice field?"

"No," Coach Toby said, poking him again in the number, emblazoned in undeniable black font, on his jersey. Making it undeniably clear what he was asking about. "What the fuck are you doing with this number? Did the equipment manager give this to you? As a joke or something?"

He and Coach R exchanged dark looks, clearly thinking Jamie ending up with Neal Fisher's old number was something like that. A bad joke gone wrong.

For a second, Jamie hesitated. He could throw the equipment manager under the bus. He could. It would be easy enough. Or he could say he'd forgotten what Neal Fisher's number was, even though that would be a blatant lie, as it felt like it was practically imprinted into his heart.

But then he reminded himself that he'd done this for a reason. He'd taken this number to make a point. And even if it was hard, even if it was really fucking difficult, he still intended to make that point.

"It's not a joke," Jamie said slowly. "And the equipment manager didn't give me this number, I asked for it."

Both of the coaches stared at him incredulously.

"I'm sorry, I thought you just said you *asked* for it. The same number of the guy who fucked us over last year."

"Maybe he missed the kick, but he's not a bad kicker. He was a great kicker, for a long time, and I chose to wear this number because I don't think enough people remember that anymore."

"He lost us the *Super Bowl*," Coach R hissed, "are you so fucking new that you don't even know what that is? What that *means*?"

"I know what it means," Jamie said. Had to bite his tongue, because he wanted to say more. Wanted to tell the head coach that Neal had spent the last six months *hiding* because of bullshit opinions exactly like his.

"Okay, that's good, then," Coach Toby inserted. "So it's easy for you to get another number."

Jamie could hear Neal's voice in his head, literally *screaming* at him: *do what he says and get another fucking number. You want to play on this team? You want a contract? Go get another fucking number.*

And finally, the most damning reminder of all: *you promised me if it came down to it, you'd give this up. And right now? Right now is absolutely the right fucking time to give it up.*

"Okay," Jamie finally said. "Okay, I can do that."

"See?" Coach Toby said, gesturing towards Coach R. "I knew he'd see sense."

But Coach Rodriguez's mouth was still pressed into a thin, angry line. "I want you to remember," he said, "I want you to remember who the winners are and who the losers are. Neal Fisher is a loser. He made us losers. You wanna be a winner? *Be a winner.*" And as abruptly as he showed up, the head coach stomped off.

Jamie stared at his retreating back. Maybe he hadn't said it out loud, but the undercurrent was obvious—Coach wasn't just calling Neal a loser. He was calling himself a loser. And for a split second, Jamie almost felt sorry for him.

Coach Toby sighed and patted Jamie's back. No doubt trying to be reassuring in the face of all that overwhelming negativity. "He's just . . . well, he's a little bitter. Having a hard time letting go of what happened last year."

Jamie stared at him. *A little bitter?* "Yeah, that isn't a surprise," Jamie said, finding his voice. "It's been somewhat of a broken record here, that missed field goal."

"Neal was a good guy and a good kicker for a long time," Toby said as they walked over towards the smaller practice field. "I don't blame you for admiring him."

Was. Jamie wanted to climb up on the retractable roof of the practice facility and yell loud enough that everyone could hear that missing one important kick in a thirteen-year career didn't suddenly make you *not* a good guy. Or *not* a good kicker. But the problem was, Jamie realized that no matter how loudly he said it, or how many times, most of the team wouldn't believe him. Maybe not Sam or Bran Phillips or Chase Riley. But enough wouldn't believe him. Enough of the coaching staff, the management and the players all were looking for one person to blame and they'd found it in Neal.

Jamie remembered his dad coming to see him his freshman year at Stanford, when he was young and terrified and sure he was going to fuck everything up because the first team kicker had torn his ACL unexpectedly right before the beginning of the season. "This is a thankless job," his dad had told him, putting both hands on his shoulders and looking deeply into Jamie's eyes. "Nobody will remember you if you do everything right, and if you mess up? Nobody will ever forget you."

At the time he'd been annoyed and frustrated that his dad's pep talk had been so un-pep-like. "Geez, Dad," he'd said. "Depressing, much?"

"Realistic," his dad had argued instead. "I want you to know what you're getting into. I want both of your eyes wide open."

Maybe they'd begun to open that day, almost five years ago, but Jamie couldn't deny any more that they were wide open now.

He'd eventually figured out how to swim and not to sink at Stanford, and now he was going to have to do the same thing here, on the Riptide. *While* proving to Toby and the rest of the coaching staff that he, not Shane, was the right choice for the future.

Chapter Ten

Neal was scheduled to fly back to LA the day before the first preseason game. The Riptide were taking on the Las Vegas Raiders, newly moved to the Sin City, and even though it was hardly a long flight, Jamie was glad that at least for this first game, when his nerves were spinning so wildly out of control, that he'd at least be kicking in a more familiar place.

Still, no matter how many of the deep-breathing exercises he'd done from Neal's mindfulness books, he felt like a wreck, balanced on the top of a precipice and wondering just how far down the bottom was.

Neal had called him a few times from New York—never really going into detail about what he was doing, or who he was meeting with—but he sounded more excited every time he called. The last time, when he'd told Jamie that he'd be back right before the game, he'd sounded *hopeful*.

"Maybe my life isn't over, after all," he'd said, like he'd believed for a little while that it might be.

"Of course it's not over," Jamie had teased. "How could it be over before you take me on this date you keep promising?"

Another common thread in their phone conversations was this idea that Neal kept clinging to that he was ultimately a distraction. "We'll go out *after* the game, and not before," Neal had insisted more than once. "I don't want you to get distracted."

Neal had not flat-out *said* they couldn't see each other in the time after he got back and before the game, but it was there, in every unsaid word, and in every awkward pause in their conversations.

"You've got this, if you can stay focused," Neal had said the last time they talked. "Gotta keep your eyes on the prize." *And off me,* Jamie had finished mentally. *Can't be thinking about me, about us, when you should be thinking about that ball, sailing right between the uprights.*

The thing was—Jamie was a smart guy. Smart and clever. He'd gotten a degree in business management from Stanford, for god's sake. He had plenty of extra brain cells, and plenty of extra attention that he could pay to Neal, while also giving football all the focus it needed.

But Jamie hadn't been able to convince Neal that was true.

He wouldn't even discuss it.

That was why Jamie had decided that the only recourse that Neal had left him was to force the issue.

He'd texted Olive ahead of time, and made sure she wasn't home. Neal had sent him her phone number when he'd left for New York, because, he'd said, Jamie didn't know anyone else in LA, not really anyway, and if anything happened or he got lonely or he wanted to meet for lunch or dinner . . .

Jamie had been touched by the gesture, and Olive had seemed equally pleased by it. They hadn't met up yet, because her classes had started in earnest, and he had practice every day, but still, they'd talked about it.

She'd even offhandedly called him "Neal's boyfriend," which Jamie wanted to tell her was a great thought, but also slightly premature, since they hadn't gone on a date yet. But he also wasn't sure how much Neal shared of his personal life, even with his niece. So he hadn't commented on her particular choice of words. But he'd *thought* about that text on and off for three days now, and it had been on the tip of his tongue *so* many times to ask Neal about it when they'd talked.

And now? Now, Jamie was basically going crazy with everything he couldn't say, and everything Neal kept assuming that they couldn't do.

Which might explain the radical step Jamie had taken tonight. First, he'd planned ahead by texting Olive, and made sure that when Neal got home from the airport, she'd be gone for the evening. Then, he'd taken a shower, made sure that his hair was perfect, thrown on his favorite t-shirt and jeans, and tried to take a few deep breaths to calm the way his heart was suddenly madly racing.

It didn't work, and by the time he got to Neal's house, parking his rental car in the driveway, his stomach was full of butterflies, his palms felt clammy and his fingers wouldn't stop trembling as he tried to lock the car and shove the keys into his pocket. He hadn't been this nervous around a guy since high school, when he'd had a terrible—and ultimately doomed—crush on the captain of the soccer team. Bryce had been a year older and funny and very cool, and almost definitely straight. That was how Jamie had ended up playing football instead. How could he face Bryce every day? See him in the locker room and know he was thirsting after something he could probably never have?

Except everything was different tonight. He could *have* Neal. He was so close he could almost taste him.

But when confronted with the front door, his courage failed him at the last second. What if Neal didn't answer? Did famous football players answer their own doors? Did famous *ex*-football players answer their own doors? Especially if they weren't expecting anyone?

Jamie took a breath and reached for his phone. He typed out a quick text. **Hey, hope you got home alright**, it said.

Neal was not the biggest texter in the world—Jamie had discovered this over the last week, as he always seemed to call when he wanted to talk. And social media? Neal had laughed for a minute straight when Jamie had asked if he had Instagram or Twitter.

Still, maybe Neal was thinking of him too. Eager to see him, too. Because he responded almost immediately. **Yeah,** his reply said, **just got out of the shower and thinking about you.**

It was the last reason that Jamie needed to make this happen. He rang the doorbell.

Nothing happened. His heart beat arrhythmically in his chest. His breath came in short, shallow pants. *Neal. Just out of the shower. Naked. Dripping wet.* Jamie could still remember exactly what Neal's wet skin had felt like against his own, when they'd kissed in the rain. His fingers dug into his palms as he tried to *not* get ragingly hard, right before Neal answered the door.

Just a sec, Neal texted again, **there's some idiot at the door.**

Jamie was about to text back and explain, *it's just me,* when Neal yanked open the front door, a disgruntled expression on his face and wearing only a loose towel wrapped around his waist.

He opened his mouth to explain but no sound came out.

Neal's eyes softened almost immediately. "You're the idiot," he said, and Jamie nodded. Still speechless. Neal's hair was slicked back from his handsome face, his eyes shining a deep mossy green. Jamie wanted him with every single molecule of his being.

"I'm definitely an idiot," Jamie croaked, finally finding his voice.

Neal gestured him inside and closed the door behind him. "I thought . . ." Neal said hesitantly, hand still gripping his towel and concern emerging in his expression.

"You thought we agreed that this would be a distraction," Jamie said. He wasn't sure where this courage was coming from, but it existed, and it kept pushing him forward. "*You* thought it would be."

"And you don't?" Neal's face had gone from mildly concerned to downright worried. "You should . . ."

"If I have to sit in that room one more moment, thinking of everything that's going to happen tomorrow, I'm gonna go nuts," he said plainly. "And thinking about you, thinking about everything that could . . ." He swallowed hard. "About what we could do, it's the most difficult and distracting of all, so let's just . . ."

"Yes," Neal said, and leaned in, pressing Jamie back against the door, as he kissed him. Unlike the hesitancy of their first kiss, when they'd never done this before, Neal dove in immediately, pushing Jamie's back against the door as he slid his tongue into Jamie's mouth, both hurried and calm, all at the same time.

Jamie's hands didn't know where to touch first. They slid through the wet strands of Neal's hair, threading his fingers through them so he could tug Neal even closer, could feel the press of his dick, rapidly hardening against the flimsy towel. Then they moved to his shoulders, to the defined crest of his muscles, to the top of his pectorals, catching on his nipples and swallowing Neal's hiss as he tweaked one.

"God, you came here for this, didn't you?" Neal said, wrenching his mouth away from Jamie's. He was breathing just as hard, his eyes huge and dark, a flush moving down his chest. Jamie was desperate to see how far it went, if it disappeared under the towel and went down even further. If he could taste it, if he put his mouth on Neal's skin, and if he could feel the frantic pulse of his blood in his inner thigh.

Personally, Jamie thought it was pretty damn obvious why he was here. The answer was right there, in the rock-hard cock that Neal kept unconsciously rubbing against. In the way their lips couldn't quite stay apart from each other, every word punctuated with a kiss or two or three. It took an eternity for Neal to even get a single sentence out.

"Yeah," Jamie said, hands sliding to Neal's hips. "I came here for you."

Neal squeezed his eyes shut, like this was both the best answer in the world, and also the worst.

"You're making it really hard . . ."

"Yeah," Jamie said, choking out a laugh. "Yeah, I really am." He arched into Neal and the pleasure as their cocks—just as hard as Neal had claimed—brushed made them both gasp.

Neal's glare was more amused than stern. "That is *not* what I meant."

"I know," Jamie said. "But it was fun anyway." He moved again, and watched as Neal's gorgeous eyes grew fuzzy, unfocused. He wet his bottom lip, already swollen from Jamie's mouth. "We could have some more fun . . ."

Reaching up, Neal cupped Jamie's chin. He was hoping it was so he could kiss him some more, but Neal just looked at him. "You really are serious about this, aren't you?"

I'm serious about everything when it comes to you.

"Yeah," Jamie admitted.

Neal leaned back against the door. "I don't want to be a distraction. Tomorrow is . . ."

"The biggest game of my career. Yeah, I get that. And like I said, if I have to sit in my room, thinking about it, for one more minute, I'm . . . I just can't do it, okay? I need you."

When Jamie had come over, he'd expected that Neal would balk. He'd expected he'd need to convince him. To *seduce* him.

Neal licked his lips again. "What would you say if I need you too?"

The answer to that was so easy, Jamie thought it didn't even need to be said. Except . . .

Jamie stared at him, at the towel that was just barely hanging on to Neal's hips, at the still-damp trail of hair leading underneath it. At his kiss-swollen mouth. The undisguised want on his face.

He skirted around the back of the couch, the same one they'd sat on over a week ago, the one they'd held hands on. The one Jamie had been desperate to mess up.

He'd dreamed about this. Fantasized about it, during a lot of those lonely nights lying in his empty hotel room bed.

Neal raised an eyebrow when Jamie sat down on the couch. "You'd want to watch TV?"

Jamie still didn't say anything. Didn't quite trust his own words. Just motioned for Neal, who walked over. Still holding that damn towel. *Throw it away,* Jamie thought desperately, *and let me see you. I'm dying to see all of you.*

"Didn't you think about this last time?" Jamie wondered as Neal hesitated in front of him. "Because I did."

Neal shrugged helplessly. "I couldn't exactly help it," he said wryly.

"Come 'ere, then," Jamie murmured. "Let me make you feel good."

One moment, Neal was staring at him, with undeniable want but also uncertainty in his eyes, like he wasn't sure what he should do, and the next, the towel was gone, and Jamie had an armful of a naked Neal Fisher, and they were kissing again helplessly, like their mouths just couldn't help but be drawn to one another. Jamie's head hit the back of the couch as Neal rubbed against him hungrily, his mouth swallowing every one of his moans. His fingertips dug into the broad muscles of his shoulders, reveling in the disbelief that any one person could feel this goddamned good.

"You're right," Neal said, between breathless, helpless kisses. "You're right. I wanted to do this." Then suddenly, he paused, and glanced down. "Except in all my fantasies, you were wearing way less clothes."

Neal reached up and tugged on the collar of his t-shirt and Jamie wasn't going to argue with getting *more* naked. He pulled it off, unable to help the gasp of pleasure as Neal's hands slid down his chest, grazing his abs, to the button on his jeans. His cock throbbed underneath the confining fabric, straining for any kind of pressure at all. Except Neal just grazed it, teasing as he made quick work of the button and then the zipper. "Lift up," he ordered, and he yanked down, leaving his jeans around his knees, and his cock pressing against the flimsy cotton of his briefs.

Neal's expression was reverent as he tucked his fingers underneath his briefs, tugging them just far enough to expose his cock. Jamie didn't think he'd ever been so hard in his life, and Neal hadn't even touched him yet.

"God, you are so sexy," Neal murmured. "I wanted you the moment I saw you."

When he finally cupped Jamie's dick, they both moaned. "Just like this," Neal said, leaning down, and slid their cocks together in one of his capable hands, sending sparks of addictive sensation streaking through Jamie.

"Kiss me," Jamie begged, already right there on the edge, and trying to hang on. Wanting to make it last. Wanting to feel Neal everywhere. He leaned down, and their kiss was ravenous, Neal's eyes fluttering closed as he stroked their cocks together, the friction agonizingly amazing.

Jamie's hands slid down his back, and dug into the gorgeous muscular curve of his ass, urging him to move faster and harder.

He was hovering right on the precipice, trying to hold back, but a particularly sweet twist of Neal's hand coupled with the realization that this was all he had ever wanted—*and* it was Neal

Fisher he was having it with—flung him off in a white-hot burst of pleasure.

Neal tensed above him, panting into Jamie's mouth as he followed after, both of them shuddering to completion, liquid streaking up Jamie's chest and mingling together.

"Fuck," Neal said, his head dropping to Jamie's shoulder. "Fuck, that was . . ."

"Incredible, amazing, life-altering?" Jamie wondered. It had been all those things for him. Maybe it was too much to ask for it to be the same for Neal.

Neal chuckled. "Yeah," he said, and like he didn't even care about the mess, slid bonelessly into Jamie's lap. "Yeah, something like that."

"Don't get me wrong, holding hands was real nice, but this was a lot more fun," Jamie said.

Pressing a kiss into Jamie's shoulder, Neal didn't say anything. "I really don't want you to worry about this," Jamie continued. "Though I guess that's asking water not to be wet." He reached out and smoothed Neal's dark, mussed hair back, finally beginning to dry in a thousand cowlicks. It was something special to be able to see him like this for the first time—not put together the way he usually was. Messed up and fucked out and affectionate in the aftermath of sex.

"It is," Neal said. He sighed. "But you're probably right. I could only take so much focus, right before. I came up with a bunch of stuff that I liked to do to distract myself just enough, but honestly, sex was always my favorite."

Jamie knew that he hadn't been the first. How could he be, when Neal looked like Neal did? Still, it made him wonder . . . *will you be the last?* It seemed impossible, in the face of everything wanting to keep them apart, that they could make a relationship work. But Jamie was helpless *not* to want it.

"I think it's my favorite too," Jamie said, nuzzling in the side of Neal's neck.

Neal sighed. "We should get up and clean up and I don't know . . . do this again in a bed."

Jamie was young, and that was almost all it took . . . just the barest suggestion this could happen again . . . but his cock valiantly twitched, clearly trying to get ready to go again.

Glancing down, Neal laughed. "Down, boy. God, I remember what it was to be in my twenties." He hesitated. "My *early* twenties."

Jamie's hand drifted down and gripped Neal's ass. Squeezed. Was incredibly gratified by the moan he made, almost like it had been yanked right out of him. "Afraid about keeping up with me?"

"A little," Neal admitted. "I am *not* in my early twenties, no matter how much I wish that was the case." He bent and found the towel, pulling back a little so he could use it to wipe up the worst of the mess they'd made on Jamie's chest—and now smeared across Neal's, too. He laughed. "I think this might just be pointless. Maybe we should just get in the shower."

"Didn't you *just* do that?" Jamie wondered, watching as Neal lifted himself off Jamie and stood up. It was gratifying to see his knees wobble a little, but he still immediately missed the press of their bodies together.

"Yeah, but this really cute idiot messed me up again," Neal said, grinning. "Come on, you're gonna love my shower."

· · · · ●· ● · · ·

It had been two weeks since Neal had stood in this very shower and dreamt about what it would feel like to touch Jamie and have Jamie touch him in return. He'd never imagined that it would really happen, or that it would feel so incredibly, unbelievably good.

Or that after, they'd laugh together in the shower as Jamie flipped through all the various ridiculous water settings on his shower system. "Do you really *use* any of these?" Jamie wondered, as the water came down in rhythmic spurts and then random patterns. He settled on a nice steady rainwater setting, and dipped his head underneath, the water flattening his curls against his skull.

"I don't use almost any of them, actually," Neal admitted.

He really was beautiful, Neal thought as Jamie reached for him, tugging him into the water, their lips meeting underneath the spray.

When they finally broke apart, Jamie was smiling, a warm steady glow that seemed to leach into Neal's own skin and heat him up just with his closeness.

"Then why do you have them?" Jamie asked, pressing more buttons, and changing the rainfall to something else. Steam was clouding up the glass shower enclosure, lending a dreamy quality to Jamie's face. He looked like a Renaissance painting, all olive-toned curves and dark hair and eyes. A sweet rose-tinted curve to his lips.

"Because I can?" Neal really wasn't sure. He'd hired a designer and a highly recommended contractor and, after some vague input, had let them make all the major decisions. He'd wanted a house he could live in, maybe even someday raise a family in, and while that family thing hadn't quite worked out, he still loved this house.

Even the ridiculously complicated shower system that the designer had insisted on putting in. "You're going to love it," she'd proclaimed. "It'll be just like going to a spa."

Neal had considered reminding her he was a football player, and even though he was gay, he still didn't really *go* to the spa, but he'd ended up liking the cool, soothing colors, and the tile and the marble, and even the huge shower, anyway. Mostly, he could admit to himself, it was because the shower was big enough for two.

Really, it was big enough for about *ten*, but Neal hadn't ever been into a group thing. He wanted one guy, whom he could love and worship and drive insane with pleasure, who would love him back. Who would watch out for him, just the way Neal intended to watch back.

Clearly that had not been Michael.

It was far too soon to know if that man could be Jamie. But there was a sharp pull, a *tug*, right there, somewhere very near his heart, that made him want to believe it anyway.

"You're a little spoiled," Jamie pronounced, smiling despite his words. "But I like it. It looks good on you."

"Does it?" Neal wondered, batting his eyes.

Jamie rolled his. "You *know* it does."

"Hey," Neal said, after he flipped the water off, and grabbed them two towels. "Hey, you know the first night we met?"

"Not something I'm going to forget anytime soon," Jamie admitted as he toweled his hair dry. "Honestly. The fact that you were not only hot and Neal Fisher and *interested* will probably be embedded in my brain forever."

"Well, you're going to like this, then. That first night? I came home and couldn't help it. Took a shower and jerked off right there, where you're standing, thinking about you."

"Really?" Jamie's face crinkled, he was smiling so wide. "God, you're adorable. Jerking off to some guy you didn't know. To *me*."

"Do I wanna know if you did the same thing?"

"Actually," Jamie admitted, "I sent you that super sappy text, and then worried for two hours that you were gonna take out a restraining order or something. But the next day? Every day after that? Oh yeah. Definitely." He hesitated. "Honestly, it was a thing I'd been doing for a while."

"No!" Neal was genuinely delighted. How could he not be? "Seriously?"

"I mean . . ." Jamie gestured to his naked body. "Just *look* at you. It was kinda hard *not* to, honestly."

"It's crazy that you're here now. I can barely even believe it, still," Neal said slowly as they walked into the bedroom. "I still feel sometimes like I'm going to wake up and discover that I can't get out of bed, and that you're not real and that . . . I don't know . . . that hope feels stupid. Pointless."

"Believe it," Jamie said, pressing a kiss to his still-damp lips. "Trust me, *believe it.*"

"I do," Neal said, discovering that he meant it. He'd been doing so much thinking while he'd been in New York—not just about what he was going to do in his future, but who he wanted to be. Who he wanted to share the life he was building with.

Despite the odds, *god*, he wanted it to be Jamie.

"Hey, you should tell me about all your big-shot meetings in New York," Jamie said, reclining onto the bed, totally naked and not ashamed at all.

Neal glanced at his half-hard cock, wondered if he'd be able to not embarrass himself—but the fact that just the thought of getting close again, of touching Jamie, sent a heated rush through him—laid that worry to rest.

Still, even though he wanted to come over there and taste how rich and perfect Jamie was, right there, in the crease of his lean, muscular thigh, he thought . . . *no, I should tell him first.*

"So, I'm going to be on Sunday Morning Football," Neal said, settling down in bed next to Jamie.

"Oh my god, *seriously*?" Jamie's eyes sparkled with excitement. "You mean like . . . next to Terry Bradshaw? Jerry Rice? *That* Sunday Morning Football?"

"Yeah," Neal said. "That's what I was in New York for, to talk about it. But they're going to film this upcoming season in LA. They're looking to appeal to a younger audience. Though it's not like I'm *young*, really. But maybe you can rub off on me, a little."

Jamie grinned. "I would love to rub off on you a *lot*."

"Down, boy," Neal said amused, but he reached out and pressed a palm to Jamie's chest, feeling his heart beating there. Strong and steady.

"I want the job," he continued, "but there's more to it than that. I want . . . someday I want to be able to put this thing with the Riptide behind me. Especially if . . ." He hesitated. He didn't know how much to say. With Michael, and with other boyfriends, it had been easy to navigate these conversations.

Maybe, Neal realized, because they ultimately hadn't mattered as much. Maybe because he hadn't wanted those men the same way he wanted Jamie.

"Especially if what?" Jamie wondered, pressing his own hand against Neal's. "You can tell me."

Looking into his dark eyes, Neal thought he actually *could*. And maybe that was the scariest thing of all. "Especially if you keep playing, and we keep seeing each other," he said. "Eventually, I don't want this to be a secret. I don't want to hide."

"And maybe if people move on, think of you differently, not like the Riptide kicker but an announcer, it'll make it easier?"

"Yeah," Neal said. "But it's also because I just want the job. It's *not* in my comfort zone, but I've been in my comfort zone so long, maybe it's time to get out of it. Forcibly."

"You've always given great interviews," Jamie said seriously. "I think you'll be great at this, if it's your comfort zone or not."

"I hope so," Neal said. "Because I want this to work out."

He watched Jamie; watched him wonder if he'd meant *the job* or *them*.

And maybe the reason he hadn't specified was because he wanted both.

"What if I don't end up on the Riptide?" Jamie wondered.

Neal had thought about that too. "Then we'll figure something out," he said. Would it be easier if they were both based in LA? Of course it would. But that didn't mean he was giving up just because something wasn't easy.

"You really mean that," Jamie murmured, and squeezed Neal's hand.

"Yeah, I do," Neal said. "And I meant the date thing too. We'll go out the night after the game, if you're free?"

"My days might be occupied," Jamie said seriously, "but my nights are all yours."

217

Chapter Eleven

Jamie was pretty fucking sure that he was going to puke.

And not like a little discreet, "hide behind the bench and throw up" kind of puke, but like full-on vomit in front of God and everybody.

He'd been nervous on game day Saturdays when he'd been at Stanford, but because of the first-string kicker's knee injury, he'd ended up being the main kicker before he'd even really understood what that meant. He'd been eighteen and raw and, Jamie could concede now, more than a little stupid.

He hadn't understood the full gravity of what he was doing back then, so it'd been almost *easy* to go out there and make his kicks and not worry about it. By his sophomore and junior year, he'd understood better how much what he was doing now was going to profoundly impact his future, but by then, he'd gained both success and confidence and so jogging out onto the field to make routine extra points and even tough field goals rarely fazed him.

He'd also never once had a serious competitor for his job in all the years he'd been at Stanford, but it was impossible to forget now that he was in the middle of one of the most intense position battles in the NFL this season. Him, against Shane Ferguson.

Neal kept saying he *knew* he could best Shane, and Jamie knew it too, which almost made it worse, because what if it didn't happen? What if he *failed* even though he knew he should succeed? It was that question that had kept him up long after he'd returned to his hotel room and his own bed last night.

It had been impossible not to think of Neal, who had been beating himself up for six months over failing when he knew, deep down, in his bones, that he shouldn't have.

How did you come to terms with that? Jamie didn't want to ask Neal to relive it. Hell, occasionally it felt like he was still crawling through all that shit, though he seemed undeniably happier than he'd been in a while. But Jamie also didn't want to *have* to ask.

The question had haunted him anyway, and it was haunting him now, making him more nervous than he'd ever been before a game. And with the nerves, came an acute nausea that made him want to lose whatever breakfast he'd choked down.

"You look terrible."

Jamie glanced up from the spot near the bench, where he was half-heartedly kicking practice kicks into the small net they'd set up. If Neal saw this footage, he'd yell at him for not being purposeful with every move he made, but he also thought if he put his body into it, his body might betray him.

He knew the guy's face and his name, but they'd never really spoken, despite both being at Heath and Sam's fateful pool party—the one he'd met Neal at.

"I feel terrible," Jamie admitted under his breath.

Chase Riley flung himself down on the bench next to where Jamie was standing. He was dressed to play in the Riptide's signature aqua and ocean blue uniform, but he wasn't wearing his helmet, and the breeze tousled his shoulder-length blond hair. If Jamie wasn't totally, completely into tall, dark-haired kickers with killer green eyes, he might've looked twice. Because Chase Riley was gorgeous.

"My first game, I definitely puked. Twice, in fact," Chase said with a grin. "It's okay to be nervous. It's a big deal."

"Thanks, I think?" Jamie said. Talking about it didn't help the nauseated roll of his stomach, but knowing that he wasn't alone made him feel less ridiculous.

Chase grinned. "You need to puke, you just holler, and I'll distract the cameras that are floating around."

"Distract them how?" Jamie wasn't sure he wanted to know, but since puking was an actual real possibility, maybe it was better to be informed.

"Oh, you know, normal shit," Chase said. "Pull my jersey up. Dance around like an idiot. Usual stuff."

Jamie had been vaguely aware that he had a reputation for slightly silly antics—it was hard to watch a Riptide game and *not* be aware of it—but he hadn't quite known what to think of Chase Riley.

But now? Now he was sure he liked him. A lot.

"You'd be a lifesaver," Jamie said. "Last thing I need is the image of me puking in HD splashed across millions of TV screens." *One in particular. Two, if he was counting his parents' TV up in Palo Alto.*

"It's no big deal," Chase said. "Any friend of Sam and Heath's is a friend of mine."

Jamie opened his mouth to explain they weren't really *friends*—but hesitated because he wasn't sure how else to explain their relationship either? *I was just a random guy they invited over to hang at their pool? I'm nobody but I'm trying to be somebody?*

"Naw," Chase continued before Jamie could get his shit together, "naw, you're a friend. We take care of our guys, if you know what I mean."

Jamie was beginning to realize what he might mean. "You mean you . . ."

"Anyone starts some shit, they'll be fucking with *us*," Chase said, digging his thumb into the number emblazoned on the front of his jersey. "And people don't usually like fucking with us."

Chase Riley was over six feet of lean, honed muscle. When his brown eyes narrowed, he almost looked dangerous. But then he gestured over to where Heath was standing with Sam. "And if they don't like fucking with me, they definitely don't like fucking with Harris."

A lot of things were beginning to make sense. There was a loose association of straight—and not straight—Riptide players who made sure that some of the homophobic pockets of the sport didn't touch them. And maybe *that*, and not Jamie's defense of Sam, was why he'd been invited to the house he shared with Heath.

"Mostly," Chase continued, "the threat's all it takes. These shitheads can dole it out, but they can't take it."

If "taking it" involved facing Heath, Chase, and maybe some of the other guys who'd been at the party, like Heath's best friend, Bran Phillips, then Jamie could understand exactly why that might be best avoided.

"Ah," Jamie said, nodding. "Well, I appreciate it."

"And you know, your boy, he was part of it, too," Chase said, leaning down to stretch. His words were muffled at the end, but Jamie was fairly sure he caught the gist of it and panic streaked through him. *His boy?* There was nobody that Chase could be talking about except Neal. Maybe he hadn't been officially or publicly out, but he'd clearly been out to the team.

But how did Chase know about him and Neal? Nobody knew, except maybe Olive, and Jamie couldn't see her exposing them. The roiling in his stomach increased. If anyone found out he and Neal were involved, there would be no competition. He would be summarily dropped from the team, and Shane would win the starting spot.

"Don't worry," Chase said with a lopsided smile as he popped back up, stretching his arms over his head. "Nobody knows. I just heard about the jersey thing, and it reminded me of something Sam said in the offseason. That he wanted to take Heath's number, to honor him, and Heath wouldn't let him, said he needed to make his own legacy, and well . . . I saw you two together briefly at their house, and well . . . no offense, dude, but your face just gave it all away."

Jamie knew he needed to work on his poker face. "Oh."

"It was just a guess, and you confirmed it. But," Chase said with an easy shrug, "like I said, your secret's safe with me."

"Thanks, and . . ." Jamie hesitated. "Thanks for the other offer too." He'd known coming out was a risk, but he hadn't wanted to hide either. He'd hoped that with Colin and Sam and Heath blazing a trail, that there'd be fewer players willing to be homophobic assholes. And it turned out he was right, just not how he expected.

"Of course, dude," Chase said with another one of those blinding smiles. "We've got your back. Now, go warm up and try to forget that all these people are watching, waiting for you to fuck up."

Jamie laughed nervously. "Does that really work?"

"Naw," Chase said. "But you'll be fine. You got this."

The next kick Jamie aimed into the net was the most confident of the day yet. Maybe he didn't necessarily feel better, but Chase had distracted him just enough that he could tamp down the worst of his nerves and get to the job at hand.

. . . ● ● . ● ● . . .

Jamie's first test came in the second quarter. This was the first preseason game, so most of the first string played one series, and then took to the bench in favor of the rest of the team, as the coaching staff tried to decide who was going to make the 53-man roster that each team was required to be at by the end of the four preseason games.

That meant that the backups were all in—and so the offense moved slowly, much more slowly than if Sam and Chase and Rashad had been in—and the Riptide didn't score a touchdown until the first half was almost over.

"You're in," Coach Toby told Jamie, pointing to the field.

That meant it was his job to kick the extra point.

"An extra point, you've got this, you've done this a hundred times. A thousand," Jamie muttered under his breath as he jogged out to the middle of the field with the rest of the kicking unit.

He went through his mental progressions the way he'd learned at Stanford—with the extra valuable additions that Neal had suggested in the last few weeks. He felt more focused than he had in a while, and as he approached his spot, Jamie didn't think he'd felt so confident *ever*. Neal was right. Chase was right. His dad was right. He *had* this.

Thirty seconds later, the long snapper pitched the ball to Ian, everything moving like clockwork, like they'd practice so many times over the last few weeks except . . . Ian didn't get a good grip on it, and the ball didn't quite get into the right place, and Jamie knew when his foot hit it, square on the laces, that the chances of it going in were slim.

He watched, fear and horror growing inside of him, as the ball went just past the right upright, and the referees indicated that the extra-point kick had been no good.

Immediately Ian jogged over and so did Jon, whose job it was to snap the ball.

"Fuck," Jon said, "it slipped a little as I was letting it go, and the timing was off."

"Yeah," Ian agreed. "It was weird timing."

As Jamie returned to the bench, it didn't help to know that it wasn't his fault. That even a review of the game footage would prove that it wasn't his fault. That hadn't saved Neal. Everyone knew that his kick in the Super Bowl had been tipped by a Piranhas defender, but that hadn't mattered at all, in the end. It had still been Neal's fault, and he'd still been fired for it.

Would this mean the end of Jamie's hopes? He didn't know, but he was desperately afraid that it might. He sank to a spot on the very end of the bench, hoping that Coach Toby would at least leave him alone for a second, so he could gather his thoughts.

Would they be asking him to clean out his locker right after the game? Everything had felt like it was falling into place for him—winning the contract here with the Riptide and his growing relationship with Neal. But maybe all that had been frantic hope on Jamie's behalf and not real.

Maybe *this* was what was real.

"Hey." Jamie glanced up and saw that Sam was standing there. His helmet was off. "Hey, it's alright, okay? Everyone could see that it was a bad snap."

For a split second, Jamie wanted to ask Sam if he had said something like this to Neal after the Super Bowl. But then he realized he didn't have to ask, because of course he had. That was Sam's way. It was clear that he didn't blame Neal, and that he didn't blame Jamie now. But was there a way for Jamie not to blame himself?

If there was, he didn't know how the fuck to find it.

"Thanks," Jamie said shortly. "I appreciate it."

"No," Sam said, surprising Jamie, "no you don't, and I get it. But I want you to know that I still support you and I still think you're the best kicker for this team."

Jamie nodded, appreciating Sam's words, even if he wasn't sure how to believe them.

Toby came over then, the kind of expression on his face that made Jamie definitely want to puke behind the bench.

"Shit happens," he said with a sigh. "I talked to Ian. He's . . . well, he's sorry, but that doesn't fix it, does it?"

"No," Jamie said simply.

"I like you," Coach Toby said. "I want you to do well here, but we've got to get these kinks worked out."

If Jamie hadn't already known he was on thin ice, he knew it now.

"Right, Coach." He knew his tone lacked confidence, but then he'd just missed his first ever NFL kick. The first kick where he could really prove to everyone that this was what he should be doing. That he deserved to be on an NFL team. And he'd *missed* it.

"The fact that it almost went in, that's actually impressive," Coach said, but those felt like empty words. He knew some kickers who practiced with bad snaps, bad holds, and learned how to make the best of bad situations. He'd never done that before. Had never had the need, because he'd worked with only a handful of guys, ever, at Stanford, and they'd always been perfect. A few baubles here and there, but nothing that stood out in Jamie's memory.

"Shit happens," Coach repeated, and gave him a reassuring thump on the shoulder. "You'll get another chance."

God, he hoped so.

If Shane kicked really well today, he might not get another one. That one kick would be his only shot, and he'd have blown it.

As the clock ticked down towards the end of the first half, Jamie tried to ignore the feeling of impending failure that was sweeping through him, but it was difficult. And the way Shane kept smiling—*gloating*, Jamie's brain supplied, *he's gloating*—didn't help at all.

. . . . ● . ● . ● . . . .

"If you're taking this job on Sunday Morning Football, then I'm confused why you're not *on* Sunday Morning Football," Olive complained, as she tucked her feet underneath her as she sat on one of Neal's couches.

"Because it's the preseason," Neal explained, "and they're still working to get everything set up for the regular season. Next week they'll make the shift to LA, and I'll join then or the next week. Today I'm just doing a short intro."

Not an interview. Neal had made sure that Alec made that explicitly clear to the producers. Just a friendly, *hey, how're you doing, I'll be joining Sunday Morning Football soon.*

Alec had told him it was a mistake not to address the elephant in the room right away—the kick he'd missed in the Super Bowl—but Neal had done all the addressing he was going to do. Their last night in New York, he and Alec had sat down with a bottle of really good Scotch and had drafted his retirement announcement. He'd vaguely addressed it there by talking about how much he owed to the NFL and its opportunities, and that he'd always tried his best to make the most of them.

The statement had been circulated to the media first thing yesterday morning, and then posted to his brand-new social media accounts, all managed by Alec's new hire, a young, savvy woman named Cailee, who was under strict instructions to delete rude comments and block any trolls immediately.

Neal hadn't had the stomach to check on her work, but Alec had called yesterday and said that the response to his statement had been largely positive, with many fans talking about how much he'd be missed. *And,* Alec had said, a wry edge to his voice, *a lot of them are curious to know what you'll be up to next.*

They wouldn't have to wait very long to find out. A camera crew had come and set up in Neal's living room. Olive had picked out a shirt for him to wear, and now all there was to do was have a complete meltdown, while he waited for this minute-long conversation that was going to change his entire life.

It wasn't a hundred percent final that he'd be joining—he had yet to sign the contract, though it was all ready. The producers were waiting for the final go-ahead after this intro, to make sure he tested well.

Neal had thought that was ridiculous—*if I'm joining, then I'm joining,* he'd complained to Alec, on the flight home, *this is dumb*—but Alec had reassured him that this was how these things worked, and everyone anticipated that his joining the panel would be a huge success. "They just have to cross their T's and dot the I's," Alec had said. "That's all this is."

"Stupid marketing bullshit," Neal had muttered. It had been easier to worry about the new direction his career was taking than to think about seeing Jamie again—even though he desperately wanted to. When he'd been in New York, things had begun to shift between them. And now that he'd come home, everything was different. It wasn't just because Jamie had come over last night and seduced him. *Wasn't very hard, now was it?* Neal's conscience teased him. *He didn't even have to try very hard.*

"Hey," Olive said, "the Riptide game is on. Jamie's going to play, right?"

Neal shot her a look as she flipped to it. "Yeah," he said shortly. "Yeah, he is."

"Well, then you should watch it," she said, turning the volume down low.

Neal didn't tell her he'd already been following along on his phone. There'd been no points scored by the Riptide in the first half so far, and so neither Jamie nor Shane had had a chance to kick either a field goal or even an extra point.

But then, Olive yelped with excitement and Neal glanced over at the TV—it was almost unbearably weird to look up and see the Riptide playing, in those gaudy turquoise and blue uniforms, and for him not to be with them—and saw that they'd just scored a touchdown and Jamie was jogging out to try for the extra point.

"Oh, this is so exciting," Olive said, hugging a pillow to her chest. "It was exciting when I knew you, and it's even more exciting now."

"Yeah," Neal said, even though he couldn't disagree more. Just watching? Especially when it was a guy he cared about—someone who not only had something to prove, but who deserved this chance?—it really fucking sucked.

And it was even worse when stupid Ian bobbled the snap and Jamie couldn't quite compensate enough, and the ball sailed just right of the upright.

"Shit," Olive said.

Neal reached for the remote and flipped off the TV. "Enough of that," he said. He didn't need to hear the recitation of the Riptide's kicking problems, which was undoubtedly coming next, and in which he'd occupy a starring position.

"That really sucks," Olive said. "He's . . . well, you know I like him, right?"

Neal glared at her, tilting his head slightly to remind Olive of the producer and cameramen who were consulting together under their breath. But Neal knew that they were still probably listening, and the last thing he or Jamie needed was a rumor starting that they were friends—or even *more*. Jamie was out of the closet, and while Neal hadn't exactly addressed any of the gossip about him, it was an open secret that he was also gay.

If a rumor started, the chances of it staying at the "friend" level were probably going to be slim.

"Oh, yeah," Olive said, in a totally normal voice. Not trying to keep quiet at all. Neal rolled his eyes. "Yeah, well, I hope he does good. Because I don't know him at all."

For a brief moment, Neal considered burying his head into the nearest throw pillow, but then it would mess up his hair, and he'd worked hard on it this morning. This was his first real prime-time coverage, and he wanted to look good.

"Well, maybe the other kicker will miss too," Olive continued. "It's not unheard of."

But unlikely. If Toby and the rest of the coaching staff decided that the bad snap was enough of an excuse to ditch Jamie, they'd do it in a heartbeat. If Shane faltered, this competition would go on another week, but Neal wasn't sure that would happen.

"Hey, we're just about ready for you," the producer said, coming over to stand by Neal. "We'll do the spot during the Riptide's halftime."

Of course they would. Neal tried to paste a pleased smile on his face. He'd told himself—and *Alec* had even reminded him of this—that it would take time for people to stop associating him so strongly with the Riptide. "You spent your entire career with them," Alec had pointed out. "You *are* the Riptide's kicker, even with what happened in the Super Bowl."

"And after?" Neal had asked, raising an eyebrow. He was referring to the way he'd been escorted out, and all the unfortunate pictures that had come out showing Terry holding on to Neal's arm, and Neal trying to push him away.

It had not been his finest moment, but then it hadn't been for the Riptide or Michael, either.

"We've got a nice setup here," the producer said as he sat down. "Your house is really beautiful."

"Thanks," Neal said shortly, sitting down in the seat she'd prepared for him. He was wearing a green polo—*it'll bring out your eyes,* Olive had claimed—but the producer had picked and chosen several decorative pieces to place behind him on the credenza, and they were all in Riptide colors. He considered saying something, but decided that this was a long-term strategy.

He wouldn't be doing himself any favors by throwing a fit right now.

"Going live in three . . . two . . . one . . ."

In the small monitor they'd set up, Neal could see the group of current panelists in their studio in New York. "Hey, guys," he said. *Be young, be hip, be cool,* he reminded himself. "How's it going so far today?"

"Could ask you the same question," Terry said. "Good to see you again, Neal."

"I think Terry wants to ask . . . did you see that kick right before halftime?" Jimmy asked.

Neal was live. He only had a split second to decide what he wanted to do. Before, when he'd done interviews, he'd still known approximately the questions the interviewer would ask and could practice answers. But this? This was going to be unscripted.

He could pretend ignorance or he could come clean. He'd been a member of the LA Riptide for thirteen years. Neal told himself it would be weirder if he *wasn't* watching it.

"Yeah, I saw it," Neal said, and carefully timed a resigned sigh. "I have to say I feel for the kid." Maybe he didn't trust himself to say Jamie's name on live TV, not quite yet, but he could use his nickname for him. "It's not easy to get on that big stage and then falter."

Terry's gaze turned calculating on the tiny monitor. "You'd know something about that, wouldn't you?"

They were going way off script now. Neal could jerk them back, but he'd look bad if he did it. And maybe he really didn't want to. Maybe this was his one chance to put all that talk to rest, once and for all. "Oh, I do," he said, with an easy smile. "I think I'd know better than just about anyone."

"But you're still retiring," Jerry added. "Not looking to find redemption."

"I don't need redemption," Neal said plainly. "I won a Super Bowl. I played for the same team for thirteen years. I made more kicks in the NFL than I ever could've dreamed of, back when I was trying to win a spot in college. But now it's time to move on, to try something new."

Terry nodded, and he looked very pleased. Like he'd gotten exactly what he'd wanted the whole time. And maybe, Neal realized, he had too.

"You think you can put up with these disgruntled old men?" Jimmy asked.

"I'd be honored, sir," Neal said.

"And we're honored to have you," Terry said. "Neal Fisher, the newest member of Sunday Morning Football, and, ladies and gentlemen, I think he's gonna keep us on our toes."

"Someone has to," Jerry said dryly.

"I'll do my best," Neal said, and then just as abruptly as it had begun, the interview was over.

Neal helped the producer pack up their equipment, which he guessed wasn't normal, if the glances she kept giving him were any indication. But Neal's parents, and then his sister, Ella, had raised him to never think he was too good to help out. That was a lesson that had stuck. By the time he was done, and returned to the living room, Olive had turned the TV back on, and the familiar blue and aqua jerseys were swarming across the screen.

"Sorry," she said apologetically, reaching for the remote, "but halftime was over . . ."

"It's alright," he said, and discovered that it actually was.

Maybe all his demons hadn't been exorcised, but he was working on it.

"Okay good," she said, "because I think that other kid is about to kick a field goal."

Neal's eyes flew to the screen. "What?" he said.

"Yeah," she said. "Forty-two yards."

It wasn't forty-four yards, but Neal had a terrible premonition that if Shane made this field goal, then Jamie's days were numbered. The coaching staff would probably prevaricate for a game or two, claiming they needed a bigger sample size of data, but Neal knew their minds would already be made up.

But then, that was the NFL for you; fairness was not often part of the deciding equation.

"Well, let's hope he misses," Neal said, his grip on his knee tightening.

Olive laughed. "Have we ever hoped that for a Riptide kicker? Ever?"

"Actually, probably not," Neal said, chuckling with her. "But there's a first time for everything."

They watched as Shane got set up. He looked confident. Sure. The snap was good; the holder placing the ball perfectly. Already he had gotten a better chance than Jamie had.

But then instead of sending the ball between the uprights, it veered wide to the left.

Olive let out a little cheer, and before Neal could even say anything, was reaching for the remote, silencing the announcers as they no doubt continued to discuss and dissect the Riptide's kicker problem.

"That was good for Jamie, wasn't it?" Olive demanded.

"Yeah," Neal agreed. "But I doubt Jamie is going to see it that way."

Chapter Twelve

It was even worse than Neal thought. Worse, and in addition, an unpleasant reminder of what *he* had spent the last six months doing.

Hiding.

"Listen," Neal said, pulling out his most persuasive tone as he leaned against the kitchen counter, phone pressed to his ear, "just tell me where you are and I'll come to you."

"No, really," Jamie protested, "I'm good, I'm just wiped out, and tired and . . ."

"And not hiding?" Neal said gently.

There was a long silence on the other end. It wasn't like Neal enjoyed pointing out the truth, but he could also look back over the last few months and wish that people had been a little more blunt with him. Would it have stopped him? Maybe not. But it would've made him think a lot harder about what he was doing and why.

"You really want to see me?"

"Did you think I wouldn't?" Neal countered.

"I . . . it was the snap, you know," Jamie blurted out.

"I saw it. And you almost compensated for it, too." Neal paused. "At least you didn't miss a field goal."

Jamie laughed then, like it had been startled out of him. "Yeah. Yeah, I guess so."

"And they didn't make either of you face the press, which is a blessing," Neal added.

"I guess they were feeling generous," Jamie retorted quietly.

"I guess so," Neal echoed.

There was another long pause. Neal didn't want to force Jamie to see him, but he also knew that avoidance wouldn't solve how Jamie felt. He had to *want* to see him. Even a little.

"Fine," Jamie said with a resigned exhale. "I'll text you the hotel address and my room number."

"Okay," Neal said, "I'll be there soon."

• • • • • • • • • •

He stopped at his favorite pizza joint, because nobody could be sad around pizza—something he and the extra five pounds currently hanging around his middle had discovered to be true—and then headed towards the hotel where Jamie was staying.

It was one he recognized that a lot of players—still unsure whether they would be staying in LA or not—liked to bunk at, and so Neal didn't walk in the front, and didn't take the main elevator, but ran up the back stairs, taking them two at a time.

He finally reached the fifth floor and the room number Jamie had texted him. Shifting the pizza box to one hand, he knocked on the door. Jamie answered it almost immediately, like he'd been standing by it, waiting.

His eyes were enormous and dark in his handsome face, and there was a disappointment and a frustration lingering in their depths that Neal recognized a little too well.

"Hey," Jamie said, opening the door wider. "Come in."

"I brought pizza," Neal said, leaning down and brushing a kiss across Jamie's lips when the door was closed. He was worried about the guy, but not dumb enough to kiss him with the door open either.

Especially not after what had happened today.

Finding out the truth would be all the excuse the Riptide needed to cut Jamie once and for all. They'd claim something incredibly fucking stupid, probably, like that Neal was cursed and had in turn cursed Jamie.

Curses might not exist, but people acting like they did often *made* them real.

And nobody was more superstitious than football players. *Nobody.*

Jamie melted into his brief kiss, winding his arms around Neal's middle. "I'm glad you came," he whispered into his chest.

Neal squeezed his eyes shut against the sudden onslaught of emotion. Was it because he was realizing he cared deeply about this man? Or because he knew exactly what Jamie was going through?

"Hey, you know, shit happens," Neal said, when Jamie pulled back, eyes glittering. "What did you say to me? *You're fine. No judgment, no nasty comments, nobody died*?"

Jamie flushed. "It feels a lot different when it's you."

"It does," Neal said. He gestured towards the little sitting area next to the hotel room's sole window. *Not* the bed. It wasn't that he wasn't *very* interested in the bed. He was. Even seeing it made his pulse speed up. What they'd done last night had been fun, but there was so much more that Neal wanted. So much more that he wanted to give.

But right now, Jamie needed more than just sex.

"Come on," Neal added, "I brought you something that's guaranteed to make you feel better."

Jamie eyed the box dubiously. "You brought me pizza?"

"Exactly. Everyone likes pizza. It's like tacos. Guaranteed to at least partially turn your mood around after a slice."

Neal slid the pizza box onto the little kitchen table and opened it. Immediately the smell of cheese and pepperoni filled the air. "I erred on the side of caution. Half cheese, half pepperoni," he said. "Next time, if you like it, I'll bring their special."

Jamie had reached in for a piece, and was already two bites in, when he glanced up. "And what's that?" he asked, his mouth full of pizza.

"Pepperoni pineapple," he said with a grin. "Not for the faint of heart."

Shuddering, Jamie shook his head emphatically. "*No*," he said, "that's a crime against humanity. An abomination. Why would you do that to poor, misunderstood pepperoni? It's bad enough that ham has to deal with the shame of being paired with pineapple."

"So, what you're saying is that I shouldn't get pizza for our date, then," Neal said casually.

"I didn't think that was what you were planning on," Jamie teased. "I thought you were trying to impress me."

"I kinda am," Neal admitted, slumping into one of the chairs, he put a foot up on Jamie's, and nudged his knee with his sneaker. "How am I doing so far?"

Jamie's smile was bright. The shadows had almost completely faded from his eyes. Neal patted himself on the back. "Good so far," he said. "This pizza is fantastic."

"Best pizza in LA," Neal said, reaching into the box and snagging himself a piece of cheese. Sometimes the purest form of pizza was the best form.

"You said you erred on the side of caution," Jamie said conversationally. "And we had chicken tacos when I was at your house.

But I do eat beef, you know. Beef and pork and basically every single kind of seafood there is."

"Okay," Neal said. "I wasn't sure." He hadn't been. He'd wanted to ask, but he hadn't wanted to pry. To dig into matters that Jamie hadn't chosen to share yet.

"I'm adopted," Jamie said matter-of-factly. "My dad is a Brit, my mom is American. I was adopted from an orphanage in Chennai when I was a baby. I don't remember anything about it. We've been back a few times, but I guess I consider myself American. Not Indian."

"Adopted, huh? That's cool." Neal finished his piece.

"I guess I don't think about it much," Jamie admitted. "My dad is my dad. My mom is my mom. Maybe they don't look like me, but they're still my family."

Neal remembered Jamie mentioning that his dad hadn't wanted him to try out for any NFL teams. That he'd wanted him to get a good job. A job his Stanford education probably would have well-prepared him for. "Your parents obviously care a lot about you, too," he said.

"What about yours? I know you have Olive . . ." Jamie trailed off.

Neal took a deep breath. It was always better to get this out in one quick recitation than it was to drag it out, painfully. "My parents died when I was fourteen, in a car accident," he said. "My sister, Ella, is only eight years older than me, but she and her fiancé at the time took care of me. By the time I went to Wisconsin, Ella and Mateo had gotten married and had Olive."

"I'm so sorry, Neal," Jamie said, reaching out, and squeezing his calf. "God, that must have been terrible for you."

"It wasn't fun," Neal said wryly. "But Ella and Mateo are both amazing. Unsurprisingly, since they raised a daughter like Olive."

"And a guy like you," Jamie said.

"You're . . . you're . . ." Neal cleared his throat. "You're really way too nice for me."

"Am I?" Jamie wondered, a teasing smile on his face. "I like to think I'm just nice enough."

"I came here to get your mind off what happened, and here you are, showering me with compliments," Neal said, standing up and going over to the sink in the tiny kitchenette, to wash the pizza grease off his fingers.

He felt Jamie come up behind him. Rest his head on his back. "Maybe it makes me feel better to do that," he admitted quietly. Michael would do what he asked, always, but the support that Jamie gave, wholeheartedly and without reserve, was something that he'd always lacked. Neal hadn't even known he'd been missing it, but getting it now? It felt like night and day.

After wiping his hands on the towel by the sink, Neal turned around. "Jamie," he said, reaching up and cupping Jamie's cheeks with his hands. "It was a bad snap. It wasn't your fault."

"I need to learn how to compensate for that. I know it can be done. Can you teach me?" Jamie asked, neatly dodging the point that Neal had been trying to make.

"Yes," Neal said slowly, "but not always. Sometimes . . . sometimes a snap just sucks, and there's nothing you can do about it."

"I don't care, I want to learn," Jamie said stubbornly. "I hate this. I hate feeling like this."

"I know," Neal breathed out, wrapping him up and tugging him closer. "Believe me, I know."

"I just . . ." Jamie glanced up. "Thank you for coming."

"I know you would've agonized by yourself all night. Not gotten any sleep. Gone in Tuesday morning, dreading that conversation. Worrying that you'd be released."

"Maybe a little less, after Shane missed the field goal," Jamie admitted. "Making two extra points in the second half helped, too, but it didn't really erase missing that first one."

"That was a tough first miss," Neal admitted. "Also, Shane didn't have the good excuse you did. It's only too bad that field goal wasn't forty-four yards. They probably would've fired him on the spot." Neal was kind of joking, but also kind of *not* joking.

"Yeah," Jamie said moodily.

"And like you said, you made two other extra points. You put that miss behind you, *and* even better, they gave you another shot in the *same* game."

"Yeah, probably only because they didn't want to send Shane out again," Jamie muttered. "And it wasn't like they had other choices. It's me or Shane. One of us has to kick."

"Exactly," Neal said. "You already know it should be you. Next game—you'll put everyone's questions to rest."

Jamie's eyes shone with something like amusement. "Oh, will I?"

"You will," Neal said emphatically. And it wasn't just lip service; he meant it, and not just because he was falling so hard and fast for this guy, but because there was something inside Jamie that reminded him of himself.

He was strong and determined and kept his eyes on the prize no matter what tried to shake him.

"Sometimes I wonder how I ended up in this position—where we forget all the wins, just to focus on the one loss."

"Believe me, a question I've asked myself a thousand times." At least nine hundred versions in the last six months alone. It was one of the reasons that Neal had known he was done. That he was ready to tackle a different challenge.

"How was your interview today?" Jamie asked, like he knew exactly the path that Neal's thought process had taken.

"It was . . ." Neal hesitated. "Different than how I expected." He didn't want to say that it had happened right after Jamie's miss. "But I think it went well."

"Yeah, I think so too," Jamie teased, eyes lighting up again. "You better believe I watched it right away, the moment I was alone. You looked so cute."

"Cute?"

Jamie laughed. "Incredibly, heartbreakingly hot, okay?"

"Better," Neal said. He leaned back against the sink, and pulled Jamie between his legs, until they were pressed together. "You didn't think I embarrassed myself?"

"I'm glad you talked about it," Jamie admitted. "I know you didn't want to."

"I didn't but . . . I realized that was just another form of hiding. I shouldn't be ashamed, and fuck anyone who thinks I should be. And the same goes for you, you know?"

Jamie tipped his head up, and instead of answering, pressed his mouth against Neal's, the kiss slow and sweet at first. He tasted like the remnants of the red flavor of Gatorade and the pepperoni from the pizza. And normally that might not have been the kind of flavor that Neal liked, but he deepened the kiss, craving more of it. Craving more of the taste of Jamie that lay just underneath.

Moaning into his mouth, Jamie moved against him, and Neal could already see what this could be like—so much like the last time. They'd get carried away, and they'd probably end up dry humping to an orgasm, but he hadn't come here to get them both off as quickly as possible.

He wanted to take his time, wanted to savor the man he was falling for.

"Hey," Neal said, after he lifted his head.

Jamie looked drunk on just kissing; flushed, with swollen lips and hazy eyes. "What is it?" he asked.

"We should take this to your bed," Neal said, leaning to nip at those tempting lips again. "I wanna make you feel good."

If it was possible, Jamie's eyes grew even wider, like he hadn't even imagined that they could do this on a bed, instead of on a couch, or against the tiny kitchenette counter. He nodded. "Yeah," he said, and Neal watched as he swallowed hard. "Yeah, we can do that."

"Alright," Neal said, reaching down, and tangling their fingers together, giving him a little tug towards the bed. Jamie followed, and when they reached the big, fluffy comforter-covered bed, Neal nudged him onto the edge.

Jamie sat down and watched with wide eyes as Neal leaned in and kissed him again. "Can I make you feel good?" he asked.

· · · ● · ● ● · · ·

Could Neal make him feel good? Jamie found himself nodding, and then watching, with a little bit of shock and a lot of awe, as Neal Fisher went to his knees in front of him, and pressed a reverent kiss to the side of his bare knee.

"Is this okay?" Neal asked. A dim part of Jamie's brain reminded him he hadn't been quite this scrupulous about consent, but then he'd just shown up at Neal's house and seduced him. Still, it hadn't been like Neal had exactly protested that particular turn of events.

"Yeah," Jamie said, his own voice going gravelly and deep. He was hard as a rock under the athletic shorts he'd thrown on as soon as he'd gotten back to the hotel room. "Yeah, anything you want."

Neal grinned and reached for Jamie's t-shirt, tugging it off, laying a strong, broad hand against his chest, right where his heart felt like it was beating so hard, surely Neal could feel it.

"God, so gorgeous," Neal muttered disbelievingly, like he couldn't quite believe that Jamie was here. And the feeling was definitely mutual. Because every time he glanced down and saw Neal's stunning face and his bedroom eyes right next to his cock, it felt like he was going to lose it before Neal could even touch him.

Neal tucked his fingers under the waistband of his shorts and tugged down, pausing as his eyes flew up, an astonished expression on his face. "What's this, kid? Going commando?" he asked, grinning like he'd just discovered the best surprise in the world. "You trying to kill me now?"

"No," Jamie said with a sharp exhale as Neal ran a fingertip up his bare cock. It twitched, precome leaking out of the red, swollen head. He wanted, desperately, to beg Neal to lean in, to suck it, to even *lick* it, but despite his current position, Neal seemed like he was enjoying taking control this time around, and Jamie had a feeling that whatever happened, it would feel goddamn amazing.

"You want something?" Neal asked slyly.

Jamie's hands dug into the bedding, curling into the cotton. "Yes," he said.

"Yeah," Neal said, his tone deep and sending a shudder through Jamie, "me too."

He leaned in then, and Jamie couldn't help it. He had to close his eyes, squeeze them shut, or else he was going to come all over Neal's gorgeous face. It was just too much to see him like this, to *feel* it as he sucked Jamie's cock down.

In more than a few of Jamie's fantasies, Neal Fisher had been fantastic at sucking cock, but somehow the reality left all those teenage dreams in the dust. His mouth was warm and soft and intense, and he devoted himself to Jamie's cock like it was the reason he'd been put on this planet. Jamie moaned, trying to hold back, trying not to come too soon, but the fact that it was Neal who had his mouth on his dick, and Neal who was sucking like he was born to do it, and Neal that was cupping his balls and tugging them just right, was like an endless feedback loop mashup of every dream he'd ever had and all this rock-hard, leaking-at-the-tip, pleasure-shuddering-through-him reality.

"Feels good, huh?" Neal said, a sudden loss of warmth making Jamie moan harder.

Jamie felt one hand close around his cock, jerking it slowly and deliberately, fingers tight around him, making sure he didn't come—like Neal had *known* he was right there on the edge, frantically trying to hold back—and then another finger slid right underneath his balls, right to his hole. It just took a brush for Jamie to feel like he was coming undone. Just the idea of Neal fucking him sent him flying apart in a thousand directions, pulsing long and hard into Neal's hand, losing himself in the feel and the thought and the fact that this dream had come true.

"Fuck, I think you want that," Neal said, all enthusiasm and no judgment.

Jamie pried his eyes open and stared down at Neal, who was wiping his hand on the kitchen towel he must've just swiped. "Fuck me," he said simply.

Neal stared at him. "You mean it. You're serious."

"Only if you want to," Jamie said in a rush. He'd been under the spell of an extraordinary orgasm when he'd asked, but he realized now that they'd never exactly covered sexual preferences. Maybe Neal preferred to bottom or didn't like anal sex at all. But if that was true, then the way he was looking at Jamie now, awed and incredibly turned on, didn't make much sense.

"I want to," Neal said, his voice unsteady. "Do you have . . ."

"Yeah," Jamie said, and rolled away, reaching into the drawer where he had optimistically stashed some lube, and an unopened box of condoms he'd bought after the first time he'd gone to Neal's house.

He set the items on the bed next to him and looked up at Neal, who was still staring at him incredulously. Like he couldn't believe this was happening. And Jamie understood, because he couldn't quite either.

"How . . ." Jamie started to ask, but Neal silenced him with a hot, heavy kiss, pushing him back on the bed and straddling him.

Kissing with Neal was so good, so life-changing, that it only took a few minutes, and Jamie could feel his cock begin to stir to life again.

"Fuck," Neal said roughly, as he felt Jamie shift desperately against him. "God, you're a fucking miracle."

"I want you," Jamie said plaintively. He didn't want to beg, but he felt like he was getting close to it.

Neal sat up and stripped off his shirt, wiggling off his jeans, too. Reaching over, Jamie grazed his palm over the rock-hard erection in Neal's boxer briefs.

"Stop that," Neal ordered, smiling. "This is gonna end before it even begins if you keep that up."

"We wouldn't want that," Jamie said with a chuckle, his laughter quickly changing into a moan as Neal slid a finger back to the same spot that had made him lose control the first time.

"Yeah, we wouldn't," Neal said roughly. "Especially when just doing this," he added, rubbing his thumb around, "was enough to make you lose it. I wanna see you when I'm deep inside."

"Yes," Jamie said on a sharp exhale. "*Yes.*"

Neal flicked open the bottle of lube and coated his fingers. Jamie squeezed his eyes shut again, trying to ignore the pleasure flooding through him as Neal worked in one finger, and then another. He already felt so full, and he could barely wait until that was Neal's cock.

"Goddamnit, you're tight," Neal groaned.

"Just . . . *come on*," Jamie begged. "I can take it."

"No," Neal said reluctantly. "I want every bit of this to feel fucking amazing."

What Neal didn't know was that probably every inch of it *would*, if he would just get on with it. But instead, he was putting more lube on his fingers, and sliding a third in, next to the other two, carefully and gently stretching him out, every second or third thrust hitting his prostate, white hot stars exploding across his vision.

Then suddenly, as full as he'd been, he was empty again. His eyes flickered open and he watched, anticipation surging inside of him as Neal stripped off his briefs and ripped open a condom packet, rolling it on with an expert motion that nearly made Jamie want to cry. *God, it was going to feel so good. Neal was going to take care of him. He was going to make him love every goddamn second.*

"Next time," Neal said, his voice guttural and so deep that Jamie could nearly feel it in his toes, "next time, you're going to fuck *me*, and make *me* feel so good I cry into the pillow, okay?"

Jamie's cock twitched with excitement at the thought, and also at the feel of Neal's cock pushing into his hole. "Fuck yes," he echoed as Neal slowly slid in. "Oh fuck, you feel so fucking good."

Neal's fingers were a vise around his leg as he gripped his thigh. Jamie bit his lip and tried to use the pain to distract him from how good everything felt, how *right*. But it didn't work, not when Neal looked like *that*, just because he was fucking him.

"God, you really like that, don't you?" Neal ground out. It couldn't have been a question, because he kept going, kept pushing in, inexorably, until Jamie felt like he was full to his throat. Jamie was speechless, wordless. *Lost.*

"I love it," Jamie finally managed to say, spitting the words out between his uncooperative lips and his fuzzy brain. Everything felt like it had short-circuited on pleasure. "Fuck me, *please.*"

Neal didn't say anything, just squeezed his own eyes shut and began to move, each thrust hitting him so perfectly that within moments, Jamie already felt his control beginning to slip *again*.

He reached for his own dick, bobbing in time with Neal's thrusts, but Neal swatted his hand away and wrapped his own around it. Jamie's back bowed as pleasure spiked through him, and his system overdosed on it, squeezing fiercely around Neal's cock, buried deep inside of him. Neal groaned, long and endless, and his head fell forward as his own orgasm overtook him.

Collapsing on top of Jamie, Neal slipped out of him, and his forehead, damp with sweat, dropped to Jamie's chest.

"Wow," Jamie said, exhaling loudly, his heart still racing. "Just . . . *Wow.*"

"I know." Neal sounded smug, but frankly Jamie couldn't blame him for that.

"I think . . ." Jamie hesitated. "I think you were right. No judgment, and nobody died."

Neal rolled over, pulling Jamie's body close against his. "What about the nasty comments?"

"You watched the game on TV, not me. I'm sure the announcers said at least *one* thing that we could categorize as nasty."

Neal chuckled. "Yeah, probably. But I didn't listen. Sometimes . . . sometimes you just don't need to hear that."

"And you didn't," Jamie said.

Groaning, Neal lifted himself out of bed. "I'm going to clean up," he said, "but yeah, yeah, no. You don't. I didn't, not for a long-ass time, you know that."

"Right," Jamie said, and sat up, waiting as he heard Neal in the bathroom, running water. He emerged with a damp washcloth, and instead of handing it to Jamie, carefully cleaned off his chest and between his legs himself. Jamie felt his heart swell with something he was terrified might be love.

Was it too soon? *Probably.* Were they risking everything by taking a chance on this? *Incredibly likely.* But it felt so good, there was no way that it could be wrong.

Chapter Thirteen

J AMIE DIDN'T KNOW WHAT to expect of the date that Neal had promised him. All he'd given away was that it was "casual," and that jeans would totally be okay, but that it was still special. *Like you,* Neal had texted him.

Neal was probably never going to be the world's greatest texter. He hated social media. He had an Instagram, but he refused to ever look at it. He'd even hired someone to do that for him. Sometimes Jamie wondered if that would eventually be him—worried that if he dared to look online, he'd see something that ruined all his attempts at mindfulness.

I'll be outside your hotel at 8 p.m., Neal had told him. **Navy blue Tesla.**

At 8 p.m. on the dot, Jamie emerged from the main hotel lobby, the doors swishing closed behind him. It had been a hot day in LA, but at this point in the evening, the air had cooled, and there was a pleasant breeze. It was dusk, and growing darker, and it took him a minute to spot the Tesla, idling at the back of the hotel parking lot. Jamie glanced around, feeling a bit like a spy, and after he was sure he didn't know anyone hanging around, made his way across the lot and opened the passenger door, sliding into the cool, leather-lined interior.

Neal was sitting in the driver's seat, wearing a black t-shirt that did incredible things for his arms and chest, and a bright, incorrigible smile on his face.

"Hey," he said, leaning over and brushing an eager kiss across Jamie's mouth. "I'm so happy to see you."

"You saw me yesterday," Jamie said impudently. Neal had snuck out of the hotel early in the morning and gone back to his own house. He'd told Jamie he had early meetings with the Sunday Morning Football producers, and didn't want to wake Jamie on a day he could sleep in. Secretly, Jamie wouldn't have minded if it was Neal waking him up, but he'd let him go because maybe it was too soon to be spending the night together.

"Yeah." Neal sighed. "It was a long day."

"What happened?" Jamie asked as Neal pulled out of the hotel parking lot and onto the freeway. He didn't know LA very well yet, but he couldn't help but wonder what direction they were going and what that could tell him about their ultimate destination.

"Just lots and lots of meetings. More meetings than you'd ever imagine it would take to host a two-hour-long show once a week."

"You've done lots of interviews before, though," Jamie pointed out. "You know how to talk on camera."

"Yeah, well, it's one thing to have some media training, which you're right, I do have. And which you should get too, by the way, if you haven't already." Neal paused. "But this is ridiculous. We had an hour-long meeting today about what I should and should not say—and you won't believe this, but a rep from the NFL was there. He had a whole freaking presentation on what we're *allowed* to say."

Sadly, Jamie could kind of believe it. He hadn't gone to the Combine, officially, but he'd gone to the NFL's three-day rookie seminar, and one of the presentations had been similar to what Neal described: what you could say and what you should absolutely *not* publicly say about the NFL. Jamie knew the rookie seminar was new, and that maybe Neal hadn't had one when he was just starting out.

"Let me guess, you're not allowed to criticize the officiating," Jamie teased.

"*No*, that's basically the number one thing we're not allowed to do," Neal agreed. "They even had us role-play several different scenarios."

"They made Terry Bradshaw role-play?"

"Well, they *tried*," Neal said with a chuckle. "It didn't work out too well."

Neal took the exit labeled Glendale. Jamie's fingers itched and he wanted to look up their route on his phone, maybe see if he could figure it out, but he reminded himself, the whole point of this was Neal wanting to surprise him. He should *let* Neal surprise him.

"What did he do?" Jamie asked.

"Terry? He spent the *entire* role play criticizing the officiating."

Jamie laughed. He wasn't surprised at all. "I bet that was interesting."

Neal glanced over, a bright smile on his face. "Honestly? It was the highlight of the day, watching him try to confound the NFL rep. I don't get how people think he's dumb, he's *so* smart. Sly and funny and always poking fun, but never in the most obvious way."

"These are the same people who thought you sucked because you missed one field goal," Jamie pointed out. "I'm not sure they're a good judge of anything."

Neal hummed, but didn't reply. Jamie wondered how long it would take for Neal to stop carrying this baggage around, this certainty that the Riptide releasing him had been the right call? He didn't know, but it physically hurt Jamie every time it came up, because he knew how untrue it was. He couldn't imagine what it would feel like for Neal, who *believed* that bullshit.

"Where are we going?" Jamie asked.

The grin returned to Neal's face. "If I told you, it wouldn't be a surprise," he said. "But I promise, we won't be bothered."

"I'm not worried about that," Jamie said, and discovered that was mostly true. What were the Riptide going to do? Release him over an unsubstantiated rumor? He'd given in on the jersey number, but was considering, because of the looser NFL rules about equipment, that he might doodle Neal's number on his shoe. It'd be small enough that most people would miss it, but he'd know it was there, and that's what mattered.

"You should be," Neal said, his voice turning grim. "They would absolutely hate this. You know it, because of what happened with the jersey. That was minor compared to what might happen if they found out we were dating."

Neal turned again, and now they were heading up a hill. There were signs, but they were hard to read in the growing dusk as they flashed by, Neal expertly handling the Tesla as it took the sharp turns smoothly and easily.

"We can't keep this a secret forever," Jamie said.

"No, I know," Neal said, and there was a guilty edge to his voice. "I'm working on it."

"By establishing yourself as something other than the Riptide's ex-kicker?" Jamie wondered.

Neal nodded. "It'll take some time . . . but I think it'll help. Maybe by next season . . ."

Next season. Jamie hadn't ever imagined that they would try to keep this under wraps for so long. Of course, that was assuming that their relationship lasted until then. Jamie knew, because he'd heard stories of in-the-closet players trying to keep their relationships secret and the inherent stress of all the required secrecy causing the relationship to fall apart. Could he and Neal last a year like this? Jamie didn't know, but Neal already meant so much to him, he didn't want to take the chance.

It still felt fantastical that this was happening at all, but at some point reality would intrude and things would change, and the last thing Jamie wanted was to find out what it would be to love and then *lose* a guy like Neal Fisher.

"You're unhappy about that," Neal said when Jamie didn't say anything, and he sounded worried.

"We don't have to talk about it now. This is our first date. We shouldn't . . . we shouldn't even be thinking about this right now," Jamie said hurriedly. He was getting way ahead of himself. But it was hard not to, when his growing feelings were so goddamn strong.

When he looked over at Neal, he saw those same feelings reflected in Neal's eyes, in the way his expression softened whenever he looked in Jamie's direction.

"No, but," Neal said as he pulled into a massive parking lot. "Griffith Observatory" was written in big block letters in front of a massive stone building with the telltale rotunda on top.

"But what?" Jamie asked, reaching over and covering Neal's hand with his own. Squeezing reassuringly. The last thing he wanted was to ruin their first date. Neal had obviously put time and thought into planning this. He'd wanted to make it special. And why else would you be so determined to make it special unless you knew that *this*, this thing they shared, was special, too?

Neal squeezed his hand back. "But there is something you should know. I . . . I dated a guy on the Riptide for a long time. We broke up after the Super Bowl."

"A player?" Jamie asked, more than a little surprised. And then he remembered the rumors he'd heard.

"Not a player," Neal said steadily. "He's the assistant VP of player personnel. It's . . . I wouldn't be surprised if you end up meeting him at some point. His name is Michael Taylor. We dated for almost three years."

Watching Neal's face, Jamie saw various emotions flit across it. Regret. Disappointment. A vague echo of anger. Resignation. "We weren't exactly a secret, but we also didn't publicize our relationship either," Neal said. "It wasn't always easy, but it worked. Until it didn't."

"And that's what you want for us," Jamie said quietly. He didn't know if he would be okay with that. But he couldn't ask Neal, who still shied away from the intensity of the spotlight, to expose himself to it, willingly.

"No, actually," Neal said, the corner of his mouth twitching up into a small smile. "Actually, not at all. I'm telling you that so you know, so when this thing becomes public knowledge, because it will someday, whether that's a few months from now or a year from now, I want you to be prepared to deal with him."

"He'll be angry?" Jamie understood that. If he'd lost Neal Fisher, he'd be pissed off too.

"He's not a . . . let's just say that our relationship didn't end well. It ended with me throwing a picture of us at his head, and him having me escorted out of the Riptide facility."

A lot of things were beginning to make more sense, falling into place when before they'd just been jumbled up in Jamie's brain. "He's the one who let you go from the team."

"Yes," Neal said.

"God, that must've sucked."

Neal's smile was rueful. "It wasn't fun. But it didn't have to be him. He *wanted* it to be him. The Riptide is the most important thing to Michael—more than relationships, more than people, more than anything. I'd fucked it up, and he was done with me after that."

"That's horrible," Jamie said, righteously pissed now. What the fuck was this guy's problem? Neal was a *human being*, not a fucking machine!

"He wasn't interested in me for me," Neal said softly. "I think he was only interested in me for what I could do for him. And, by extension, the team."

"I don't, I would *never*," Jamie said fiercely. "Never, okay?"

"I know." Neal reached over and laid a hand across Jamie's chest, right where his heart was beating. "I know you wouldn't. I wouldn't be here with you if I thought you only cared about what I could give you."

Jamie reached up and curled his palm around the back of Neal's neck, smoothing down a few stray hairs. He tugged him closer and their mouths met over the center console. The kiss was slow and sweet and also felt like a promise.

"We're never going to be like that," Jamie swore, when he finally broke the kiss. "I want you to know that."

Neal tipped his head and their foreheads pressed together. "I know," he said. "I believe you."

"Good," Jamie said, feeling satisfaction swell inside of him. And something else, that he was very afraid might be love. "Now, let's go on this fabulous date you promised me."

Neal grinned. "Your date awaits," he said, gesturing, and opened his car door.

• • • ● • ● • ● • • •

It had been forever since Neal had been on a date where he *cared so much* about making a good impression. Not because he thought he needed it. The way Jamie gazed at him made it clear that his crush was definitely growing serious.

And Neal's own? Undeniably serious. He'd put a lot of time and energy into this date, because there was a persistent voice inside of him that kept saying that if he didn't, he'd regret it. He'd be standing up at his wedding, a few years down the road, or twenty years later with his kids, and he'd be forced to admit he took the love of his life on a basic first date, to something like dinner and a movie.

It was that voice, and also the way he knew Jamie was going to matter, that pushed Neal to get creative. He'd also been forced to find something that he could conceivably restrict to just the two of them.

Olive had suggested Griffith Observatory, and when he'd called, it turned out that the museum director was not only a huge Riptide fan, but they also felt sorry for him. Neal was definitely not above using his position—or his *ex*-position—to get what he wanted.

The director had agreed to shut the museum and observatory down two hours early, and promised to be the soul of discretion when he personally showed them the various telescopes that the Griffith owned.

"This is so cool," Jamie said, grinning widely as he got out of the car. "I've always wanted to come here, but never had the chance."

Neal found himself smiling just as widely as he reached for Jamie's hand. He looked up, a slightly puzzled expression on his face. "It's alright," Neal said, "it'll just be us and the museum director, and he's a fan, so I think he'll be discreet about it."

"Oh, that's nice," Jamie said, and Neal took his hand, wrapping their fingers together and squeezing.

"I want this to be a real date," Neal said, leaning over, and brushing a kiss across Jamie's cheek. "So that means I can kiss you whenever I want to."

"I thought you were supposed to wait til the *end* of the date," Jamie teased as they walked up the vast green lawn towards the front of the observatory.

"Who wants to do that?" Neal asked. "That sounds terrible. If I'm into you, and I'm *definitely into you*, babe, I'm gonna want to kiss you all the time."

Jamie flushed, his eyes wide and full of joy. "I'm into you, too," he said.

Neal ducked close, taking in the citrus, woodsy scent of Jamie's cologne, and under that, the smell of *him*. His cock twitched, and he wanted so much to find some dark corner they could get lost in, but this was about more than just sex. Not that the sex wasn't incredible; Neal had never been so absorbed before, not in all his years, and all the guys he'd been with. Jamie made him feel special; like he was brand new.

"I'll let you in on a little secret," he said, punctuating his sentence with a quick nip of Jamie's ear. He shuddered and Neal filed that little tidbit of knowledge away for later use. "I don't think I've ever felt this way before," he said.

Jamie's eyes widened, then went soft and dark. The moment stretched out between them, pulling them close and tight. "I thought..."

"I've dated plenty of guys before," Neal admitted. "But it's never been like this. I feel . . . breathless and silly, almost, waiting for the next time I get to see you. And every time I leave you, I want to turn around and stay."

Jamie reached up and cupped Neal's cheek. "Then you should stay," he said.

"Maybe I will," Neal said.

He didn't know how he could, but he wanted to, desperately. And he knew then, despite the precautions, there was no way this was staying under wraps until next season. They'd be lucky to keep this under wraps until Jamie had secured his long-term deal—even though Neal was determined that he wouldn't be the reason the Riptide didn't offer it to him.

"Hi there," a voice interrupted them. Neal glanced up and saw a middle-aged man in slacks and a polo walking over to them. "I'm Curt Rafferty, the observatory director."

"Hi, I'm Neal," he said, "and this is Jamie."

If the director recognized Jamie, which he probably *did*, because he'd specifically told Neal what a huge Riptide fan he was, he didn't show it. He shook both of their hands, his grip firm and his smile genuinely friendly.

"Thank you for shutting down a few hours early for us," Neal said, as Curt led them down the main walkway towards the observatory. "We really appreciate it."

"Oh, no problem. I get it, you know," Curt said. "I bet some fans can be real invasive, when you're just wanting to be left alone and enjoy something."

"Not always, but recently, yeah," Neal said, which was about as close as he was getting to talking about the last Super Bowl.

"I was thinking that you could spend some time looking through the exhibits," Curt said as they walked through the main doorway. "I set up everything you requested in the planetarium, and then after, we can take a look at the stars."

"That'd be great," Neal said, shaking his hand again. "What time in the planetarium?"

"Just show up in about an hour and we'll be ready for you," Curt said, eagerly shaking his hand again. "I'll be giving the planetarium talk myself. It's such an honor for you to be here." He paused. "For you *both* to be here," he added.

Neal felt Jamie tense next to him.

When Curt walked away, Jamie turned to him, obvious concern on his face. "He recognized me," he said. "I knew he'd recognize you, but I thought . . ."

"What? That after what happened at the Super Bowl and then afterwards, and *then* the crazy competition this year, that one of the finalists to be the new kicker could fly under the radar?" Neal teased. "That ship has sailed, babe."

"I think you must be exaggerating," Jamie said, rolling his eyes.

"Maybe," Neal said, nudging him with his shoulder. "Or maybe I'm telling the truth. Regardless, Curt is right. Sometimes you just want to be left alone."

Jamie reached out and took his hand again, squeezing it. "Not alone," he said. "I'm good just like this. With you."

Hand in hand, they wandered through the various exhibition halls, stopping to read the different placards that were set up. Neal had hoped that Jamie would find the observatory interesting, but he had apparently underestimated just how interesting he would find it, because at some point, he glanced down at his watch. "Crap," Neal said, "we have the planetarium show in five minutes."

"What's the show we're seeing?" Jamie asked, as they followed the signs through the vast marble hallways.

"I don't know," Neal said, not sure he wanted to admit the instructions he'd given Curt.

"I really don't believe that," Jamie pointed out. "You arranged and planned all this, and you left the choice of the planetarium show up to the guy running it?"

Neal felt his blush reach from the edge of his hairline, to the tip of his nose, down his neck, and into the open collar of his shirt. "Uh, not exactly," he admitted.

Jamie's smile grew bright. "What exactly *did* you tell him, then?"

"I told him to make it a romantic one," Neal murmured, turning and pulling Jamie flush against him, before they could quite reach the auditorium where the planetarium show was shown.

"Romantic, huh?" Jamie asked. "Does that mean you wanna make out with me during the planetarium show?"

"I didn't think you'd want to miss a minute of it," Neal said seriously. Maybe he *had*, at one point, back when he'd had his initial conversation with Curt. But now? He could see how much Jamie was enjoying the observatory. He wanted to stop and read every single placard, take in every single glass case, every single rare picture the staff here had captured with their powerful telescopes.

"So, really," Jamie said, reaching up and pressing a quick kiss to Neal's mouth, "what you're saying is that you're trying to butter me up for later."

Neal already knew he didn't need to. They could barely keep their hands off each other. It was like once he'd let it happen between them; the floodgates had broken, and the craving that they'd kept barely contained now overflowed any normal control and threatened to take over everything.

Maybe Jamie had been paying attention to the exhibits, but Neal had been paying attention to Jamie. He couldn't help it. He'd meant every word he'd said before; with Jamie, everything felt brand new—fresh and wonderful and unique. Like he was getting to fall in love for the first time all over again.

Because that's what this was, wasn't it? He was falling in love.

He'd never been sure that it could happen again, after the fallout with Michael had left him so bruised and battered and burned that he hadn't been certain he was even capable of it again. But trusting Jamie was so easy, it was like breathing.

"Do I need to butter you up for later?" Neal asked, even though he already knew the answer.

"No," Jamie said honestly. Bluntly. "I'm yours."

"And I'm *yours*," Neal said firmly, kissing him again.

They only reached the planetarium five minutes behind schedule.

Neal's lips were still tingling from their kisses, and every nerve ending felt raw and sensitive. He felt exposed; and it wasn't just the sudden realization he'd had about Jamie and just how much he cared about him.

It was being close, but not close enough.

But the auditorium would be dark. They wouldn't be alone, but they'd be alone enough.

"Welcome," Curt said, standing by the door. "I have the refreshments set up inside."

Jamie shot Neal a look. "Refreshments?"

Neal shrugged helplessly. "Is it a first date if there isn't champagne?"

Jamie rolled his eyes, but looked terribly pleased as Neal led them over to the small table covered in a black cloth. He popped the cork easily and then poured them each a glass of the chilled wine that he'd sent over earlier that day. It was one of his special stock, and even though Jamie might not realize it, it was one of the most expensive bottles he owned.

The wine was dry and just the perfect amount of sweet on his tongue as he sipped from his flute. "How is it?" Neal asked Jamie.

They hadn't discussed wine before; Jamie probably didn't even know about Neal's cellar or his extensive wine collection.

There were so many things they'd barely discussed. Was it too soon to think about falling so deeply and so hard for a man he was still getting to know? With Michael, Neal had taken his time. Or at least, that was what he'd told himself. Now, he wasn't sure he'd ever really been in love at all. Because what he'd experienced with Michael was a faint echo of what he was feeling now. They'd been compatible—both in bed and out of it. But with Jamie? Neal felt like he'd suddenly been plugged into an electrical socket and he was trying to control the flow of overwhelming feelings that kept cascading through him.

"I like it," Jamie said, taking a sip of his wine. "I like it a lot."

They took seats in the middle row, almost exactly in the middle of the auditorium. Neal nobly resisted the urge to suggest they sit even further back, so they could fool around.

The lights dropped and Curt began to narrate the story of the aurora borealis, using the interpretations of the Vikings. It was just as Neal had asked for—sweeping and romantic, the music swelling over them, the incredible visuals flashing in front of their eyes.

Halfway through the show, Jamie leaned over and brushed his lips over Neal's cheek. "This is perfect," he murmured. "Incredibly romantic."

"Just wait til after," Neal whispered back. "Trust me, it's gonna make this look like amateur hour."

It was dark, so it was difficult to make out Jamie's exact expression, but he was sure it was full of disbelief. This *had* been a great date so far, but Neal had one more trick up his sleeve.

After the show was over, Neal grabbed the bottle of champagne, and Curt led them through the museum again. Full dark had fallen, and he took them outside of the building, down the steps and onto the vast lawn that surrounded the observatory. Los Angeles, in all its sparkling splendor, was laid out like a carpet of lights underneath them.

"This is pretty damn romantic," Jamie crooned, reaching up so he could whisper the words almost directly right into Neal's ear. He shuddered as Jamie did almost exactly what Neal had done earlier, nipping him gently in the earlobe before shooting him a knowing smile.

"Just you wait," Neal promised.

Curt led them around the building, and there was a mobile telescope set up. He checked the settings, and then glanced through the viewfinder. "Yes," he said, nodding to Neal. "You're all set."

Jamie glanced at him in confusion. "What's all set?" he asked, as Curt waved and took off, leaving the two of them alone again.

"I wanted Curt to find a particular star," Neal said, setting the champagne bottle on the ground, next to his flute. "A special star."

"What's special about it?" Jamie asked, clearly amused.

"Well, why don't you take a look at it?" Neal said.

Jamie bent down and looked through the viewfinder. He was quiet for a few moments, then lifted his head back up. He still looked puzzled. "It's a beautiful star," he said, "bright and shining, but I don't see what's so special about it."

Neal reached for Jamie's hand and squeezed. "It's special because it's your star."

Eyes widening, Jamie let go and, bending down, looked through the telescope again. "That's . . . that's *my* star?" he asked incredulously.

"It's yours, it's even named for you," Neal said smugly. "I thought it was only right that you should have a star named for you, considering how bright you're gonna shine." *And because you told me I was the brightest star in the sky, and I know you meant it.*

Jamie stared at him, still disbelieving. "You bought a star for me?"

"Yeah, I did."

Was it too much? *Maybe.* Yes, it was only their first date, but Neal already knew that unless the unexpected circumstances surrounding their meeting derailed their relationship before it could even begin, this date wouldn't be even close to their last.

Jamie reached out and hugged him tightly. "You are too much," he whispered into Neal's shoulder. "Way too much, and I love it."

I love you, Neal thought, wonder spiking through him as the words settled into place, real and true and immovable. *Now what the hell are we gonna do about it?*

Chapter Fourteen

The next Riptide preseason game took the team to Green Bay, Wisconsin, to face Aaron Rodgers and the Packers.

On one hand, Jamie didn't think he could possibly be *more* nervous than he had for the last game, but even though the stakes had not really changed—if anything, they'd gone *up*, not down—he definitely felt less nerves surging through him as he got warmed up on the sideline.

One of the few benefits of flying to Wisconsin to play the Packers, always a dangerously good team, was the fact that while his friend Dylan hadn't managed to totally supplant Mason Crosby, the Packers' kicker, he'd done well enough to make it onto the Packers' practice squad. It wasn't quite the same as being officially on the team, but it was better than nothing.

"I see you emerged the winner out of all that crazy shit," Dylan said, as they clasped hands and hugged.

Jamie shrugged, tilting his head to point out Shane, on the other end of the sideline. "Not yet, but I'm close to making it," he said.

"I told you, he doesn't have game-time mentality," Dylan said, shoving his hands into his shorts. He wasn't dressed to play, because practice squad members didn't. But Jamie knew from the texts he'd exchanged that he hoped that if Crosby faltered at all, he might get a shot.

"Well, he isn't the one who missed a fucking extra point last week," Jamie grumbled.

"Yeah, he missed a field goal, *and* he didn't even have the excuse you did. That was a fucking horrible snap."

"It wasn't great," Jamie admitted.

"You shouldn't worry about it," Dylan said confidently. "I think you've got this. He's got this haunted look in his eyes. I saw it. He knows his days are numbered."

"Are you sure about that?" Jamie didn't think that was true at all. Shane had gotten cockier since the first preseason game.

"Trust me," Dylan said conspiratorially. "He's done, and he knows it."

Not for the first time, Jamie thought Dylan and Neal would get on like a house on fire. But whenever he considered telling Dylan that he was not only dating an ex-kicker but *Neal Fisher*, he stopped himself, because Dylan would *lose his mind*.

He could already imagine all of Dylan's concerns, and it wasn't like they were even *wrong*. The Riptide would hate it if they found out about him and Neal, and the chances of Jamie winning the contract after that would be slim.

But on the other hand, what kind of relationship was it if they had to keep it secret?

"Well, I guess we'll see," Jamie said. "Coach says I'm doing field goals today, so as long as I don't get hit with the unlucky number, I think I'll be okay."

"Oh, come on," Dylan said, thumping him across the shoulder. "You've probably kicked a forty-four-yard field goal so many times in the last month, you could do it in your sleep."

"Maybe," Jamie said. He still didn't want to have to *try*. Especially not after all the ridiculous emphasis the coaching staff had put on that particular distance.

"Make a fifty-plus-yarder for me, though, alright?" Dylan said, grinning. "And don't forget, I'll be watching."

"You got it," Jamie said. "Don't be a stranger."

"Should be sayin' that to you, future big shot," Dylan shot back with a wild grin on his face. "I'm not the one about to sign a long-term contract with one of the best teams in football."

· · • ● • ● ● • ·

Coach Toby had pulled him and Shane aside the day before they'd flown to Wisconsin, and had informed them that this time,

Shane would be kicking extra points, and Jamie would take all the field goals.

"What if we don't get into field goal range?" Jamie had complained to Neal that night over a dinner that he'd picked up on his way over to Neal's house. "Am I just supposed to sit, useless, on the bench?"

Jamie hadn't missed the smile that Neal had quickly tamped down. "It's gonna be fine," he'd said, "but if you want me to call up Sam and make sure he stalls out a few drives so you can get your kicks in, I can do that."

Jamie had whacked him on the shoulder, and they'd both shared a laugh about how Sam would react to such a request.

"I think Heath might be more offended than Sam," Neal had said with an amused chuckle. "Sam knows the preseason games don't really count, but Heath? He wants to win everything, no matter what."

"Some things don't change, I guess," Jamie had decided.

"And some things do," Neal promised.

It was still just as hard as Jamie had expected, to sit on the bench, on the far end, and watch as Sam drove the offense down the field and hit Chase Riley on a nice crossing pattern to score a touchdown. It was even harder to watch as Shane set up for the extra point attempt, and unlike the last game, when Jamie had been the one kicking, he nailed it right through the uprights.

It was the icing on the cake when Shane jogged back to the sideline and flashed Jamie a smug, egotistical grin, showing just how confident he was that he was ultimately going to win the contract.

Maybe he will, Jamie thought with resignation. *I can always get a job, there's surely plenty of jobs in LA. Maybe Neal wouldn't even mind it if I stayed with him awhile, while I was looking for one.*

But then, right as he was beginning to wonder what that kind of life might look like—he could imagine himself settling in to a new job, coming home to Olive's taco experiments, nights cuddling on the couch with Neal—he realized that Sam and the offense had just stalled out.

"Wright," Coach Toby barked in his direction. "You're up."

Jamie jerked his attention back to the job at hand—he wasn't ready to give up just yet, especially when Shane was so goddamn smug about it. There'd be nothing he'd like more than to wipe that smile off his face. *Permanently*, if that was possible.

And you can do it right now, Neal's voice echoed in his brain. *Get your head out of the clouds and focus on this kick, damnit.*

"Yes, sir," Jamie muttered under his breath as he and the rest of the field goal unit jogged out onto the field.

Quickly calculating the distance in his head, he realized that he was going to be dedicating this one to Dylan—it was fifty-one yards.

Surely, if he could make this, it would go a long way to proving how good he was, how much he deserved to be the last kicker standing.

Any idiot could make a bunch of extra-point kicks.

But Jamie was going to nail this fifty-one-yarder and make the coaching staff of the Riptide seriously consider what they were throwing away if they let him go.

He got set up, and this time, the snap was perfect, Ian got the ball down and flawlessly situated and Jamie knew as his foot connected that not only was this going to go in, it was going to go in with room to spare. And it *did*.

"Fuck yes!" Jamie said, pumping his fist, and this time it was *his* turn to shoot Shane a superior smile as he jogged back to the sideline.

When he returned, and after Coach Toby had given him a reassuring and approving pat on the back, Jamie glanced over and had to laugh, because Dylan was giving him two very exaggerated thumbs up and grinning wildly, like Jamie had already won the spot.

And Jamie thought, if he could see Neal, he'd be doing just about the same thing.

· · · • · • · • · • · ·

Altogether, Jamie made two field goals in the game—fifty-one yards, and another one, a little chip shot of about thirty-two yards. Both of them were dead straight, and as he packed up his bag in the locker room, he knew his confidence was back, and he wouldn't be going down without a huge fight.

"Great kicking today," Coach Toby had said after the game, giving him a brisk smack on the back. But then, Jamie had watched him go up to Shane, the coach's actions nearly identical. Because despite that he was only kicking extra points, Shane *had* kicked well too. He'd made three extra points, each ultimately uneventful.

Jamie had a feeling that the competition between them would come down to something small, something normally insignificant, and to win, he was going to have to be on his toes all the time.

"Hey, dude." Jamie glanced up as he walked out the locker room door to see Chase jogging after him. "Great kicking today. That fifty-one-yarder? That was a fucking *beaut*."

"Thanks," Jamie said. "It felt good."

"Well, it sure looked good," Chase said as they walked out of the stadium towards where the buses were idling in the parking lot, ready to take them to the airport and back to California.

Neal had agreed with Chase's assessment. "So pretty I almost cried," had been the exact wording of his text.

"Do you think that other kid could kick that?" Chase asked as they stowed their bags and then climbed onto the bus. Jamie kept half-expecting Chase to move on, to go sit someplace else, but he seemed determined to stick by him. Jamie didn't really know *why*—he was just Jamie Wright, and he didn't even have a deal yet.

By the season kickoff, he might be wondering what had happened to all his well-laid plans.

But Jamie didn't really think so. Not anymore. It seemed that Chase had decided the same thing.

"Well, yeah, we can *all* kick like that," Jamie pointed out as they sat down. Chase tucked a strand of slightly damp, dirty blond hair behind one ear, propping his knee up against the seat in front of them.

"It's doing it in a game, right?" Chase said. "Not many ideal factors in a game."

"As many as we can get our hands on," Jamie said with a grin.

"I always play better in games. But then, I fuckin' hate practice," Chase said wryly. "So I guess that makes sense."

"You hate practice?"

Chase shrugged. "Drills, man, they don't teach you *jack shit*. Anyone can catch a ball thrown to you in the ideal circumstances. That's what you're supposed to do, right? It's like you guys—you wouldn't have made it this far if you didn't have that shit *down*. But to do it in a game? When the situation isn't ever ideal, and three defenders are about to clock your ass into next year? That's a skill. And you can't teach that."

Jamie had watched Chase make plenty of incredible catches over the years. It was kind of his signature.

"You're telling me you don't practice those catches? The ones with one hand and falling down and backwards and . . .?"

"I mean I *do*, because Coach wouldn't let me get away with not practicing. But it's pointless."

"It's not for me," Jamie said.

"I wondered." Chase sounded like he was actually genuinely curious, and that curiosity added another interesting layer to the guy, a complexity that Jamie hadn't realized he possessed.

He hadn't ever ascribed to the belief that all football players were big dumb brutes, but then he'd watched lots of Chase's interviews too, over the years, and Jamie had a feeling that he'd been deliberately dumbing himself down in the public eye. For what purpose? Jamie didn't know. He'd have to remember to ask Neal what he thought.

"I caught Neal's interview from Sunday Morning Football," Chase said casually, and Jamie had to wonder if this was the real reason that they'd ended up sitting next to each other as the bus filled with players.

"Did you?" Jamie said hesitatingly. He knew Chase had promised not to tell anyone—and it wasn't like he had much evidence to back up his theory—but the fact that he knew made Jamie nervous. Maybe he should've told Neal about his conversation with Chase, but the right time hadn't come up yet. They were both so busy—and when they weren't focused on work, they were focused on each other.

Chase nudged him with his shoulder. "It's all cool, man," he said, lowering his voice. "I told you, your secret's safe with me."

Jamie nodded. Hoping he was right. Desperately afraid that he was wrong.

"He sounded good," Chase continued. "At peace and all that shit."

"Yeah," Jamie agreed. He'd watched the interview way too many times to admit to, even to Neal. He *had* sounded good. *At peace and shit*, Jamie thought with an inward chuckle.

"We all tried, you know?" Chase said. Jamie realized that not only would it have been Heath and Sam and Bran Phillips trying, but Chase had been part of that group too, and he'd tried his hardest to get Neal to stop blaming himself for what had happened. And it not only made Jamie like Chase even more, but it made him really wonder what it was that made this guy tick. The persona he presented to the public definitely wasn't all he had going on.

"He wasn't ready to hear it," Jamie said.

"Maybe," Chase said with an irrepressible grin, "I just wasn't cute enough."

Jamie rolled his eyes. "Yeah, I think that was it. Neal didn't secretly want in your pants, so he didn't listen to you."

"Hey, you know, maybe he was just waiting for you," Chase said. And with that final parting shot, the bus pulled up to the airport.

Jamie opened his mouth to protest—Neal hadn't been waiting for *him*, he'd been waiting for . . . *time*, Jamie would guess; because that was what always healed, right? Time?—but Chase was already halfway off the bus, throwing an arm around Sam's shoulders as they walked off.

"He wasn't waiting for me," Jamie said under his breath as he gathered his bag and walked towards the plane. "He was waiting for *himself.*"

But even he wasn't quite convinced as he boarded the plane. Maybe that was because deep down, that was what he desperately wanted to believe. Jamie knew that Neal had begun the healing process himself, but the idea that Jamie was the one who had made him *want* to? It filled his heart with an impossible joy.

He sat down in an empty row, still unused to the luxurious and cushy leather seats with their turquoise trim. He pulled out his phone and texted Neal. **Headed home on the plane now,** he texted. He wasn't exactly expecting that Neal would invite him over—it was late and it would be even later by the time they landed, but there was a part of him that wanted Neal to ask anyway. That also seemed to be the same part that was convinced, despite the fact that they didn't know each other all that well yet, that he was in love.

Neal's reply came back when they had already taken off and were smoothly flying through the night sky. **It's gonna be late,** he said, **but I want to ask you to come over anyway. Even if I'm dead on my feet. Which I am. I don't know how Terry and Jimmy do it at their age. I'm exhausted and I'm not even forty.**

Yet, Jamie texted back. He'd already resigned himself to seeing Neal tomorrow. He'd promised him brunch. **But it's really not that far away. Better prepare yourself.**

You're such a brat, Neal texted back. **But I'll see you tomorrow. For brunch?**

I'll be there, Jamie said, and forced himself to put his phone away. He could text Neal all night long, despite that Neal didn't really enjoy texting, but he was clearly worn out and needed to get some sleep.

The plane had quieted after taking off, with so many players and coaches sleeping after a long day. There was Wi-Fi on Riptide flights, among various other luxuries, so Jamie booted his laptop up and was just about to pull his headphones out so he could watch the highlights of Neal's first Sunday Morning Football appearance when Sam unexpectedly stopped right at his row. "Hey," he said, sliding into the empty seat next to Jamie, "how's it going? That was a *great* kick today."

Jamie didn't roll his eyes, even though he kinda wanted to. He'd made one great field goal today—even he wouldn't deny it—but Sam had made perfect throw after perfect throw, throwing two touchdowns and looking poised and confident.

"Thanks," Jamie said. "You played great, too."

"Yes, well," Sam said, rolling *his* eyes, "Heath is *very* proud."

"I'm sorry," Jamie said, "was it Heath out there and I somehow missed it?"

Sam threw his head back and laughed. "I like you," he said. "You get it."

"Thanks?"

"Seriously, you do. I had to get up and take a break because Heath is Heath and sometimes he's insufferable. I love him anyway, but *ugh*, insufferable."

"What did he do?" Jamie wondered.

"Oh, he just always thinks he knows best. And maybe," Sam said, shooting him a lopsided smile, "maybe he does, but it's still annoying."

"I bet it is," Jamie acknowledged. He didn't think Neal would do that, but then he was still getting to know Neal. Though, even he could admit that Heath Harris was pretty intense. Calmer now that he'd retired and gone into coaching, but still intense.

"I love him, but sometimes I just need a break," Sam said. "Hey, he mentioned that Olive said you'd been over to Neal's house a few times." His smile grew unexpectedly sly. "*And* she mentioned that there might've been a big date last week."

Jamie blushed. "Maybe," he said.

"Well, we're rooting for you," Sam said. "For Neal too. But you, too. Just so you know."

"Thanks. I'm rooting for me, too," Jamie said dryly. *More than you realize.*

"You should come over Thursday night," Sam said. "We're having another pool party, and we'd love to have you *and* Neal come."

"So you can gossip about us some more?" Jamie wondered.

"Exactly," Sam said with a knowing grin as he slid out of his seat and paused in the aisle. "See? You've already figured this league out. We love to play football, but we *live* to gossip."

"I'll keep that in mind," Jamie said. And couldn't help but wonder, as Sam wandered away, towards the front of the plane, if it was a mistake that already so many Riptide players knew the truth.

It wasn't that he didn't trust Chase or Sam, he *did*, but he knew how strongly Neal felt about keeping their relationship under wraps. So instead of watching Neal on his laptop, in the middle of a crowded plane of Riptide players and staff, he decided maybe it was better if he read.

He put his laptop away, pulled out his phone again, and opened his reading app, letting himself get lost in the latest mystery novel he was reading.

An hour later, they were still about halfway home, and Jamie paused, stretching, and decided to hit the bathroom while he found another water bottle, since he'd polished his off and good hydration was important.

When he stood up, he stretched again, and then turning to make his way to the front of the plane where the bathroom was, something caught his eye. A dark blur that made him tilt his head back to get a better look.

And that was the moment he realized that sitting directly behind him, with only a cushy seat in between them, was Shane.

Panic streaked through him. He and Sam hadn't exactly been keeping their voices down, and with only the seat between them, the chance of Shane overhearing at least *some* of their conversation was high. Why hadn't he been smarter and cut Sam off? Told him they'd talk about it later?

Because you wanted to talk about it, he realized uncomfortably. *You wanted to be able to talk about it with* someone *and Sam already knew, and you're like a sappy, crushing teenager who can barely control himself. You think about Neal all the time; you want to talk about him all the damn time, too.*

Maybe, Jamie rationalized, maybe Shane hadn't been paying attention. Maybe he was sleeping. Maybe he had headphones in.

Maybe he was safe after all.

Jamie took half a step back, and that was all he'd needed to get Shane's attention. Who wasn't wearing headphones. Who wasn't sleeping. Who was now staring right at Jamie, and this time his smile wasn't only unbearably smug, there was an undeniable knowing edge to it. And then, the final icing on the cake. Shane put a finger to his lips and then shook his head slightly, an ugly gleam in his dark eyes.

He knew.

He knew, and the first thing he was going to do when he got off this plane was tell everyone who would listen to him.

Sure, he didn't have *proof,* but he'd heard enough, and if push came to shove, and Coach R called Sam into his office, would Sam lie for him? Did Jamie even want him to?

He wasn't sure. Without saying another word, Jamie hurriedly walked to the bathroom, shut the door behind him, and tried to calm his suddenly racing heart.

There were other Neals in the world, of course. Other Neals that Jamie could be dating. As he thought through the conversation he and Sam had had, he knew that neither of them had mentioned Neal's last name. There was plausible deniability there.

But would the coaching staff even want to have the conversation? Would they even bother? Or would they just take the rumor and couple it with the stupid idea Jamie had had to wear Neal's old jersey number and come to the correct conclusion?

Jamie couldn't imagine that Shane *wouldn't* tell anyone what he'd just overheard. Surely he realized that this was a surefire way to essentially eliminate Jamie from the competition. From what Jamie knew of Shane, it wasn't like he was exactly the kind of scrupulous guy who wouldn't want to win that way. He'd do anything to best Jamie, he felt that truth in his *bones*.

Staring at his reflection, hair mussed and eyes wild, in the mirror, Jamie knew he was going to have to do something. What, he wasn't entirely sure.

He could tell Neal. He *should* tell Neal.

Maybe Neal would have some advice on what Jamie should do.

But every time Jamie thought about what he would say or how he would say it, all he felt was completely fucking stupid. It had been dumb in the extreme to blab about his growing relationship with Neal to another Riptide player *on the Riptide plane, sur-*

rounded by Riptide players. Jamie could imagine Neal looking at him with disbelief, and saying some form of, *what did you think was going to happen?*

Jamie knew that Heath and Sam had kept *their* relationship under wraps for almost an entire season. What did it say about Jamie that he hadn't even managed to make it through the *preseason*?

Nothing good, Jamie decided firmly. It said nothing good, and he couldn't tell Neal. Not until he'd figured out how to fix this, first.

Maybe he could catch Shane before they reached the Riptide facilities. Before he could decide exactly what he was going to do with the information and before he could actually *do* it.

"You're good, you're awesome, you can *do* this," he said, giving himself a little pep talk. "You can convince him he heard wrong. That he misheard you, even."

But Jamie didn't *feel* all that sure that he could. Still, what else could he do?

You could always tell them first, an unhelpful voice that sounded unpleasantly like his father pointed out. *If you told the Riptide first, you could control the circumstances and the delivery and maybe even the consequences.*

Jamie shook off the idea, and after doing the business he'd came in there for, walked back to his seat, feeling like he'd made the right call.

First, he would try to convince Shane that what he'd heard wasn't what he *thought* he'd heard.

If that didn't work, then he would try something else.

• • • • ●•● • ● • • •

Jamie couldn't get back into his book. He was too nervous, too agitated. Too busy running through the conversation he'd had with Sam, looking for anything he could use to prove to Shane that he'd heard wrong. And then, he spent way too much time obsessing over what exactly he would say. Should he pretend ignorance? Should he try to work his way up to the topic? Or should he just assume that they both knew what Shane had assumed?

In the end, it was painfully simple.

It was Shane who made the first move; beckoning to Jamie to sit next to him on the bus when they finally disembarked from the plane.

"Hey," Jamie said uneasily. He'd been confident. He'd told himself he needed to be confident, but now, faced with Shane's knowing face, he didn't *feel* particularly confident.

"You're an idiot," Shane said bluntly.

Jamie wasn't exactly going to disagree with that assessment, not right now anyway. But he shook his head, because the whole idea was to convince Shane he was wrong. "What are you talking about?" he said, playing ignorant.

"You're fooling around with Neal Fisher," Shane said bluntly.

"What?" Jamie said, hoping his false shock was convincing enough. "I don't know what you're talking about."

"Yes you do," Shane said steadily. "I heard you talking to Crawford about it."

"Oh, yeah," Jamie said. "I *am* dating someone named Neal, but trust me, it's not Neal Fisher."

"Okay, so it's not Neal Fisher. But it's someone named Neal that Sam Crawford and his boyfriend know. Someone he'd want to invite to his house."

"It's not Neal Fisher," Jamie said weakly, and knew just how unconvincing he sounded.

"Sure it's not," Shane said dryly. "Like I said, you're a fucking idiot."

"I . . ."

"Don't even bother," Shane said with a sneer. "Just . . . don't bother."

"Alright," Jamie said, anxiety blooming in the pit of his stomach. Maybe he wouldn't say anything. Maybe he'd keep quiet because what he knew was just a rumor. But rumors could do just as much damage as facts, and Jamie was terrified that Shane would use this like the weapon it was.

How was he going to tell Neal?

You're not going to, that voice said firmly, again. *You're going to fix this, and you're going to do it by getting ahead of it.*

Growing up, Jamie had discovered that his dad was right about almost everything. Usually the only thing he was dead wrong about was football. But in this case, Jamie was afraid that he wasn't. At all.

Should he do it right now? Try to catch Coach Toby as the bus pulled into the facility? Before he went to his car?

No, he should wait. Wait at least a day or two.

Maybe until they came back to the facility for Tuesday morning practice.

"But then," Shane said unexpectedly, "Coach Toby is an idiot, too."

Jamie cracked a smile, even though he wasn't feeling it. "Yeah," he agreed. Wondering if this was Shane's olive branch. Maybe he wouldn't tell after all. Maybe Jamie had been wrong, and he wasn't the bad guy.

But the thought lingered anyway.

• • • **•** • **•** • • •

When Jamie was in the car headed back to his hotel for a much-needed night's sleep, he called Dylan. It was late in LA, and probably even later in Wisconsin, but Dylan picked up right away. He'd always been a night owl, and it seemed nothing had changed.

"Jamie?"

"Is Shane a bad guy?" Jamie demanded before Dylan could ask why he was calling so late.

"I don't know, is he?" Dylan sounded bewildered. "He's kind of a jerk, but he's also a football player."

"Would you trust him?"

"With what? You're not making any fucking sense here. You call me up at three a.m., wondering if some random kicker you're not even friends with, is a bad guy. You're gonna have to give me some context here, man."

Jamie tapped his fingers against the steering wheel. He didn't really *want* to give any context, but maybe it was unavoidable. He'd been wanting to tell Dylan anyway, about him and Neal, and maybe doing it was the only way to figure out what he should do.

You know what you need to do, that voice reminded him, but Jamie pushed it away.

"You know that party I went to at Heath and Sam's house?" Jamie asked.

"Yeah, what about it?"

"I met Neal Fisher there." As soon as the words were out of Jamie's mouth, he was glad—and relieved—that he'd said them. He'd had to tell someone, someone he could really talk to about it, and Dylan not only felt like the right choice, he was probably the only choice.

"You met Neal Fisher," Dylan said incredulously. "Why didn't you tell me?"

Jamie opened his mouth to explain, but Dylan kept talking. "Wait, don't tell me," he said. "Is it because it was Neal Fisher and he was the evil villain and he might ruin you, or because he's hot and you *want* him to ruin you?"

Jamie couldn't help it. He laughed. "Uh, both?"

"So did he?" Dylan's question was casual, but pointed.

"Ruin me?" Jamie took a deep breath. "Jury's still out on that one."

"But you're hooking up, right? You wouldn't be telling me this story if you weren't."

"We are. We're . . ." Jamie hesitated. They were more than hooking up. It was serious. Definitely serious. "We're dating, actually." *I think I love him.*

"Wooooo, get it, Wright," Dylan hooted into the phone, his voice echoing around the compact car's interior. "I know I say this a lot, but I'm proud of you."

"For dating Neal Fisher?"

"For saying *fuck it* to the world," Dylan corrected.

"Well, about that . . ." Jamie hesitated. "It goes without saying that it's a secret. Or it *was* a secret."

"Shane found out, didn't he?" Dylan said. He was sharp. One of the many reasons Jamie had liked him from the moment they met.

"He did," Jamie admitted. Hoped Dylan wouldn't demand to know *how* Shane had found out.

"Well, I guess the best thing you can do is hope that he doesn't want to be a dick. As to whether I'd trust him . . ."

"Would you?"

"The jury's still out." Jamie could hear Dylan's shrug over the phone. "He's not good enough to win the job, not really, but would he use what he knows to get you into trouble? Maybe? It's hard to say. What's your take on it?"

"At first, I thought he wouldn't even wait til we were off the plane. But then? Then I wasn't so sure."

"I'm assuming I'm your second call," Dylan said. "And Neal was your first. What does he think?"

Jamie bit his lip. "I haven't told him yet. I don't . . . I don't know if I can."

There was silence on the line as Jamie pulled into the hotel parking lot.

"You haven't told him yet?" Dylan finally exclaimed.

"It's my fault. I feel embarrassed. I feel humiliated. All I had to do was keep my mouth *shut*, and not brag about it like some lovesick teenager, but I couldn't even do that."

"If you're dating," Dylan pointed out, "it's highly likely that he is *also* behaving like a lovesick teenager, and it doesn't matter. He's not going to blame you for what happened. Shit happens, you know that."

"He's not. He's calm and collected and romantic and a fucking *grownup*," Jamie grumbled. "And the last thing I want to do is go running to him so he can fix all my problems."

"Ah," Dylan said.

"What does that mean?" Jamie wondered.

"It means you're letting the age difference fuck you up," Dylan said.

"How do you know there's an age difference?"

"You can't see it, but I'm rolling my eyes at you. There's definitely an age difference. He was in the league for thirteen years. You probably had your sexual awakening to him or something. Anyway, I also just looked it up. It's fourteen years. That's not like . . . cradle robbing or anything."

"It's not," Jamie insisted.

"But what I'm saying is that you guys, no matter the age difference, you've got to figure out how to be partners. Real partners. If you want to have a chance in hell of lasting."

"You want me to tell him."

"Of course I want you to tell him." Dylan sounded exasperated. "You *should* tell him."

"I'll think about it," Jamie said. He would, that was the truth, but he already knew he wasn't ready to tell Neal yet. Not until he tried to fix it himself.

"You're a stubborn asshole," Dylan muttered.

"Yes, well, you love me just the way I am."

"And so does Neal Fisher," Dylan retorted. "But God forbid you actually believe that."

CHAPTER FIFTEEN

FOR THE LAST FEW days, Jamie had been incredibly tense and Neal couldn't figure out why. Was it the upcoming third preseason game? Neal didn't think so. But he'd been tense ever since he'd gotten back from Green Bay. It didn't make much sense to Neal, because based on performance alone, he was fairly certain that Jamie had a serious edge over Shane. That gorgeous fifty-one-yard field goal had been the nail in Shane's coffin. Jamie just had to keep it up for another two games, and Neal knew the job would be his.

So why was he so edgy? Quiet and withdrawn and even short-tempered at points?

Neal had tried asking a few times during the week. "Is it Shane?" he'd tried first, on Monday morning when Jamie had come over for brunch and had looked like he'd barely slept, dark circles under his eyes. But Jamie had brushed him off. "No, of course not. I'm not worried about that guy," he'd claimed.

"What about your parents coming?" Neal had asked on Tuesday night when they'd been cuddling in front of the TV, despite the impression that Jamie was barely watching. Jamie had arranged for Dave and Lila, his parents, to come down to LA for the next preseason game, and had even suggested that Neal join them for a late dinner after the game. He'd been thrilled at the suggestion, because that showed that Jamie was just as serious as Neal was about this relationship, but then, Neal realized, how serious could it be if Jamie wouldn't confide in him?

It was Thursday now, and despite asking several times—both subtly and directly—Neal still hadn't figured out what was wrong.

The thing that helped, that prevented Neal from going out of his mind and out of his skin with worry, was that he *knew* it had nothing to do with him. Jamie's smile felt like it grew brighter and wider every single time he saw Neal, and he could almost always pull him out of his funk, by relaying a funny story about Terry's latest antics or by kissing him until neither of them could breathe properly.

Still, it bothered Neal, because he cared about Jamie—*you love him*, that annoying voice reminded him, *you don't just care, you're no-holds-barred, fling-yourself-off-a-cliff in love*—and the last thing he wanted was for him to be upset or stressed about something. Especially something that he wouldn't tell Neal about.

"Are you sure you're okay?" Neal asked, as he parked across from Heath and Sam's house. "You've just been so quiet lately. I know this is a big moment for you, and I don't want to trivialize it . . ."

"I'm fine," Jamie said before he could even finish. "I'm really fine. Sorry, I guess I have been a little stressed about the upcoming games. The last month has felt like a roller coaster, and it's not over yet. Not by a long shot."

Neal wanted to believe that was all it was, because this *had* been a roller coaster, and Jamie was also right because it *wasn't* over yet. But there was something else, he *knew* it. He just didn't know how to convince Jamie that he was worthy of being his confidant.

When he'd frustratingly wondered out loud how he could get Jamie to trust him the other night, Olive had looked at him with galling sympathy. "He does trust you," she said. "Do you think he'd be doing any of this if he didn't? This a big fucking risk for him."

"I know," Neal had said miserably. "I'm way too aware of that."

"You've got to give him time," Olive said, sounding much wiser than her nineteen years. "He'll come around. What are you in such a hurry for anyway? You're still getting to know each other."

Neal supposed he should be glad that Olive had yet to figure out he'd fallen irrevocably and completely in love with the last guy on earth that he should've developed feelings for. God knew, she wouldn't pull her punches if she knew. She might even pull out the big guns and call her mother, who would undoubtedly fly to LA and try to talk some sense into her baby brother.

The last thing Neal wanted was to try to explain to Ella that he'd let himself get so carried away that the consequences of this relationship had paled compared to the pain of pushing Jamie away.

But now, Jamie glanced at him, like he was worried about *Neal*. "You've asked me that question half a dozen times in the last week," he said as they got out of the car. Jamie grabbed the six-pack of beer they'd picked up at the store on their way here, and they made their way up to Heath and Sam's house.

Neal glanced over at the spot where he'd been hiding the first night they'd ever met.

"I know," he finally admitted. Jamie turned to him and didn't knock this time. "I know I've asked you a bunch of times. It's only 'cause I'm worried about you."

"Why?" Jamie asked, even though he *had* to know. He was the only one who knew at this point.

Neal shoved his hands in the pockets of his swim trunks and knew it was not the right time to confess his already-serious feelings. But he wanted to.

"I care about you. You're stressed. This is a crazy time." It was everything Neal could say that wasn't *I'm in love with you, that's why*.

Jamie's smile was soft and sweet, and a few of the shadows hiding in his dark eyes fled into the dusky night. "I care about you too," he said quietly, reaching up to cup Neal's cheek with his palm. If Jamie slid his hand further, he'd be able to hear Neal's heart pounding away in his chest.

There was a part of him that still wanted to rip his shirt off, to tear open his chest, to expose his wildly beating heart to Jamie's eyes. To *show* him, instead of just tell him. But he didn't, because even though Neal hadn't been unable to prevent himself from tumbling head over heels, he still wondered if it was too soon.

You don't want to scare him away. He's a rookie. A kid, practically. He has his whole life spread out before him, a hundred wondrous possibilities. A thousand. Why would he want to waste it on some washed-up ex-kicker who still isn't sure what he wants to do with his life?

That voice wasn't totally right—*I do think I know what I'm doing with my life,* Neal thought rebelliously—but it was right enough that it held him back, even still.

"Should we go in?" Neal asked, finally, the silence stretching out between them until he wasn't sure he could resist anymore. Was it undeniable affection in Jamie's expression? Reflected in his dark eyes? The enticing, intoxicating scent of the bougainvillea surrounding them? The fact that they were standing in the exact same spot they'd met in nearly a month before? Neal wasn't sure, but the moment felt dangerous.

Jamie reached up and brushed a kiss on Neal's mouth before pulling away. "Yeah," he said. "We should."

Not that he *wanted* to, but that they *should.*

Neal understood that a little too well.

This time, after Jamie knocked, it was Heath himself who answered the door.

"Slumming it these days?" Neal asked, raising an eyebrow as Jamie handed the bigger man the six-pack of beer.

"Not hiding in the bushes these days?" Heath retorted as they followed him through the foyer and into the kitchen.

"That's unfair. True, but unfair," Neal countered.

Heath flashed him a smile. "Never promised to play fair."

"He really never has," Sam said, coming up to them with a bright welcoming smile on his face. "Glad you guys could make it."

"I am too," Neal said and discovered that he meant it. Glancing around Sam, he noticed that it was a much smaller group than usual. He didn't see Felicity or Sam's parents anywhere. Bran and his wife were lounging by the pool, their little girl, Sara, nowhere to be found. Chase was sitting on the other side of the pool, chatting with Rashad. There were no madcap games of Marco Polo happening, and the grill was quiet.

"Less people here tonight," Jamie pointed out.

"I just thought we could chill out and relax," Heath said with a shrug. "Believe it or not, sometimes it's nice to not have a hundred people in our backyard."

"What he means to say," Sam said, slinging an arm around his boyfriend, "is that this season is stressing my guy out, and he just wanted a chill evening."

"I can't argue with that," Jamie said wryly.

"Yeah, if anyone needs it, it's probably you," Sam agreed. "How're you feeling? I really meant it—that field goal last game was a *beaut*."

"It was," Heath agreed, popping open a couple of beers and, after sticking them in foam coozies, handed them to Jamie and Neal. Neal glanced down and almost laughed out loud when he read what was written on his bright purple one.

"Mr. Always Right?" Jamie said, raising an eyebrow, and then looked over at Neal's. "And Mr. *Thinks* He's Always Right?"

Heath flushed bright red. "They were a gift from Felicity."

"An *appropriate* gift from Felicity," Sam teased.

"I won't even ask who's always and who thinks he's always right," Neal said dryly, "because I'm afraid I already know the truth."

Sam shrugged. "I think it's pretty obvious," he said with a bright grin.

Heath elbowed him in the side. "I don't *always* think I'm right."

"That last drive on Sunday?" Sam asked pointedly. "I was right, and you were wrong."

"Maybe that one time," Heath acknowledged begrudgingly. "But usually when you run around like that, with the ball like a fucking loaf of bread under your arm, you're going to lose it, and then that's a turnover the team can't afford."

"Yeah, yeah, sure, Coach," Sam teased. "Why don't you drill me in fumble drills next week, and you'll see how unlikely that is."

Jamie leaned in towards Neal. "Why do I feel like everything they say is a double entendre?"

Neal chuckled. "Probably because it is." He held up a hand to Jamie's ears and shot Sam a faux-reprimanding look. "You're scorching his ears, guys. He doesn't want to hear what you get up to, and frankly neither do I."

"Really?" Sam said with wide, disbelieving eyes. "I thought everyone wanted to watch us have sex."

Heath grabbed Sam's arm and steered him towards the kitchen, leaving Jamie and Neal to head out towards the pool.

They stopped by Bran and Frankie, and Jamie got caught up in a discussion of the offensive line with Bran. Neal considered going and looking for Heath, wondering if he should ask him if he'd seen anything particularly weird this week at practice. Anything that might explain why Jamie had been so anxious. But then Chase raised his hand, waving Neal over, so he went to pay his respects to one of the best wide receivers in the league, and also someone that he'd count as a good friend.

"Hey," Chase said, gesturing with his beer. "Take a load off, old man."

"I'm not old," Neal retorted.

"Not these days," Chase said with a wild grin. "Not from what I hear."

It was not exactly a state secret to this small group of friends that he and Jamie were involved—after all, most of the people here tonight had been here for their first meeting, and they *had* arrived together tonight. But still, Neal froze. Was this the problem? Had someone found out about him and Jamie that was on the team? Were they threatening to tell the coaching staff about what they would undoubtedly consider an "inappropriate relationship"?

"Who told you?" Neal said, his tone suddenly growing super intense, no matter how he tried to downplay it.

"Did someone have to?" Chase said, still relaxed despite Neal's demanding question. "It's kinda obvious, Fisher."

"Yeah, well, it needs to be *not* obvious. You know that, and you know why."

"Hey," Chase said, raising his hands in mock surrender. "Tell your guy that. He asked for your number and then, after he gave it up, doodled it like a love letter on the toe of his cleat."

Neal glanced over at where Jamie was talking animatedly with Bran. The rest of the shadows that had clung to him for days had seemingly dissipated, but Neal knew, from experience, that at some point, they would return. It was inevitable, and Neal was convinced it would keep happening until Jamie confided in him and they figured out a way to fix his problem *together*.

Even if it was technically unfixable, Neal was still going to try.

"He did that?" Neal hadn't known about the number Jamie had written on his cleat. He was both terrified and frankly, totally thrilled that Jamie would do that. For *him*.

"Yeah. You know, he talks a pretty good game about how much he respects you, about how much he looked up to you his whole kicking career, but it's still obvious, you know? Especially if you're looking for it. He's got a shit poker face."

"It's hard. I don't know what to do about it," Neal said. "He just needs this contract, and then maybe in a little while, if he proves himself, maybe it won't matter who he dates."

"You could fix things," Chase said, surprising the hell out of Neal.

"Me?" Neal couldn't believe it. He was the one who'd been fired after thirteen *good* years. He was the one who Michael had been a complete disloyal dick to.

"Johnny Lyon doesn't hate you, Neal," Chase said, referring to the Riptide's owner. "Even Coach R has *mostly* moved on. But you're still stuck there, and so is Michael. You know how tight he and Toby are. He's fucking up this team with his resentment."

"Believe me, there's nothing I can do to change Michael's opinion of me," Neal said testily. "Except maybe invent time travel and go back to the last Super Bowl and not miss that kick."

"Deflected. It was deflected. You know that." Chase nudged his knee with his own. "I'm not saying it's your fault. Or that you should apologize. But if you want a future for you and your boy over there, it might not be a bad move to at least move on. Publicly."

"Do you really think that would work?" Neal didn't trust any of the Riptide. He definitely didn't trust Michael. He wasn't sure how any of them would react.

Chase shrugged. "You care about him, don't you? It's worth a try."

"He's been tense lately. Worried about something." Neal took a deep breath. "Do you think Michael found out and is making things hard on him?"

"This would be hard on him, period," Chase pointed out. "But no, I don't think anyone knows. They're all still too busy over-thinking this whole kicker thing. They're looking but not really seeing."

"You noticed," Neal pointed out.

Chase laughed. "Yeah, except I actually *look*."

Neal knew that many people thought Chase Riley was a big dumb player who was really good at catching footballs and faster on his feet than his huge frame should've allowed. But Neal knew that Chase Riley was a smart, intelligent, *observant* guy.

Maybe nobody knew yet, but at some point, the Riptide would settle on a kicker, and they'd stop obsessing and start watching. And suddenly, just like his brand-new boyfriend, Neal felt his anxiety spike.

Maybe Chase was right, and there wasn't one thing in particular that was bothering Jamie. Maybe it was just this whole fucked-up situation.

. . . .

"I want to toast to our amazing son," Jamie's dad said, raising his glass and watching as the rest of the table did too. Jamie glanced over at Neal, who was grinning, and just as enamored with his dad as he knew he'd be. "Because he kicked ass today."

"Ugh," Jamie groaned as they all clinked glasses. "That's horrible. How long have you been waiting to use that?"

Dave smiled. "A few years now. I knew we'd be here and I knew this would be the right time, *but* I didn't know we'd be lucky enough to share it with another kicker."

"Ex-kicker," Neal said gently, but looked incredibly pleased nonetheless.

"Oh, honey," Lila said, sweetly patting him on the arm. "Once a kicker, always a kicker, right? You know we don't blame you at all for what happened. That ball was tipped."

Neal's smile was rueful. "So everyone keeps wanting to tell me."

"You know, I'm not much of a football fan, or at least I *wasn't*, before Jamie decided that was what he wanted to do with his life, and I know enough now to say, unequivocally, that ball was tipped," Lila said.

Jamie knew how much Neal hated talking about last year's Super Bowl. He'd watched him flinch and avoid the topic at least half a dozen times now. But he was nodding along with his mother, interested and absorbed in what she had to say on the topic.

And that, more than anything, should have put his worries and his concerns to rest, but how could it? Was he supposed to feel better he'd finally met a great guy—the *right* guy—and he not only was hot and funny and sweet but that he got along great with his parents, and that somehow, his arch rival had the ammunition to destroy everything?

So far Shane hadn't said a word, but Jamie wondered how long he could keep silent. Especially when today, in the third preseason game, Coach Toby had again had Jamie kicking field goals, and even two of the extra points, Shane relegated to cleaning up in the fourth quarter, when the score was high enough that it hadn't mattered if he'd made those kicks or not.

Jamie knew he was the front-runner now. Felt it in his bones. The only thing that might dislodge his grip on the position was the knowledge that Shane was holding in his back pocket. Would he keep the secret? Or would he expose Jamie at the very worst moment, at the moment when Shane's chances finally evaporated completely?

Jamie didn't know what he'd do—he couldn't exactly *ask* him—and he knew for the last week he'd been tense and anxious about the worst-case scenario coming true. Neal had sensed it, and had kept asking what was wrong, but Jamie still didn't know how to tell him how stupid he'd been. How absolutely fucking cocky he'd been, to assume that he could get away with having everything.

Maybe he *should* have told Neal, but if he did, what could Neal even do? It wasn't like Jamie could even figure out what he could do to save himself.

So he'd done the only thing he could—keep quiet and keep his head down and keep making all his kicks. Become so indispensable that even if Shane told, even if the Riptide found out the truth, they'd still award Jamie the contract.

For a moment he'd considered trying to pull his dad away at some point during the short time his parents were here, and confessing the truth and asking his advice, but Jamie already knew what it would be. *Tell them before Shane can,* he'd say. *Get ahead of it.*

But doing that, when Jamie wasn't sure if Shane *would* tell, would mean taking an enormous risk. What if it didn't matter how he'd kicked today or in the other preseason games? What if the Riptide didn't give a shit and cut him anyway?

Maybe it was selfish, but getting a taste made Jamie really, desperately want to have it all.

"Tell us what you're doing now," Lila said encouragingly. "Jamie mentioned something about television?"

Neal smiled proudly, and squeezed Jamie's hand, which he was holding under the tablecloth. This was a fancier restaurant than Jamie had envisioned when he'd suggested they take his parents out to dinner after the game, but Neal had insisted, saying that this particular restaurant was discreet and had a back room where they could dine in peace. *Without anyone finding out,* was the unspoken conclusion to Neal's insistence that he take care of the reservation and the details. And Jamie had let him, because *more* people didn't need to discover their secret. Not until they were ready for it to happen.

"I'm joining a panel on ESPN that usually airs before the Sunday morning games," Neal said. "It's called Sunday Morning Football."

His dad looked like Neal had just hit him over the head with a large hammer in one of the cartoons he'd loved to watch as a kid. "You're going to be on Sunday Morning Football?" he said with wonder. Considering his dad was originally from England, and had originally considered "football" to be a completely different (and superior) sport, Jamie was proud of how much he'd learned about American football and how enthusiastically he'd taken to it, when Jamie had first started playing. Now he thought his dad might be more of a fan than Jamie himself.

"You're sitting with Terry Bradshaw? And Jimmy? And Jerry?" Lila looked impressed.

"I'm surprised you're familiar with it," Neal said modestly.

"It's *way* better than the crap they have on FOX," his dad said. "Those guys don't know what they're saying."

Neal laughed. "Well, in their defense, we don't really know what we're saying either."

Jamie thought of some of the outtakes that Neal had recorded on his phone as they'd practiced together and knew that was a fairly accurate statement. Maybe it was nonsense, but it was entertaining nonsense, and Neal had not only fit right in, but with a new purpose, Jamie could see him coming back to life. Every day he smiled more, and laughed more, and teased Olive—and now Jamie—more.

It's not just the show; it's you, too, he wanted to believe, *he's falling in love with you and it's making him happy.*

And if Jamie believed that, then how could he let Shane ruin everything?

His mom reached over and patted him on the shoulder. "You're looking so pensive," she said, and he could hear the concern in her voice. "I know you're stressed, but surely you've done everything you can do?"

Jamie would have agreed with her, a hundred and ten percent, only a week ago.

"He has," Neal said firmly. "He's navigated this situation with more determination and cool than anyone could have. It's why I'm sure he'll be the one left standing at the end of all this."

Jamie's dad leaned back in his chair and rubbed his hand across his face. "And how do you fit into this?" he asked bluntly.

Jamie flushed, semi-mortified that his dad was going to do this now, but not really surprised. When his parents had found out who he was dating and who he wanted them to go to dinner to meet, they had been incredulous. "Isn't that . . . isn't that the kicker who missed the field goal in the Super Bowl?" Lila had asked hesitantly. "It is," his dad had answered. "And he's the guy Jamie's trying to replace."

Jamie supposed he should be lucky that the conversation hadn't taken this particular turn immediately. He knew his dad was concerned about how it would look. *And he's not alone.*

Neal glanced over at him, concern and affection both evident in his expression. "I don't think we were ever supposed to meet. Under normal circumstances, we wouldn't have. But my old teammates are annoyingly persistent, and we both ended up at the same party, and the rest is history."

"Is it?" Dave wondered. "Is that why we're eating in a back room of this restaurant and you two didn't come in together?"

"Dad," Jamie warned.

"No," Dave insisted. "You're on the verge of an incredible opportunity, and you have to know this might kill it dead. I raised you to weigh your decisions, and obviously Neal here is a smart man, too. That's why we're here. That's why we can't sit out on the patio. Because this isn't public knowledge."

"It's still new," Jamie tried to argue, but it was no use, because his parents knew.

Liked Neal maybe, but didn't necessarily approve of the risk they were taking.

"I care a lot about your son," Neal said calmly, like he had expected this and had prepared for it. "I'd agree; the situation isn't ideal. But we're determined to make it work, because the alternative is worse."

"Worse?" Dave echoed.

Neal's hand squeezed his under the table again. "We fit together," he said simply.

Jamie watched as his mom's eyes grew soft and wistful, and knew she'd been won over. His dad still had faint frown lines on his face, but he looked way less convinced this was a bad idea than he had been a minute ago.

"This isn't a fling," Jamie said firmly. He'd known it but the way Neal gripped his hand, like he was a lifeline, when he said it, made him believe it even more. "We care about each other, and like Neal said, the situation isn't ideal, but we're not planning to hide forever. We're working on a plan."

"I hope the plan is to at least wait until Jamie has his contract and he's established with the team," Dave said.

"It is," Neal said firmly. But all Jamie could think was *God, I hope so too.*

CHAPTER SIXTEEN

Two days later, Neal was sitting in the living room, enjoying a glass of red wine and contemplating putting the TV on while he waited for Jamie to come over after a late meeting with his agent.

Olive was studying with some friends in her separate apartment, so it was dark and quiet.

He was still contemplating flipping on ESPN, not because he was actually interested in what they had to say about the upcoming week of games, but because he'd been watching as much as he could, to prep for his first week on-air, which would be the last set of preseason games. But before he could reach for the remote, the sound of the back door opening and closing distracted him. He nearly called out for Olive to ask her what she was up to, but the chatter accompanying the door made it clear she was still with her friends.

"This is your uncle's house?" the girl asked—Neal thought her name might be Marcy, but it was hard to keep track of all of Olive's friends.

"Yeah, don't you know her uncle is Neal Fisher?" a guy asked. He was someone Neal didn't recognize, and there was an edge to his voice that Neal wasn't sure he really liked.

He could hear them rustling in the kitchen, opening and closing the pantry door and the refrigerator. Obviously searching for snacks and sustenance to get them through their study group.

"I know who Neal Fisher is," Marcy said.

"Yeah, everyone knows who Neal Fisher is," the guy retorted. "The whole fucking world."

Neal's fingers tightened around his wineglass.

"Yeah, that field goal he missed," Marcy said.

He knew Olive was there. But he also was surprised she hadn't said anything. Did he expect her to defend him? He *had* missed the field goal.

Just as he was trying to decide what it *was* he expected from Olive, another voice he didn't recognize piped up. "What's the point of making so many, if you're only going to miss the one that matters?" another guy said, and his tone *was* belligerent.

Neal tensed.

"It was deflected," Olive finally said, but her tone was reluctant. And the way everyone laughed at her words made him think this wasn't the first time this conversation had come up or the last.

"He *missed*. It doesn't matter how he missed," the first guy said.

Neal realized, with blinding clarity, that Olive—and maybe his sister and Mateo—dealt with this shit, same as him, every single day.

"Yeah, my dad lost a fucking *fortune*," the second guy added. "Hey, Olive, grab me those chips, why don't you?"

"Grab them yourself," she said, sounding snippy. Annoyed. And Neal couldn't blame her.

Neal stood and, setting his wineglass down with a click against the glass-topped coffee table, walked into the kitchen. He leaned against one of the sets of floor-to-ceiling cabinets and crossed his arms over his chest. "I'll get them," he said casually, like they hadn't just been talking about him, in his own goddamn house.

The two guys, young and looking just about as stupid as they sounded, gaped at him.

Marcy was the only one who spoke up. "Hi, Mr. Fisher," she said nervously.

"Hey, Marcy," he said, pleased that she'd greeted him. "Where's Olive?"

"She's in the pantry, I think," she said, still sounding semi-terrified despite that he thought he'd kept his temper pretty well in check.

"Alright," he said. When he turned to glance back, he was not surprised to see the back of those jerks that Olive was spending too much time with. The door shut behind them. Neal sighed and went into the pantry, looking for his niece.

Her hands were full with a few bags of chips, a box of animal cookies, and a two liter of Mountain Dew.

"Fuel for studying?" he asked, and she glanced up in surprise.

"I didn't realize you were home," she said, and instantly looked guilty.

"I know you didn't, and neither did anyone you were with," he said gently.

He was angry, but not at her, because it wasn't her fault. God, his first inclination was to blame *himself*, still and always, because that was the reason she was dealing with this shit, right? *Him*?

"I . . ." Olive stared at him, like she didn't know what to say, and really, that made two of them, didn't it?

But then it hit him that wasn't true at all. He knew what he wanted to say. What he wanted to ask her. What he *needed* to know.

"Do they do this all the time?" he asked.

"Do what all the time?"

"Talk about me like that. Harass you because you're related to me," he said carefully.

"I mean, not *all* the time. Sometimes, I guess . . ." The way she trailed off and wouldn't quite look him in the eye told Neal everything he needed to know.

"I'm sorry I didn't defend you," she added, suddenly fierce, "I do, usually, you know. I do, I just . . ."

"Get tired of having to do it?" Neal finished for her.

She stared at him.

"I missed the field goal. You don't have to defend me." But if she didn't, Neal didn't know what he would do. He had loved her from the very first time he'd seen her—a tiny, red, squalling child with a shock of dark hair and eyes that reminded him of his and his sister's. He'd held her and rocked her until she calmed and fell asleep. Maybe he wouldn't have children of his own—that was still up in the air—but he had always known that he had Olive.

"I do," Olive said, and suddenly, she was dumping the snacks in her arms onto an empty shelf and flinging herself into his embrace. "God, I'm so sorry you had to hear that," she whispered into his shoulder. "You don't deserve it."

"Neither do you," Neal said, stroking her hair back. "And I'm sorry you have to deal with it."

"Don't be," she said, pulling away. That fierceness in her eyes was back. "It's not your fault. You didn't do anything to hurt them, not really, but they're stupid idiots who think that winning a game is all that matters."

"They're not alone in thinking that," Neal said wryly.

"I know," Olive said, beginning to load her arms back up with the snacks she'd gathered. "But you're so much more than that, you know? You're my uncle. You're funny and smart and kind and you have great taste in boyfriends—well, at least *now* you do."

"Thanks, I think?" Neal said. "It's funny how you didn't tell me how much you guys didn't like Michael until it was over."

"Mom said we were being supportive," Olive said.

"She would." Neal sighed. "But really, I am being serious, Olive. You don't have to defend me."

"How about I'm pointing out how incredibly brainless it is to think a game is all that matters?"

"Alright, then, you can do that, if you feel inclined," Neal agreed, barely managing to hold his smile back.

"Good," Olive said, nodding sharply. "Those guys aren't my friends, anyway. They're these idiots in my sports bio class, and between you and me, I'm kinda hoping they end up dropping out."

Neal raised an eyebrow.

"I told you," Olive repeated with a grin. "They're idiots."

·   ·   ·   ●   ·   ●   ·   ●   ·   ●   ·   ·

Jamie came about an hour later, after Neal had finished his wine, rinsed his glass, and had retreated to his bedroom. About a week ago, he'd given Jamie the code to the front door, and he'd started letting himself in. Jamie *would*, but he almost always texted something like, **I'm here, and I'm coming in**, like he wasn't sure if he'd be arrested for breaking and entering. Or if he wasn't sure he belonged.

Neal wanted him to feel like he did, but he also knew there was nothing else he could say or do to convince Jamie; he had to convince himself.

There is one thing, his brain supplied. *You could tell him you don't just care about him, that you don't just like him, that you . . .*

Neal stopped that voice right in its tracks.

"Hey," Jamie said, appearing in the doorway. "There's some cars out front, I wasn't sure . . ."

"It's Olive's friends," Neal said, as Jamie walked in, sitting at the edge of the bed. "Well, maybe not *friends*. Study partners, I guess."

"Oh?" Jamie wondered.

"They didn't know I was home, and proceeded to break down what a shitty job I did in the Super Bowl," Neal said wryly.

Jamie's expression morphed from interested to concerned. "They *what*," he exclaimed, hands clenching into fists like he was ready to go out there and demand retribution from anyone who'd wronged Neal. If he was going to, Neal thought, that list was going to be a hell of a lot longer than Jamie probably anticipated.

"They're just dumb kids," Neal grumbled, but the realization still stung. Their words had still hurt him. And even worse, they'd hurt Olive. Olive, whose only crime had been to be related to *him*.

"I'm sorry," Jamie said, reaching for him and pulling Neal tightly against him, hugging him close. "People suck."

"They do," Neal mumbled into his shoulder. He would *not* cry, even though he wanted to. "Sometimes . . ." He swallowed hard.

"Sometimes I think missing that field goal isn't something I'll ever get over. Not really."

"I don't think you *have* to get over it," Jamie said softly, slowly. "I think you might just learn to live with it better. One day at a time."

"I'm just so tired of feeling guilty," Neal said, and despite how much he'd tried to hold back, a tear dripped down his cheek.

"Maybe you need to learn to forgive yourself," Jamie said.

Neal knew he was right; knew that forgiving himself for missing the kick was something he'd have to do—if he was going to learn to live with it or if he was ever going to have a chance of moving past it.

"I don't know if I can," Neal admitted.

Jamie raised his head and looked Neal right in the eye. Right in his watery, tear-filled eyes, and he didn't flinch, didn't look disgusted. Accepted all of Neal, the same way he had accepted all of Neal from the moment they'd met. He reached out and wiped the dampness of his tears off his cheek.

"I say this because I care about you. But I'm not sure you've tried very hard." Jamie's voice wobbled slightly, like he was unsure if it was the right thing to say—or the right moment—but what he didn't know was it *was*. Deep down, Neal knew Jamie was right.

"I'm not sure you're wrong," Neal said quietly.

Jamie hugged him tightly. "I'm not," he said firmly. "But that doesn't mean you can't start now." He hesitated. "Do you want to talk about it?"

"The miss?" Neal felt himself inwardly shudder at the thought. He didn't even like *thinking* about it, even though it was hard to avoid.

"Yeah," Jamie said.

"Uh, *no*," Neal said, finding himself chuckling, despite the tears still wet on his face. "What is there to talk about?"

"You do know it was deflected, right?"

Neal rolled his eyes. "I've only been told about a thousand times."

"I kind of assumed you hadn't watched it again," Jamie said. "So I wanted to double-check."

Neal took a deep breath. "So yeah, it was deflected. Does that make me feel any less guilty? Not really. It doesn't change the outcome. It doesn't change how I feel about it. It sure doesn't change how anyone else feels about it, either."

"I get it," Jamie murmured. "I didn't feel any less bad when Jon fucked up the snap."

"How about I start tomorrow?" Neal said with a chuckle. "Tonight . . . tonight I just want to forget."

Jamie's eyes were soft. Intense. *Loving*. Even though Jamie hadn't explicitly said how he felt, there was no doubt in Neal's mind what that look meant. It meant Jamie would follow him, shining his light, no matter how many dark places Neal fell into.

"I can help you with that," Jamie said and kissed him.

. . . ● . ● . ● . . .

All it took was the kiss. Jamie instantly felt overwhelmed and overcome, and decided that he didn't want to just help Neal forget—he wanted to forget too. To let down his guard, to stop worrying for one precious night that all of this might evaporate the next time he opened his eyes.

Neal tasted rich and heady, like wine, and Jamie felt drunk on him, as he straddled Jamie and just like the first time they'd had sex, he deliberately rocked against him, their hardening cocks mirroring the way their tongues brushed together, indulging in a playful, intense dance that Jamie knew would only end one way.

He was panting when Neal broke off, the green of his eyes reduced to a single narrow ring around his dilated pupils. "I want you to fuck me," Neal said with determination.

Jamie moaned a little, because *yes*, that was something he wanted. Something he'd been dreaming about long before he'd ever met Neal Fisher.

Long before he'd ever met him or discovered the man underneath the name.

But he'd also been dreaming about something else.

"How about I make love you to you, instead?" Jamie said, hearing the unsteadiness of his own voice.

Neal smiled, warm and bright in the dim light in the room. "Is that what you want?"

"Yes." Jamie was more certain now. On much more solid ground. "I love you, but then I think you know that already."

"I . . . I love you too," Neal said and his smile grew even brighter, his eyes shining like stars. "I really, really love you. And I want you to make love to me." He leaned in and nipped Jamie's bottom lip with his teeth. "Fucking. Making love. I want all of that."

"All of what?" Jamie asked, gazing up at him. He was so beautiful, so precious, Jamie's heart contracted at the thought he didn't see himself the same way. Maybe he would, someday, but he didn't, not right now, and that hurt more than Jamie had expected it would.

"You feeling good. Me making you feel good," Neal said.

"I thought you wanted to forget," Jamie wondered as Neal pulled off his shirt and started to work on Jamie's.

"You make me forget," Neal said, and kissed him again. Deeply. Intensely. And for a second *Jamie* forgot too, forgot everything that worried him. Forgot about Olive's stupid friends, forgot about Shane, forgot about the Riptide, forgot about everything that wasn't the man surrounding him.

The man he loved, who loved him back.

Neal gasped as Jamie reached up and pressed a palm against his cock, a hard line in his athletic shorts. "Let's get these off," Jamie said, "and I'll really make you feel good."

Neal's cock twitched against his hand, and Jamie knew what he wanted to do. What he *could* do. Jamie nudged Neal over to the side, and let himself slide off the bed, to the floor, so he was kneeling right in front of Neal.

He reached up and tugged Neal's shorts off, his dick bobbing against his abs, leaving a wet streak behind. Jamie rose up and licked it, savoring the taste of Neal's skin, and loving the way he tensed, his muscles flexing under his mouth.

"I'm gonna make you feel so good you don't know anything else," Jamie swore, and watched as Neal's fingers dug into the comforter, his eyes squeezing shut.

It wasn't the first time Jamie had sucked his cock, but each and every time, Jamie felt like he could get lost in the taste and the smell and the *feel* of it, the way even Neal lost himself, his hand reaching down to grab on to his hair and *tug*.

He slid Neal's cock into his mouth, reveling in the intimacy of the moment, and the way Neal spread his legs open, wordlessly asking for it. Jamie slicked up a finger with his mouth and found the furl of his hole, wonder pulsing through him as he opened up for him, one long stroke at a time, as he continued to suck on his cock.

"Another," Neal begged, but Jamie knew if he was really doing this—if *they* were really going to fuck, then he needed more than just saliva. Reaching out, he blindly opened the drawer next to Neal's bed, and was rewarded when he pulled out a half-used tube of lube, slicking up his fingers and then giving Neal what he'd asked for.

"God," Neal groaned as Jamie slid a second finger alongside the first, fucking him slow and steady as he kept sucking, tightening his mouth around him, precome blurting onto his tongue.

"God," Neal repeated, his head falling back. "Fuck me, god, *please* fuck me."

Jamie felt his own cock pulse in his jeans, hard and suddenly desperate to replace his fingers. He pulled them out and, shedding the rest of his clothes, grabbed the lube and was about to reach into a drawer for a condom, but Neal's hand stopped him. "We don't need that," he said softly. "I'm negative. Have you been tested? I want to feel you. *Really* feel you."

"I am," Jamie admitted. He'd been tested for everything as part of the pre-draft process, and he hadn't had sex since then. He leaned in, and kissed Neal, feeling every ounce of his longing. "I want that too."

"Come on, then," Neal said, sliding back on the bed and opening his legs. Jamie swallowed hard, slicking up his cock and joining him on the bed, running a reassuring hand across his thigh, and pushing him open the last bit.

From the moment Jamie slid inside Neal, he was lost.

Nothing else existed. Not their star-crossed relationship. Not the contract he'd worked so hard for. Nothing but the inexorable, tight press of his cock inside Neal's body, and the way Neal moaned when he finally came to a stop, fully seated inside of him.

Jamie squeezed his eyes shut, trying to stay controlled and not let the overwhelming pleasure consume him whole. "God, you feel so good," he ground out.

"Please," Neal begged, and that was all he needed to know before he began to move. Neal was so tight, so slick and hot and fit so perfectly around him it was all Jamie could do to set the pace and then hold on for the rest of the ride, as Neal arched up to meet every thrust, and then reached down to wrap his hand around his own cock, furiously pumping as Jamie shuddered and emptied into him in a dizzying rush.

"Fuck," Neal groaned as he exploded, clamping down around the tail end of Jamie's orgasm and drawing out the pleasure just a little longer.

Neal finally stopped pulsing between them, and Jamie gazed down at him, seeing the love in his eyes, and feeling his own, warm and certain and *real*.

"I really do love you, you know," Jamie murmured as he pulled out and used Neal's t-shirt to do a cursory cleanup.

"I love you too," Neal said, smiling up at him. Seemingly not in a big hurry to move yet. "We'll clean up in a minute, I just want . . . I just want you."

"You just had me," Jamie teased, as he discarded the t-shirt and climbed back in bed, cuddling up next to the man he loved. "I'm young but you're still gonna have to wait another few minutes til I'm ready again."

"A few minutes," Neal deadpanned. "Fuck, what am I going to do with you?"

"I think . . ." Jamie hesitated, pressing a kiss to Neal's chest. Right where his heart was beating. "I think you're doing it."

• • • • • • • • • •

Neal gradually woke up the next morning as the sunlight filtered into his bedroom. He stretched and turned over, not surprised to see that Jamie was still there. Except he was surprised to see that Jamie wasn't sleeping—he was wide awake, staring at the ceiling.

"Hey," Neal said, wrapping his arm around Jamie's shoulders and tugging him close. "Couldn't sleep?"

"I did, but I had a bad dream, and woke up and couldn't go back to sleep," Jamie admitted.

"What was the dream?"

Neal didn't think it was his imagination that Jamie went pale. Maybe if he was lucky, Jamie would finally tell him what was going on, what had made him so anxious recently.

"It wasn't really a dream. It was a nightmare, and it wasn't . . ." Jamie took a deep breath, his entire body shivering. "It wasn't really a nightmare either, it was too close to reality. I . . . I think I need to tell you something."

"You can tell me anything."

But Jamie looked at him like he wasn't sure. Like he didn't know how Neal would react, and that hurt more than Neal was willing to admit to.

"I mean it," Neal repeated firmly. "I love you. Nothing is going to change that."

"What if I told you I left the Riptide and decided to look for a different kind of job?"

Neal was shocked—but not unpleasantly. "How could I judge you for that," he said slowly, "when I've done the same thing? You know, I'll support you, no matter what. You can stay here with me, if that's what you're worried about. Is looking for another job what you want to do?"

"No," Jamie said miserably. "But I'm not sure I'm going to have a choice."

"Why?"

Jamie glanced away. "Someone knows about us. Someone who . . . let's just say it's someone who has everything to gain by speaking up about it."

"Shane." The answer seemed painfully easy to guess, and suddenly everything clicked into place. "He found out during the game last week."

"Right after," Jamie said, picking at a thread coming out of the hem of the sheet. "It was an accident, I swear, I was just talking to Sam . . . and I didn't think, and well, I feel so dumb about it."

Neal sighed. "Don't. It was bound to happen. Neither of us wants to live our lives with our relationship buried in the closet, so to speak." He paused. "But the good news is he's known for over a week and he hasn't said anything yet."

"That I know of," Jamie said.

"Have you talked to him about it?"

Jamie nodded. "A little. He didn't say whether he'd keep quiet or not. It was . . . he wasn't clear about it. I'm sure that was on purpose. Maybe he's trying to throw me off my game."

"Maybe." But Neal wasn't convinced. "But that hasn't worked, has it? Because you kicked better last week than you have all preseason. You were *so* solid, and the coaching staff gave you chances—chances they didn't give Shane."

Neal had been so sure after last week's game that the competition was virtually over, and that Jamie was going to win the long-term deal, but then this wrench in their best-laid plans had suddenly appeared.

"If they knew, they wouldn't keep me around," Jamie said bluntly. "They threw a huge fit about your jersey number."

"Maybe. Maybe not." Outwardly, Neal knew he sounded calm. Inwardly, he was raging.

Jamie shot him a look. "Hey," Neal said, "we don't know one hundred percent for sure."

"No, but we have a pretty good idea," Jamie said, and looked up at the ceiling. "I just wish I knew what to do to fix it. Or if I knew whether Shane would go to the coaching staff and tell them."

"I'm assuming he just overheard you talking, and he doesn't have proof?" Neal asked.

"No proof," Jamie said. "But I'm not going to lie if they ask me."

That wasn't a surprise; Neal wouldn't have expected him to.

"I've also considered telling them first," Jamie continued. "Like . . . getting ahead of it."

"But what if Shane wasn't going to actually do it? Then you'd have jeopardized everything for nothing."

Jamie said nothing, just stared moodily at the ceiling.

Neal had promised himself when he fell asleep last night that he would work harder on eradicating his constant feelings of guilt and responsibility. It wasn't entirely his fault that the Riptide had lost the Super Bowl. If Sam had converted that third and long to a first down, Neal wouldn't have had to kick a field goal in the first place. If Chase hadn't dropped the pass before it, it would've been an easy touchdown. If the defense had stopped Colin O'Connor and the Piranhas better, it never would have come down to Neal at all.

He'd been thinking about all of this; about how he was going to move past it, when he'd woken up and Jamie had dropped his bomb.

Maybe it was Jamie who was responsible for Shane finding out, but Neal didn't think he could live with himself if he not only lost himself the Riptide kicker job, but lost it for Jamie too.

It would be too much. Too much currency that he couldn't ever pay back.

Neal took a deep breath. Thought about what he could really do. Thought about what Chase had said the day before. Considered going to Toby. Considered how unpleasant it might be to beg Michael to save his new boyfriend's job and gave that up almost immediately, both because of how truly unpleasant it would be and also because Neal didn't think it would work.

There was only one solution.

"I think you shouldn't do anything right now," Neal said cautiously. "I think you should just sit tight. If Shane was going to say something, he'd have done it by now. He has to see the writing on the wall; you're *going* to win this job, and I'm not sure there's much he can do about it."

"You really think so?" Jamie didn't sound convinced, and Neal was fairly certain it wasn't because he thought he wasn't a better kicker than Shane. It was because this secret had the power to destroy him.

Destroy them both.

"I do," Neal said. And he was going to make sure of it.

CHAPTER SEVENTEEN

JAMIE LEFT AFTER BREAKFAST, heading to practice, and after a few minutes, Neal grabbed his keys and followed him.

He hadn't told Jamie what he was doing, and he didn't particularly want to get caught, but he thought this might be his only chance to corner Shane.

As luck would have it, when Neal pulled into the Riptide practice facility parking lot, he spotted Shane, recognizable from all the YouTube clips he'd watched over the last month, just getting out of a small silver compact.

Neal pulled up behind him, and sunglasses in place as a slight disguise if anyone happened to glance over at him, lowered the window.

"Hey," he said, and Shane looked up. And then looked again. Probably because the last person he was expecting to see in the practice facility parking lot was Neal Fisher, who was technically banned from Riptide property.

Shane didn't have to say it, because Neal knew it was fucking crazy. Knew that he had officially crossed over into lovesick territory.

"What are you doing here?" Shane hissed, coming over to stand by Neal's car. "You're not supposed to be here."

Neal was surprised that he was surprised, considering what Shane supposedly knew.

He watched as the realization hit him. "You're here to talk about Jamie," he said.

Neal nodded. "Get in the car," he said. "You're early. I'll have you back in time."

"Not gonna take me to some abandoned warehouse and knock me off?" Shane asked, smiling. The joke almost made Neal like him, but then he remembered the sword that was metaphorically hanging over Jamie's head.

"Don't tempt me," Neal said, after Shane slid into the passenger seat.

"I would ask what you want, but I think it's obvious," Shane said. "I kept expecting Jamie to do it, but then it's Jamie. The guy doesn't have a cutthroat bone in his body."

It's why I trust him; it's why I love him.

"You don't want to win this job because they released Jamie for some dumb-ass reason, like who he's dating, do you?" Neal asked, trying to be as non-threatening as possible. He didn't *want* to threaten the guy. He just wanted him to see reason, see that he shouldn't use what he knew just to become the Riptide's new kicker.

The problem was, Neal was afraid that was exactly what Shane was prepared to do.

"I don't?" Shane didn't look convinced.

"You don't," Neal said firmly.

"You promising me a starting job someplace else?" Shane wondered.

"You know I can't do that."

Shane's glance was a challenge. "Then why do you think I would just let this go? I'm going to see it through to the end."

Exactly what Neal was afraid of. But then he *hadn't* told yet, when he easily could've, over a week ago. Neal wished he could ask Shane why that was; wished that if he did, Shane would give him an honest answer.

But Neal wondered if it was because Shane himself didn't know.

Neal took a deep breath. "You want money?"

Shane stared at him like he'd grown a second head. "What?"

"Do you want money?" Neal repeated. He felt dirty offering it, and even dirtier having to say it twice, but he'd driven here, hadn't he? He'd come here, determined to shut Shane up, no matter what it took, and if that meant bribing him, then he'd do it, even though he wasn't sure how he'd live with himself afterward.

But then, how could he live with himself if he cost Jamie this job? He'd already lost it for himself. He couldn't lose it for Jamie, too.

"I want a job in the NFL," Shane said. "And not because of the money. So, *no*."

This made Neal like Shane better than he wanted to, because obviously Shane was a purist who wanted to play football because he loved playing football. Neal wished he hadn't come here, because even he knew there was nothing he could offer that Shane would take—except the spot that Jamie wasn't willing to give up.

"Alright," Neal said. "I suppose appealing to your better nature is out of the question, too."

"Maybe you should've thought of that before you got into his pants," Shane said.

He should've. But then, he'd tried to resist. He'd tried to tell both of them they couldn't be involved, even as every molecule in his body tugged him in Jamie's direction. And then it had seemed easy enough—surely, they could keep this one secret.

"I did, actually," Neal admitted.

Shane looked contemplative. "Well, aren't you two some real Romeo and Juliet shit?" he asked.

Neal laughed, despite the anxiety that threatened to blow the top of his head clean off. "Yeah, I guess we are," he said.

Shane glanced at the clock in the dash. "I've got to run. Team meeting in a few," he said. "But good talk."

As he got out of the car, Neal could only think it *hadn't* been anything close to a good talk, because he still didn't know what Shane was going to do.

The one takeaway from the entire conversation was that he wasn't sure *Shane* knew what he was going to do. And that was more terrifying than anything else.

· · · ● · ● ● · · ·

"I just met your boy," Shane said, sliding into a seat next to Jamie in the big amphitheater where the Riptide held their team meetings.

"What?" Jamie glanced at him in shock. *"What?"*

"I met Fisher," Shane said casually, stretching his legs out, like running into Jamie's boyfriend was a routine occurrence that happened every day.

But Jamie knew better. Jamie knew it couldn't possibly be a coincidence that he'd run into Neal. Neal must have made sure they met. And Jamie could think of only one reason why that might be.

"I'll say this, he should stay in TV. Negotiations aren't his strong suit," Shane said. Didn't sound angry. Didn't sound annoyed.

Jamie wondered what the *fuck* Neal had said to him. "But then," Shane continued, still pensive, like he still wasn't sure *what* to make of their meeting, "I don't think his heart was really in it, either."

"It wasn't?" Jamie didn't know what to think. He wanted to pull out his phone and send a text, demanding to know what the hell Neal had been thinking, to corner Shane like that.

"I think . . ." Shane let out a deep breath. "I think he cares about you. That's all."

Jamie stared at him. That was again, not what he was expecting Shane to say. He wanted to ask more, to ask why Shane thought that, but at that moment, Coach Rodriguez appeared and the room silenced.

It was an interminable hour, during which Jamie knew he should be paying attention. The last preseason game was coming up in only a few days. He needed to handle the kicking side of things, or else it wouldn't matter what Shane did or didn't say—he wouldn't have a job in a week. But it was impossible to pay attention, when so many questions were buzzing away in his head.

Finally, the meeting ended, and Jamie only realized it because Shane nudged him and said, "Come on, we've got to get going, Coach T wants to talk to us."

"Yeah," Jamie said, still distracted, as he grabbed his bag. "Yeah, we can do that."

Shane shot him an odd look as they exited the auditorium. "You okay?"

Jamie thought it was ironic that it was Shane asking him that. When Shane was the one who held the cards to destroy everything he'd worked so hard for. But then, he hadn't yet, had he?

"Yeah, I'm good," Jamie said.

As he'd expected, Coach Toby wanted to discuss the game plan for the last preseason game against the Giants. And as Jamie also expected, Coach Toby informed him he'd be taking the brunt of the work during the game. Shane didn't say much, but Jamie still breathed a sigh of relief when their conference ended, and they went to change for practice. But then, what had he really expected? That when confronted with Jamie's clear status as the front-runner he'd just blurt out, "Jamie is fucking Neal Fisher"?

He hadn't, and Jamie wondered if he wouldn't. But then, you didn't know what anyone would do when their backs were to the wall. Maybe he still thought he could beat Jamie if Jamie faltered.

Considering Jamie had no intention of faltering, it was impossible to say what Shane would do when he had to face the realization that he definitely hadn't won the job or the contract.

Jamie changed quickly, and grabbing his phone, jogged out to his car. Once he was safely inside—he wasn't risking *anyone else* overhearing this conversation—he dialed his dad.

"Jamie!" Dave exclaimed when he answered the phone. "I thought you'd be at practice."

"I am at practice," Jamie admitted. "I . . . there's something I need to tell you. Something I need advice on."

"Is everything okay?" his dad asked, voice concerned. "You don't sound too good."

Jamie laughed, a little hysterically. The pressure was getting to him, and he knew it. Not just the pressure of trying to be the best every single day—every single *moment*—but also the pressure of not knowing what Shane would do.

"Uh . . . actually no, I'm not good. I'm . . . someone found out about me and Neal," he said in a rush. "Someone on my team. Actually . . . the guy I'm competing against for the kicker spot."

"Your competition found out about you and Neal," Dave said slowly.

"Yes," Jamie said. "And I . . . I don't know what to do."

"You don't know if he's going to tell anyone or not." His dad sounded worried. "I knew this was a bad idea, you dating that man. It's going to end . . ."

"Don't." Jamie cut him off. "I know you think it's a stupid move, but I care about him. I . . . I love him."

Dave was silent for a long moment. "Then I guess you need to decide what you're going to do."

"I would if I could figure out what Shane's going to do. I can't get a read on him at all. I don't think he'll tell, and then I catch him looking at me, and I wonder, if he finds out he hasn't made the team, will he use it as a last-ditch attempt to discredit me?"

"He could," Dave said thoughtfully. "Here's the thing, son. You can't control what Shane does. That's on Shane. But you *can* control what you do. And I think what you should do is tell the truth now. Present the situation as it is to your coach. It might be better coming from you."

It was exactly what he had expected his father to say. Jamie thought maybe that was why he'd needed to make this phone call the whole goddamn time. Because he'd just said what he needed to hear. The same thing the voice in the back of his head had been encouraging him to do since Shane had found out his secret.

"What if they release me?" Jamie asked.

"Then they release you, and you either find a new team or you use that incredible brain you have, and that education you were lucky enough to get. You're smart. You can get a job. I know you want to play in the NFL, but you have options. You always have options."

He did, Jamie realized. He'd just wanted *this* so badly that it hurt to even contemplate giving it up. Especially when he'd trudged through all this hell to get to the other side.

"And," his dad added, "you don't know what the Riptide will do. Maybe they won't care."

"You haven't been here during camp and the preseason," Jamie said. "All they care about is not repeating the mistakes of the past. And to them, that mistake is Neal."

"They were always going to find out at some point," his dad said gently. "Isn't it better that they find out now?"

Maybe his dad was right. Maybe this was inevitable. It was just the timing that had been left up to fate. And honestly, Jamie was tired of letting fate—and Shane—control what he was going to do.

"Thanks," Jamie said. "I think . . . I think you might be right."

"You knew what you needed to do," his dad said. "You just needed me to say it out loud."

His dad, like always, wasn't wrong. He had known; he'd known the entire time.

"Well, thanks for saying it out loud, then," Jamie said.

"Let me know how it goes," Dave added. "And you know you can always come home, if you need to."

"I know," Jamie said, and knew he was lucky. Not everyone could go home. Not everyone had a rich boyfriend who'd offered to let him stay with him.

· · · · ● · ● · · · ·

After practice ended, Jamie pushed down the sudden swelling of nerves and anxiety, and jogged over to where Coach Toby was talking to Coach McMahon, the offensive coordinator.

"Hey, Coach," he said, trying to stay casual, but his voice came out high and squeaky. *Nervous.* "Can I talk to you for a minute?"

"Sure," Toby said, and they walked together across the field towards the locker room. "What's on your mind?"

"I need to tell you something," Jamie said, "and it's important that it comes from me. And that you understand that this isn't just a passing thing."

Coach stopped in his tracks and looked Jamie dead in the eye. He nearly quailed and gave up and said *never mind, it's nothing*, but he didn't, he *couldn't*, because it wasn't nothing. It was the opposite of nothing. "What's this about?" he asked.

Jamie took a deep breath and took the plunge. "I met Neal Fisher when I came down here to try out for the team," he said.

Coach frowned. "You met Neal Fisher?"

"I met Neal Fisher, and then, I started dating him."

If Jamie had ever wondered if Shane had already told and it hadn't been a big deal, the complete astonishment on Coach Toby's face set the record straight once and for all. Coach hadn't known. But he knew now.

"You're . . . *dating* Neal Fisher . . ." Coach trailed off. "Like . . . the Neal Fisher that was our kicker for thirteen years? *That* Neal Fisher?"

Jamie nodded. "That Neal Fisher." Like there could ever be more than one.

"Well, fuck me," Coach Toby said. "You certainly don't like to make things easy on yourself, do you?"

"No, sir," Jamie said, holding back a laugh. Even if things went sour, even if they went as badly as they possibly could, even if he was escorted off the premises the same way that Neal had been, telling the truth had lifted an enormous weight off his shoulders.

In that moment, Jamie knew he'd done the right thing.

"I'll be honest," Coach Toby said, taking off his cap and rubbing his partially balding scalp, "I don't really know what to do with this. You know how we feel about him."

"Yeah, I know," Jamie said.

"But on the other hand, we wouldn't normally give a shit *who* you date," Toby added. "You obviously know about Crawford and Harris."

"I do." Jamie decided there was no need to drag them into this. Coach didn't need to know that he'd met Neal at their house.

"I'm . . . I'm going to talk to Coach Rodriguez about this," Toby said. "But stick around. He'll probably want to talk to you, too."

Jamie wasn't surprised. He'd expected that at *least* Coach R would want to talk to him about it. Maybe the director of player personnel, too. And maybe even Neal's ex, who Jamie knew was his assistant.

"I'm . . ." Coach stopped in his tracks and turned back. "And listen, Jamie, I'm glad you were honest. And you should know. Neal's a good guy."

"I think so," Jamie said. "I've always thought so."

· · • · • · • • · ·

It was still hard to sit around and wait for the ax to fall.

Would it be his neck on the line? Jamie might have made his peace with it if it was, but it was still painful to sit here, and not be sure one way or the other.

But even though it was tough, Jamie still felt relieved that he'd finally done it. Once this was over, and he knew, one way or the other, he would call Neal and tell him.

Maybe he'd be mad, but if he was, Jamie couldn't fix that. The same way that Neal hadn't been able to fix *this*. The only way Neal could've done that was to not come find him at Sam and Heath's pool party, all those weeks ago. But then, what would they have sacrificed instead? Jamie wanted a lot of things—this kicking job for one, but Neal was not something he was prepared to compromise on.

It was almost half an hour later when Coach Toby came to get him from the locker room, where he'd been sitting so long his muscles had grown cold and stiff.

"Coach Rodriguez wants to talk to you," Coach said, his expression so controlled that it gave nothing away. "He's up in his office."

Jamie followed Coach Toby to the elevator, and they rode it to the top floor, where the head coach's office overlooked the practice fields.

He'd only been in this office once or twice—generally Coach Toby handled all the special teams, and there wasn't much of a reason for Jamie to visit the head coach.

Except for today, on what might be his *last* day.

Jamie wiped his damp palms on his shorts and followed Coach Toby into the office.

It was huge, nearly triple the size of Coach Toby's own office, on the lower level, and not only had an enormous desk on one side, but an entire sitting room on the other side, complete with two chairs, a couch, and a large coffee table covered in stacks of printouts and several tablets.

But most surprising was the fact that Coach Rodriguez was sitting with Heath, discussing something in low voices, so low that Jamie couldn't quite make out any of the words as he walked in.

Coach R looked up when Jamie walked in, and so did Heath. The latter smiled at him, in what Jamie hoped was an encouraging way, but Coach Rodriguez's expression was flat. Totally impenetrable.

"So," Coach R said, "I hear that we have a situation."

Jamie swallowed hard. Was it a situation? At least Coach Rodriguez hadn't called it something worse.

He nodded.

Coach R continued, drumming his fingers impatiently on the arm of the chair he was sitting in. "Not the first time I'll probably have one, and not the last, I'm sure, but at least you did us the favor of not falling for one of the guys on the team."

Coach's voice sounded wryly regretful, and Jamie could see how Heath and Sam could've made things difficult. Jamie was also sure that Heath was trying to hold back a laugh. Maybe that was a good sign?

"No," Jamie said. "Neal isn't on the team anymore."

"But you want to be."

It was a statement, not a question, but Jamie nodded anyway. "I do," he said.

"I know we already talked to you about the jersey number. We're trying to move on, move past what happened last year, but you just seem determined to bring it all back again."

This moment right here was why Jamie had been determined that he was the one who had to do the telling—because he could set the record straight about everything. Ultimately, he couldn't convince Coach Rodriguez that what he was saying was the truth, but he could at least try.

"I'm not trying to bring anything back," Jamie said firmly. "I met Neal Fisher accidentally. I don't think either of us intended for anything to happen, but then it did. I meant what I told Coach Toby. I care about Neal, and he cares about me. I know this is hard to understand, because of the position Neal was in before, and that I want the same position now, but what we share has nothing to do with football."

"Nothing?" Coach R raised an eyebrow. "Am I really supposed to believe that you've never talked about what happened last February? That he's never given you advice?"

It was the watershed moment. He could lie. He could tell Coach Rodriguez and Coach Toby what they wanted to hear—that Neal had never given him any kicking advice, that he'd never helped him, that he'd never *tainted* him with his own failure.

But what would Jamie be saying then, really, underneath his words? That they were right. That Neal was flawed, that he was damaged, that he could *ruin* Jamie, just by association. And Jamie knew that he could never participate in that kind of character assassination. Neal had missed a field goal. He hadn't murdered anyone. He hadn't insulted anyone. He hadn't done anything wrong, except not do his job perfectly on the one day it mattered more than any of the previous thirteen years.

"He's Neal Fisher. Of course I've asked him for advice," Jamie said steadily.

"And he gave it to you," Coach Rodriguez said.

"I was lucky enough that yeah, he gave me some advice. Taught me a few tricks of the trade. But then," Jamie added, "so has Coach Toby."

"That's Coach Toby's job. That's what he's here for," Coach R retorted.

"Yeah, but you can't tell me that if you were lucky enough to meet Vince Lombardi that you wouldn't ask him for a few pointers."

Coach R got up suddenly, and Jamie flinched. But instead of firing him immediately, he began to pace in front of the windows overlooking the practice field. "I really like you," he said. "You've got grit. You've got determination. You're a great fucking kicker, Wright. But you're making my job harder than it should be."

"I know. I'm sorry for that." Jamie knew that the head coach set the tone for the season and for the rest of the coaching staff.

It would make sense to assume that of anyone on the Riptide, the person who'd struggled the most with losing the Super Bowl had been Coach Rodriguez. He'd lost his chance at history, and that was a hard thing to come to terms with.

"I think you actually mean that," Coach R said, sounding like Jamie had surprised him. "Which . . . I may regret this. Occasionally I also regret how that *other* situation turned out, but most of the time, I'm actually pretty glad those two crazy kids worked it out, so instead of going with my gut instinct, I'm going to go against it. I'll let you continue to prove yourself. You're a great kicker. You make those kicks for us on Sunday, and we'll see after that."

Jamie couldn't quite believe it. He hadn't been released? Coach was still giving him a chance to make the team?

"Really?" Jamie asked incredulously. He'd been so prepared to be told to clean out his locker that the opposite didn't quite make sense.

"We came into this season looking for a kicker who could get the job done, who we could depend on. We still want that. Regardless of who he's dating. But I have to admit, this threw me for a loop."

"It threw me for a loop too, sir," Jamie acknowledged, and this time Heath couldn't hold his smile back.

He found himself relaxing in fractions as Coach came up and shook his hand. "It means something that you wanted to be honest, despite the risk you took in telling the truth," he said. "That means a lot to me, personally."

Jamie shook his hand in a daze. "Thank you. I appreciate it. I don't plan on letting you down."

Coach R even smiled. "See that you don't."

"Come on, let's get out of the coach's hair," Coach Toby said gruffly.

They were back in the elevator when Toby turned to him. "Don't take that lightly," he told Jamie. "He could've recommended you be released immediately. But he believes in you. He thinks you're possibly a great fit for this team."

"I know," Jamie said. He couldn't quite believe it himself.

He'd been so sure that the conversation he'd have to have with Neal would be of the "well, that sucked" variety, but it turned out that maybe the Riptide weren't all bad, after all.

"And you should thank Harris," Coach T added. "He spoke up for both of you, and he didn't have to do that."

"He did?" Jamie was surprised. Of course he'd met Heath a few times, but their paths crossing occasionally hadn't gelled into a friendship yet. Sam, he felt a lot more sure about. Heath still felt like a bit of an unknown entity.

"He spoke up for Fisher too, last February," Toby said gruffly. "Not that it did much good. Coach had already decided the moment that ball hit the upright."

"It'd be a hard thing to get over," Jamie said cautiously. "I know that, because even the few misses I have haunt me."

Coach Toby turned to him. "And you see what it's done to Neal," he added. A sentiment that Jamie hadn't felt comfortable confessing.

"Yes," Jamie admitted.

"I know what you've been trying to do," Toby admitted as the elevator dinged open on the ground floor. "It's misguided, but I can see it."

"I meant well," Jamie said.

"I know," Toby said, slapping him on the back. "I care about him too, believe it or not."

Jamie must have looked slightly incredulous at this because Coach chuckled then. "I did coach him for thirteen years, you know," he said.

"Right," Jamie said.

"He know about this stunt you pulled today?" Coach asked.

Jamie sighed. "No."

"He's gonna be pissed about it."

"Probably," Jamie had to admit.

"But it was the right thing. Don't let him tell you any different."

• • • • ●•● ● • • •

When Jamie texted Neal, asking where he was at, Neal replied back simply, **the practice field.**

Jamie assumed immediately that it wasn't the *Riptide* practice field, but Neal's own, and set off to meet him there.

When he pulled into the parking lot, he saw Neal, dressed in a cutoff tank top and loose athletic shorts, sitting on one end of the field, his knees drawn up against his chin.

Jamie parked and got out of the car, jogging over. "Hey," he said, when he approached Neal.

When Neal glanced up, his expression was wry. "Not expecting to find me here?"

"Not really. I thought you had meetings today. Getting ready for the first week of the season," Jamie said.

Neal glanced over. "I could say the same about you," he said guardedly.

"I finished early," Jamie said, and sat down next to Neal. The grass was warm and soft and the view here was different than he'd expected, the uprights rising like gigantic monoliths above them. "I talked to Coach Toby today, and then Coach Rodriguez," he added, decided that maybe it was best to just rip it off quickly, like a Band-Aid. Maybe Neal would be less pissed. Maybe it would hurt less if he was.

"You told them," Neal said on a quiet exhale.

"I decided it was better to share my truth my way than let Shane try to intimidate me into silence."

"How did that go?"

"They weren't *happy* about it, but they didn't release me either. So, I guess it went fine?"

Neal didn't say anything for a long moment, just kept staring up at those huge uprights above them. "They don't seem so big when you're standing forty yards away," he said finally.

"Are you okay?" Jamie asked cautiously. He didn't really *seem* okay. "Are you still upset about what happened with Olive and her friends?"

Neal sighed. "Yes. No. I'm upset about that. I'm upset how my actions affected my family. I'm upset that they affected the Riptide. And you. And I'm disappointed that neither of us could find it in ourselves to be honest with each other."

Jamie felt a pulse of guilt. He *hadn't* been honest. Not when Shane had first discovered the truth, and not today, when he'd made the unilateral decision to tell the coaching staff about their relationship. But then Neal had also gone behind his back by talking to Shane.

"I just thought," Neal said, "when I fell in love, like *really* fell in love, with someone I wanted to be around forever, that it would be different. Maybe it can be. But we haven't done a very good job of it so far."

"We haven't," Jamie admitted. "I'm sorry. I got . . . scared? I was embarrassed too, humiliated that I'd gotten found out because I was gossiping like some silly crushing teenager."

Neal turned and grinned at him. Jamie felt that same jolt he did, every single time, the same bone-deep realization that this was *Neal,* and Jamie loved him, and Neal loved Jamie back. "I wouldn't have blamed you. How could I? I'm just as bad as you are."

"Maybe you're better at hiding it."

Neal shook his head. "No way. I'm just as embarrassing as you are, I promise. If you ever doubt it, just ask Olive."

"I might," Jamie said, smiling back.

Neal reached out and took his hand, squeezing it gently. "We can do better though, I think. I have to believe we can."

"I want to," Jamie said earnestly.

"Let's make a promise here," Neal said. "Let's promise to be honest, even if we're scared."

"Even if we're embarrassed?"

Neal grinned. "Especially then. I promise, I do plenty of humiliating, embarrassing stuff. Just wait til I'm on TV in two weeks, and then you'll have plenty of material. Or, like I said, you could always talk to Olive. I think she has a whole collection of my embarrassing moments."

"Maybe I want you to show me yourself," Jamie said.

"I can do that." Neal let himself fall back to the grass, and Jamie followed him, hovering above him, the green of Neal's eyes vibrant against the grass surrounding him. "I want us to have lots of time so I can," he said softly.

"Me too," Jamie agreed.

"And I guess . . . I guess I got scared that we wouldn't. That's why I went to reason with Shane. But I should've talked to you first."

"I should've told you the first night about Shane." Jamie lay down next to Neal and put his hand on his chest, right over where his heart was beating. "I fucked it up. I just . . . I didn't want you to solve all my problems for me."

"And then I went and tried to solve all your problems for you," Neal said wryly, chuckling. "Wow, we suck at this relationship thing."

"But we can do better," Jamie said.

"We can. We should. Because I meant it." Neal's gaze pinned Jamie. "I love you."

"I love you too," Jamie echoed, cuddling up against him. Feeling the reassuring beat of his heart. Feeling like they'd already promised, they just hadn't said the actual words. But maybe they'd said something more meaningful, more lasting.

"I'm glad Rodriguez didn't just kick you off the team," Neal said. "I was afraid he would, if you told him."

"I was afraid too, but I was willing to take that risk. I didn't want to lie anymore."

"I told my agent that I might come out sometime soon," Neal said. "It doesn't have to involve you. Telling the Riptide is one thing, telling the world is another."

"Yeah, it is," Jamie said, but he already knew that he wanted to be supporting Neal when he did it. "And ESPN is okay with it?"

"Okay with it?" Neal asked wryly. "They're *thrilled* about it. They said they wanted to find a new audience for Sunday Morning Football, and I guess not being old and not being straight is exactly what they're looking for."

"And maybe," Jamie said hesitatingly. "Maybe I won't even be on a team when it happens."

Neal rose up and stared at Jamie. "You're kidding me, right? You've got that job nailed up. You told them you're dating their much-hated ex-kicker, and they didn't tell you to go clean out your locker. You're a shoo-in for the job."

"Maybe." Jamie wasn't quite convinced. "Coach Toby said they were still deciding."

"Trust me, it's a formality," Neal said.

"I just have to get through this last game," Jamie said.

"Well," Neal said with a sudden bright grin, "you're here. You might as well get some practice in."

Jamie groaned.

"Seriously," Neal said, grabbing him around the waist and lifting them both up together. "Can't waste this great field, and the sunlight."

"You sound like Coach Toby," Jamie argued.

"The question is," Neal said, sparkling brighter than Jamie had seen him in a week, "do I sound like Toby or does he sound like me?"

Chapter Eighteen

Jamie was just finishing getting ready for the last pre-season game walk-through when one of the assistants popped their head into the locker room. Jamie was still new enough that he didn't recognize all of them or know who all of them worked for.

"Hey, Jamie Wright?" the guy said, and when Jamie nodded, he said, "Mr. Taylor wants to see you in his office."

Jamie shot him a look. "I have a walk-through starting in twenty minutes."

"It won't take long, he just wants to show you something."

Taylor. Suddenly Jamie was sure he knew who wanted to see him. It was Michael Taylor, the assistant to the director of player personnel. And Neal's ex-boyfriend.

"I'm Gavin," the guy said, reaching out and giving Jamie's hand a perfunctory shake as they headed towards the elevator. "I don't think we've met yet."

"No, I don't think so." Jamie hadn't spent much time with any of the administrative side of the Riptide, but he supposed that if he made the team, officially, that would change.

Maybe it was already changing.

"Mr. Taylor is excited to meet you too," Gavin said, as they walked into the elevator.

Jamie could bet that he really was.

"Do you know what this is about?" Jamie asked as they watched the floor numbers tick by on the screen. There was a part of him that was nervous that Coach had changed his mind, and he was being let go after all—because Michael Taylor might be the one who'd do that kind of dirty work—but deep down, Jamie knew that wasn't what was happening.

He wasn't headed to Michael Taylor's office because he was one of the two kickers left on the Riptide, he'd been requested to visit Michael Taylor's office because he was dating his ex.

"Just something that Mr. Taylor thought you should discuss," Gavin said nebulously. And Jamie wondered then if Gavin even knew what the purpose of this visit was.

The elevator doors dinged open on a floor lower than the one he'd visited just yesterday. Which made sense. Michael Taylor might have power here, but he had *less* power than Coach Rodriguez. Jamie felt heartened by that reminder, and he kept his head high—metaphorically and literally—as he followed Gavin into Michael Taylor's office.

He was handsome, but older. Maybe as old as Neal, or even a few years older than that, with blond hair graying at the temples, and cold blue eyes that stared Jamie down as he walked into the plush, comfortable office.

"That'll be everything for now, Gavin," Michael said, dismissing his assistant, who closed the door behind him, leaving Jamie alone with the man.

"Sit down, please," Michael said, and Jamie sat, even though he really didn't want to.

Michael's voice was icy at the edges, almost as cold as his eyes. Jamie found it hard to believe that Neal had ever been happy with this tightly controlled, standoffish man. Yes, he was good looking, but he didn't look capable of laughter. And Jamie knew how much Neal loved to laugh. As a result, Jamie had been so determined lately to pull Neal out of his shell and bring more humor and lightness into his life.

Maybe he'd been taking himself way too seriously long before last year's Super Bowl. Maybe the root of that problem lay with the man standing in front of Jamie.

"I have a walk-through starting in fifteen minutes," Jamie said when Michael just continued to stare at him from behind the desk.

"I pulled up your file, you know," Michael said, like Jamie hadn't even spoken. "You're twenty-three years old."

"Yes," Jamie said. Unsure where this was going, but afraid that deep down, he already knew.

"I heard Coach Rodriguez talking to my boss today. Apparently you made a big, *romantic* confession in his office yesterday. About you. And Neal Fisher."

"I did," Jamie said. Maybe he should've denied it, but knowing Michael was Neal's ex, it was painfully obvious where this was going, and maybe not obvious to Michael, but obvious to Jamie, that whatever wrench he tried to throw into their relationship wasn't going to work.

"Then you should see this before you go all noble sacrifice for him. Know what kind of violent asshole your new *boyfriend* is," Michael said, and turned the laptop on his desk around, and suddenly Jamie was staring at a security feed video of this same office, of Michael just as he was now, but instead of Jamie, it was Neal facing him down.

The Riptide are going in a different direction next season, Michael said on the recording, and Jamie felt the impact of it right to the sternum. He was watching the moment Neal was let go from the Riptide, after he'd missed the kick in the Super Bowl.

"I don't need to watch this," he said, looking up directly into that frosty blue gaze. "This isn't something I need to see."

But Michael just stared at him. "Maybe you should wait to see if that's actually true."

"No," Jamie said steadily. "I don't need to see it because nothing you can show me would change my opinion of who Neal Fisher is."

And you? Neal asked on the video.

Me?

You, that's what we're talking about, right? Because every single fucking sports reporter, when they're not covering Colin O'Connor's victorious retirement, is predicting how fast the Riptide is going to release me.

That was when Jamie realized with a horrifying start that this video didn't just show a breakup between Neal and the Riptide, but it was also evidence of a much more personal breakup.

He stood abruptly. "I'm done. This has nothing to do with me. This doesn't even have anything to do with Neal. This is all about *you*."

"Oh, I disagree." Michael's smile was a grotesque masquerade of concern. *How did Neal not see through this guy?* Jamie wondered. "You wouldn't be here today if this hadn't happened."

"Maybe not," Jamie acknowledged.

"Don't you want to see why I had to have him escorted off the property?" Michael asked, his lips curling cruelly.

"No," Jamie said. He thought about what Neal had told him that night, the night of their first date, when he'd told Jamie about his past and about this relationship. "But let me guess, he throws a picture at your head."

For the first time since Jamie had come into his office, Michael looked surprised. "He told you?"

"He told me," Jamie said smugly. Maybe he should've gone high when this asshole went low, but it was too hard to resist.

Michael stared at him, incredulous.

Jamie would never know what his response would be, because the door burst open then, and Coach Toby strode into the room, red-faced and looking fairly pissed off.

"What are you doing?" he demanded, and to Jamie's shock, the Coach directed the question at Michael, not at him.

"What am I doing?" Michael asked, recovering better than Jamie had.

"There's no reason for you to have Jamie up here," Toby said. He glanced at the laptop on the desk, and just then, on the screen, Neal threw a picture at Michael's head. Jamie was only a little disappointed that he missed.

"I was just trying to make sure he was informed," Michael claimed.

"You're hung up on this," Coach Toby said, which Jamie thought was ironic—because it definitely hadn't felt like Michael was the only member of the Riptide organization hung up on Neal and the Super Bowl. "You're hung up on this," he repeated, "and it's pathetic." He turned to Jamie. "Come on," he said, "you've got a game to prep for, and there's nothing this guy has to say that you need to listen to."

Jamie turned, following Toby out of the office, and he only glanced back once, when he was just about to pass through the doorway. Michael was staring at the video, and Jamie was almost certain that the expression on his face was regret.

When he and Neal had first met, he'd wondered more than once what it might feel like to get close to Neal Fisher, but never really have him. What it might be like to love him and then lose him.

What it would be to lose him and realize you'd never deserved him in the first place.

Jamie realized that Michael's expression was exactly what that must feel like.

· · · ● · ● · ● · · ·

"I met your ex today," Jamie said as Neal drained the pasta into the sink. He nearly dropped the heavy, hot pot at Jamie's confession but re-gripped at the last moment. He glanced up at where Jamie was sitting on one of the barstools, watching as Neal finished making dinner. It wasn't anything fancy—"just a carb load for tomorrow," Neal had explained when Jamie had walked into the kitchen—but he thought it'd be nice for them to have one nice quiet evening before tomorrow's game. Before everything changed.

"You met Michael?" Neal said, giving the pasta in the colander a last shake to get the rest of the water out.

"Yeah, he's a real piece of work. You mentioned you threw a picture at his head when he fired you, but you neglected to mention he's a stone-cold dick," Jamie said.

Neal felt a thread of worry curl inside of him. They'd made promises that they would be more honest with each other, that they wouldn't hide things, that they'd approach their relationship like a team, but why did hearing about Michael now make him worry that the man might have gotten to Jamie?

"He wasn't always like that," Neal said, sighing. With some perspective on the relationship, he hoped that was true. At first, right after the breakup, he'd been convinced that Michael had been using him the entire time, that it had never really been real, but now? He wasn't sure. "But the NFL is a tough place to work. And it's much tougher when you're someone that people are predisposed to dismiss."

"Because he's gay?" Jamie asked.

Neal nodded. "I think it made him hard. Uncompromising. That didn't do him any favors. But he was sweet, and kind, at first. I don't know when that changed, but it did, and after the Super Bowl, I realized it."

"Yeah," Jamie agreed. "A guy who'd play his ex's new boyfriend the security feed from their breakup is a hardcore asshole."

"He did that?" Neal felt that frisson of worry expand. "I'm sorry . . . I wasn't . . ."

"No," Jamie said, sliding off the barstool and walking up to Neal, and pressed a hand against his mouth. "No, you don't get to apologize for hurling *anything* at that asshole. I'm mostly sorry you missed, honestly."

Neal felt a surge of laughter bubbling inside of him. Jamie looked so fierce, so proud, that he almost wished that he hadn't missed on purpose. But then if he hadn't, God knew Michael probably would have done something even crazier, like file criminal charges.

"I am too, a little," Neal admitted.

"He didn't deserve you," Jamie said. "I'm not sure I do either, but I'm working hard to be worthy. Because I love you."

"He didn't, you know," Neal said. "He said he did, but he didn't really love *me*. He saw us as some kind of sports LGBT power couple. Sometimes I think he liked the idea of me more than he liked the actual me."

"I love the actual you," Jamie said seriously, leaning in, brushing a kiss across Neal's mouth. "Every single part of you."

"I love you too," Neal said. *In a way I never loved Michael. I wasn't capable of it, not until now, not until I met you.*

He didn't say the words, but he felt them deep down, way down in his heart, that Jamie heard them anyway.

"Sometimes," Neal continued, after taking a deep cleansing breath. "Sometimes I wish he'd get punished for it. For all the shit he's done. All the shit he put me through. All the shit he put *you* through."

"But he did," Jamie said matter-of-factly.

"But he still has his job."

"Yeah," Jamie said, "but he lost you. That's enough punishment for a lifetime, right there." His smile was as bright as the sun, and Neal couldn't believe just how much it warmed him, just standing here and basking in it.

For a long moment, they stood there in his kitchen, holding each other, and Neal finally, reluctantly broke away, towards the stove where he'd been heating up marinara sauce for their pasta. "Can you grab the garlic bread out of the oven?" he asked.

"Sure," Jamie said, pulling the oven open and using the edge of a dish towel to grab the foil-wrapped bread.

A few minutes later, they were settled at the table. Neal had poured himself a glass of wine, but had given Jamie a firm look when he'd asked for some. "Night before a game," Neal said. "What would Toby say if he could see you now?"

"That I'm dating a man with extraordinary taste in wine and I should enjoy it?" Jamie said, picking up the bottle and pouring himself half a glass. "It'll be fine," he said, with a wink. "Tomorrow, we'll really celebrate."

Neal hoped that was true. Hoped that they would have news worth celebrating. But he shook off the last of his uncertainty and grinned at his boyfriend as he dug into his pasta.

"I was thinking about something today," Neal said after they'd finished their meal.

"Oh?" Jamie asked, as he rinsed off his dish and then took Neal's from his hand.

"I was thinking about retiring formally, before I start on the show," he said.

"I thought you put out the statement?" Jamie wondered, putting the dishes into the dishwasher. Neal never left them for Maria anymore. In so many ways, Jamie made him a more thoughtful man; a more conscientious one. A chill raced up his spine whenever he thought of what might have happened if he'd resisted the urge to go inside Heath and Sam's house; if he'd resisted the urge to meet the intriguing man with the head full of dark curls.

"I did, but it doesn't feel like enough. Not enough closure." He hesitated. "I was thinking of trying to put something together with the Riptide."

"Do you think they'd go for that?" Jamie asked cautiously. He would know; he'd been there the last two months. He'd seen every single reaction and counter-reaction to what Neal had and hadn't done.

But Neal knew that he'd hadn't talked to the one person who could make anything happen, regardless of what the coaching staff or Michael's executives thought of it.

"I'm going to ask Alec to talk to Johnny Lyon for me," Neal said. Johnny had always liked him. Maybe Johnny didn't anymore. It was hard to say for sure, unless Alec found out the truth. But Neal had decided that discovering that truth was more important than the chance of rejection.

"Wow," Jamie said, leaning back against the counter. "You really want to do this?"

"Give a press conference, possibly in conjunction with the Riptide, and open myself up to the media asking questions?" Neal took a deep breath. "Sometimes yes, sometimes no. But I know I haven't moved on, and neither have the Riptide. Not really anyway, and maybe we both need closure."

"Maybe." Jamie still sounded dubious. But then he smiled, suddenly. "You might find an unexpected ally in Toby," he said.

"Really?"

"The moment he found out Michael had called me into his office for all that bullshit, he came charging in there, ready to defend my honor. Or maybe yours." Jamie paused. "Yeah, definitely yours."

"When I talk to Alec, I'll let him know there may be someone else who can help us," Neal said.

"I'm proud of you," Jamie said, reaching down to shut the dishwasher. "Doing this will take guts."

"Maybe," Neal admitted. "But I kinda feel like I've been hiding for long enough. Time to face it all. The good and the bad."

· · · ● · ● · ● · ·

The day of the last preseason game dawned clear and hot, the sun shining relentlessly down onto the field as Jamie went through his regular set of warm-ups.

The extreme nerves of the last few games had faded away, leaving some uncertainty hovering in the vicinity of his stomach, but the apprehension he'd felt was replaced by excitement and a bred-in-the-bone certainty that he could *do* this.

After the anthem had been sung, and the coin toss, Coach Toby came over to him and pointed to the field. "You get the kickoff," he said, "and make it count."

Jamie intended to. He intended every single one of his kicks today to prove that he was the right choice for the job. No matter who he wanted to date or who he *was* dating.

The kickoff went smoothly, as Jamie kicked it right through the Giants' end zone, making sure there was no chance of their kick returner taking it to the house for a touchdown.

Neal and the books he'd shared had taught him this; to focus on every little detail. To let the big picture wash past him and focus on the task he had set in front of him. Every kick was *the* kick, because Jamie had realized you never knew when *the* kick was going to come.

The first half passed uneventfully. Sam and the offense were moving the ball well and scored two touchdowns. Coach Toby sent Shane out to kick one extra point, and Jamie out for the second one, right before the end of the half.

Sam came over to him as they jogged into the locker room. "Sorry about the lack of field goals," he said with a lopsided grin. "I'll see if I can miss a few throws to get you into range," he added, the teasing glint in his eye making it obvious that he wasn't quite serious.

"Thanks," Jamie said dryly. "I'd appreciate it."

"I heard," Sam said, his voice dropping in volume and growing serious, "about what you did."

Of course he had. Heath had been there, and Jamie assumed there was very little they didn't share with each other.

"Yeah," Jamie said.

"It was brave."

"Maybe not as brave as making out with your boyfriend after winning the Super Bowl," Jamie pointed out.

Sam shrugged. "Bravery is bravery, okay? But we've got your back."

"I know Heath . . ." Jamie trailed off.

He'd meant to find Heath after practice, and then again before the game, to try to thank him, but Heath had been busy, getting Sam ready for the last preseason game. There hadn't been a spare moment yet to pull him aside and tell him just how much Jamie appreciated having someone in his corner.

"Heath still feels guilty that he wasn't able to save Neal," Sam said, interrupting him. "So this time he did what he could to save you. And honestly, he hates seeing competency wasted, and everyone knows you're the better kicker. Who gives a fuck who you're dating."

Jamie smiled. "Hopefully way less people after today."

"You can do it," Sam said, clasping him quickly on the shoulder as they entered the locker room. "I have faith in you."

And Jamie knew it too, from the sincere tone in Sam's voice, and he knew others felt it too. He got a reassuring nod from Bran Phillips as he passed him in the locker room. Chase didn't even say a word, just nodded from across the room, and Jamie heard his voice, practically like it was in his ear, saying, *you've got this.*

After halftime, and the Giants' opening drive stalling out mid-field, Sam and the Riptide offense took the field again, driving towards the end zone. Rashad had a couple of great runs, and Jamie watched from the sideline intently, waiting for another shot to make his case to the coaching staff. But then, unexpectedly, the tables turned. Sam was sacked. Then they had a holding penalty, and suddenly it was third and *very* long, over twenty yards, and Jamie quickly calculated how many yards a field goal would be, approximately, and felt his breath catch in his throat.

It depended entirely, of course, on how many yards this next play got. They wouldn't be going for a first down, only enough to make the field goal easier to kick, but as Jamie stared apprehensively at the field, he knew what might happen if they didn't make up any distance.

And like fate had predicted it, had moved the pieces on the board so that Jamie would have the most challenging course possible—*and also the most convincing,* Neal's voice in his head added, *if you make this, you're on the team, no questions asked*—Chase couldn't quite haul in the short screen pass Sam threw him. The resulting field goal? Forty-four yards on the nose.

Jamie never even questioned if it would be him kicking it. He already knew it would be him. He glanced over at Shane, who looked sick, like actually physically *ill* at the thought he might have to go out there and kick a forty-four-yard field goal and exorcise all the Riptide's demons in one unavoidable moment.

Coach Toby came over, a contemplative expression on his face. "I don't need to ask who's gonna do this one," he said simply. "Because you look ready for anything." He pointed to Jamie. "And you look like you're going to vomit," he added, gesturing towards Shane. His expression was a cross between disgust and disappointment. The self-recrimination in Shane's eyes said it all. He knew he'd failed. He knew Coach Rodriguez wanted this to be an easy, clear-cut decision, and if Jamie made this field goal, he couldn't make it any easier on him.

You make this, and you're in, Jamie thought as he jogged out towards mid-field. He felt the pressure begin to build inside of him, relentless and unyielding, but he shrugged off as much of it as he could as he stopped, with the rest of the field goal unit, at the spot. He checked the wind, and even, in a new part of his routine, glanced down at the turf, making sure there were no stray pieces sticking up that might impede the snap or the hold.

"Let's get this done, boys," Jamie said, and gave a reassuring nod to every member of his team, from Jon, the long snapper, to Ian, who'd hold the ball after Jon released it.

They looked nervous. Jamie wondered if he looked nervous too, but he pushed that thought away too.

One thought was harder to push away. He could imagine Neal sitting on his couch, Olive next to him, fists clenched by his sides, eyes glued to the TV, not really wanting to watch as Jamie attempted the same kick that changed everything for him, but not able to look away either.

But then he pushed it away because, Jamie realized, this wasn't about Neal at all. It had never been about Neal. Maybe him making this kick today would exorcise the Riptide's demons. Maybe it might exorcise Neal's. But for Jamie? It was validation. Validation that he could walk through all the hell that the organization had thrown at him, all the doubt and the soul-searching if this was the right path, that he could *do* this. This was what he'd been born to do.

The official blew the whistle, and Jamie let everything fade away. The crowd, the team watching, the future that was possible if this kick went through the uprights, and he just did what he'd done a hundred times before. A thousand.

Jon snapped the ball, Ian caught it and turned it, just as Jamie's foot connected. The rhythm, perfected through so many drills in practice, was flawless.

The ball left his foot exactly as he'd wanted it to, and Jamie watched, heart in his throat, the world filtering back one thought at a time, as it soared right through the uprights.

It was unbelievable, he thought, that a future could be so different between one moment and the next. One second, it was just out of reach, and you were stretching to find it, to grasp it, and the next? It was solid and in your hand, and you were holding on to it so tightly that you knew nobody could take it from you.

Chapter Nineteen

After Jamie got back to the sideline, someone—Jamie thought it might be Coach Toby, or maybe it was even Heath, hugged him. It was hard to tell, because he was surrounded by players and staff, patting him on the back, on the helmet, even on the ass. Telling him without words, because football players had never been particularly known for their ability to vocalize emotion, that they believed in him. That they trusted him. That what he'd just done had meant something more than just three points on the board.

When Jamie finally managed to sit down on the bench, the third quarter had nearly ticked away.

"Hey," a voice said.

He glanced up to see Heath standing in front of him. Heath pointed to the ball in his hands. "Thought you might want that," he said, tossing it to Jamie, who caught it neatly. He said a little prayer of thanks to Neal for all those ball drills he'd suggested he do.

"I do. Thanks," Jamie said. Hesitated. "And thanks for everything else, too."

Heath shrugged. "It was stupid, and someone had to tell Coach R that. Someone who wouldn't get fired for saying it."

"And you were that guy?" Jamie wondered if, despite his claims, Heath still might've risked his job for it, because even the famous ex-quarterback wasn't *that* impervious.

"I was this week," Heath said firmly.

"Well, I appreciate it," Jamie said.

"Don't thank me. You earned the spot all by yourself," Heath said. He smiled and pointed to the ball. "And don't lose that."

"I won't," Jamie said, wondering if Heath meant more than just the football in his hands. If he did, then Jamie was determined not to lose that either.

For the first time since he'd been about to make the kick, he let his mind go to Neal.

How had he reacted? How had he dealt with it? He would have to ask him the moment he saw him tonight.

But it turned out, that wasn't how it happened after all.

After the game, Jamie was in the locker room, finishing packing up his bag, when Coach Toby showed up.

"Coach R wants to see you," he said.

Jamie gathered his stuff and felt Shane's eyes boring into him from the other side of the room. He was definitely pissed, and

Jamie wasn't even sure he could blame him. The Riptide had created this situation, and then after forcing the players to endure it, could simply dismiss them, like they hadn't meant anything at all.

Jamie almost went over and said something, but he didn't know what he *would* say. He'd won this job, fair and square, and he wasn't going to apologize for that, and he wasn't going to give it up either, and that was probably the only thing Shane was interested in hearing right now.

Coach R was in his office, sitting on the couch, much as he had been the last time Jamie had been up here.

"Great job today," Coach said, getting up and shaking his hand briskly. "I'm . . ."

That was as far as he got, when suddenly the door opened and Shane came striding into the room, followed closely on his heels by Coach Toby, who looked more upset than Jamie could remember him being.

"I need to tell you something," Shane spat out. "I think you don't know anything about this guy, and you're about to hire him."

Jamie was not particularly surprised, but he was still disappointed. He'd hoped that despite the inherent suckiness of losing out on the kicking job, Shane would take it better than he was. That he wouldn't make some painful last-ditch attempt to discredit Jamie.

Jamie sent a silent word of thanks to his dad, who had convinced him he'd needed to tell the truth, so he didn't need to be afraid of Shane anymore.

Because he wasn't, at all. Jamie just felt sorry for him.

Coach R turned towards Shane, and he didn't bother to hide his frustration. "Did I ask you to come up here?" he demanded of Shane.

"No," Shane said, "but I needed to tell you something. There's something you don't know."

"And that is?" Coach Rodriguez asked, exchanging looks with Toby, who was still hovering in the doorway.

"Your great new kicker," Shane said with a sneer, "he's playin' both sides. Pretending that he's part of the Riptide, part of trying to move on and make something great, but he's fucking Neal Fisher, on the side, too."

Jamie frowned. He had never clarified with Shane that it wasn't just sex between them. That they were more than just fucking. Shane had even told him, just a few days ago, that he thought Neal really cared about him. But apparently all of that subtlety had been lost in favor of framing his revelation in the most shocking way possible.

"What you're saying is that Jamie is having a consensual relationship with a player who is no longer on our team. Is that correct?" Coach R's voice was deceptively calm, but Jamie could hear the venom in it.

"Yes," Shane said, shifting his weight from one foot to the other, suddenly seemingly uneasy.

"We know about it," Coach R said.

Shane looked over at Jamie and there wasn't really anger in his look. It was something more like resignation. "He already told you?"

"He already told us. He was honest. He was a teammate. He said he didn't want his dating Fisher to distract from what was important, and he thought if he set the rumors straight, then it wouldn't. And he was right. It didn't. He made that field goal today. Maybe he didn't win us the game, but he proved he was a team player."

Coach Rodriguez paused, pinned Shane with a sudden, fiercely uncompromising look. "Are you a team player, Ferguson?"

Shane hesitated, which was his whole mistake. Actually, Jamie corrected, his whole mistake had been coming up here at all. His mistake had been relying on fear, instead of overcoming it.

"You're not," Coach Rodriguez answered the question for him. His voice was flinty, hard. Relentless. "You're not a team player, because a team player wouldn't take a loss like this. Wouldn't take the first opportunity he had to stab another player in the back. Even if he'd just won the job he'd wanted."

Jamie watched as Shane swallowed hard. "It's a conflict of interest, sir," he said, making a last-ditch stand, which Jamie supposed he had to give him some amount of credit for. At least he hadn't just turned on his heels and run away. A lot of much tougher guys, when faced with Coach Rodriguez in a mood like this, might've cut and run.

Shane hadn't, but then Jamie wasn't sure if that was misplaced bravery or just plain stupidity.

"Maybe it is, maybe it isn't, but I sure as hell don't like your way of dealing with it. I didn't much like Jamie's either, but at least he was honest about it. You, on the other hand, tried to sell out a teammate." Coach Rodriguez shot him a look, making it abundantly clear that he did not approve of the way Shane had handled it. "We had already decided that Jamie was going to be our kicker, but you just put another nail in your coffin, Ferguson."

"I was trying to help you," Shane said sulkily.

"Yes, well, some advice for the future. Have your teammates' backs. That's all the help a coach needs." Coach Rodriguez glanced over at Toby, who gave him a nod.

"Come on, Ferguson," Toby said with resignation. "We need to get your paperwork together, and you'll need to clean out your locker."

Jamie didn't look at Shane as he walked out of the room, humbled and broken.

"Well, then," Coach said, turning to him. "That was fun." He sat down on the couch again and beckoned for Jamie to join him.

"It made me glad I told you before he could," Jamie admitted.

"Integrity means something," Coach agreed. "A lesson he's going to have to learn the hard way. But one," he added thoughtfully, "you already know."

"Thank you, sir. It's all my dad, honestly."

"I'll have to meet him one day. Make sure they come to some games this year, eh?" Coach said. "Rick, our VP of player personnel, he'll be in touch with your agent with the contract, but it's like we talked about when you first came here. It'll be three years, with an option for a fourth year."

"That's fantastic," Jamie said. An option for a fourth year? For a rookie kicker who hadn't been drafted, this was like winning the lottery.

But then that wasn't exactly true, was it? Lottery implied luck. And there had been some luck involved, but Jamie had worked hard. He'd done everything he could to win this job.

Even ask Neal Fisher for advice, all those weeks ago.

"We'd like to announce it in a press conference this week. Give the media a chance to get to know you."

"Alright," Jamie said. And suddenly he had a thought. "Though, there's something I'd like to ask for, if that's okay."

"Is it something I'm going to like?"

Jamie shook his head. "Uh, definitely not," he admitted, but Coach R was still smiling. Still pleased. He sighed.

"Does it have to do with the situation I'm currently tolerating?"

"Yes," Jamie admitted. "Yes, it does. But I think it'd be good for everyone, honestly. Good closure. Good media spin. I think you'll like it."

"I think I'm probably gonna hate it," Coach Rodriguez said, resigned. "But I'll hear you out anyway."

"Good," Jamie said, and outlined his plan.

$$\cdot \: \cdot \: \cdot \: \bullet \: \cdot \: \bullet \: \cdot \: \bullet \: \cdot \: \cdot \: \cdot$$

"I cannot believe I let you talk me into this," Neal said, even as he straightened his tie, and then reached over and tried to straighten Jamie's.

"This is what you said you wanted, right? You told me you wanted to do this," Jamie said. "You wanted a chance to retire as a member of the Riptide and you wanted a chance at closure." He looked way too pleased with himself. Like every piece had fallen into place just-so, and Jamie was responsible for all of it. Which, Neal had to concede, maybe he was.

Neal looked around, at all the Riptide personnel milling around. Some of them had smiled at him, one or two had even greeted him, but most were still keeping their distance. Like what Jamie had done in the last preseason game still wasn't enough to erase their memories.

And maybe it wasn't enough to erase theirs, but Neal was working on erasing his own. Erasing the guilt that always accompanied it.

"Yeah, I did," Neal agreed. He'd been shocked the moment Jamie had called him up, with Darla, the PR rep, alongside him. He hadn't quite believed them when they'd outlined the plan, but since he was currently *back* in the Riptide facilities, and this was all actually happening, it was hard not to believe it anymore.

"You can always change your mind," Jamie said cautiously, patting him on the shoulder reassuringly. "You don't have to do this . . ."

"But I do," Neal said firmly. He'd known it when Chase had brought it up. Known it when he'd lain in bed and thought about what Chase had said over the last week. Had believed it when he'd told Jamie over dinner a few nights before. He owed it to himself to take this step. And maybe he owed it to the Riptide, too. "I mean technically I'm already retired . . ."

"Yeah, but now you're going to retire a member of the Riptide. And that means something to you. I know it does."

Neal sighed, because Jamie was unfortunately one hundred percent correct. "It does, but I didn't want you to spend all your newly won goodwill getting me that chance."

Jamie shrugged, seemingly unconcerned that he was already pissing his brand-new team off. Which, Neal realized, he probably was. "They want me to kick for them. They want me to sign the contract. I said I would, but that I wanted them to do this for me, first."

Neal wasn't sure whether he wanted to laugh or cry—he *was* sure he wanted, desperately, to lean in and kiss his boyfriend. To try to tell him how much this gesture meant to him, even as he worried about its implications for Jamie. "You're wonderful," he finally said. "Way too fucking good for me, that's for sure."

He reached out and surreptitiously squeezed Jamie's hand. Neal had a feeling that everyone in this room already knew they were dating, but he was trying, maybe not very hard, to keep that under wraps officially for a while longer.

"No way," Jamie said, eyes sparkling, smile as wide as Neal had ever seen it. "You're just right for me, and you know it."

"I definitely know that I'm too old for you, too washed up, and probably not nearly as good of a boyfriend as you hope I'll be," Neal said. "But I'm gonna take you anyway, because I love you."

"Good," Jamie said, squeezing back. "I love you too."

Darla, the Riptide's public relations guru, walked over to them. "We're just about set," she said, including both of them in her warm smile. "You two ready?"

"As ready as I'll ever be," Neal said, and Jamie nodded.

It was the truth. He still felt a bit like vomiting, at the thought of the questions he was undoubtedly about to get, but Jamie was right. He'd desperately wanted this chance. A chance maybe not at redemption or at wiping the slate clean, but a chance to end his career on a more positive note.

"Good," Darla said. "I'm sure there'll be lots of questions, but only take the ones you're comfortable with, and take your time with your answers. There's no rush."

"I gave him that advice, which is good advice, by the way, kid," Neal said, nudging Jamie. "Take your time, especially."

Darla rolled her eyes. "Of course you did. You're already behaving like an overprotective boyfriend," she teased.

"Who said anything about a boyfriend?" Jamie asked.

Darla laughed. "Oh, honey," she said, "you didn't have to."

Neal thought again, *everyone knows, why are we trying to keep this a secret?* Jamie had made the same argument when they'd made the arrangements for the press conference, but Neal had suggested that there were enough life-changing events happening today. They should leave something for later, he'd told Jamie. But now, suddenly, he wasn't sure that had been the right call. His heart definitely hadn't been in his arguments before, and it definitely wasn't now.

But before he could pull Jamie aside and discuss it, Darla was leading him up to the table set up in front of all the press. There were two Riptide helmets on either side of him, and a microphone in front of him. Neal swallowed hard and sat down.

"First, before the questions, I'd like to read a statement," Neal said. It was a modified version of what he'd posted on his social media, and what they'd sent out before he'd taken the job with ESPN. But back then, he hadn't felt comfortable saying anything about the team he'd left, not when their relationship had ended so acrimoniously.

But now? Sitting in a Riptide facility, wearing a turquoise tie and flanked by Riptide helmets? Neal could say it. Could make everything that he'd held back before known.

He read the entire statement, and then concluded it, as he hadn't before, with a new paragraph. "Lastly," he said, his voice not as steady as he would've liked, "I want to thank the Los Angeles Riptide for taking a chance on me, just out of school, an unknown rookie who didn't know anything about anything, and for making me part of their family for thirteen years. I wish . . ." Neal felt his voice catch, but plowed on. "I wish that I could have ended our relationship on a better note. I wish, more for them than for me, that I could've given them their chance at the history books. But I'm grateful that I can sit here now and express my appreciation and how honored I was to be a part of the Riptide for those thirteen years."

Neal had known this would be an emotional moment. But he hadn't anticipated that all the emotion of the last year—the kick and its aftermath, meeting Jamie, coming back to life, finding a new purpose—would wash over him in one enormous wave. He steadied himself by taking a sip of water, as Darla called on the first reporter.

Neal recognized him, because he'd been around for years—just like Neal himself.

"Neal," he asked, "how do you feel about the Riptide's search for a new kicker?"

Neal chuckled. "Had to start with something hard, didn't you?"

The reporter just shrugged.

"Well," Neal said, considering the question, "I can't say I blame them, honestly. I spent six months after the Super Bowl so depressed and overwhelmed with guilt over what had happened that I could barely get out of bed. I needed someone to forcibly jerk me out of feeling sorry for myself, and you know? I think the Riptide needed that same reminder. Life isn't over. The future still looks bright."

"And you think Jamie Wright is part of that bright future?" the reporter asked.

"I do," Neal said firmly. "I think he's a great fit for this team, and I couldn't be more pleased with the player who's going to be kicking for the Riptide."

The next question wasn't much easier. Neal wished he hadn't worn a tie; it was currently feeling like it was choking him. "Would you have considered retirement if the Riptide had won the Super Bowl?"

"I don't know, because that didn't happen," Neal said bluntly. Sometimes honesty was the best policy when dealing with the media. "I'd considered it. But I hadn't found anything I loved as much as football back then."

Another question. "And you have now?"

"As you probably know, I'm lucky enough to be joining ESPN's Sunday Morning Football as an analyst. I've talked for years about how they didn't have any special teams players or anyone with that perspective on the panel. But now, I'm going to change that, and it's a tremendous honor."

"Who's your favorite person on the panel?" another reporter asked.

This one was a little easier. Neal took a deep breath. "I have to say Terry Bradshaw, because he always keeps me on my toes."

"Do you have anything to say about a rumor that you're going into coaching?"

"No, I'm not going into coaching," Neal said firmly.

But that particular reporter wasn't done. "I've heard rumors that you've been coaching Jamie Wright."

Neal wished that Jamie wasn't behind him. That he could see his eyes. "Unofficially," he said with a wide grin.

"Do you care to elaborate on that?" the reporter asked, just as Darla appeared, shooting him a reprimanding look. And maybe he shouldn't have said it, because now the rumor mill was only going to shift to a higher gear, but there was a huge part of him that just didn't give a shit.

"Let's thank Neal for his time," Darla said.

There was a chorus of applause, and then Neal stepped down, just as Jamie was walking up. He stopped, momentarily caught off guard by the brilliant smile on his boyfriend's face. "Couldn't help yourself, could you?" Jamie murmured as he passed by him.

He really couldn't.

Jamie's part of the press conference was much more straightforward. He signed the contract, while the flashbulbs of many cameras recorded the moment for posterity. The questions were also way less personal, probably because unlike Neal, Jamie was new to them.

At least until one reporter decided that there was something juicy worth digging for.

"You came out as gay in college," she said, "but you've never had a boyfriend publicly. What do you think about NFL players dating each other? Is that something you would be interested in doing? Do you think it should be allowed?"

Right now, of course, it wasn't. Not technically. But then Neal had also retired, so he *wasn't* a player.

Jamie grinned. "I think it can be a distraction to date someone on your team. So, no, I don't think the rules should be changed. Bent, occasionally? Maybe?"

"Who would you bend them for?" she asked, and Neal fought back a grimace.

"Oh, I wouldn't bend them for *me*," Jamie said, seemingly unconcerned about the minefield he was stepping through. "I've never met a player I wanted to date. An *ex*-player, maybe," he said with a teasing grin, shot right in Neal's direction. Temping him. Making it clear what he wanted Neal to do.

Darla visibly paled where she was standing next to Neal. "What is that boy doing?" she hissed under her breath.

"Making your job harder?" Neal suggested.

"Yes," she grumbled.

"Who would that be?" the female reporter asked Jamie, her interest now piqued.

He'd captured more than a few reporters' attention now. Neal could see their intent gazes switch from Jamie to himself. And he knew that the game was just about up.

Neal glanced over at Darla, wondering if she would stop this. Stop *him*. But Neal knew enough about PR in general to know that any publicity was *usually* good publicity. That suddenly this must-watch press conference might just become historic.

Neal walked over to where Jamie was sitting. He didn't seem surprised to see him at all. Looked pleased about it, in fact. And Neal knew he'd made the right call. How could this have really turned out any differently, in the end?

"I think I've found him," Jamie said with a grin, gazing up at Neal with so much love in his eyes that Neal felt weak, felt blessed. Felt a million other conflicting emotions that all turned into one inescapable reality. He hadn't been looking for his future, but he'd found him, anyway.

Neal leaned down, and kissed him.

EPILOGUE

NEAL WASN'T NERVOUS. HE really wasn't nervous. Except the way that Terry Bradshaw was smirking next to him would make *anyone* nervous.

"You ready to talk to your boy?" Terry asked, while they were still on the last minute or so of commercial break.

"Of course," Neal said. "I talk to him all the time, don't I?" *Except never on live television with millions of people watching.*

"That's right, you do," Terry said. "I like him a lot, you know. Good kid."

Neal didn't hold back his eye roll. "You've only said so about a thousand times, *and* he's not a kid."

"Tell him that the Riptide needs to find him a better long snapper. He's pissing me off," Jimmy Johnson said, inserting himself into the conversation. Which was really all it needed, Neal thought bleakly. Nobody got Terry going like Jimmy. They were the Laurel and Hardy of football analysts.

"You can tell him yourself," Neal said, amused not only because Jimmy was way too right, but because his new co-workers had adopted Jamie the same way they'd adopted him—unequivocally, and with as much interfering and "helpful" advice as they could dole out.

"Oh, I will," Jimmy said.

"Ian never fucked you over that way," Terry said. Suddenly, since Neal had joined the Sunday Morning Football panel, Terry thought he was an expert on special teams.

Neal raised an eyebrow. "He didn't?"

"I had Cory look it up, made him sit through six seasons of you kicking and Ian snapping. I think he might be having dreams of murdering me in my sleep." Terry cackled. Cory was his research assistant, and Neal personally thought Cory wasn't planning on ushering Terry out quite that painlessly.

Nope. He'd make it slow. And make sure Terry was awake the whole damn time.

"He's gotten sloppy," Neal agreed. "But he did it to me, too. More than once."

"Jamie needs to make sure Rodriguez takes care of that problem. How you gonna win games if you don't give your kicker the best chance to succeed?" Jerry Rice added.

"I hate to tell you, but a rookie kicker doesn't exactly have Rodriguez's ear," Neal said, which they all knew perfectly well. "But I'll be sure to let him know," he added dryly when a trio of incredulous expressions stared back at him.

"Back from commercial in three . . . two . . . one," the producer said into their earpieces.

"Welcome back to Sunday Morning Football," Jerry said, because he was the only one the producers could routinely count on to adequately handle the introductions and the transitions. Neal had seen, live and in-person, how difficult it was to marshal any of these legends on a regular base. Six games into the regular season, and he was frankly impressed they looked as professional and organized as they did, considering the chaos just behind the scenes.

Still, it was a chaos he honestly *enjoyed*. He was lucky as hell. He got to sit between Terry Bradshaw and Jimmy Johnson once a week and soak up their football prowess and also provide a body between in case things went south.

Which they had. More than once.

"Our next guest might be a rookie, but he's become legendary for turning around the Riptide's kicker problems without breaking a sweat, and also because well . . ." Jerry shot Neal a knowing grin. "Well, we'll let Neal answer why else he might be legendary."

"Thanks, Jerry," Neal said wryly, and then smiled, because Jamie's bright, happy face had just appeared on the monitor, and *he* was smiling, which made it impossible for Neal not to.

"Awww, look at how cute these two are!" Terry crowed.

"Hi, Jamie," Neal said. He'd practiced saying that in the mirror when Jamie had been at practice this week. Embarrassingly, more than once. He'd hoped he'd sound a little more professional and a little less lovesick teenager, but he gave a mental shrug. He *was* kinda like a lovesick teenager. Truly, completely, utterly in love for the first time in his thirty-seven years. Maybe he should just own it.

"Hey, Neal. Hey, Terry, Jerry, Jimmy," Jamie added, blushing. "It's so great to be here."

"I tried to get Neal to bring you along, but he protested that you weren't a dog he could drag around on a leash," Terry said.

"That is not what I said, exactly," Neal said firmly.

"I paraphrased," Terry said. "You heard of paraphrasing, Jamie?"

"A few times," Jamie said, his smile still plastered across his face. It was hard to deal with Terry and *not* be alternatively amused and homicidal.

"Let's talk about the Riptide's record, Jamie," Jerry said, changing the subject to what they were *actually* supposed to talk about. Neal wasn't under delusions they'd actually *stay* on topic, but he admired Jerry's dedication to dragging them there. "Four and one so far. And that one loss was a heartbreaker."

"It was," Jamie agreed. "I wish I'd gotten to go out there and win us the game."

He hadn't been able to because instead of setting them up for the game-winning field goal, Sam had pushed the offense a little too hard, and had ended up throwing an interception instead of getting them closer to the end zone. Neal knew that Sam—and Heath, of course—were still beating themselves up over that.

"Still, winning four games out of five. You're on pace to be just as good as you were last year," Jimmy pointed out approvingly.

"Hoping we'll be better, actually," Jamie said earnestly. Then flushed. "Not that there was anything wrong with last year's team. They were incredible and did incredible things. But I wouldn't mind having a ring to match my boyfriend's."

Terry laughed. "I bet you wouldn't." He turned to Neal. "How do you keep up with him?'

"I do okay," Neal said. "He hasn't complained yet."

"Keep up with me? How about keeping up with *him*? Did you guys hear about the renovated sports park he's opening with the Riptide next year? He's out there all hours, supervising the work himself," Jamie said, neatly turning the tables. Neal wasn't surprised at all. Even dismissing how incredibly biased he was when it came to his boyfriend, he knew just how smart and quick Jamie was. Every day he woke up and couldn't believe that he'd gotten so lucky.

The sports park project was one of the bonuses of making peace with the Riptide and with Johnny Lyon. Neal had gotten his dream after all. His private field would always be his—and Jamie's. But the rest of the park was on its way to being restored, thanks to a partnership with the Riptide organization, and hopefully next year, there'd be a new, safe place for the local kids to practice and play.

"I didn't know you were taking such an interest, Fisher," Terry said, even though he knew very well, because Neal kept trying to get him to dedicate the park himself, when it opened.

"It's an important initiative, and I want to do my part to give back to the community that's been my home for the last decade," Neal said.

"Jamie, what's the deal with your long snapper?" Jimmy said, asking as he'd promised he would. "You've got to get him to cut that crap out."

Jamie looked regretful. He'd missed two extra points and a field goal because Ian, the long snapper, had apparently developed a bad case of fumbling the football. Neal knew how pissed Jamie was, because those misses were counted against *his* reputation. But still, he'd cautioned Jamie from speaking out too negatively about the guy.

After all, Neal knew exactly what it felt like when the world condemned you for something you couldn't really help.

"We're working on it," Jamie said. "Ian's doing his best. We're still getting our rhythm down, working on it a lot during this bye week, and I know that we're going to get through this."

Jimmy nodded approvingly, and Neal knew then that the question had been a test. Would Jamie throw his teammate under the bus? He already knew Jamie wouldn't—he'd consistently and utterly refused to ever judge Neal on what had happened last year—and now the rest of the world was discovering it too. Jamie was a solid teammate and, impossibly, an even better person.

Yeah, you're not biased at all, Neal thought wryly.

Except it really was true. Jamie was as true as he was wonderful. He'd never expose a sordid hidden side, like Michael did. He wasn't capable of it. Neal knew it, and that was why he trusted him completely, with every little bit of his heart and his soul.

"Don't let Crawford beat himself up too much about that interception," Neal said to Jamie, even though he'd said those exact words to Sam himself. Sometimes he knew it was hard to listen, and he also wanted to put out he was publicly supporting the Riptide quarterback. If anyone knew what it was to be slammed in the media, it was Neal.

"Of course, we've got his back," Jamie said earnestly. Then he grinned wildly. "And yours, too, Fisher."

Terry cackled next to him, and Neal couldn't believe he'd ever worried that this panel of football legends would ever buy into homophobia and reject him or Jamie for their relationship. They were more excited about it than anybody else.

It was endearing, and maybe a little bit annoying.

"And I've always got yours," Neal said. "You gonna be home when I'm done here?"

Jamie nodded. "I've got the nachos all ready, and I think Olive's making tacos."

"That sounds perfect," Neal said. "I can't wait."

• • • • • • • • • •

Make sure you check out the next (and last!) Riptide book, **The Red Zone**, about Alec, agent extraordinaire and the much-misunderstood Spencer Evans. Available now on Amazon & Kindle Unlimited.

• • • ● • ● • ● • •

Want to read Chase's book? Check out **Hit the Brakes** now. It's book two in my Food Truck Warriors series, but can be read as a standalone.

INTERESTED IN READING MORE OF
BETH'S BOOKS?

CHECK OUT A FULL LIST OF TILES
BY SCANNING THE QR CODE
OR VISITING HER WEBSITE

WWW.BETHBOLDEN.COM/BOOKLIST

WANT TO FOLLOW BETH?

MAKE SURE YOU NEVER
MISS A RELEASE?

SCAN THE QR CODE BELOW
OR VISIT HER WEBSITE
FOR A SOCIAL MEDIA LIST,
NEWSLETTER SIGNUP,
AND SO MUCH MORE!

WWW.BETHBOLDEN.COM/ABOUT